Honey & Spice

Also by Bolu Babalola:

Love in Colour

Honey & Spice

BOLU BABALOLA

HEADLINE

First published in 2022 by Headline Publishing Group

First published as an Ebook in Great Britain
by Headline Publishing Group in 2022

Cataloguing in Publication Data is available from the British Library

Hardback ISBN 978 1 4722 8638 3
Trade Paperback ISBN 978 1 4722 8639 0
Ebook ISBN 978 1 4722 8640 6

Senior Commissioning Editor: Katie Packer
Copyeditor: Aruna Vasudevan
Cover illustrations: Jovilee Burton
Cover designer: Siobhan Hooper
Proofreader: Vimbai Shire

MIX
Paper from
responsible sources
FSC® C104740

HEADLINE PUBLISHING GROUP
An Hachette UK Company
Carmelite House
50 Victoria Embankment
London
EC4Y 0DZ

www.headline.co.uk
www.hachette.co.uk

For my babygirls, my babyghels:
soft and savage and sweet and strong and tender
and tough and exquisite — so exquisite.

CHAPTER 1

'Do you like that?'

I shifted on the bed as the fifty-thread count sheet scratched against my calves. Biggie was staring down at me from across the room in 24 x 38 form, half-peeling, half-clinging to the wall with contraband Blu-tack, his crown wonky. An apt display of the indignity of being stuck as a witness to everything that went down in a twenty-year-old guy's uni room. My guy – not *my* guy, but My Guy – was using my left breast as a stress ball and OK, yeah, it was mid-term, so we had a ton of assignment deadlines, but take up yoga or something, lift more at the gym, but please do *not* take the pressure out on my tender tit. (It was day fourteen on my twenty-eight-day cycle. Hence why I was here. Ovulation sometimes makes decisions for you.) My Guy's vodka-spiked breath was hot and curled around my neck, suffocating me. Above us, Biggie's eyes looked bemused, brows furrowed in concern. *I feel you, Big Poppa.*

This really wasn't as much fun as I'd hoped. As much fun as it used to be. The newness, the thrill, had worn off, and exposed the fact that My Guy really had no clue what he was doing. He relied on his status as campus hottie to do his work for him, trusting his squinted hazel eyes, which counterfeited intensity and interest in you – the real you, Ma – to do all the work for him. He didn't engage with his attraction to you because he was so sure of your attraction to him, and why bother trying to make you feel good when he assumed everything he did would automatically feel good to you?

My Guy had asked me a question, but he wasn't waiting for the answer. He moved to suckle at my neck aggressively, toothily, still using my boob as a distraction from the 3,000-word essay on macroeconomics he had due in about nine hours.

Honestly, why do so many guys mistake vigour for technique? Like, OK, you want me – this much is clear and, frankly, under-standable – but what are you going to do with it? Where is the finesse, hun? The clear understanding that you are handling a masterpiece?! You've got this far. Appreciate it.

I shimmied beneath him and for a few seconds the movement deluded him into thinking he was doing something right. He groaned an 'Oh is it, Babe?'– until he realised I was shimmying out from under him to sit up straight, snap my bra back on, slip on my T-shirt, pull down my tan corduroy mini and shrug on my leather jacket.

It ain't, *Babe*.

'Babe?' His hazel eyes were soft with confusion and, bless his soul, I got it. This didn't happen to him, usually. This shouldn't happen to him, according to his calculations. (All collegiate dating interactions were calculations, and his were Him + Girl = Whatever He Wanted It To Equal, because look at him for fuck's sake, how could she not want what he wanted?) This abrupt change clearly took some adjusting for him, like it took some adjusting for him when he finally realised that I was the one who didn't want to be seen in public with him, who chose the hours we were together, who didn't want to sleep over. It turned his little world inside out that he wasn't the centre of mine. And part of his attraction to me was fascination, exploration of the unknown, a Girl-Who-Don't-Wanna-Be-Cuffed-By-Me safari.

I untucked my braids from the back of my jacket, slipped on my boots. 'I hate it when you call me that. Don't call me "Babe". I've told you before.'

I moved to the mirror pinned against his wardrobe. It was smeared with antiperspirant smatter that hadn't been wiped and was framed by vaguely sexual-sounding motivational workout slogans: 'Rise and Grind', 'Beast Mode', 'Feel the Heat'. I stared at the mirror, then slipping out a baby wipe from my leather satchel, I wiped my lips, disinfecting them, removing the organic, locally produced lip gloss known as My Guy's saliva for something more fruity smelling.

'Look, I've been thinking—' I dabbed on my lips with a doe-foot wand, '—we should cool off with this. You know? I'm busy with uni and the show, and sneaking around has been fun but—'

'You're ending this, Kiki? Really?'

I flicked my gaze from my reflection to his. Pure disbelief. Brow furrowed, pouty, pink lips slightly agape. It would've been kinda cute if it wasn't based on arrogance. He was topless, his firm body panting, recovering, asking his true question, spilling the real tea: *You gonna deny this? Really?* The thing is when you make going to the gym six days a week your personality, it must be hurtful when it doesn't melt the knees it's supposed to, fails to work its tried-and-true magic. But after a while, it just wasn't enough. His body wasn't much of a conversationalist, didn't ask mine what her interests were, her favourite song, which spot was the softest.

I looked at his reflection. 'OK, let's be real . . . there was nothing really to end. There was no beginning to this. It just happened and I – we – kept letting it happen.'

'And I'm glad it happened.' He got up from the bed, came up behind me and looked at himself in the mirror as he wrapped his arms around my waist, pulling me back against him so I could feel just how glad he was. He looked at us in the mirror.

'Look at how good we look together.' He removed an arm to lift my chin up, as if I'd asked him for help. 'People respect you. People respect me. Think about how we would rule this place, babygirl? Looks and brains. Light and dark.'

Babygirl. It sounded foreign on his tongue. He'd gone to a boarding school in Sussex, where he'd only had white friends, and he was still fleshing out this new flavour to his personality.

I raised a brow. 'Which of us is which?'

He smiled, tightened his grip around my waist. 'See, funny, too.'

It only took a few seconds for his gaze to flit from me, from us, to his own reflection. His bottom lip had tucked in. It was honestly like a very uncomfortable threesome where two people were way more into each other than they were you, eventually leaving you to watch them doing their thing, fascinated. I presume.

My Guy's eyes were still on his own. He kissed my neck. 'A peng power couple.'

I bit my lip to keep my laugh in, but from the way his grip tightened on me, I think he misread it as a sign of arousal. Oh, man. I knew enough about him (enough was enough) to know he was serious. This had been fun, but I was done.

I unwound his arms from around my waist. His weight against me now oppressive. It was kinda disturbing how, despite his heat, I wanted to shudder within my leather jacket. His room smelled of weed, Dior Sauvage hastily sprayed to cover up the weed, and the heady, musky spoor that could only be described as 'boy'. The cocktail was making me a little queasy. I picked up my satchel, forcing his arms to drop to his sides as I turned to face him. 'Do you want me, or do you just want me to want you?'

My Guy kissed his teeth and groaned, ran a hand across his face impatiently. 'Man, for fuck's sake, see like, here you go again, Kiki. Speaking in riddles. Just be straight with me.'

'I always am. I told you from jump what this was. You were cool. You said you preferred it. You do you. I do me.'

My Guy looked at me with almost the same intensity that he'd been looking at himself in the reflection a few seconds before. He was doing it again, hoping the fact that his eyes were hazel and his skin caramel were enough to work for him. If I hadn't chosen him specifically because there was no risk of falling for him. I guess it could have worked if I hadn't already bitten into him, felt the crunch and discovered that his sexy was fake.

'Yeah, but maybe . . . I didn't realise how much I'd like it when I do you.'

I knew how My Guy thought it sounded in his head. His voice had lowered into a purr, his eyes calculatedly heavy, constructed to elicit the image of him on top of me, his voice against my neck. It was meant to weaken me – and it had worked so many times for him, I'm sure – but I had an in-built resistance for that kind of bullshit. I'd been through it before and now I had immunity. He snapped out of intoxication mode on hearing my incredulous laugh, his eyes widening, mild annoyance and confusion slipping into them.

I shook my head. 'You haven't *done* me.'

'I mean, basically.'

'I mean, basically, we've only had a few spicy cuddles.'

'And whose fault is that?'

I smiled. 'I have to go.'

'You're shook and I get it, but you're different from the rest, Kiki. It isn't the same with you. You know I cancelled on Emma from Hazelwitch Hall for you tonight?'

I turned from my way to the door and pressed my hand against my chest. 'Oh, you shouldn't have. Really.'

My Guy nodded, rolled his tongue in his mouth, laughed humourlessly. 'You're really kind of a bitch. You know that?'

I grinned. 'I do. Thanks though. It means a lot coming from you. If a guy like you doesn't think I'm a bitch, that means I'm fucking up somewhere.'

He laughed heartily, with the energy of someone who hadn't understood a word I'd said, and went back to his bed, reclined, abs flexing, white boxer-briefs tighter than normal. It was like he had to physically remind himself that he was hot. As if he was actually capable of forgetting. 'Be like that. You're gonna be back.'

'Well, if I did leave an earring, you can toss it. I never wear my good shit here.'

OK, so it was a good exit line, and I was proud of it, but I'd jinxed myself. As I did my ritualistic double-checking of my bag (I couldn't leave any evidence of my presence) as the door to My Guy's flat clicked behind me, I realised I'd left my lip gloss. Shit. Actually, it was Aminah's lip gloss that she told me to look after in my bag and I'd forgotten to return a month ago. Despite the Best-Friend Bylaws stating that there is a statute of limitations in relation to make-up reclamation, I'm pretty sure she would be pissed at where I'd left it. She'd rather I'd flushed it down the toilet. After peeing on it. I couldn't have left it. I rooted for it as I absent-mindedly walked towards the lift, praying that God would forgive me for my recent transgressions. (Did it help that My Guy had a tattoo that said *In God We Trust* on his chest? In cursive, above a Tupac quote, '*Real eyes realize real lies*')

I hit a very firm, warm wall, my nose squishing against the soft cotton of a slate-grey shirt. 'Shit! My bad—'

'Nah, it's cool, don't—'

The voice was low and smooth, thick like honey sunk to the bottom of a tumbler of cognac. I looked up – but not enough because I found I'd only reached his nose: it travelled down his face narrowly and then curved out, drastically, majestically. I mean, it was quite enough to look at, but I thought I'd try again. I tilted my head a little further up till I hit black quartz gazing at me, glinting.

He was looking at me like he knew me. That was weird for a number of reasons, including but not limited to the fact that I knew everybody in the Black caucus of Whitewell College. I knew each clique, sub-group and faction and, granted, it was the third week of second year, so there was a bunch of new people, but even so. I flicked through my mental Rolodex of mandem and came up blank. He wasn't part of the Nigerian Princes (sons of Nigerian politicians); the Faux-Roadmen (studying Pharmacy at a redbrick university is not the same as dealing, sweetie); the Future Shiny Suits Who Read (a group that could include any of the above, but usually studied something finance-related, sought to work in the city, wanted an educated girl who 'knew her place', quite fine and included My Guy). Nor the Water into Wine (at the clerb) Bible Study Boys . . . nothing. Looking at his face seemed to actively contribute to my mind blankness, which was bizarre because my mind was never blank unless made purposely so. Like when My Guy was trying to talk to me about the *48 Laws of Power* one time.

He blinked and cleared his throat even though when I heard his voice the first time, it didn't sound like it could get any clearer. 'Uh, don't sweat it—'

Funny he should mention that, because I was. My skin was

tingling. This was intriguing. I didn't really sweat, and when I did (like the time I went on the elliptical for two hours while watching Beychella on my phone), it was like this, a slight prickle.

'I don't sweat. But thanks.' I started to move past him to the lift, encouraging him to do the same, towards his destination, his destiny, away from me, when he stopped suddenly, turned around, dark brows furrowed.

'Uh, I'm sorry, I just . . . did you say you don't sweat?'

I cast a gaze across the hall, partly to obnoxiously demonstrate the fact that no one else could have just said that and also to double-check that nobody was coming out or coming in. I knew every Blackwellian who lived on My Guy's floor and timed my visit, knowing that two of them were at Bible study, one at football and another at a friend's birthday dinner. There was nobody. I wouldn't be seen. I looked back at him, hitched a shoulder upwards.

'Yeah. Why?'

He nodded, eyes squinting, concentrating the light, the corner of his plush mouth quirking up. 'Sweating is a regular biological human function.'

'What's your point?'

'So, you're saying you're not a regular human.'

I smiled, slid my head to the side. 'Do I look like a regular human to you?' Trick question. He would stumble or leave. Stumble and leave. It was fun, tangling my words around their ankles, without them realising, and then watching them trip.

He inhaled deeply, like he was considering the question. He stepped back a little and assessed me, flicked a quick gaze down me that felt like he was striking a match against my body. Something flared under my skin. His eyes rose to meet mine again.

'Nah. Definitely not regular.' He smiled, and my pulse stuttered. 'Just not used to seeing another superhuman about, so had to double-check. It makes me feel less lonely, so thank you.'

Uh *huh*. I held still. That wasn't supposed to happen. I knew this game, this game was mine, and normally I knew how to lose those who attempted to chase. I'd expected to lose him. In fact, I'd wanted to lose him, to shake off whatever had been clinging on to me in the two minutes we had interacted, the gliding of energy on my skin that was making me fizz (I knew having a latte past 3 p.m. was a bad idea, I am mad sensitive), but not only had he followed me, it was like he already knew where I was going. It was like we were going the same way. He shot me a half-smile, sloping, something that managed to be tiny and also have the power to elevate his face, soften the steep angles. The sharp glare of the industrial lights in the hallway had nothing on it. It made its way to the pit of my belly and tugged.

Our eyes stayed on each other for a few seconds longer, as I attempted to figure out what the hell was happening, when a door clicked open somewhere in the near distance. Both of us jumped as if we'd been interrupted, as if there had been anything to interrupt, and turned to the direction of what would have been disturbance, as if there was anything to disturb.

Zuri Isak stood at the door to Flat 602 (I'd just left Flat 601) in a crop top and leggings, curls glossy and loose. Cute, casual. Purposely cute and casual. Zuri wasn't meant to be here. She was meant to be at her friend Nia's birthday dinner at Sakura in town. I knew this because there was a social media countdown designed to make people who weren't invited feel like they were missing out on the Groupon dinner, at a place where sugar daddies took their babies to dinner. Anyway, this was particularly interesting because Nia and Zuri had recently undergone a power shift in their clique, whereby Nia had usurped Zuri as Queen Bee by organising a group trip to Barcelona to stay at her stepdad's villa over the summer while Zuri was visiting family in Michigan. She could have easily reorganised it for when Zuri returned, but she didn't want to do that. It was a power play. A coup. And judging by the light mascara, dab of lip gloss and smidge of blush – I flicked my gaze over to Fellow Superhuman, only just noticing that he was holding a bottle of rosé in his hand – something told me that Zuri skipping the birthday dinner to Netflix and chill was also a power play.

Zuri nodded at Fellow Superhuman, who definitely wasn't as lonely as he made out to be. 'Hey you! I didn't hear you knock so thought I'd come check—'

He smiled at her. It was interesting. Objectively, as a scientist (fuckboiologist and mandemologist), it was different to the smile he gave me. The smile he gave her was mainstream, pop, radio-friendly. The smile he'd given me was the single released after an artist had established themselves, found their voice, could speak directly to their target audience. The smile he'd given me had more R&B to it.

He walked towards the open door. 'Sorry, the lift took its time—'

Zuri nodded absent-mindedly, throwing her gaze to me. 'Hey Kiki, wassup?'

She wasn't suspicious – I wasn't a threat; I was never a threat. I was known as The One Who Didn't Date – but that was precisely why my presence there was curious. I didn't have a clique and I lived with my best friend. Weren't nobody for me to visit. I'd thought this through, though. I had an alibi in a girl (not a member of the Black caucus) I had a political communication module with, and who also happened to live in Flat 604.

'I was just picking up some notes from Ilana.' I patted my satchel. 'Missed a lecture today. Cramps.'

I briefly wondered if the detail was overkill, but Zuri had stopped listening halfway through my sentence, anyway. Her hand was already curving around Fellow Superhuman's sturdy arm and she was looking up at him, long lashes batting. 'Cool. Awesome. I'm just . . . going over a tutorial too. Can't wait for your next show!'

She pulled him into her flat, but not before he threw me an inscrutable look. I shook my head, smiled, and pressed the lift button. Yeah, something was gonna be studied that night. A relief, really. My understanding of fuckboiology had fallen out of whack for a second. It was nice to have it reset. Whoever he was, he was just like the rest. That was comforting.

CHAPTER 2

Whitewell College Radio, 9.30–11.00 p.m. slot, Thursday, Brown Sugar Show

I snuck into the cramped campus radio studio, hoping that the fact that I'd opened the door gently would make a difference to the fact that I was late to my pre-show meeting with radio tech, producer (informal capacity) and best friend (formal capacity) Aminah. However, as soon as the door clicked open, she whizzed around on the bright-blue Office Depot chair, from where she was sat at the radio desk, twenty inches of wavy hair, swishing with the movement, a badass Bond villain with an exceptional ass.

She rose an immaculate brow. 'Where you been, bitch?'

'Library.'

'Lying.'

I grinned and shrugged my jacket off. 'Yup.'

'Do I wanna know?'

'No.'

Aminah narrowed her eyes. 'But I know.'

'I know.'

Aminah shook her head with kind concern, looking like a reality TV show therapist, pressing lilac gelled nails against her chest. She wasn't about to let this go.

'You know, Sis, it really isn't healthy to purposefully emotionally disinvest from intimate relationships—'

I furrowed my brows in mock confusion as I threw my jacket on the worn leather sofa against the wall. 'I'm sorry, I forget, are you a psych student or marketing?'

Aminah shook her head as she relinquished the seat by the desk and moved to the sofa, smacking my butt on her way over. 'All right, I don't like attitude. Very hostile. And actually, I took a psych module this term, but that's not the point. I got that from Auntie Jada Pinkett Smith's talk show—'

'Speaking of shows – can we prep for ours?'

Aminah smirked humourlessly. 'Nice pivot. Very well done. So now you wanna work? After being late for the staff briefing?' She grabbed a packet of plantain chips from the stash we kept in the cupboard in the corner of the room and sat herself on the sofa, pointing at me like a disappointed Nigerian grandma with a hand on her wrapper-wrapped waist. 'No snacks for you.'

I resumed my rightful place in front of the desk, slipped the headphones around my neck and tapped the laptop alive. 'I didn't wanna eat, anyway.' Another superfluous lie. 'And also, we *are* the staff. And it's fine, I know the topic I'm gonna cover and you *know* all we ever do in these meetings is talk shit—'

She popped a plantain chip in her mouth. 'Cffrucial for staff-bonding—'

'We live together—'

'What's your point?'

I laughed. 'You know what? I don't have one. You're right. I'm sorry . . .' I paused and cleared my throat, schooling my voice into nonchalance. I mean, I was nonchalant, but I wanted to be very clearly, unequivocally nonchalant because my best friend had emotional X-ray vision. 'Hey, real quick, um . . . I bumped into this guy earlier, and I've never seen him before, which is weird because—'

Aminah had brought her tablet out of the expensive structured bag she had laying on the sofa, presumably scrolling the show's page for today's topic. She immediately pulled down her black-rimmed designer spectacles and smirked, doing precisely what I hoped she wouldn't do, making my casual inquiry into a thing.

'Oh? Kiki Banjo intrigued by someone? Well, put me in a grey double-jersey sweater/jogger combo outfit because the world is clearly ending.'

In another life, Aminah Bakare – who was currently wearing a checked blazer together with a matching mini-skirt and a black polo neck – could easily have been Supreme of the Naija rich bitches at Whitewell College. Her parents ran a Nigerian snack empire called ChopChop (source of our endless supply of plantain chips), and up until the age of fifteen she'd been schooled in a prestigious international British school in Lagos, where everyone inexplicably spoke in an affected Valley-girl accent that she eschewed out of principle. ('Why would I choose to sound Kardashian? What kind of recolonisation?') Her parents thought that finishing her education in England (where she was born but not bred) would help her when it came to applying to university, so she ended up in a private boarding school in Sussex for a few years, which she'd hated. ('It was full of literal landed gentry and Freemasons, Kiki. You know what Freemasons are? It's white juju. The most wicked kind. I was the only Black girl and I swear to you my English teacher looked me directly in the eye and said the word 'nigger'. Yes, we were discussing *Catcher in the Rye*, but is that the point?!') She left to complete her A Levels at a state school on the east London/Essex border while staying with her aunt, achieving the straight As her parents swore she wouldn't be able to get without a school that counted Margaret Thatcher's grand-child as its alumnus. It was to Rosewood Hall's relief. She'd made their existence very difficult by levelling formal complaints about racialised comments made by staff members and students alike, refusing to wear a Remembrance Day poppy and questioning why they learned about the British Empire without criticising its brutality. The point is, that despite being a relative renegade and a Bad Bitch who rejected all expectations and presumptions, on a granular level – my best friend, my sister – Aminah Bakare was a princess who could detect the presence of a pea beneath a custom memory-foam mattress and, therefore, would not be caught dead wearing grey double-jersey out in public.

I rolled my eyes. 'All right, a little dramatic. Oṣe, Halle Barely—'

Aminah almost choked on a plantain chip. 'Wow—'

'Look, it's just for the social database, so we know what's going on in the uni. For work purposes. How can I talk about what's going on if I don't know what's going on? It's just weird because I've never seen him before and he was going to see Zuri Isak—'

Aminah pulled her glasses down further. 'Uh huh. Zuri Isak, who just so happens to live in the same building and, I believe, the same floor as—'

'You know what? Forget it. Let's just get ready for the show. We got ten minutes. Can you shoot me over some of the questions, please?'

Aminah smiled and turned her gaze back to the tablet screen 'OK, I'm gonna pretend to move on, but . . .' Her slickly shaped brows suddenly knitted in curiosity as she scrolled.

My brows instantly did the same, because when Aminah frowns, so do I. It's instinctive. 'What's up?'

'Hmm . . . so, this is weird. All the advice questions this week are super . . . specific? "How to make a guy wife you?"; "How to make a guy choose you?"; "How to be a priority?"'

I wheeled my chair over immediately. This was alarming and unlike Blackwellian women. They knew better – I'd made sure of it. True, we mainly dealt with relationship dilemmas and I primarily gave out romantic advice, but we'd never received a lump *genre* of question before. Nothing this focused.

Since First Year, when I started this show – R&B and soul punctuated with advice that tied into themes of songs – the Blackwellian babes and I had been through a lot. Together we dealt with Boys who said 'You're moving kinda mad still,' when you asked them the simple question of 'What are we?' I'd helped guide them around Mandem who elongated their 'wows', to questions that were veiled iterations of 'If you profess to like me, why don't you fucking act like it, you prick?'

That 'woooww' was a tool, I told the girls, the extra syllables added to buy the boy time to figure out what lie to tell you when you queried why you got a 'good morning, beautiful' text from him when your girl said he'd been seen coming out of Teni's flat this morning. I broke down how to handle guys who would then turn around and ask, 'Why u preeing for?' like you were the crazy one when the day before he had drawled, voice rumbling through collar bone, 'You're different still, you know that, babes. Never met anyone like you.' We had grown, developed in our studies of fuckboiology, my syllabus strong. So it seemed strange that suddenly they were preoccupied with being chosen. We were the choosers, we never begged.

Aminah had pushed her glasses back up, inspecting the comments with scientific attention: 'The comments are clique-wide: the Vegan Cupcakes, the London Gyaldem, Naija Princesses, Bible Study Babes, and all with the same kinda question. Plus, they're interacting with each other. Badly. There's no "You got this sis". It's . . . savage. It's "Stay away from him"-type shit.'

I took the tablet from her to examine it for myself. She was right. Instead of the usual supportive comments that littered the page, there was in-fighting, sniping – 'have you considered that maybe he ain't want you sis?'; 'sis, wasn't your man just caught in the bed of one of those white girls that always crash our motives dressed as rebore Kim Ks? Maybe take time to recover??' Sheesh.

'Sis' was a powerful, potent word, one that had the power to build up or destroy with the same intensity; it was a sword that could either be used to knight or slice. There was a bloodbath in the Brown Sugar comment section, even worse than when someone said they 'didn't really *get* Beyoncé' during a debate session at a Blackwellian meeting.

This was bad.

Since its inception, Brown Sugar was the glue that gelled the female factions of Blackwell together, the show was where we virtually communed and our social page was a safe space where girls would put aside their differences to bond with double-tap-likes over dickhead drama. Groups that didn't really fuck with each other during Blackwell socials (other universities had African-Caribbean Societies, we flipped the name of our institution and made it our own), would coalesce in the comment section to drag a Wasteman who replied to an errant 'I love you' with, 'safe, babes'. This was deep.

I passed the tablet back over to my best friend. 'This is over one guy. There's a unifying source here—'

Aminah nodded. 'Right, but this hasn't happened before. I mean, we've had girls fighting over guys, but not like this. And I really don't think the demographic of the Blackwell mandem has changed that drastically in the past year, and— Why do you have that look on your face?'

Of course. It had to be. Fellow Superhuman from earlier wasn't like the other guys. No, he was smooth, actually, genuinely smooth. Or at least extremely skilled at seeming genuine. He was warm, looked you in the eye. I had built up an immunity, and he had almost got me. He had looked at me, and I had felt it under my skin – and if he almost got me that meant that he definitely had got some of the other girls.

I nodded at Aminah. 'I think I know who it is. Do you have a way of checking if the girls have had a mutual follow on social media recently?'

Aminah smirked. 'Do I own every single item from Fenty Beauty? Let's not ask silly questions. I study digital marketing. I am good at what I do. I am a social media savant, sweetie.' She said all this while swiping and tapping like a maestro conducting an orchestra, effortlessly subduing technology with a perfectly manicured hand. She stopped abruptly, and held the tablet up to her chest, mischief peppering her face.

'Keeks, the guy you met before, was he tall, dark and handsome? Looks like he walked out of a nineties' romcom? Looking like some sort of stem-cell experiment between Kofi Siriboe and Morris Chestnut?'

I would have laughed if the description wasn't so creepily accurate. 'You found him?'

Aminah flipped the tablet around: it was zoomed in on the ProntoPic page that had Fellow Superhuman staring at me, on a beach, topless, pink board shorts with palm trees on them, a red cup in hand. His chest was all ridges and slopes. I was never really a fan of extreme sports, but hiking suddenly seemed like a cool thing to try.

Aminah's smirk broadened. 'I think we found the reason our girls are moving mad. His name is Malakai Korede. Transferred in September from Northchester University. So, we know he's smart. Smart enough to have you wondering who he is—'

I narrowed my eyes and took the tablet from her, scrolling through his pictures. His selfies were sparse, so we knew he wasn't overtly vain. He was confident, breezy with his looks, and when he *did* take selfies, they were purposeful. They were neither the badly angled close-ups of nostrils that made a sis quickly rush to say 'He's better in person', nor were they the cringey mirror poses, the squinted eyes, slight pout, captioned with a lazy trap lyric that boasted of money, bitches and swag the dude most likely lacked. Nah, Fellow Superhuman's – sorry, *Malakai's* – photos were interesting. There was one of him in front of the Mona Lisa..

I asked what she's on tonight and she side-eyed me. Curved by a 516-year-old, I can't believe it. #notageist

A smile I didn't agree to release slipped out. Unnerving. Huh. OK, so he somehow managed to be part of the 0.001 per cent of the male population that was vaguely amusing. I could see how that might rattle our girls. I was pretty sure the majority of guys in our uni thought satire was a way of describing an outfit.

I swiped a little more and came across a picture with the most cherubic little girl with rich black clouds at the side of her heart-shaped face, annotated with:

She's the boss of me. #uncleniecebonding #PrincessAliyah

So, he was good with kids; had a softness to him. The most dangerous thing about that was clearly it wasn't performed: there was no way he could fake the adoration with which he looked at that angel. With that obnoxious display of genuine cuteness, he was speaking directly to a bunch of young women whose mothers had told them that they were to graduate with a diploma in one hand and a future Obama in the other. The case of Malakai Korede was solidifying. He was a catch – fresh manna from heaven in the form of a man from Brixton (gleaned from tagged locations). And we, the girls of Whitewell, were in a romantic desert. Who were we to question God's boon, an oasis to satisfy our thirst? The comments on his photos ('go off king!') were from members of the same clique. The most recent photo featured heart emojis from Nia. And he was also desirable enough to be used as a pawn within inter-squad politics. Yeah, this was worse than I thought. He was evolved. He wasn't a cookie-cutter player, dumb but affable. He had a personality, ridges and hard edges and quirks and he still managed to be apparently generally palatable enough to be attractive to all the men-loving, femme sub-groups in Blackwell.

It was early October, but the scope of his reach in the female cohort of the ACS was already impressively wide – more than your regular, tall, dark, handsome headache could hope to achieve in six months. There was something about him, a different kick to his sauce. Our girls weren't fools; they were wary, tough. Sure, Malakai was fresh meat, but if they found him unpalatable, they would have spat him out pretty fast. But this boy remained undragged on social media, managing to fly under my radar, somehow safely untethered, despite having some sort of link to a spice from every Blackwellian female clique. No other boy on campus could have got away with it. Somehow, he was turning our girls on each other. Like an infection, he had to be drawn out.

I passed the tablet back to my best friend. 'I'm gonna deal with this. He's messing with our girls. Plus, they're our core demographic. We're a space of peace and truth and if he's causing discord within them, that's an issue for me.'

Aminah cackled and threw a plantain chip at me, which was mainly annoying because I hadn't managed to catch it with my mouth. A waste. 'Yeah. I'm sure you want him to cause discord in *your* core demographic—'

I wheeled myself back to the desk. 'OK. Well, I see you're not taking this seriously enough. Also, that doesn't even make sense—'

Aminah shrugged. 'I thought it was poetic.'

'Can we start the show?'

I smiled into the mic and adjusted the headphones on my ears, slid a knob on the mixing desk down and switched to a soft neo-soul instrumental, turning it down low.

'Good evening fam, that was D'Angelo and you already know what it is, kickin' it with Keeks and throwing it all the way back this Thursday night, giving you the finest, smoothest, sexiest tunes to vibe to – as always, because I care about you guys. I want you to have the best in all things. Now, with that being said, tonight I have something in particular I wanna discuss with my sisters. Fellas, stay if you want – but if you're easily rattled by women acknowledging their power, then please, to the left, to

23

the left. Take this as a health warning. If you start beating your chest so hard it becomes concave, my guy, you will only have yourself to blame.'

I smiled and glanced back at Aminah as she smirked, gave me a thumbs up in encouragement. I turned back to the mic. 'Now, with all health and safety concerns addressed I think I'm clear to tell you that I wanna talk about the concept introduced by tonight's theme song by our patron saint D'Angelo, with 'Playa Playa'. That's right. We're talking about *The Player*. Did you like how I said it? Like it was a monster or some shit.'

'Kiki—', Aminah admonished within her capacity of producer and person who had to make sure I adhered to university broadcast guidelines so we didn't risk our show being taken off air.

I grinned. 'Sorry. What I'm about to issue is a PSA. A public service announcement. A warning. It is crucial for our well-being, sisters. Now see, many people think of "player" as a gender-exclusive term. It's a guy smooth with his tongue . . . in a couple different ways. Don't act shy, you know what I mean. This is a safe space, girls. Let your savagery unleash. We are red-blooded women and we have needs, OK?'

Aminah laughed as she clicked her fingers above her head like she was at a spoken-word recital. 'Go ahead, Sis. Tell it.'

I allowed my voice to slip into an exaggerated spoken-word cadence, low and silken, 'It's a guy with so much sauce he has you swimming in it. Has your head spinning in it so you don't know which way is up and which way is down – so you don't even realise when he has you trippin' for him.'

Aminah let out a loud hum as if she was in church, and I turned to see her, eyes closed, hand on heart, shaking her head as if she was receiving the word.

I stifled a laugh, rolled my eyes and turned back to my mic, my voice becoming sombre now, morphing into my ten-o'clock-news-bulletin voice, 'But allow me to ask a question, my sisters. If he is a player, are we games? Or are we consoles to be used to help a guy navigate his way to being a man? Our buttons being pressed, being turned this way and that for his progression?'

Aminah hummed louder and raised her hands in praise.

I leant closer to the mic even though no one could see me, because I knew the effect would be felt, the punctuation would ripple through the airwaves. 'Aren't you tired of mandem using your hearts for sport? I ask this now because I heard there's a new player in town. And I won't lie, he's kind of cute too. A snack. A *beverage*. But you guys know that too much coffee is bad for you, right? Keeps you up all night, bad for your heart, makes you thirsty and occasionally, if you're extra sensitive, gives you the shits. This analogy went left, but you catch my drift.

'In a similar manner, there is a tall, hot, dark presence in Whitewell that has our ladies moving hectic. Giving them the shakes, making them snappy, dehydrated and irritable. Be wary of the Wasteman of Whitewell, sisters. It's cuffing season and feelings are infectious, I get it, but get your immune system up, take your shots (I myself am partial to bourbon), listen to Megan Thee Stallion twice a day, and take your antihistamines to ward off the dusty. Because you know what I think, ladies? It's time to flip the term "player" on its head. This thing called romance ain't a one-player game. Let's reclaim our power.

'Wastemen are aptly called so because they waste our time. Waste our energy. On purpose. They sell us dreams and then take them away, so we end up chasing them as if it was ever a reality. They're bad at communication, texting us good morning every day and then leaving us in the cold of blue ticks when we ask them where they're at, leading to us to jumping to conclusions, and let me tell you, that kind of cardio isn't good for our hearts. It takes us away from us. Wastemen are thieves. What was it that my king D'Angelo said in his parable of a bop, 'Playa Playa'? They rob you of your glow, queens. See, that time and energy that they take from us could be used for realising our power. Stop us from seeing how beautiful we are from soul through to skin, because he has you wondering why you aren't enough. Now ain't that a bitch? If you ask me, I think we should be bigger bitches.

'Sisters, I'm not suggesting anything radical. Just that we take our control. The game will always be the game, but make sure you're at least an equal player. At best, a better one. Call it karmic restitution. Make them sweat you and don't ever let them catch you slippin'. Until next time, stay sweet, ladies. Yours always, K.'

CHAPTER 3

'Ms Banjo! You're early.'

I smiled as I entered Dr Miller's office. She dusted some brownie crumbs off her fingers. Somehow, the action was elegant, in line with the dreads wrapped up in an ochre headscarf, large crescent bronze earrings and the brown-plum sheen of her lips. I plopped myself on the chair by her desk and threw my satchel on the floor. 'Which is why I'm your favourite student.'

'It's not appropriate to have favourites.'

'So you admit it, I am your favourite.' I passed her the flat white I'd picked up with my latte from the campus coffee shop, Beanz.

My most hallowed female authority figure, aside from Beyoncé and my mother, adjusted tortoise-shell frames on a flawlessly composed blank face. 'I'm technically not allowed to take anything from students. I absolutely cannot drink this.'

She motioned at me with a single finger, capped by a gleaming, wine-coloured nail and bearing a hefty, intricately designed silver ring – instructing me to put the coffee down on the desk. '. . . It's wonderful how I just found a flat white on my desk, randomly. Can't let it go to waste.' She picked it up, took a sip, smiled. 'Thank you.'

I hitched up a shoulder. 'For what?' I held up my coffee cup and smashed it against hers in a toast to tutor–student boundaries.

Dr Miller and I weren't thrown together as a mentor–mentee duo by chance. I studied Politics, Media and Culture and she taught an Intertextual Media and Culture module. She also happened to be the only one of the two Black lecturers in the entire institution of Whitewell who looked after undergraduates. The other Black lecturer was a man who once gave a speech to the boys of Blackwell during Black History Month on how the best way to avoid trouble was not to look like trouble (no saggy trousers, no looking 'Black'). Earlier statement revised: Dr Serena Miller was the only Black lecturer in my university.

I decided that she had to be my mentor in first year, in my third seminar. During a class discussion on the cultural power of social media crossed with art, where I cited *Lemonade* as an example, a Barbour-wearing boy called Percy, who I once heard describe the class as 'community service' – for him, 'the diversity stuff looks good on the CV', interrupted to inform me that the visual album was an example of 'convoluted fluff pandering to identity politics and contributing nothing to society at large'. I opened my mouth to call him an uncultured, narrow-minded, racist prick, but thought better of it and instead practised some breathing exercises I'd learnt from my favourite YouTube lifestyle guru, Coco, from The Chill Life with CoCo.

'Don't you feel like—' (*deep breath . . . inhale . . . exhale . . .*) '—you're speaking from a rather limited sphere? (*Seriously, Kiki, deep breath . . . exhale.*)

'As a white male, your culture is the norm—' (*am I speaking weirdly slowly?*) '—and it's likely that that is the reason why you—' (*are a fucking prick*) '—think that any deviation from that is lesser than. Why you think anything "other than" *is* "lesser than".'

The class fell silent and Percy went precisely the colour of his confectionery counterpart from M&S. Dr Miller's face was ostensibly expressionless, a stoically impartial monarch, dangling earrings adding gravitas, bronze lips pressed in a manner that almost obscured the slight flick in them. The curve would have approximated pride or amusement, or both, if I didn't know better.

She cleared her throat and continued, 'I think what Ms Banjo is trying to suggest is that what you're saying aligns with what critics unable to think outside of the confines of their self-imposed racial rigidity would say. And that racial rigidity often leads to bigotry and prejudiced opinions. Let's be wary of that.'

Dr Miller paused before continuing, giving us the space needed to digest that she had, indeed, used the language of academia to call Percy a racist prick, her intelligence and expertise protecting her from lawsuit and sanction. 'However, it does open up a discussion,' she said, walking the breadth of the lecture hall, pen tapping against her palm. 'What do we think? Has social media led society closer to a post-racial society? An interracial society? Or are we more segregated than ever?' She opened it up to the class, but not before throwing me, the only Black girl in the tutorial, a sturdy, small smile.

Although we had an African-Caribbean Society through Blackwell, Whitewell College was still a liberal arts university in pastoral southern England and, therefore, a minority set to task in validating the use of the term 'diverse' in the prospectus. We were a world unto our own when concentrated together at a student house party, with the lights turned off, elbow-to-elbow and butt-to-groins in constricted corridors. But, in actuality, we were scattered across the university, across disciplines, across years, all feeling like rebels because instead of straight up professional degrees (law, economics, whatever-will-put-you-in-corporate-wear-and-a-nine-to-five-and-make-immigrant-parent-sacrifices-worth-it), we mixed it up with funky minors that our parents thought frivolous.

We thought we were so edgy with our interdisciplinary courses, our economics and art history degrees that made African parents wonder where they went wrong, but the price we paid for being such deviant rebels, in pursuit of higher education, was being even more minoritised, in a space where we were already pretty marginalised. So, when Dr Miller looked at me that day, I knew she was saying we had to stick together, knew that I had to write a letter asking to be switched from my assigned tutor, who'd informed me they were relieved that they could call me Kiki instead of my full name, Kikiola. Due to the kind of benevolent racism you can count on – your white friend trying to set you up with the only Black guy she knows – I didn't need to plead too much before my wish was granted, Dr Miller becoming my personal tutor, and quickly part of my university survival kit.

'So,' Dr Miller reclined in her seat. 'You are objectively one of the highest-achieving students that I teach—'

'You can just say the—'

Dr Miller released a small, demure smile. 'Well, you've had a little competition lately—'

Impossible. 'That's funny, Dr Miller.'

Dr Miller's face betrayed no evidence that she was joking. I straightened. I took the 102 version of her class because it was the only module where: a) I was being taught by someone who saw me; and b) I could talk about Aunt Viv being replaced in *Fresh Prince* and relate it to racialised desirability politics. It was where I thrived, where my mind felt both at ease and challenged and where I also just so happened to virtually get straight firsts in every assignment. Dr Miller's revelation was humbling.

Dr Miller's smile broadened at the look on my face, and she continued, 'This is actually what I wanted to talk to you about. As you know, NYU Brooks Media & Art Institute is our sister college and every year every professor can nominate one second-year student to qualify for their summer programme of choice. It looks good on the CV, will boost you in the hunt for grad jobs and it's a chance to experience something new, to expand your horizons. I know their Pop Media programme is perfect for you. Candidates will be paid and given the opportunity to rotate departments at a media house that includes audio, digital, television and print. Many people on the programme went on to work at the very organisations they shadowed. Have you heard of Temilola Lawal?'

I swallowed. 'Um, the culture journalist who just became the youngest person to win a Pulitzer for feature writing?'

Dr Miller nodded. 'She went on the programme. I think you'd be a great candidate.'

'Wait, Dr Miller, are you serious?'

It was too much – of what I wanted to do, exactly what I had been waiting for – and it filled my chest till my giddiness spilled out of my mouth. The summer before university I'd missed out on a competitive media internship in London due to reasons I liked to file under 'personal'. Too many feelings had hampered my ability think straight last time, my mind was too messy and my heart was too unharnessed. I had myself together this time. I was collected, controlled. In other words, I wasn't about to fuck this up.

Dr Miller's eyes glinted. 'I'm not joking. Jokes are rather tedious, don't you think? I'll email you the forms. Deadline is January. Now, I know you'll do fine with the essay part of the application. It's about the power of media and your personal con- nection to it, but you will also need an exceptional media-related, extracurricular project—'

'Oh, easy—'

'And I know you already have that with Brown Sugar,' Dr Miller continued with a pointedly quirked brow, 'which is wonderful, but your task concerns . . .' She clicked on her laptop with a red, polished nail and pushed her glasses up. '"Building, creating or growing. The candidate will need to pursue and achieve tangible growth of a media project or platform, by diversifying the format or by building from scratch." It's about evolving what you already have and recording how you did it. A project plan—'

'Brown Sugar is already one of the most popular media platforms on campus—'

'Your base is commendable. Decent. Loyal. I've seen the numbers. But there is still room to grow. It's a great show but there's plenty of ways to improve it, if you want to. It might be worth doing some sort of survey to find out why the people who don't listen, don't listen.'

I nodded, sat up, 'OK. I mean, of course, I'll do what I can to lift up the ratings, but surely, it's not my job to *chase* listeners, right? They're either with me or they're not. I can't contort myself into something I'm not—'

Dr Miller smiled, a genteel glimmer of a sword. It told me she was about to sweetly read me, drag me, or both. '*Kikiola*,' the force of my full name informed me that I was right. 'Media is about staying true to your voice, of course, but it's also about interacting with the people you're communicating with. It's not about talking *at*, it's talking to – with.

'What do people want? How can it align with what you're trying to achieve? Are you generating conversation or just providing didactic answers? You may have blind spots – in fact, I know that you do – especially when it comes to opening up to other people.'

I usually didn't mind Dr Miller using the operative word in 'personal tutor', but in this instance, it jarred. Couldn't she just awkwardly ask me how I'm 'coping' with university and shove some pamphlets about student alcoholism my way, like a regular one?

'Dr Miller, I work in groups all the time in seminars!'

Dr Miller raised a brow. 'Kiki, when you're put in a group, you don't give space for other people's ideas.'

'But in our mass media presentation Harry suggested that books should have the ability to be ingested through a serum we inject. It was worrying. Also, we need to talk about the counselling system in this school—'

'It was out-of-the-box thinking. Why don't we question traditional modes of information? It was worth discussing, even if you did conclude that it lent itself too easily to eugenics and indoctrination,' Her lips were a wry slant. 'Another issue is that you do all the work and divide it among the group,'

'I do n—'

'I know your voice, and I hardly think a Patricia Hill Collins quote is coming from Percy. Kiki, I really want to be able to put you forward for this programme. You're the perfect candidate. But I also want to see all you can be for it, and that means challenging yourself. Brown Sugar can be bigger, and I think that may include figuring out how you can work with the needs of your community.'

My shoulders slumped, and I sat back in my chair. This wasn't a stipulation, this was a glitch, a catch, like yes you have free tickets to a Drake concert, but you have to listen to white dudebros rapping it in your ear at a party for three hours straight beforehand. The formula worked. People wrote in and I responded – how else could I work with my community?

I sighed. 'Dr Miller, I hope I don't sound arrogant here, but I know what I'm doing with Brown Sugar. I'm good at it. Can't I figure out some other way to boost ratings?'

Dr Miller's lips pulled into a subtle smirk. 'Kiki, it's not arrogant to know what you're good at. It's arrogant to think you don't need to grow. Find out what more you can do for your people. I know you'll find a creative way to do it. I mean, every seminar you find a way to call Percy the same thing using different words.' She sipped her coffee, hiding her tongue in her cheek.

I tried to balance my elation that she believed in me with the fact that she was basically asking me to do the impossible. Brown Sugar was my space. Yeah, I shared it with other people, but I was safe behind it. Inviting other people's opinions meant it was likely to fall out of my control, become messier. It meant I could mess up. I wasn't in the habit of doing that.

Dr Miller smiled widely. 'What a sweet look of torment on your face. Look, I have something fun that could help. The student in my other seminar—'

Ah, my nemesis.

'—is working on a new film. I'm their personal tutor too. They came to me asking if I thought the film was a good idea, and I do. They're just missing something, and I think talking to you would help them. Likewise, I think you talking to them might help you come up with ideas to reach people. They're personable, friendly—'

'Dr Miller, are you saying that I'm n—'

'You're a delight, Kikiola, but people use consultants in media all the time. This student is bright and sharp. They're also new, so I think you would be able to help them settle in. This person is different to your fellow seminar students, they're more . . . your wavelength. You'll work well together—'

'Oh, so they're Black?'

Dr Miller ignored me, possibly because answering that question would have risked her suspension. 'I'll email you some of their work. I think you'll find it interesting.'

I rubbed the bridge of my nose, prickling a little at my phantom academic nemesis. I wondered if she could pull off sideboob? Probably. It was tragic, perhaps, but school was my thing, my skill at it an anchor, and now, apparently, I needed a helper to achieve my goals.

Dr Miller's amber-brown eyes filled with warmth as she assessed me. 'I want you to go to New York for this programme, Kikiola, and I really want to be able to give you the best shot of getting there. Give it a chance.'

I wasn't sure if Dr Miller liked me or secretly hated my guts. Why go out of my way to entangle myself with other people when I was doing fine by myself? This was my fault for choosing a liberal arts university in England. Who does that? It's not even the norm and now, because I didn't choose to do biochemistry or law like a good Nigerian daughter, I had to suffer through some kind of holistic abstract learning experience with a stranger?! Put me through a Tort tournament, please. Maybe this was actually my parents' fault. Their understanding and relative liberalness gave me the freedom to opt for a degree I'd enjoy rather than one that would set their mind at ease. Quite short-sighted of them to value my happiness. Being a lawyer wouldn't even have been that bad. Sure, my soul might have become a calcified husk, but I would look great in a formal pencil skirt. I have a great butt.

'You have three months. Plenty of time. I'm looking forward to seeing what you come up with for Brown Sugar.' Dr Miller silenced any potential questions by putting her coffee down for the last time. 'That's enough for today. Enjoy your student party tonight. And thank you for not bringing me a flat white.'

'It wasn't my pleasure at all.'

She lifted her empty cup in salute.

CHAPTER 4

An Afrobeat song was playing; skipped beats and melodies that smoothed around waist and hip, cajoling them to come out, come play. I wanted to come out, come play – or at the very least not think about New York or some irritant getting in the way of it. A rugged, low, sexy West African mandem voice pleading with babygehl not to kill him with that load she's carrying (the load, if it wasn't clear, is her butt) was pulsating through the speakers and mingling with the crisp autumn night. Aminah and I, positioned as the babyghels, moved through it, hips swaying, heels clicking and clopping against the asphalt as we walked the path to our gritty student bar, shabby on the outside, but the hottest rap video club on the inside. To us, anyway. Everything we did as Blackwellians, we did as a pastiche of the luxe life.

Aminah and I walked with linked arms into the party, through the small, loose crowd that was kissing, laughing, smoking by the open backdoor of the little room annexed behind the Student Union. It parted to make way for us. Aminah and I weren't popular or unpopular, we just *were*. Though previous experience had made me wary of making friends, Aminah and I formed a natural unit.

We were placed in the same halls in first year and met four days after we moved in. We were taking out our bins at the same time one morning, both in our PJs – which happened to both be jersey shorts and tank tops – hair wrapped in satin scarves. We gave each other polite, silent nods and smiles, acknowledging the intrinsic kinship derived from makeshift pyjamas and Black womanhood, when a toga-clad drunken straggler who looked like his name was Chad, or possibly Brad, swayed past us in the courtyard, releasing fumes of alcohol. Like we could sense what was coming, we exchanged a glance. He smirked at us and called out, 'Oi Destiny's Child! Shake what your mama gave ya! Show me if I'm ready for this jelly!' As if in rehearsal, both of us immediately dropped our trash bags and started cussing him out in sweet, tight harmony. ChadBrad started to sway away, startled, alarmed, but alcohol had slowed down his motion, so he had ended up staggering like a poisoned rat. This allowed Aminah to step forward and yank the hem of his toga, ignoring his yells, and leaving him naked bar a pair of boxers. It was then I realised that I was in love. She smiled, and I immediately beckoned at her to toss it to me. She did, trusting my instincts, probably encouraged by our riveting rendition of 'Who the fuck do you think you are, you prick?' earlier. I caught the reeking bed sheet between my thumb and forefinger and tossed it into the giant wheelie bins outside our building. We both immediately ran inside the glass doors, falling over ourselves, wheezing, grabbing each other for stability. She said to me that day, 'You're my friend by force now. I really don't have the energy to go and make any more, so shall we just see how this goes?' And so, we were friends by force, and I was grateful – I wasn't sure I would have found the courage to be her friend without her declaration. I'd come to university bruised.

Now, we stood outside of the cliques and the Blackwell industrial complex. We were a core unto ourselves, Brown Sugar lending us immunity from being too involved, and because of that, we found ourselves acting as intermediaries, ambassadors and impartial judges when called upon. This garnered us some respect, if not exactly warmth. It worked for me: I didn't need to be too involved. I didn't need a group; I didn't want to be entangled in friendships that were just ways to run away from loneliness. I had Aminah, and I had Brown Sugar, and that was my community. I wanted to get my degree, secure my future and leave. That didn't mean that I couldn't have a good time along the way.

The bar was steamy and dusky, smelling like Hugo Boss, fruity body sprays, Brazilian bundles toasted straight and the chemically floral-scented melange of hair products. Grease, spritz, gel and mousse used to primp to perfection. Amber and umber lights lit up the dark and saw twilight and sunset finding a home in heavily moisturised brown skin, making it glow with delicate force. The music seemed to make the walls of the old university bar pulsate, like it wasn't already thrumming with the energy of around a hundred-odd kids overstuffed into its every crevice and cranny, waved on cheap vodka and dark liquor and arrogance, the kind of arrogance you get intrinsically when you're young and fine. Guys with sharp shape-ups. Girls in dresses that flaunted their curves. Both feeling confident that they were likely to find someone to feel them as much as they were feeling themselves.

This was our kingdom, where we came to unwind, escape, put our defences down every Friday after a week of our housemates, Ellie and Harry, asking us where we were from-from. This wasn't the main student union party, where we had to have our shoulders braced and brows pre-arched as certain people who were so used to having access to the whole world couldn't comprehend the cordoning off of one little peninsula and dropped 'nigga' like the '-a' wouldn't curdle into an '-er' in their mouths when they were rapping along to Kanye. If we got into a fight, it would be *us* that got kicked out, like we were the ones who started it – like this particular fight hadn't started a long, long time ago and it was proven, irrevocable, historical fact that we weren't the ones to throw the first punch. Nah. None of that.

This was *our* space.

FreakyFridayz.

When I first arrived at Whitewell, the only events we had were overstuffed house parties in the home of a grad student who was far too old to be rubbing shoulders (etc.) with freshers, a few town hall meetings, where people just discussed what happened at the last house party, and a Black History Month 'talent show' that consisted mainly of us having to sit through mandem's mediocre raps and bad spoken word. We were the only society on campus with no demarcated space. No land, no stake. The Rugby Society had the bar on Wednesday afternoons, the Young Conservatives had their afternoon tea parties on Thursdays, and the Whitewell Knights had their gin and (C)oke nights there on Tuesdays.

Early on, Aminah had dragged me to a Blackwell Society meeting. ('Let's just try to be social. For once. See what happens. Kofi said they're ordering pizza today. If you break out in a rash, I promise I'll carry you away on my back.'). I sat in the back of the lecture hall, legs hunched up against the seat in front of me, listening to the president, Zack Kingsford, half-English, half-Nigerian, fully a prick, fully a snack, asking for donations to rent a place in town for a party (fifty each, far more than would have been needed). When a voice called out, 'Why do all that shit when we could throw a club night?' I thought that someone else had the precise thought I had at the exact same time, until I realised that everybody in the lecture hall was staring at me and that the voice had sounded eerily like my own. I didn't come to these things. I barely spoke to anybody outside of the confines of Brown Sugar and so I guess people were shocked to hear me. I was shocked.

Zack stared at me, his eyebrow with a single slit in it, arched with curiosity. Zack was president, reigning Monarch of the Mandem, and your position in Blackwell was meant to be defined by whether you wanted to be fucked by him, loved by him or friends with him. I wanted none of the above and it confused him. He looked up at me from his podium.

'Kiki Banjo. I see you've taken a break from bashing men on your cute show to come join us today. You wanna come down? State your position?'

I smiled. 'I'm good. You can come up though.' A snigger rippled through the crowd and I felt Aminah settle into her chair next to me, whispering, 'Here we fucking go.' We were only two semesters in but we were already spiritually married and Aminah knew that now I had just exposed myself, there wasn't any way I was going to back down. She also undoubtedly found Zack's discomfort delicious.

He was second-year incumbent – technically against the bylaws of university societies, but who was watching? Zachary Kingsford was used to giving orders, he never received them. He thought his name gave him jurisdiction over all. And technically it did. A middling business studies and sports science student, his place at a top liberal redbrick university was assured by the fact that he was a boon to the university athletics department, a star in the university rugby leagues – that and his daddy was a very rich benefactor. Zack was not smart, but he was slick with words, bolstered by nepotism. He was the perfect politician. He smiled something strained in my direction, hazel eyes glinting with irritation. I'm sure it hurt. He preferred conversations with girls who giggled and said he 'kinda looked like Drake'. He was so gassed on that he'd changed his ProntoPic username to CognacDaddy à la ChampagnePapi.

'No problem.' But the vein popping on his temple stated otherwise, 'Nothing wrong with a woman being on top. Actually, I prefer it.' The offence was in his predictability.

I rolled my eyes as the sniggers got louder. This was why I never liked to get involved with petty collegiate political shit. It was so needlessly tedious. I nodded slowly. 'That was cute. Rehearsing for your future sexual harassment case at the suit-wearing drone job your daddy got for you?'

Zack's tan cheeks flushed deep. The room erupted, low and rumbling and Aminah uttered a proud, adulatory 'Killa Keeks.' When the noise died down, I managed to speak before he did, still reclining in my chair, boot hitched on the back of the empty seat in front of me.

'All I'm saying is that we don't need to spend money when we should have our own space for free. Every month on a Friday, we throw a club night here. Obviously, open for all, but it will be thrown by us, for us. On our terms. Our music. No bouncers saying we're not dressed right. Or there are too many of us in a group. We're treated as guests here. People to fill up quotas. Like they're doing us a favour. Let's make ourselves at home.'

The room thundered. So did Zack, but in an entirely different way. Even though he was several feet away from me, I could see he was rattled. Something about his discomfort turned me on.

Zack wasn't used to acting like a president. He'd never really had a platform beyond looking hot. During his second election – the one I was around for – he'd taken a bunch of freshers out to an R&B night (the only one in town) and bought them shots, which helped him win by a landslide. In another context this might have triggered an intervention by the UN, but here, in the instance of collegiate politics, it was a tale of rightful victory, one of generosity, real love for The People. Zack was here for image, not real action.

I could see Zack attempt the math in his head. Public rejection of my idea would look bad. He swallowed awkwardly, nodded. 'I hear you. You've raised some valid points.'

Oh. I hadn't realised it was going to be that easy.

'All those in favour of Kiki Banjo taking charge of this project—' Zack boomed across the room.

I froze. 'Wait, what? No, no. No, no, no.'

Zack grinned at me widely. Prick. He was smarter than I thought. He was deflecting, hoping that putting the focus back on to me would mean that he wouldn't have to follow through with it.

'—say *yeaaaaaaayahhhhhh*.' His voice swept low and deep and picked up at the end of his sentence like this was a call-and-response rap song and not an impromptu appointment into his cabinet.

I started to panic. 'This is your job. This doesn't even count as a proper vote! Whatever happened to democratic integrity?!' My voice was drowned out by the overwhelming sound of an entire lecture hall – around 150 of my peers – shouting 'Yeeeeeeahyah!'. I swore under my breath.

Zack, the bitch, had smiled and winked at me, arms spread wide as he bowed sarcastically. 'Your job now, Queen.'

And because I was Nigerian, a chronic over-achiever and proud as shit, I accepted. And, if I said so myself, I killed it: FreakyFridayz became the hottest night on campus.

It was bustling now, loud and, despite the raucousness, the bellow of, 'Oi. Tia and Tamera!' rang clear and true. Only one person used that nickname for us – due to Aminah and I being as insepa-rable as twins, though lacking the syndicated sitcom we obviously deserved. Sure enough, a few seconds later our boy Kofi inter-cepted us. Kofi was a business student by day, and FreakyFridayz DJ by night. He transitioned from old school bops to fresher beats later in the night, often slipping in his own creations from his side hustle as a bedroom producer.

He bent down to kiss me on both cheeks, then reached for Aminah's hand to press it to his lips. Kofi's full-time 24/7 calling was to feen for my best friend. She rolled her eyes and shook her head, playing her role, swallowing her smile, giving him a little to savour but not enough to commit. Their relationship was one of push and pull, cat and mouse, where one was never really sure who was the cat and who was the mouse at any given time. Kofi was a cute, well-liked Ghanaian prince from south London and Aminah was a Nigerian princess from west. It was a Pan-African diaspora fairy tale waiting to happen, one for the ages, a pending peace treaty for the continual Jollof Wars, the West African cousin conflict that raged at weddings and birthday parties ('Basmati or plump? I heard you guys put nutmeg in yours – sorry, is it dessert?'). But Aminah was a fellow stush Yoruba princess and, as such, ascribed to our own particular brand of feminism: a man had to earn attention, so when he got it, he cherished it.

I cast an eye around the party, readjusting the chain of my bag on my shoulder. 'What's it saying tonight, Kof?'

Kofi let out an easy grin, looking directly at Aminah. 'On mute till you guys pulled up.'

Aminah tilted her head, her wavy tresses falling further down her shoulder. She stepped forward, gently gripping his chin. 'So, you missed the sound of my voice?'

Kofi smirked. 'The sound of your voice, the sight of your face . . .' His eyes dropped to her lips. Aminah rolled her eyes, pushing his face away as Kofi laughed. I cleared my throat. I loved them both but the sexual tension was getting stuck in my throat. Second-hand sexual tension has a kind of tangy aftertaste.

Kofi glanced back at me, his smile more affable, less besotted. 'Nah, seriously, been waiting for you. Can't start my set without my girls—'

I quirked a brow and smiled. 'What you *mean* is, you can't start your set without asking me if you can play more than one Blaq Kofi original tonight. Right?'

The deal was that FreakyFridayz would be a collaboration

between Brown Sugar and Blackwell Society. I was in charge of sorting the music and events, and Blackwell was on logistics.

Kofi grinned. 'Sis. This is the one. I mean it. You'll love it. Have I ever let you down?'

I reached up to squeeze his cheek. 'That time you tried to set me up with your finance bro – cousin who said "Females like you" in conversation—'

Kofi rose his hands up in surrender. 'That was my bad. Vincent drives an Audi and is always in Dubai and you're kind of fancy to me, so I just thought—'

I smiled. 'Kofi, I'm playing, you know I love your stuff.' And I did: it was spacy and electronic but still somehow soulful, still somehow euphoric. 'But if we play it now, it's not gonna get the attention it deserves. People are waved and they're just going to hear something that isn't the new Burna and be pissed. The atmosphere has to be right. Let me play it on my show next week, get people familiar and then you can play it at the next FreakyFridayz—'

'My G.' Kofi gave me a goofy grin, put his hands together and bowed before me. He turned to Aminah. 'Your girl is a genius.'

Aminah smirked. 'Obviously. I only keep company with greatness.'

Kofi bopped closer to Aminah, and she shot him a sly smile as he said, 'Is that a compliment?'

'It's a challenge.'

Just like she'd written, Kofi swiftly, gently, reached out for her arm, 'Come Queen, let me treat you to a beverage before my set,

I tell you my five-year plan, you tell me yours, and I'll see where I can fit in.'

I grinned as Aminah threw me a knowing look while Kofi led her to the bar, her arm looped through his. This was my cue to resume my post as Chief-Tone-Regulator of FreakyFridayz.

CHAPTER 5

'**D**id you see her walk in just now? Fuming.'

As I was about to situate myself in my usual corner, where I could oversee without participating, two Blackwell girls – Bible Study Babes – walked past, voices gleeful.

'I know. Bless. This is what happens when you don't approach relationships spirit first. It's sad. Poor thing.' There was a respectable pause before true gossip-thirst was revealed. 'Let's go see.'

I slowed in my tracks. While I often let disruptions diffuse and dissipate on their own – a little tension helped to thicken the passion and excitement in the air – it was a delicate balance, and a sleight of hand (or a slap of hand) could contaminate the whole vibe and bring it to an abrupt end.

Just as I moved to follow the girls in the direction of the potential source of drama – was it a frenemy fight, a ting tussle? – a strong scent of reality-star-branded perfume, hairspray and distilled

hateration wafted past my nostrils, swiftly followed by a sicken-
ingly syrupy voice saying, 'Oh hun, you must be lost or something:
this is our spot.'

I turned to the left of me to see precisely what I'd expected to
see: Simi Coker in terror mode. She was stood in front of a girl
I knew to be a First Year, who, along with three of her friends,
had made the mistake of occupying one of the shabby, beat-up tan
leather sofas that comprised a 'booth'. Due to the fact that this
wasn't actually a high-end lounge but a gritty student bar it wasn't
technically possible to reserve a booth, but this was irrelevant to
Simi, who believed she owned it by virtue of being ex-president,
self-appointed Baddest Bitch on Campus. (It was on her ProntoPic
bio, '*Ex-President of Whitewell College ACS, and self-appointed Boss
Bitch on Campus, Booty & Brains*', lest we got confused.) And the
fact that she had sat there, week after week, sipping Malibu and
pineapple with her security detail (the four specifically selected
girls who were interchangeable 'besties').

The First Year blinked and immediately jumped up from the
sofa, yanking her Back, crushed-velvet body-con dress down
and immediately gestured to her squad to do the same. They
grabbed plastic cups and hitched bags on shoulders as the First Year
said, 'Oh shit, my bad, Simi. I didn't realise—', with deference.
Although this girl was only a month and a half into university
life, she knew what Simi had worked hard to establish: she had
authority on campus.

Having had a taste of the power and loving its tang, Simi had
transferred her legacy from the political office to social media,

and concentrated all her clout in The TeaHouse, a forum she had launched that kept all the Black caucus up to speed with which events and house parties were coming up. It also – and this was crucial – functioned as a gossip machine that spilled high-grade, steaming Campus Ceylon, mainly revealing who was Cuffed Up (usually proven by a blurry picture taken at Nando's) and who had been caught cheating (usually proven by a blurry picture taken at Nando's). Simi Coker could make or break you. Naturally, with me being asocial, she hated me. I represented everything she was against. I offered romantic clean-up while her business was situated in romantic mess, and my platform happened to be as big as hers. Both our voices held sway, and she saw me as her only known threat.

Simi smiled, shimmering lids batting, before she slid a smug look to her posse. 'It's OK babes. You weren't to know—' Her voice was a sugar and wasabi dip.

This wasn't any of my business, and I wasn't in the mood to face Simi. I was on a mission – Disturbance Detection – and yet, despite myself, I snorted.

Simi turned a fraction, bum-length water waves swishing elegantly. Simi, of course, was beautiful, the kind of beautiful that had always been told it was beautiful: smooth butterscotch skin, with a sweetness that didn't quite seem to sink into her personality.

'Kiki.' Her hand was flicked out, a Gucci number hanging off the crook of her arm, her Unfriendly Black Hottie energy dialled to ten. 'Can I help you? Is there a reason you're minding my business instead of yours as a pretend club manager?'

I sighed and smiled. 'Funny you talk about people minding their business when you literally have a gossip-porn website. Didn't you split up three couples last week?'

Simi rolled her eyes. 'I'm a truth teller. It's my duty as a leader in our community.'

'Uh huh, and we thank you for your service, Sly News – but as a leader, could you maybe be less of an agbaya to the First Years—'

Simi's smile froze on her lips, swiftly translating the Yoruba for 'bully'. Her eyes narrowed as she eked out a smile that was uniquely bellicose in its beauty. 'Me? Agbaya? I'm as gracious as can be. Do you see me talking about how your braids and your nose ring look dated like you're tryna do Edgy Black Girl by force and you should live a little and get some bundles? No. Did I call you Poetic Injustice? No!'

I grinned to myself. *Do I use questions as a means of passive-aggressive attack?! Yes!*

I bent my voice to match her faux-sororal sweetness. 'Thank you so much for your restraint, Simi. I feel it. I appreciate it. And, I mean, it's not like *I* said that your leopard-print body-con with those shoes makes you look like a forty-five-year-old Real Housewife of Lekki married to an oil and gas man who takes his ring off every Friday night . . . We're on the same page!'

Simi's face froze as if she'd taken injectables like the fictional Lekki Housewife. As she went to reply I cut in, 'Simi, FreakyFridayz is supposed to be an open space. They're freshers. You remember what it's like. I mean, I get that it was a while ago for you, but—'

'Settle down.' Simi narrowed her strip-lashed eyes. 'I'm a year above you—'

'It's hard. The least we can do is let them know that they can come here and turn up without being terrorised over a ratty sofa.'

I glanced at Head Fresher, stood frozen in the booth, eyes wide – stuck in stasis, trying to decide whether it was safe or not to move. 'I like your dress.'

Head Fresher released a small, hesitant but pleased smile and tugged at her dress, self-consciously. 'Th-thanks. Um, I love your show, by the way. Your "Fresh So Clean" episode where you gave fresher tips on dating and broke down the kinds to avoid? Lifesaver. Stopped me double-texting a guy who called me the wrong name when we were making out.'

I murmured something about being glad it helped, because although I was comfortable behind a mic, the spotlight made me uneasy in my skin, something I had a knack for forgetting until I was under it. Inconvenient. I cleared my throat and turned to Simi, who was still, her face prettily blank, but I saw the wheels turning. Luckily, my social life was quiet enough to deprive her of ammunition. I was safe. Even with this knowledge, I still felt a chill that almost impressed me.

After a few moments she nodded slowly, tilted her head to her squad. 'Let's go. Some postgrads invited me to a house party tonight. Might be more our level.'

Free now, I turned away from the small stir Simi had caused towards a tidal wave. Drama was mounting. And it was coming from a throng stood a few metres from me. A smile slipped out and my brows shot up as I approached. I knew I smelled something savage.

Malakai Korede. Or rather, Shanti Jackson. Our resident beauty blogging queen was standing in front of Malakai Korede, clapping in his face as she told him about himself, her lilac, faux-fur cropped jacket falling off her shoulder, flicking her flowing ombre locks to the side dramatically as she read him, 'Malakai, you need to explain what the fuck is going on. Do I have mug written on my forehead or something? Is that why you think you can pour bullshit into me and I'll allow it, or what?! Let! Me! Know!'

Each word was punctuated by a clap, and yet Malakai, unlike any other guy in his position, didn't look ruffled, didn't retaliate, didn't tell her she was moving mad. He watched her calmly, as he leant against the wall, his eyes genuinely intent, like he was *really* listening to her. He was a developed player in the game, the final boss you encounter after defeating them all. He knew how to mimic a Good Guy so closely that, to the untrained eye, you wouldn't be able to tell otherwise. He was a top-tier knock-off, and, obscenely, he looked good doing it.

He was dressed in a fitted white T-shirt that showed off strong clavicles perched on shoulders that were athletically broad, sloping deltoids that slid into arms that almost put my waist-to-hip ratio to shame, pronounced even underneath the denim jacket he was wearing over his top. A gold chain, which sat sublimely between delicate and thick, dipped into his shirt, glinting off his dark skin. He was a well-crafted uni boyfriend. Artisanal. Malakai Korede was like the Dior Saddle bag my Auntie Wura had got me from her 'travels' (a Turkish market) last year. If you looked closely, you would see that it actually read Dirr, but it was such good quality that its fakery was near undetectable.

Shanti, leader of the London Gyaldem, acrylics long, patience short, hair premium Peruvian, attitude premium south London, ran her eyes up and down Malakai's form, and clacked gleaming claws in his face. 'Nah, Malakai. I don't know if you've forgotten who I am, but allow me to reintroduce you . . . I! Am! Not! The! One! To! Play! With!'

I couldn't help but smile. He was trapped. Maybe my PSA had landed and our girls were recognising the threat Malakai posed.

He watched her calmly, and said something that could have been, 'I understand that.'

She paused for a second, momentarily thrown off by his placidity, before launching in again. 'So, if you "*understand that*", how can you tell me I have qualities of the kind of girl you see yourself with, and then next thing I know, I see your wrist on Chioma's ProntoPic stories? How do we have the same qualities? The girl dresses like a bootleg Erykah Badu. She's an Erykah Badon't!'

My brows shot up as low jeers and cackles came from the gathering audience. That was a pun I'd used on my show once – but not in that context. As the crowd shifted, I saw that Chioma 'Chi-Chi' Kene was stood next to Shanti, glowing and glowering with her waist-length, dirty blonde–brown faux dreads and a septum piercing. Chi-Chi was head of the Incense and Almond Milk Babes, who I lovingly dubbed the Vegan Cupcakes. They ran the spoken word night, believed that 'vibes' were a state of being

56

and optimistically brought Cauliflower BBQ 'wings' to summer cookouts. It was really a testament to Malakai's wide-ranging appeal that he'd managed to attract two entirely different girls, especially since most of the guys that looked like Malakai said shit like, 'Yeah, Chi-Chi is fine as fuck, but I don't know about those vegans, man. Where am I gonna take her, if I can't take her Nando's? Stress.' I was grudgingly impressed.

I knew Malakai was different to most of the guys at the university, but this complicated it further. This man had range. He moved with so much style and flair that he had somehow caused Chi-Chi – one of the most chilled-out, Zen girls on campus – to trip so hard for him that she was now rolling her eyes, sticking a wide-spread, heavily bangled, bejewelled hand in Shanti's face. 'Bitch, are your bundles sewn in too tight? Who are you talking to? Don't you have some poop-diet tea to tout on the internet?'

Well, shit. Chioma might have been vegan, but she had a taste for blood.

'Drammaaaa!' The voice of my best friend sang in soprano over some new Skepta, a signal that Kofi had taken over the booth. Aminah passed me a drink as she settled in beside me, leaning against the wall with her own. I assumed that both were courtesy of Kofi. I sipped at my Diet Coke and whiskey and ran my eyes across Malakai Korede's form, his handsome face a midnight lake, barely a ripple despite the storm he had caused. I took a sip of my drink. 'Yeah, and I think I know who the director is . . .'

Aminah cackled, shook her head slowly and grinned. 'What a demon!' She bit her lip and assessed him as the girls gesticulated in front of him. He was nodding intermittently, but speaking very little. Aminah released a low sound of satisfaction. 'Mm. A fine demon—'

His eyes flicked in my direction, like he knew where I was. His eyes glinted sharply, as he raised his glass to his lips. If I didn't know better, I could have sworn he had tilted it in my direction. When he moved the cup away from his lips, I saw that they were slanted at a dangerous angle, a tiny smile I knew was directed at me. My breath hitched somewhere in my throat and before I could get it loose he had torn his gaze away from me, back to the irate ladies in front of him.

My heart had never been compelled into competitive sports by boys and yet here it was, acting like an Olympian, beating like its name was Serena. I'd worked hard to be immune to Wastemen; I'd taken my shots, but Malakai Korede was a new and evolved strain, one that could melt down the usual standard range Wasteman Detectors with the heat of a single glance. I'd done the right thing with my warning on the show. I wasn't special. He didn't *know* me and yet he was looking at me like he did. He wasn't even turning anything on for the game, none of the R&B smouldering narrowed eyes My Guy utilised. This was just his look. The girls had been in more danger than I'd presumed.

I cleared my throat. 'Demons are often fine, MiMi. That's why they're demons. They look like angels. But you gotta remember they were cast out of heaven for a reason.'

Aminah smiled. To my relief, she hadn't noticed the silent exchange. 'All right Phony Morrison—'

My mouth sagged. 'Excuse me?'

My best friend sipped her drink and smirked. 'Oh, you thought you were the only one with bars? Anyway, he's a little too tall for me. A bit too lean. I like my men a little stockier. Me-sized.'

Aminah was five foot three and Kofi was about five-eight and thick with muscle.

I nodded. 'Uh huh. Ghanaian too? Cute dimple? Obsessed with you? Is that your type?'

Aminah shot me a flat look before turning back to the scene before us, pointedly ignoring me. Chi-Chi's bangles were now adding percussion to Skepta's north-London growl, mingling with the rumbling grime beat, as she waved her hand in time with her words, punctuating whatever she was saying. Shanti shook her head, smiling sarcastically, arms folded across her ample cleavage, bolstered up in the V-neck of a bright-yellow body-con dress.

Aminah pulled a face. 'Yikes. Those are two of the finest girls on campus. I've never seen anything like this. You gonna stop it before gold hoops, balayage inches and Kanekalon hair go flying? Before people start slipping on shea butter? The Vegan Cupcakes and the Baddies look like they're about to square up to each other.'

On either side of Chioma and Shanti stood loose crowds of their respective squads, conch-piercings and culottes versus bundles and body-cons. At some point beyond this place the two cliques might merge, become one, conflate, but for now identities were distinct. They had to be, lest you got lost. At the moment they were just observing, sizing each other up, maybe laughing or rolling their eyes to add wind to jabs thrown, but I could sense the potential of a blow-up.

I slid my head to the side. 'I don't know yet. I kind of want to see how it plays out.'

'Malakai, I don't understand. Honestly, I don't,' Chi-Chi was saying, 'You take me to Root—'

My brows shot up. I was right. The boy did have skills. Root was the only vaguely fancy vegan restaurant in town. They had cloth napkins.

'—We *vibed*, like I genuinely felt like we'd maybe met before in our past life – I told you that – and now I find out that you been taking this one to chicken mortuaries—'

Aminah choked on her drink. 'Is she talking about Nando's?'

I didn't have a chance to reply because Shanti had stepped to Chioma's face. 'Babes, you better send some prayers up to your ancestors right *now*, tell your girls to burn up some incense or whatever the fuck you witches do, because let me tell you, you're gonna need their help—'

Chioma laughed. 'Cute. Omo, listen. I may be vegan, but I eat bitches up for dinner. Don't get confused—'

The crowd surrounding them erupted. I looked around to notice the audience for this episode of *Love and Grime, Whitewell* had broadened out. The ripple effect was widening; it had escalated, was souring. Malakai had still barely said a word, like he wasn't the one responsible for this mess. It made my blood boil, but I had no time for my wrath to focus and sharpen in his direction. A full-on fight was going to break out on my turf, and if I didn't stop it, no one else was politically neutral enough to.

Aminah turned to me, her big, darkly lined doe eyes made wider. 'Now?'

'Yup,' I nodded.

I stepped forward just as Malakai finally deigned to speak. He pushed off against the wall he had been leaning against, put a hand on each of the ladies' arms, and spoke to them at a decibel level I couldn't catch. I paused, stepped back and watched both girls immediately relax, their breathing slowing as Malakai spoke to them with an affable, casual face, as if a minute before the whole ecosystem of the party hadn't been put into jeopardy. The belligerent looks on both women's faces faded as they listened to him, their frowns slackening as they began to nod grudgingly, throwing each other wary looks of respect. Eventually, their tight, petty faces loosened enough to release smiles and jocular eye rolls, the three of them engaging in ostensibly friendly conversation for a few more moments before Shanti and Chioma hugged each other, smiled at Malakai and then migrated to their respective tribes, rejoining the main body of the party.

My jaw almost sagged. That had never happened before. Not in our ecosystem. Crossing two girls? Malakai should have got eaten alive. I had no idea how he had managed to finesse that situation.

'Um,' Aminah's voice piped up over a new Wizkid song. 'What did I just witness? Did he just calm Brandy and Monica down? After his very cute yansh was on the line?'

'Jeez, Aminah—'

Aminah cackled filthily. 'What? It's right there, Kiki; I have

61

eyes. He has *bum*. Nothing wrong with appreciation. Love the peng, hate the sinner—'

'Not a thing.'

'Totally a thing. As someone from a blended Christian and Muslim home, I am qualified to say it. It's in the Koran and the Bible.'

I shrugged. 'OK, well. Pretty sure that's double blasphemous.'

Aminah smiled. 'No offence, but you're from a mono-religious background and therefore less cultured than I am. Anyway, how did he do that?'

I held still and sipped my drink as I watched Malakai immediately get distracted by one of his boys coming to greet him, hand claps and back slaps exchanged, palms sliding across each other and punctuated by a click, a universal mandem handshake, all smiling, white teeth glinting in the violet and pink lights. He was quickly joined by another one of his boys. He nodded, playfully squaring up, not missing a beat in the exclusive dance of Cool Boy Social Interactions. You couldn't be taught the moves; it wasn't something you learned. It was something that lived in you and was brought forth. He'd only been here about a month and somehow he was the alpha of a crew. He was making a statement: he was comfortable here, he was playing with me.

Malakai was slick, so silken in his movements, that when his gaze snatched in my direction again, it was so casual it took me a moment to realise that it was *weird* that he was looking at me like he was – the light in his eyes bounding in its deep dark setting, lips curved dangerously. It was a continuation of a conversation.

He mouthed, 'Hi', through lips that curled into something like a hook that curved into the bottom of my belly and yanked a sharp, searing feeling through it, right up into my chest. The corner of my mouth flicked up despite myself. This was slightly alarming. Was I *smiling back*? Why was I smiling? How did I stop?

I tore my gaze away from him, the feeling in my belly subsiding to a mere warm tingle, hoping that the break would force my smile to dissolve. When I glanced back again, he was still looking at me. His smile beamed something beautiful, something lethal, as white as the light you probably see when you die. This was apt, because I was sure I was going to. I couldn't believe he'd caught me doing a double-glance at him, like I was *interested*, or something equally heinous. My face felt hot. But then he looked back to his friends, jumping back into conversation with them, like the silent exchange between us had happened in a suspended vacuum that existed outside of reality. Now he was back in his reality, where beautiful girls ran up to him; him smiling easily, politely. It wasn't the same smile he gave me though. It wasn't the R&B smile.

'Um, Ma'am, you just eye-fucked.' My best friend's voice brought me around. Sound seemed to rush back in – rap, laughter, jeering, screeching, and the cheering for a dance battle going on in the corner, all mingling with the heartbeat pounding in my ears.

I cleared my throat and shifted my feet on chunky-heeled ankle boots. 'What?!'

Aminah's shiny, plum lips were spread apart in glee. 'And it was hot too. The two of you, with your seductivitis eyes. Oozing lust.'

'First of all, gross. Secondly, I don't know what you're talking about. I just happened to be looking in his direction and he just happened to be looking in mine. What you just saw is literally just how eyes work. It's biology.'

Aminah's long, dark, mascaraed lashes narrowed into pincers as she shot me an incredulous look. 'Oh? Sorry, Ma. *Biology*. Is it also biology that you're blushing right now? I know it's dark and I know you're a chocolate honey but I can tell when you're blushing. It's one of my superpowers. It happens so rarely. Last time was when we watched that new Michael B. Jordan action movie where he was running around, tiddies out.. I could feel the heat just, like, *radiating* off you. Made me sweat out my edges . . . Tell me, Keeks, do you want Malakai to help you sweat out your edges?'

I swallowed my snort. 'I'm putting you on a time out.'

Aminah made a sudden scoff of disgust, which doubled as a warning alert as to who was approaching me. I smiled through gritted teeth as Zack stopped in front of me. He was looking at me through heady hazel eyes, bottom lip tucked into his teeth in a way that would have been sexy if I didn't know it came from an assiduous desire to be sexy, a pre-calculated equation, tried and true. He was wearing a pale-blue shirt with a tiny man playing polo embroidered on it, his pungent cologne swilling through the air.

Zack stood back, silently allowing his gaze to scan my form up and down and up again in slow strokes. He wanted me to know what he was doing, biting his lip like that, looking at how my body poured into a black bandeau crop top and black midi-skirt, the perkiness of my ass kicked up a little by my boots. I calmly watched him perform his thirst. Finally, he dragged his eyes back to mine, shook his head slowly and hit me with the pièce de résistance. 'So, you really just came here to murder me tonight.'

'One can only hope.' Aminah's voice was drier than cassava as she levelled an even, unimpressed stare at Zack, a boy she hadn't been able to stand since the time they went to the same boarding school.

Zack chuckled, rolled his tongue in his mouth and nodded slowly. 'Aminah. How are you? I didn't see you there. Blind to bad energy.'

My eyes flicked up to the ceiling. Aminah slid her head to the side, an arm under her breasts, an elbow propped on it, sharp-taloned azure nails wrapped around her glass. 'That makes no sense, you goat. Also are you nose-blind to bad energy as well? Is that why you can't smell the stink of your own cologne? What is it, Eau de Prick?'

Zack stilled, his smile stiffening. His charm was defective around us and it always threw him off. It was like he forgot every time, and every time he went through the same kind of reckoning that to us, he wasn't an automatic knee-weakener and panty-wetter. I grinned as Aminah turned to me and kissed me on the cheek, whispering, 'You good?'

I looked back at Zack. 'I can handle him.'

She nodded, threw Zack the stinkiest side-eye and kissed her teeth, as she walked past him, flicking her hair as she made her way over to Kofi's DJ booth.

Zack stepped closer to me. 'You didn't wanna come say hi to me? I know we had a fight but I thought we'd have a truce, seeing as it's my birthday.' I called Zack Kingsford 'My Guy' because I thought it would distance me from the reality that I had been hooking up – even admitting it to myself was embarrassing – with a truly jarring person. Didn't work. We all had our vices.

In the far corner of the bar, by the DJ booth, were three beat-up leather sofas arranged in a C-shape with a black centre-table in the middle, three artificial candles flickering on it, a self-designated VIP area. Every month I tried to discourage its creation and tried to open it up and every month it was colonised by the same squad before anyone else got a chance to sit there – Zack's boys, dressed in weaker iterations of his outfit. With them, in between them, leaning against walls, sat on the arms of the populated sofas, on the laps of Zack's tribe, were the pretty girls who had made the contraband banner that was stuck on the wall above them. It read, in nineties' hip-hop-style graffiti, 'Happy Birthday. King Zack', with a wonky crown slipping on the axis of the 'A' in his name.

I smiled. 'I had no idea it was your birthday, and it wasn't a fight, Zack. Also, you know this is not what we're supposed to do with our access right? This is meant to be a communal area. No VIP shit.'

Zack shot me back something sly, nodded and rubbed his chin. 'You're a VIP to me, partner. Speaking of which,' he stepped closer, 'you left something at mine during our last . . . meeting.' He reached into his pocket and pulled out the smooth cylinder that was Aminah's designer lip gloss. I darted a quick glance around to make sure nobody was watching and snatched it from him, slipping it into my bag swiftly. There was no reason for him to do that in public. Except to be a dickhead.

'You're a dickhead.' I kept my smile sweet, conscious of the fact that we were surrounded by people.

'You're in denial,' he countered.

I gritted my teeth. This was way more drama than I'd bargained for with this whole deal. That was the entire point of Not Dating Zack. Not to feel obliged to dedicate time to him. Yeah, he had a body that was just muscle and skin and made for sin, but he was not the best talker. And that worked for me – I couldn't get thrown by anything like a personality, a sense of humour or intelligence – but it also meant that I found his tongue tedious when it wasn't in my mouth.

My arrangement with Zack had started shortly after the infamous town hall incident a year ago when late-night meetings in a booked-out, tiny study room to figure out the logistics of FreakyFridayz with him led to my butt being pressed up against the desk. He was boring because, like every boy who was used to not working for what he wanted, he liked that I didn't like him. And *I* liked that I didn't like him. It was the perfect situation. He was attractive and fulfilled what I needed him to do – and nobody had to know.

Romance was a waste of time, a form of manipulation utilised by boys who didn't wash their bed sheets regularly. It existed, sure, but I wasn't surrounded by anyone I believed engaged in it properly, with *respect* for the object of their affection, rather than a thirst to claim; a triumph of acquisition, rather than a triumph of winning affection. With Zack, it was clinical, uncomplicated. There was no risk of catching feelings. I had someone to make out with, without having to commit to anything longer than the duration of a Netflix movie. But this year, Zack had switched up on me, my lack of sustained attention now presenting itself as an affront that he needed to correct.

My eyes drifted beyond Zack's shoulder, landing on Malakai again, and somehow, by coincidence or God, or the same energy that hop-scotched between us, it happened to be the exact same moment he looked up. I cleared my throat and forced my gaze to switch back to Zack, whose arm had somehow made its way above my head, his palm flat against the wall, boxing me in.

I looked up at My Guy. 'Seriously. What do you want, Zack?'

He shot me a slow grin. 'Still mad at me? I don't get no "Happy Birthday", no card—'

Nobody would blink twice at what was going on right now. Zack was known for being flirtatious, and we worked together. We were hidden in plain sight.

'Happy Birthday.' I sighed. 'Zack, I'm not mad at you. We had a good time. It was what it was. And now it's over.'

Zack arched a brow as he ran his eyes over me, voice dropping to a burr. 'You telling me you ain't gonna miss me?'

He was sexy, but his sexiness had run its course with me, a stick of bubble gum chewed on for too long. 'You've got plenty of company, hon.' I flicked my gaze towards the sofas – his fan club was already shooting me evils through heavy-lashed eyes. I smiled up at Zack. 'You'll be all right.'

He chuckled, because my words gliding off his skin, tickling him as they fell. 'They're not you.'

I laughed at his attempt to be romantic. 'OK. Say I say yes. Would you want me to go on dates with you in public? Be on your ProntoPic feed? Be your girlfriend?' I knew being in a public relationship with me wouldn't serve him. I wasn't sweet enough, pliable enough, not the right kind of popular. I was transgressive enough to be an exciting sidepiece though.

'Why you thinking about *labels*, Kiki?' Zack shook his head. 'We're more than that. All I know is that I want *you*. You're peng, buff—'

'That's the same thing twice, Zack.'

'Sexy, fine—'

'Thank you for seeing me, man. Really.' I pressed a palm against my chest. 'I contain multitudes.'

Zack smiled and swayed a little. He was drunk.

'And I can help you contain more—'

I groaned. 'Really, Zack? That actively made my vagina drier. Kinda like pussy silica gel. Know what I mean?'

Zack's eyes shone, and he stepped closer, voice dropping. 'I see you're into that freaky shit. That BDSM ting. Shit-talk me to get me worked up. I'm into it—'

He did *not* know what I meant. I stared at him for a few seconds in sheer disbelief before laughing and shaking my head. 'OK, I don't know what you're on right now, but I'm going to need you to back up. I don't have the time for this. Go drink some water. You're acting really thirsty right now and it's not attractive.' I patted his chest with the back of my hand, but he didn't budge. My hackles immediately pricked up.

'Kiki, listen. You make me better. I make you better. I mean,' he gestured around the bar, the laughing, the dancing, the joy, 'look at this. You did this. I pushed you to do this.' Zack reached out to stroke the back of a finger across my jaw.

My eyes narrowed. 'I will bite you.'

He grinned. Oh, gross. He liked that. I kept my breathing steady. I was becoming nauseated by him. This thing between us was already turning rancid when I ended it, but now it had a stench to it: it was growing into something sinister.

I gulped down my warm drink, had pushed myself off the wall Zack had me cornered against to move past him, when he snatched at my arm, his fingers pressing firmly into my flesh. I halted, rolled my eyes and rubbed the crease between my eyes. Not today.

Zack had his bottom lip tucked into his teeth and was looking at me with eyes that were dilated and thick with something I didn't need to see through to see through. 'Do you want to die today?!'

Zack oozed out a broad smile that made the whisky and Coke in me revolt. He yanked me towards his body and I crashed stiffly into him. 'Do it slowly.'

I tilted my chin and levelled my gaze, trying to calm my racing pulse, flared by anger, not fear. If Zack wanted to be a predator, then I was going to be a force majeure, the lovechild of Şango and Oşun, thunder, lightning, a flood.

'Let go of me now, and I'll do you the favour of pretending that you losing your fucking mind is down to drugs. Otherwise—'

'Do *me* a favour?' The corners of his mouth kicked up in a snide snarl. 'Babe, *I* chose you. You're not even my type. I usually go for girls who,' his eyes ran across me, 'are more on my level. This was charity.'

I nodded. 'Oh, I see.' There it was.

Zack's sneer melted a little and his smile faltered as he noted the look on my face. I was grinning widely, manically. 'Kiki, look, I was just chatting, I'm sor—'

I shook my head, and wrestled my arm from his grip, still smiling, like he'd told the funniest joke, which was somewhat close to the truth in that he was a fucking joke. Malakai's friends were laughing at something, carefree, unaware. Malakai didn't join them. His brows were furrowed slightly as he looked at me, eyes bright, glimmering at me in the dim, violet light. I swore they were saying something. I swore I heard them say what I was thinking.

Zack took my silence for softening and tried to place a hand on my waist. My stomach turned and the safeties came off my inner glocks. I put my empty cup down on a nearby table, looked back at up to him and smiled. 'Yes, you are sorry.'

CHAPTER 6

I found my legs, striding towards Malakai, weaving deftly through the crush of twined bodies. Kofi was playing a song that sampled Floetry's 'Say Yes'. We had entered a slow-jam section of the night and so backs were pressed flush against fronts, faces were in necks and arms were wrapped around waists, as hips swayed to the sultry song, making it relatively easy to make my way through what would normally have been a thick crowd.

Malakai pushed himself off the wall immediately. My heart slammed against my ribcage with the full weight of itself, in protest of what I was about to do, but there was no backing down now. He was looking at me with calm curiosity. He'd moved a little away from his friends and into a corner that was slightly obscured, but still visible to eyes that were purposely seeking and trailing. He flicked his head at me to follow suit. I stepped up to him, ignoring the interested eyes of his boys, and the gentle jesting calls of 'Jeez, is that you, yeah, Chief Malakai? A whole Kiki Banjo, ya kna? How much did you pay in dowry?'

Malakai directed a middle finger at them while looking straight at me, his plush mouth bent slightly in intrigue, his eyes sparkling. He had to be kidding me with this. How were they so dark and so bright at the same time? I didn't think horoscopes were my thing, but his eyes really looked like stars and I suddenly wanted to be an astrologer, to learn how to read them as they flashed at me.

'What do you need me to do?' His voice was low, gravelly.

A thrill ran through me but I had no time to assess it. I rose on tiptoe, wrapped my hand around his neck and said, with a breath into his ear, 'Kiss me.'

He smelled good, a dark musky, woodsy fragrance with the clean, sweet scent of whatever lotion he used, and I took it in deeply to distract myself as two long seconds ticked by in which he said nothing. The length of our bodies weren't touching, but I was close enough to sense his surprise. The adrenaline from my war-surge was beginning to thicken and slow enough for embarrassment to creep in. I wanted to humiliate Zack in the language he understood, twisting his toxic machismo and shoving it down his throat, but now *I* was the one choking.

I let go of the back of Malakai's neck and began to retreat, accepting my defeat, prepping my 'shit-sorry-forget-I-said-anything' speech, when he put both hands on my waist and drew me to a halt. A shot of heat rushed through my entire body. His fingertips rested lightly on the top of my skirt, just below where the slip of skin exposed by my crop top began. It was a comfortable pressure, politely light, respectful, and yet the pit of my stomach flared, impolitely, disrespectfully. The slip of skin itched for his hands to move a scintilla upwards. What had I got myself into? I needed to be in control, always, but the way my skin seemed to be feening for something it had never had before was beyond mine. He had barely touched me.

Malakai lifted his head so he was looking right at me. I was on my tiptoes still, and if he hadn't been holding me I was pretty sure the intensity of his gaze would have been enough to knock me off balance. My heart wasn't beating like war drums anymore; it was carnival drums. My body had been ready to move into combat, but now, strangely, I wanted to dance.

Malakai nodded, the corner of his deep and delicious-looking mouth flicking upwards. 'OK.'

I only saw a flash of Malakai's eyes amping up in wattage, the increased gradient of his crooked smile, before my bottom lip nestled between his and I slowly, gently pressed, causing his own mouth to part immediately, welcoming me into a dark and decadent warmth. His lips moved in a motion that was in deep conversation with mine, filling in the cadences, an instant response to my calls that sent a thrill so sharp through me I almost stumbled. I pushed my body closer, and he took it as permission to draw me in with teasing languidness.

He was good. And not just one-size-fits-all good, but good enough to match me. He was feeling me out, taking the lead gently when it was clear I was ceding power. I could taste that he was having fun with it, deepening the kiss before lightening up, making the increasingly frantic heat gathering inside my stomach rise and then simmer. I could feel a new brand of adrenaline kick up inside of me. He was challenging me. This was a duel. Fine.

I drew back slightly, and twirled my tongue, and I could tell by the low vibration in my mouth that it had the intended effect on him. He pulled away and looked at me, slightly stunned, an impressed brow quirked.

Huh. Good work, Keeks. Me: 1, Malakai: *Oh.*

His eyes twinkled, and he brought his mouth back to mine, transforming my smug smirk into a small moan. Fuck. It occurred to me that this might have been my first honest kiss. Both our motives were plain. We were engaged on the same level for the same purpose: to feel and be felt. The raison d'être might have originally been to make Zack sweat, a mutual decision to destroy, a wartime treaty (Zack and Malakai were natural enemies, after all), but with every little gentle sweet motion of suction and lip grazing I could tell the kiss had morphed into something different. Still an assertion of power, but this was a power shared, ceded and reclaimed in the same breath, a friendly battle of thrills and a test of will. My heartbeat was drumming a frenetic, syncopated rhythm on internal djembes that got me thinking that our ancestors were being summoned to approve of whatever the fuck was going on here.

I detected that Malakai was beginning to lose his grip on reasoning by the ever-increasing heaviness of his breath and, truth be told, I was too. This wasn't the kiss I'd planned – this was fun and my body was engaging in it far more than I'd intended. I didn't have to look back to know that Zack was watching us, and sure, that meant other people might be watching us, but at this particular moment I didn't give a shit. I felt powerful.

Besides, public making-out at FreakyFridayz wasn't a big deal. As it was, I could guarantee at least eight other couples were dry-humping at various corners of the room — it is a truth universally acknowledged that university club nights are one of the horniest places in existence. But even without the cloak of invisibility that general shamelessness provided, I felt good about the fact that though this guy had control, I had what it took to make him lose it. I slid my arm from around his neck so I could curve a hand around his neck and rest my thumb on his jaw, and deepened the kiss, gently slipping the tip of my tongue into his mouth. I felt the pressure of Malakai's hands on my waist increase automatically in a way I knew he couldn't help and then I pulled away. Just in time. Before the kiss took us someplace else.

Malakai's smile sloped out slowly. 'Well, shit.' A surprising grin snuck out of me in response. I bit my lip to curb it.

Then I heard it. Low and resounding whoops curling around us, bringing me forth from whatever vacuum had been created when we stood together and our lips touched. I closed my eyes as realisation dawned. That would have been the inevitable audience that gathered when Kiki Banjo made out with the new Sweetboy just after he'd had a run-in with two other queens, narrowly avoiding a civil war. I never got involved with inter-politics. I tried to settle things from the peripheral, and now I had situated myself smack dab in the middle of a particularly spicy sandwich.

When I had approached Malakai, I hadn't thought deeply about

76

the collateral fallout, just that I wanted to make Zack implode and Malakai posed the perfect weapon. I hadn't expected it to be like *that* – a whole world created in a kiss, let there be light, and it was . . . good. To my gratification, Malakai looked equally surprised by the presence of other people, eyes dancing around and above my head as if the crowd surrounding us had just magically appeared. But when his eyes landed on me, they were back to being confident, easy, as he maintained my gaze.

'Ignore them.'

'Don't tell me what to do.' It was automatic, spit out of my mouth like a bullet, and Malakai smirked like the bullet had just lit him on fire instead of penetrated through skin.

'Didn't you just command me to kiss you?'

'The question was implied. And you agreed. Enthusiastically.'

Malakai paused, eyes flashing brighter with the light of a swallowed smile before clearing his throat. 'Trust me. Turning around now is bait. It means you're self-aware, that the kiss was for a purpose and you're checking to see if it lands. You'll blow your cover. Zack will take it as a win. You want that?'

His voice was level and warm, and the conspiratorial tone told me this was for my benefit. He was on my side. Like it or not, we were teammates, and I had no idea why he decided to join forces with me, but he was right. I couldn't turn around. For this to work I had to pretend I didn't care about anyone watching, had to act like I was into this for its own accord. Besides, if I stayed still, if we stayed talking as if this was a thing, people would get bored, the ripple would subside. This was a power move.

'Fine. We stay like this.'

The one improv class I had taken in first year (Dr Miller suggested it as a way of improving expression: obviously, it was hell. The studio smelled like feet, and everyone insisted on massaging each other for no reason like were in a university-sanctioned sex cult) must have worked because I really sounded like that was going to be a chore. I stood back and held on to his forearms, strong and taut with a smattering of light hairs that buckled under my touch. This was throwing me off. I've been around hot guys, I *dealt* with hot guys, but this was more than facial symmetry, and a smile so bright I felt like I could see my future in it. My pulse was still trying to simmer back into regularity.

Malakai nodded. 'We could stay like this, sure. Or we could get a drink.'

I laughed. 'You serious?'

Malakai's grin was mischievous. 'We're at a party. You're here and I'm here, there's good music, playing and your man over there looks like he wants to bottle me, so we might as well have fun with this.'

Of course. This was tactical game playing. Malakai probably wanted Zack's spot as Alpha, and I was a pawn to him as much as he was a pawn to me. I wasn't in trouble. This reminder calmed and cooled me. 'He isn't my man.'

Malakai's eyes became less playful. 'Yeah, yeah, sorry. It didn't look like you were into whatever that was. I was gonna jump in when he—' His jaw tightened. 'I was waiting for some kind of signal from you. You looked like you had it in hand.'

So that was why he had been ready when I'd turned to him. He'd been watching. He'd been checking to see if I was OK. The idea sent something simultaneously warm and sharp through me. I forced it to mellow. So, he was *objectively* decent. If that was enough to entrap me then the bar for straight men was subterranean.

'I did have it.' I paused. 'But thank you. For looking out. And being, you know, there.' Because how else do you say, 'Thanks for letting me kiss you to ward off a dickhead! Thank you for knowing what was happening.'?

Malakai barely nodded, his eyes trained in on me, as if he were studying me. It occurred to me that he was still checking if I was OK. It made my skin prickle. That wasn't his job. None of this was his job. What was I even doing?! I cleared my throat and let go of his arms. My palms almost smarted as the balmy air of the bar smacked against them, cool in comparison to the heat of this man's skin.

'Look, um, this has helped, but Zack is . . . well, he's a Neanderthal, and he's probably going to be more pissed at you than me, so . . .'

Malakai's smile was breezy, but his voice had an edge. 'So?'

I stilled. Why was his recklessness so hot? I was falling for hypermasculine heterosexual tropes like some porcelain-skinned damsel in a Mills & Boon.

'*So*, I don't want to cause trouble for you.'

Malakai laughed outright. 'We both know that's not true.' His smile slanted up in a way that made my core tighten in a manner

I didn't approve of. 'Besides, trouble always ends up finding me anyway.'

He couldn't have been serious. My brows perked, ignoring his implication. 'Oh, you mean like when Chioma and Shanti were in your face? That kind of trouble?'

'A misunderstanding. It's sorted.'

'Uh huh.'

The curve of his lips broadened. 'You don't like me.'

'I kissed you.'

The chuckle that Malakai rolled out ironically sounded exactly like chocolate-dipped trouble. I wanted to bite into it.

I smiled reluctantly, twitched a shoulder, conceded the silent point. Kissing meant nothing. I had, after all, actually allowed Zack's tongue in my mouth. I tried again.

'Fine. I don't know you.'

Malakai nodded casually. 'Right. See, I thought that. But for some reason you're moving like you do know me. Kiara.'

His face had been straight, and I resisted the immediate bend in my lips. The deliberate slip-up on my name had been casually done, expertly executed. Shit, he *was* funny. More dangerous than I suspected. I adjusted my summation of him accordingly in my mental Fuckboi database: Fuckboi with jokes.

'You been watching me move, Micah?'

'I feel like we've been watching each other. And it's Michael, actually.'

Malakai's flattened voice created the perfect platform for my laugh to slip out and skid across. Malakai didn't miss a beat; he caught my bait between his teeth and tossed it back to me with ease. If this was a game, then it was fun to play with someone who could challenge me.

I stepped closer to him. 'OK. I'm sensing that you have something you want to get off your chest. Am I wrong?'

Malakai's eyes were still dancing. He didn't look annoyed, but he didn't look pleased either. His gaze sparkled like he was about to jump into a duel. My pulse spiked remembering the last time we did that.

'The Wasteman of Whitewell.'

I was kind of proud of it. It sounded like one of the mediaeval romance novels I used to love. *The Cad of Canterbury*. *The Richmond Rake*. *The Vicious Viscountess*. *The Wasteman of Whitewell*.

'Oh, you're a fan of my show? Thank you so much.'

Malakai's face didn't twitch. 'I am, actually. I listen to it every week.'

Oh.

My attempt to be a brat flopped. I swallowed down this titbit of information he had revealed down in an attempt to ignore the fact that it made my pulse skitter, but the fact that it tasted sweet on its way down made it decidedly difficult to ignore the fact that I liked that he listened to me. The show was my main source of confidence but also coyness. He tapped into both at the same time.

I cleared my throat. 'Thanks.'

Malakai shrugged, matter-of-fact. 'I wasn't saying it to gas you. It's good. It's good energy, good music and I like what you say.

I mean, I really like what you say. Until last week . . . You know what happened last week?'

I hitched a shoulder up and narrowed my eyes in polite curiosity. 'No. What happened?'

Malakai released a slow smile and nodded, 'You were describing this dickhead that breaks the hearts of gyaldem and I was like, *rah*, who is this guy? Prick. But then all of a sudden, my phone starts chiming. Messages from girls cussing me out, telling me they were about to reclaim their time. Calling me a Wasteman, saying that I'm trash. And then tonight happens. Two beautiful girls I've gone on dates with suddenly turned on me like I married them both then abandoned our twelve children.'

I moved to lean against the wall in front of him, fold my arms across my chest, stare up at him inquisitively. 'Huh. At the same time? Like was there a whole polygamy set-up? Old school Naija?'

'No, like, international businessman with one family in London and another in Houston-type deal. New school Naija.'

'What kind of business is taking you to Houston? Do you sell Bibles?'

'If I was a Bible salesman, that would actually make the whole two-family storyline even juicier.'

We each smiled, then stilled, apparently both as disconcerted that our words had fallen into rhythm in the same way our bodies had. So, the first time we met wasn't a fluke.

Malakai cleared his throat, his voice now sounding formal. 'Anyway. I've been doing damage control all week. As you can imagine, it's all been wildly distressing.'

'Wildly? Distressing?' I laughed, then stopped when I realised he wasn't smiling. He was serious. 'Wait, are you – you're fucking with me, right? You're upset because I disrupted your little *harem*?'

Malakai shook his head. 'Nah, I'm upset because you're a hypocrite—'

I raised a brow. 'Excuse me?'

'Kiki, we're the same. The same way I assume you were seeing Zack casually—'

'Wait—'

'So, you weren't coming from his flat that night we met?'

I swallowed, my skin prickling with new exposure.

Malakai shook his head. 'Look, no stress. I didn't tell anyone. It's none of my business, and honestly, I don't give a shit. My point is, the same way you were seeing him casually is the same way I was dating the girls. Similar, anyway. Because I actually liked them, and it's clear you can't stand Zack. Don't get me wrong, that's your prerogative and you can do whatever you want, but I don't appreciate being judged for doing the same thing you do. All the women I talk to know what's up from the beginning. I make that clear. That's why I was able to sort that shit out with Chioma and Shanti earlier. It's why me and Zuri are cool. I didn't lie. I never lied. They're great girls that I wanted to get to know. No commitment was promised. I told them that I understood their feelings, but I just thought this was a healthy way of doing things. There was communication there. You were getting involved in things you don't know about.'

My mouth parted. Was he accusing me of . . . slut-shaming?

Me, the feminist, who had words of Audre Lorde and bell hooks seared into her heart? Who knew the entirety of the prelude to 'Flawless'! I was never lost for words and this time wasn't any different, but it definitely took me a while to retrieve them. When I found them, they came out like bullets. I stepped closer to Malakai, eyes narrowed and seething.

'Oh, there was *communication* there? That's why everybody knew who I was talking about on the radio – because all the women knew where they stood? Please. Look, just because you were able to spin something that smoothed over that mess between Chioma and Shanti doesn't mean you're innocent and it doesn't mean I'll buy it. You clearly did something for the girls to believe that they meant more to you, something that made them retroactively question your behaviour. And for *your* information, what I did with Zack was not the same thing. Dudes have been doing what you're doing since the beginning of time. Having their cake and eating it too. Well, guess what? The patisserie's *closed*.' So maybe that last part was overkill. I continued talking, hoping to erase any damage that corny line had done to the gravity of my point. 'What I'm doing is levelling the playing field. There is a difference, Malakai, and I don't need to waste any more time trying to explain that to you.'

'*Patisserie?*'

Oh, for fuck's sake. 'Can we focus?'

His lips bent in an irritatingly inviting manner. 'I'm focused.'

'You're mocking.'

'Nah. It was clever. Literary.'

He was definitely mocking. Zack didn't quite have what it took to get under my skin, but this guy was burrowing like he knew where to go. It almost made me want to stay as much as it made me want to go. Which meant I had to go.

'You know what? We're probably done here. I think Zack's got the message. People will have lost interest by now. It's already been a long night and I don't have the energy for whatever this is going to turn into. Thanks for the emergency kiss, but I think I'm gonna—' I went to walk past him.

Malakai stepped to make way for me but his eyes flashed, 'I'm sorry.'

'What?' I stopped in my tracks. Men who looked like him and acted like him and, OK, fine, kissed like him, did not apologise. Even men who didn't have his credentials didn't apologise. Was the music really that loud? I really needed to sort out the sound system because it was clearly a health hazard, causing me to hear things that did not—

'I said, I'm sorry. You're right, I hear you. I shouldn't have compared the two situations when I really don't know you like that. But here's the thing,' he rubbed the back of his neck, 'I want to. Been wanting to. Since the first time we met.'

My breath hitched, but I forced myself to breathe, for the expression on my face to stay the same. Cool. I hadn't been ready for that, but it was fine. He did this all the time. Evolved. Player.

'The first time we met you were going to Zuri Isak's room—'

'The first time we met you were coming out of Zack Kingsford's room.'

85

Touché. I didn't know if it was great or terrible that he was reasonable. Hot and reasonable. He was also kind of a dick, the same way I was kind of a dick. It was slowly occurring to me that perhaps he wasn't The Wasteman of Whitewell. The Wasteman of Whitewell wouldn't have helped a girl who called him The Wasteman of Whitewell get revenge on another guy (a guy infinitely more fitting of the title). He wouldn't have noticed her discomfort. Granted, he could have had his own agenda to shame me, but there were easier ways. He could have let me squirm, turned it around and used the opportunity to embarrass me, leave me pouting into the air, but he didn't.

Malakai cleared his throat in the silence between us.

'You know what? You probably want space. I'm gonna go. And yeah, that kiss was . . . That kiss was something, but it was also nothing. I wanted to help. Me wanting to hang out with you has nothing to do with it. You don't owe me shit.'

Either he was a preternaturally talented actor, or he was telling the truth.

'I know I don't.'

Malakai took it as a dismissal. He inclined his head deeply, pressed a hand across his chest like he was excusing himself from my court, and shot me a tiny smile. 'It was an honour to be your sidekick in making a dickhead squirm, Fellow Superhuman.' He winked and stepped away from me, ready to go. My stomach flipped and spurred my hand to reach out for his wrist.

He looked down at my hand and I found my gaze travelling there too, because I could not believe I'd just done that. My body was in rebellion tonight, acting without permission from my mind. When I looked back up, his eyes were glinting down into mine, asking a question. I nodded. I was here now. I might as well follow through. I dropped his wrist and any pretence that I wasn't curious.

'I know I don't owe you shit. Which is why you're buying me a drink and not the other way around.'

Malakai's smile widened. That was two shots of dark liquor on its own.

'Yes, Ma'am.'

He looked like a bad decision. The best kind of bad decision.

CHAPTER 7

I watched Malakai elegantly move through the teaming, steaming crowd, a rum and Coke in one hand, and what looked like a straight whisky in the other. I had gone a year at Whitewell Uni drama-free, keeping myself to myself and Aminah, comfortable going from studio to class to dropping by at FreakyFridayz. Now I was sitting in Cuffing Corner, waiting for a guy to get me a drink. A guy with an extremely good butt. I bit the inside of my cheek. I was the one who'd issued a warning about this guy and now I was ogling him like some kind of smitten First Year. This was just an investigation. Surveying the threat posed to the girls of Blackwell. This was due diligence.

Malakai passed me my drink as he settled next to me on the beat-up, maroon leather sofa, our knees just inches apart. The level of the music was low enough for conversation, but here, at the corner of the party, it was even lower. Cuffing Corner was so-called because it was where potential couples who were at FreakyFridayz for a date night came to chill. The light was dimmer here and there were coffee tables with fake candles on, for a bootleg grown-and-sexy atmosphere. It was the only place in the party for us to sit and talk in relative privacy; it was a practical choice, but it still elicited a necessary eye roll when Malakai suggested it.

I took the drink and flicked my eyes across him. 'You're dangerous.'

'Dangerous how?' Malakai lowered his tumbler of something dark and strong from his lips, and something dark and strong in his eyes told me he already knew exactly what I meant.

'Dangerous like, right now, without even looking I know there are probably at least six girls in this party who want to choke me out for even breathing near you, let alone sitting in Cuffing Corner with you.'

Malakai shook his head. 'It's because I'm new. I'm still fresh. It isn't real. It will wear off in a few weeks. If anyone's in danger, it's me.'

'What are you talking about?'

Malakai laughed incredulously, and then faded into a smile when he realised my face hadn't flinched. 'Shit, you're serious.' He nodded, bit his lip and rubbed at his jaw in a way that was obnoxiously attractive and exemplified the aforementioned danger. Malakai shifted closer to me, 'I promise you, half the mandem in this room are wondering how I got Kiki Banjo's attention.'

I rolled my eyes and with it, pushed away the flutter in my chest that came with his proximity. 'They don't talk to me. They're scared of me.'

'Those two facts aren't mutually exclusive. They don't want to put in the effort that it would take to secure you, because they know you see through their shit, so they make out like it's impossible, that you're stush. They'd rather act like there's something defective with you than be the guy that's worthy of you, because that would mean they have to face their own shit – and if there's anything mandem hate it's facing their own shit – so they leave you alone. And you? Well, you like it that way. No mess.' He said it all casually, voice even and matter-of-fact.

It unnerved me that there was nothing I could genuinely unpick. 'How do you figure this?'

'The same way you know everything you talk about on the radio. We watch from the outside. We know how the game works. I don't know you like that but I know enough to know that.'

I turned to him fully, folding my leg up beneath me and leaning my arm against the back of the sofa. Our knees knocked. Neither of us moved.

'OK, Mystic Malakai. Let's play a game. See how far your skills stretch. You down?'

'Hit me.'

'Zack and I are not a match. Obviously. In fact, if I focus too hard on his personality, I find myself actively repelled. Given these facts, why was I hooking up with him?'

Malakai rose a brow. 'Is this meant to be challenging?'

My smile widened. 'You're kind of a dick, aren't you?'

'Yes. Not a Wasteman though.'

I rolled my eyes and swallowed my grin. 'Answer the question.'

Malakai laughed and nodded. 'All right. You hooked up with him *because* you were disgusted by him. My guess is, you weren't really looking for a relationship and you figured you might as well hook up with someone you have nothing in common with. No distractions. No risk of complications.'

I stilled.

As if reading my mind, as if detecting my discomfort, Malakai shook his head. 'It's not that you're easy to read. Like I said, I noticed you. Wait, that sounded . . .' He faltered. 'I meant, I know what to look for when I'm looking at you.'

I slid my head to the side, and a smile tipped out. He paused again. Brought his knuckles to rest on the tip of his nose as he stared at me. 'Fuck. I sound like a creep. Let me do that again.'

The insecurity broke into his voice, betraying a surprising softness that made me smile. 'Hey. Don't run away from your truth. Listen, if you want a lock of my hair, I'd appreciate it if you just asked instead of plucking it next time? It hurt when you did it while we were kissing.'

Malakai caught my grin and tilted his head like something had been revealed to him, 'Oh wow. *You're* a dick.'

I nodded and sipped my drink. 'Ah, you noticed. So many guys judge me by my looks and not enough by the fact that I'm a huge arsehole.'

Malakai pressed a flat palm to his broad chest. 'Not me. I see you. The real you. Angel face, demon heart.'

'Thanks for understanding me.'

We punctuated our conversation with deep, grave nods before both erupting into laughter. I found I had moved closer to him on the sofa, so my bent knee was almost on top of his. I was physically tipsy, but I also felt like my soul had had three shots. I felt lighter, somehow more snug in my skin and though I knew I was on a mission to figure out what was drawing me to him so I could cut it off, whatever was drawing me in was addictive and delicious and impossible to find the root of. I kept stopping to savour it. I cleared my throat. 'Since you're all-knowing, you're probably aware that this is going to be our last conversation.'

Malakai smiled. 'I get it.'

He was consistently surprising. The lack of obvious ego-bruising only stoked a reluctant curiosity in me. 'Really?'

He hitched a shoulder like what he was about to say was the most factual, logical thing in the world. 'You're afraid that I'm not actually who you made me out to be. That you might actually like me.'

'*Huh.* You ever tried Pilates?'

'Every Wednesday morning just after I drop the kids at school. Why?'

I nodded. 'Oh OK. Figures. I just feel like someone whose head is so far up their own arse would be flexible enough to be good at it.'

Malakai's eyes sparked as he sipped his drink and shook his head. 'You're an assassin.'

'And yet here you are. Still breathing. Despite my best efforts.'

'Don't take it personally. As we've previously established, I'm superhuman. Like you.'

I tried to restrain my smile at his sly call back to our first meeting, but it must have leaked out because, eyes twinkling, he began gesticulating as if he was explaining a profound truth.

'Yeah, as you obviously know, in the old days we were known as gods – which, of course, was ridiculous – but now we're known as what we really are: stupidly good-looking humans with special abilities.'

I huffed a laugh into my drink, creating ripples in the sweet–sour liquid. I brought my glass down. 'Uh huh. What are yours again?'

'Many, but they include the immunity to Kiki Banjo's many attempts to kill me.'

I released a light snort. 'How super can you be if you have to build a whole defence system against me?'

Malakai's eyes flitted across me deliberately as he leant back, assessed me. His voice dropped. 'Oh, I'm very super, I'm Black Panther-meets-Şango. It's just that your level of lethality is unique. I have to adjust to your power.'

I narrowed my eyes. I'd tried to remain contained, repressed, but somehow he was pulling me out of myself. 'Do me a favour and let's keep this whole superhuman thing between us, yeah? People find out and they start freaking out, treating you differently—'

Malakai nodded with understanding. 'And it becomes this whole thing where they try to get you to form an inter-galactic crime-fighting collective—'

I extended an arm and spread a hand out in agreement. 'Right?

93

Right? And who has the time? I'm just trying to get my degree. Learn how to master eyeshadow. And sure, I can carve out a Wasteman's heart with my eyes, but it's not all I am. Besides, I hardly ever do it because the clean-up is too stressful. I hate blood.'

Malakai's smile broke through, lighting up his face. I was used to my jagged edges scraping up against people, but Malakai seemed to click into mine, slot right into rhythm.

His eyes glittered. 'Mad. That's what I mean. That right there.'

'What?'

'*That.*' He gestured to my face, my form, the air around me in awed bafflement. 'That's what I mean by you being an assassin. Have you seen your fucking smile? You can make a man do anything with that shit. You're a straight-up villain.'

Malakai's eyes sharpened, their brightness now concentrated, as they grazed my face. It instantly sparked something in me, like there was a friction point between us and we hadn't known it existed until we had got close enough to collide. I was light-headed despite the fact that all I'd had was half a glass of watery Jack Daniel's and Coke and . . . was I having fun? With a boy? With *Malakai Korede?*

I was undercover in the open. I was *investigating* the truth of the Fuckboi, but all of a sudden I realised the risk I'd taken, that I'd underestimated my defences. My heart was pounding a hole in my emotional fences. If that wasn't enough to break them down, then the heat from Malakai's eyes would have been enough to erode them. We inched closer to each other at the same time, pulled by

94

the same energy that crackled between us during our first kiss – an hour ago? Half an hour? Five minutes? I didn't know: alcohol had slowed time or maybe this potent thing between us had.

He was looking at me with an intensity so heavy it dropped to the base of me and disturbed the peace. I felt myself responding in kind. Just as Malakai drew nearer, I caught the shape of my best friend in the corner of my eye. She stormed into the area, stepping over the clusters of couples cosied up on sofas, before striding over to us.

'Hi, yes, hello, I'm Aminah, the best friend.' She flicked an appraising, amused look across Malakai as we jumped apart and I cleared my throat.

Malakai nodded, and held out a hand. 'Hi, I'm—'

Aminah looked at his hand then back up at him and laughed, 'I know who you are,' she looked at me with a small grin. 'Cute. Shaking hands. Polite. Not Wasteman behaviour at all.'

Malakai turned to me, raising his eyebrows, as if Aminah had proved his point. I rolled my eyes and looked up at my best friend pointedly. 'Aminah. What's up?'

'Ah, yes.' She settled between us on the sofa, scooting her butt on the seat and forcing Malakai and I apart. 'Sorry about this. But you guys sitting so close to each other is part of the reason I'm here—'

I frowned. 'Minah, what are you talking about?'

'I'm getting to it! Calm down! Can I have a sip of that please?' She grabbed my glass from my limp hand, taking a large swig before handing it back to me. 'Thank you. So, as your best friend, I'm loving . . . this.' She gestured between Malakai and me. 'It's great. Get it, girl. And that kiss? Superb. Almost had me climbing up on Kofi—'

'I'm sure he'd be gassed about that,' Malakai laughed.

Both mine and Aminah's necks tilted at the exact same degree. Aminah rose a brow, 'Excuse me? You're cute, but not cute enough to avoid getting smacked.'

Malakai raised a hand, eyes wide. 'Yo, sorry, no disrespect. It's just that Kofi's my boy. Grew up together. I wasn't being sarcastic.'

'Oh.' Aminah visibly relaxed, then smiled as she realised that this revelation meant that Kofi had spoken to Malakai about her. 'Cool . . . Anyway, I am not just here in a best-friend capacity, I've got my producer/manager hat on.' She turned to me, her eyes as serious as tipsy double-strip-lashed eyes could look. 'And as your manager, I am seriously worried. I have heard things at this party. And the Brown Sugar account has lost fifty followers since that kiss. The Blackwellian queens aren't happy.'

My blood ran cold. 'What do you mean? Why?'

Aminah inhaled deeply, pulled out her phone from her bra and slid a thumb across it a few times till a ProntoPic account The TeaHouse flashed on her screen. Simi. My breath tightened.

Malakai and I both peered at the screen, and sure enough there was a grainy, dark picture of my arms around his neck, his hands at my waist. You couldn't see our faces, but the inspired caption, 'Seems like Brown Sugar is into Dark Chocolate', made my involvement pretty clear. Underneath the picture were dozens of comments – snake emojis, apparently meant to denote the fact that I was a sly bitch.

Even when Simi wasn't there, Simi was there. She had eyes everywhere in the form of First Years desperate to please her and Second Years who thought that the closer they were to her the less likely it was that they'd be stung. She had an army of spies, and of course, she would have had someone watching me, waiting for me to slip. It was stupid of me not to think about that. She saw my show's popularity as a threat to her power, even when I clearly had no interest in said power. All I wanted to do was get my fellowship and play bops. Her surveillance had never been a problem before because nothing I did gave her minions any grip. But now I had actively antagonised her and given her something to hold against me: Malakai.

'Fuck.'

Aminah nodded grimly and placed her phone back in her bra with the same gravitas that a lawyer would have had snapping her briefcase shut.

'Fuck, indeed. Keeks, we have an image problem. It doesn't look great when the campus romantic advisor, the one who told girls to reclaim their time and play players, not only made out with one of the most eligible players on campus but is also cuddled up in Cuffing Corner with him. Do you know what I mean? That affects your credibility. Which affects our show. You know if we consistently dip below a certain number of listeners, we lose it right?

'Simi is a snake and I know she has it out for you, but you know her clout. She has connections in nearly every girl group on campus. They're going to mobilise and boycott and we're going to drop listeners. I need a media extracurricular for my internship, and if I don't get it, I'm going to have to go to Nigeria and work for my dad this summer while he tries to set me up with his best friend's son, who wears a sovereign ring on a pinky finger, trilby hats and too-short trousers. Kikiola, I *cannot* . . .'

And it would cost me New York. I had no clue how I would grow the show, but I had no chance if there wasn't a show to grow. Besides that, the idea of losing Brown Sugar freaked me out. It anchored my university experience. I needed it to keep me moored. I put my drink on the coffee table, swallowed my own rising panic and rubbed my hands up and down my best friend's arms. 'Breathe, Minah. Countdown from ten—'

'Regular ten or Beyoncé ten?'

'Beyoncé ten.'

Aminah shut her eyes and nodded, exhaling air through tightly pursed lips, reciting lyrics from the Beyoncé song, 'Countdown.'

Malakai leant forward and peered at me over my best friend's meditating form. 'Sorry – am I missing something? This seems kind of ridiculous. Is this a real problem? We just kissed. It's no one's business. Who's going to believe the dumb theory that the radio thing was just a ploy to get me? I mean, I get it. I'm a catch, but . . .?'

Aminah's eyes flickered open and looked at him like he was scuff on brand new heels, her panic making her snap, 'I'm sorry is this a *joke* to you?'

Malakai blinked. 'No, I just – this seems like an overreaction.'

Aminah glowered. 'Oh yeah, because of course we hyper-sensitive, emotional women would be *overreacting*. It's not like we understand the inner mechanisms of the social ecosystem of our school because we've been here for a year and are integral cogs to its functionality—'

Malakai's eyes widened. 'Wait, I didn't mean—'

Aminah raised a hand. 'Of *course* it matters, Newbie. The girls run shit here. Simi is a cow, but she is a cow with clout. She is ex-ACS President. She's like the anti-Kiki, and people listen to her almost as much as they listen to us. Even if they don't think they believe her, the suspicion is enough. Reputations are at stake, and reputations are currency here. I mean, *think*. Kiki doesn't date and a week after she issues a PSA telling everyone to basically back up off you, she's suddenly doing tongue twerks in your mouth?'

I exhaled deeply, swallowing. I was so stressed I couldn't even interrogate my best friend's use of 'tongue twerks'. She was right. This was bad. And irresponsible. I didn't even really know Malakai and I still hadn't actually received a feasible explanation for him making two of the baddest girls in school trip for him simultaneously. If anything, sitting with him – shit, *kissing* him – sanctioned his actions. I sat back, looked up, and realised that narrowed, frosty glares were being thrown my way from various points in the room. Reality descended on me, eroding the last remaining light and warmth from my time with Malakai. I went cold.

'You're right. It looks like I tried to alienate him on purpose because I fancied him. Which is so, so, *so* far from the truth.'

Malakai frowned. 'OK, we get it. Why so many *sos*—'

'I only kissed him to shake off Zack . . .' The panic crawled up my throat as I fanned my face to subdue the sudden, inexplicable, uncomfortable heat that was rushing through me. 'I just thought he was the best bet! I assumed he would be down because I thought he was a hoe.'

Malakai quirked a brow. 'Excuse me?'

I rolled my eyes. I had no time for feelings. I didn't care about being liked, but I did care if the Blackwell babes lost respect for me because they thought I'd double-crossed them. I also really cared about my show.

'Oh please. It's not sexist if it's directed at a man. Women deserve sexual liberation, and guys like you do not. You can't be trusted with it. You misuse it.'

Malakai rolled his tongue in his mouth, his eyes glinting with irritation. 'Ah. So we're back to you acting like you know me again. Cool. I missed that. That was a good time.'

I laughed humourlessly, and scooted forward on the sofa. 'Oh. Oh, I see. So you can presume shit about me, but I can't about you? That's the same entitled crap that probably led you to date multiple girls at the same time and not expect any emotional investment. Don't act like you don't know what you're doing. It's manipulative.'

Malakai released a slanted, dry smile. 'Remind me why we kissed again? Was it love at first sight or was it to piss off Zack? And listen, I rate it, I get it, but what I don't get is you acting like we're so different. And you kissing me proves that. Everybody saw that you're exactly what you preach against. It's like I said before. You're a hypocrite, Kiki.'

I froze. 'OK, wow.'

Aminah's eyes widened as her head whipped between Malakai and me, her hair swishing in my face in the process. Something flitted across Malakai's strained face and he flattened his lips. It looked like it might have been a small dose of regret. He cleared his throat.

'Look . . . let's just calm down. I didn't mean to—'

I held up a hand. I had stopped floating a while ago, but now I crashed to the ground. I had been so stupid.

'Oh, I'm calm. Who's not calm? Don't try and do that . . . gyaldemwhisperer thing to me. It won't work. And don't try and backtrack because you just exposed the real you. Now it makes sense. You didn't agree to kiss me to help me. Why on earth would a guy like you do that?'

Malakai's smile was now a sardonic curve. 'Guy like me?'

I ignored him. 'You did it to call public bullshit on what I said on my show. You wanted to show me up. Expose me. You played me.'

Malakai sat back. He nodded slowly and his demeanour shifted with a shrug of his shoulder. 'What if I did?'

Hot fury turned the words in my mouth into ash. A heavy silence dropped between us. I shook my head in disbelief. It was almost a relief to know that it was just a seduction ploy to make me look dizzy. The part of me that wanted to believe that what had just happened between us couldn't have been fake only worked to convince myself that it had to be. This was exactly what guys like Malakai did. When you fell into the trap, they'd tell you that you should have been watching where you were going.

Aminah cleared her throat. 'Wow. That was hot.'

'What?' Both mine and Malakai's voices were incredulous, our eyes snapping into each other's almost as quickly as we tore them away.

Aminah shook her head sloppily. 'I mean don't get me wrong, I am vexed. I wanna cuss Malakai out.' She threw him an irritated look. 'But it was compelling. Juicy. Better than my favourite reality show, *Romance & R&B.*'

Malakai stared at her. 'What is happening right now?'

I picked up my bag. 'I'm leaving.'

Aminah placed a hand on my arm, steadying me. 'Seriously. I would watch this. Or listen to it.'

I nodded sarcastically. 'Yeah. OK. Let's do a radio show where I let Malakai break down all the benevolent ways being a Fuckboi actually helps women.'

Aminah gasped and her eyes widened. 'Kiki Banjo, you beautiful, talented superstar. This is why I manage you! Opening up the lines of gyaldem-to-mandem communication. Fuck, I'm a genius. I mean, technically you came up with the idea, but I definitely led you to it. Wow, even when I'm not trying, I'm on it. Why am I studying Marketing and Business when I could just teach it?'

Aminah's hands were suspended in the air as she pantomimed the frames in a screen in which she could apparently see her future as some sort of public relations fixer. I nodded, pulled Aminah's hands down and hopefully, with it, her excitement for the idea.

'All right. Calm down, Olivia Nope. There is no way I'm doing this; can we go? I'd rather listen to Camila Cabello singing

Beyoncé songs acoustically on loop than be around him for one more second.'

Aminah gasped. 'All right, I know emotions are high but, please. Don't put evil like that into the universe. Our tongues are powerful. We're Nigerian. We know this.'

I reeled myself back in. Anger had pushed me too far. 'No, sorry. I wasn't thinking straight. My brain is just all out of whack because the girls think I played them for nineties' Morris Chest*not*.'

Malakai sat up. 'You think I look like Morris Chestnut?'

I shot him a withering look. 'Has the inflated size of your head made your ears shrink or something? I said *not*.'

Malakai's hitched right shoulder and half-smile simmered my blood.

'You used him as a reference. You're clearly thinking of me in the tangential direction of a nineties' heartthrob. I'll take it.'

I rolled my eyes. 'Prick.'

Malakai didn't blink. 'She-demon.'

My smile was a pastiche of innocence. 'What happened to angel face?'

'I didn't specify if the angel was fallen or not.'

I narrowed my eyes and yanked an increasingly waved Aminah up with me, rattled by the fact that I was rattled. I'd had enough.

'Have a nice life, dickhead.'

Malakai smiled brightly and reclined, sipped at his drink. 'It will be. As long as we never have to do this,' he gestured at the space between us, 'again.'

I paused. *Inhale. Deeply. That's it. And exha*— I was picking up the glass of watery remains of my drink. I'd intended to down it, hoped that even in its ultra-weakened state the rum would drown my irritation, but as I lifted it up, I found my hand tilting away from me, in the direction of Malakai Korede, so that the cold watery drink trickled down in to his lap. He jumped up, eyes so shocked that the light in them sharpened to a blade.

Aminah gasped. So did I. A little bit. So, I decided the best thing to do was to lean into my actions.

I smiled sweetly at Malakai's shocked face. 'Don't worry. We won't be.'

I stalked out of Cuffing Corner, my best friend staggering gleefully behind me, while I made the determination that any mild kindles of warm feeling I had felt towards Malakai were simply the result of looking directly into the enchanted eyes of The Fuckboi Supreme.

CHAPTER 8

Brown Sugar Show: Archives

Ladies,

I am a believer in the power of 'moving mad'. You know what I mean? When a dude has you so fucked up that he has unleashed the power of a thousand goddesses. Usually it comes with a simple, 'Fine. Do you then, innit.' Or a 'Cool'. That's my favourite. See when they move mad the trick is to move madder.

There are, by my calculations, two modes of moving mad. There is the 'killing them softly' approach. The quiet storm. Step back. Cut them out. Leave them on read. Two blue double ticks cooling in the breeze. Give them the time they think they need to breathe so they realise that . . . actually? They can't breathe without you. Now you got the dude wondering. You got him stressed out. You got him thinking, Why don't she care? Why is she taking my fuckery so well? *Babes, they get shook. The power is flipped over on to you. You will not be a victim and your silence will either force them to confront how they had you fucked up and apologise, or they'll take it as an excuse to bounce. Either way you're good, you're free, the ball is in your court. Either way, you know what you mean to him.*

Now, the second mode is moving actively mad. That's even more powerful and should only be reserved for special occasions, wielded with the most delicate care. You have to be sure of yourself to use it appropriately. We've seen it in Jazmine Sullivan's 'Bust Your Windows'. The video for Queen Bey's 'Hold Up'. OK, our producer Minah Money is saying, apparently, I cannot advocate for destruction of property on the radio for whatever reason. Why is she looking at me like that??! Whatever. You get my drift.

Sometimes these men move so mad that they have us moving mad chaotically. They've got under our skin. There is power in leaning into that. Embracing our emotions. Show them peppeh. Make them regret fucking with you — but note that if you decide to go this route, you have to have direction. Purpose. It has to be dosed correctly. Misuse the power of moving mad chaotically and you might end up being the one apologising, overtaking his official offence so much that you end up being in the wrong. So, be careful with it. Although, if he stays after you've poured bleach on his Yeezys you'll know he's really into you. If he leaves, he leaves. Either way you've displayed your truth.

Stay sweet ladies,

Brown Sugar x

'Rise! And Shine! And give God the glory, glory!!'

I grunted and pulled my covers over my head, as my best friend, totally unsurprisingly, took my response as a welcome and opened the door to my room, bounding in. Aminah always entered a room with a faint scent of a light Dior Oud, her signature, so even if I hadn't heard her voice, I would have known she was there. It clouded my room, permeated my Ikea bedclothes. The bed depressed slightly as she sat down next to me and yanked the covers off my head.

'Troublemaker. It's 11 a.m. and we have brunch plans.'

Shit.

Aminah and I had brunch at Wisteria & Waffle once every month. A student version of The Ivy, it was in town, did two-for-one on cocktails and Prosecco from 9 a.m. to 3 p.m. on weekends and was supremely social media-friendly in a girl-boss sort of way, with floral walls, an LED light fixture that read 'Vibes,' excellent bathroom lighting and unreasonably peng waiters, like some kind of culinary version of Hollister. The black tee and fitted trouser/skirt combo the waiters wore seemed especially tailored to elicit thirst – an ingenious marketing ploy to make us order more cocktails, because we did, every time.

There was one waiter in particular who Aminah and I both crushed on – a postgrad: a tall, bearded, cinnamon-skinned spice. He had an Eye of Horus tattooed on his firm forearm that winked along with him when he brought us our mimosas. He was known as AJ, but he informed us in a conspiratorial, low voice that we could call him Aaron: a bizarre, but nevertheless sexy invitation I'm pretty sure he extended to all the Whitewell women. Because of this, W&W was also the baitest place to be on a Saturday morning. It would be rammed with respective cliques trying to rejuvenate after a night at FreakyFridayz. That meant it was the *last* place I needed to be after the previous night's antics. They kept replaying in my mind, swirling around my head with the alcohol.

We'd got home at 3 a.m., manoeuvring past the death glares that were being thrown my way. Aminah had insisted we had a few more shots at home to 'cheer me up' despite being waved herself, and we dissected what had happened – her gleeful, me regretful. Somewhat regretful.

Was I wrong for pouring my drink into Malakai Korede's lap? Probably.

Had he deserved it? Almost definitely.

On the other hand, had he helped me stick it to Zack by kissing me like a pirate who'd discovered the real treasure was within his lady love the whole time? Fuck, yes. It was unnerving that part of the reason for my sleepless night was the reliving of that kiss. The thrill that ran through my body when he'd held me close. How it felt like he'd wanted me. How it felt like I'd wanted him. I also had to contend with the fact that the Blackwellian girls all probably thought I was a two-faced bitch. My mind was in disarray.

Less important, but nevertheless pertinent: I'd slept in my make-up and forgotten to do my skincare routine before bed, so I also had to reckon with the fact that I was likely to break out today. All of this meant that there was absolutely no way I was leaving our flat this weekend.

My best friend tried to haul me up, but I batted her away as I hoisted myself up. I always forgot that Aminah and I had far, far different tolerances to alcohol. She was as chirpy as a Real Housewife who just got word that her nemesis's husband was cheating on her. Immaculate in her matching pink monogrammed satin gown and headwrap, Aminah actually did look like she belonged in a reality show for the elegant and luxe. It was fascinating. I didn't even know how she was *standing* – just a mere few hours ago she'd been texting me 'ofggggg the room is spinningggggg' from her bedroom next door.

I readjusted my oversized shirt and scooted over so she could nestle next to me on the bed. 'Why don't we have brunch at home? Save money.'

'Because we have half a plantain and two slices of bread left, and we were meant to go grocery shopping after brunch. Why don't you want to go? Is it because you think everyone's going to be staring at you after last night's scene? . . . They will. Revel in it.'

I shot her a humourless smile. 'Thank you so much for that. Give it to me straight, though, now that we're both sober—'

Aminah pulled a face in a way that indicated that she might still have been a little drunk and I made note of my own slight wooziness. 'OK, now we're both relatively sober . . . how mad did I move last night?'

'Kiss or the drink?'

'Both.'

Aminah grinned. 'I thought the kiss was sexy as hell. The drink spill . . . OK, it was a *tiny* bit extra.'

I picked up another pillow and buried my face in it as I leant back against my headboard. If Aminah was saying I'd been 'extra' that meant I'd moved chaotically mad. I felt a tug on the pillow. Seconds later, Aminah managed to pry it from my hands, forcing me to look at her. She bashed me in the face with it.

'Oshey, Nollywood, can I finish? It was a little extra, but it was exciting, Keeks. You lost control. I have never, ever known you to lose it like that. Even when you're pissed off it's, like, *measured*. This was different. I loved it. You let go and let that drink *flow* into Korede's lap. It was kind of iconic.'

I rolled my eyes at her bad poetry, despite knowing that she'd been right about the control part. Malakai getting under my skin so easily was freaking me out. He was essentially a stranger and he'd also proved himself a Fuckboi by saying he'd used the kiss to prove a point. So why was I letting him get to me in a way that had me acting out in public? That wasn't me. I was never at the centre of campus drama, yet within a few days of meeting him I'd drawn attention that I couldn't control. It wasn't directly his fault but there was something unbridled in the energy between us.

Aminah nudged me. 'Have you seen what they're saying about you on the socials?'

I groaned again. Thankfully, I'd had the presence of mind to put my phone on flight mode before I went to bed. I rubbed the bridge of my nose. 'Aminah, I get it. They think I'm a back-stabbing snake. Can we talk damage control on Monday, please? I cannot deal with it right now.'

My best friend slinked her phone from a silk pocket as her fingers tapped and slid across, deftly conjuring information up. 'Um, no. I mean, last night it was definitely that, don't get me wrong, but look at this.'

She pried my hand from my eyes and forced me to look at her phone screen. I peeked at it tentatively, immediately faced with a gif of me pouring the drink on Malakai's lap, the caption above it, 'Maybe Kiki snapped! I have to stan!'

Aminah's grin was wide, as she nodded excitedly. 'Uh huh. Look at the Brown Sugar socials – people *love it*. When they saw you kissing, they thought you snaked them, but when they saw you turn on him, they saw it as vengeance. The tide turned pretty quickly after that. The girls love it. I bet Simi is livid. It backfired beautifully. People are saying that Malakai got a taste of his own medicine and you were the perfect person to dose it.'

I frowned, trying to process this information when my gaze snagged on another picture. It was a picture of Malakai and I sitting together, my legs crossed, head tilted, with a smirk on my face. Malakai was looking at me intently, smile sharp and slanting. Our knees were inches apart. It was blurry but I saw it clear as crystal, felt it clear as crystal, the warm heat in my belly returning at the memory of how light and easy our conversation had been. I forced it to cool. It was all bullshit. Part of his game, and it was my fault for being duped.

My eyes dropped to the caption and I read it out loud: 'Two can play that game.' I raised an eyebrow and smiled reluctantly. 'Huh.'

Aminah smirked. 'Hot, right? The sexual tension in this picture is mad. Look at the way your eyes are lit up —'

I held up a hand. 'OK. First, it was the flash; second, with love, you are so annoying, third—'

'Has Killa Keeks got an idea?'

'How do you know?'

Aminah grinned at the look on my face. 'Last time you got this look we joined the French society so we could get a subsidised trip to Paris, because you found out it was on the Beyoncé tour.'

The plan worked, too. Yeah, we'd missed a 'team-building dinner' with fellow students called things like Penelope Arbuthnot and Barclay Harington, but somehow we got over it. It was a win–win situation. We got to go see Beyoncé, while also having the opportunity to re-enact the 'Apeshit' video in front of the Louvre.

'OK, so . . .' I turned to face my best friend properly, swivelling myself on the bed and crossing my legs under me – she did the same, listening, expertly filing her nails without looking, her face warm with interest.

'I was just thinking that all this attention would be a cool thing to harness. Remember I told you that the summer programme Dr Miller wants to put me up for requires me to build or grow a media platform? I could use this to generate more ratings somehow.'

'You mean . . . like you mentioned the other night? The thing I encouraged but you shot down?'

I smiled at her pointed brow. 'Not exactly that. I mean that was going to be a debate, a battle of the sexes thing. We need a hook, a story. I've been thinking about how popular Simi's blog is and it's because people love a narrative, and they also *love* love. Or its idea anyway. Imagine how interesting people would find it if I was actually dating Malakai? And that thing at FreakyFridayz was just . . . like a fight. What if I capitalised on that interest that surrounds new couples? Actually make our "relationship" the show? Feeding the gossip straight to them, instead of going through a third party like The TeaHouse.'

Aminah froze. 'Stop. I'm getting chills.'

'Right? The only complication is that it's Malakai. Not only can we not stand each other—'

'Is that true though?'

'I definitely poured a drink on his crotch.'

'OK, so, the fact that you poured it there and not on his head shows where your mind is at, like maybe you thought there was a fire there that you needed to extinguish.'

I stared at my best friend, bemused. 'You are not taking another psychology class. I forbid it. Anyway, there's no way he will agree to it . . . Let's move on. Wassup with you and Kof?'

Aminah immediately rose from my bed, adjusting her gown around herself primly. 'I don't know. What is up with me and Kof?'

'Oh. So that wasn't you up there last night by the DJ booth being his hype-woman?'

'Hype-woman? Ew. I am his muse. Also given that the music really determines how live the party is, all I was doing was making sure people were having a good time by bringing the best out of Kofi. It was an act of kindness. I'm basically Angelina Jolie. A devastatingly beautiful humanitarian.'

'Right.' I couldn't really argue with her reasoning. Aminah Bakare was truly amazing. My sis was a mistress of marketing, a PR princess, a spin savant.

Aminah twitched a shoulder in petty triumph and flounced towards my door. 'I'm giving you forty minutes to get ready, bitch. Aaron awaits and I have a line I wanna test on him. 'Is that a PIN machine in your pocket or are you just happy to see me?'

I laughed. 'Poetry. I think I'm just gonna trace his tattoo slowly and go, 'Did that hurt?'

'Can't wait to be sister-wives!'

I opened my laptop to stream music as I got ready. 'Only person I'd want to do it with, Babe.'

From: S.Miller@WCU.ac.uk
Subject: Study Buddy

Or if you prefer, 'Academic Acquaintance'.
Here is a link to the other student's work. I have sent them your work too. Let me know what you think. I really think your ideas complement each other.

Dr M

I stared at the email blinking at me on my laptop screen. It had popped up as I switched on my Saturday Soul playlist, just as Jill

Scott asked me to take a long walk with her. So, Dr Miller hadn't forgotten. It was a Vimeo link. A film. Pretentious.

I stared at my D'Angelo poster on the wall for guidance. It was his *Voodoo* album cover, body hard, eyes soft. Slight smirk, lips looking tender, gaze beckoning. It didn't help. All it did was make me slightly horny. Ugh. I felt irritated about the fact this stranger was apparently good enough for me to seek help from. I didn't need help. I had this on my own. Maybe I needed to look at their project to prove it to myself. Besides, Keep your academic enemies closer. I clicked the link.

It was called *Cuts,* a fifteen-minute short about a Black barber-shop. It was terrible in that it wasn't terrible. It was good. Really good. Really, irritatingly good – and not the artsy, derivative, pandering shit on toxic masculinity I expected it to be. It showed quick, sharp shots of men bantering and barbering, moralising while doing-the-mosting, regaling while roasting, straddling the line between shameless sin and sanctimony, telling the crassest stories, lines that sounded like poetry: 'She was sweet plantain, soft like mango'; 'God is good all the time. He turned my life around man, can't lie' and 'I'm not religious like that. Respect it, though. My mum's house is church. Her bills are my tithes.'

It was grainy, the soundtrack a song that was somehow a mish-mash of neo-soul and grime. Eyes soft, body hard. Aunties coming through with shopping trolleys singing, 'meat pie, fish pie, puff-puff', adding musical dimension to the pirate radio station playing in the background. Boys coming in to get a trim for their first dates, the old guys calming their nerves by sharpening the edges on their foreheads, while making fun of the sizes of their heads, telling them their own first-date stories with their missuses.

There was mix-tape selling, jewellery hawking, shit-talking, confidence-constructing . . . It was good. Maybe it needed a little work with narrative, but maybe it didn't. I felt it. I wanted to know this person. I suddenly felt embarrassed. I'd been a petulant prick. Why was I threatened by someone being better than me? I was a nerd but I never ever figured I'd be *that* kind of nerd. The irritation began to ebb out of me just as the credits rolled across the laptop screen. Stark white letters against a black background, stars on a clear dark night, just like his stupid eyes.

A Malakai Korede Film.

I slapped my laptop shut. I needed fifteen mimosas.

'I am extremely uncomfortable right now, Minah. I have to say.' We were sat at a window table of W&W, me with a half-English breakfast, Aminah with a stack of pillowy pancakes and summer fruit.

She shrugged and picked up her mimosa. 'If I were you, I would lean into it. Let people stare. Besides, you look good. How do you know it's not because of that?'

I glanced down at my outfit – a men's black T-shirt with Fela's face graffitied on it that had 'Expensive Shit' scrawled beneath it in haphazard brushstrokes, worn as a dress, with tights and combat boots. I thought I looked good. That perspective changed, however, if I met the decoratively eyeshadowed eyes of the girls shooting me curious gazes in between dainty mouthfuls of waffles and whispers.

'I just know,' I said, as I speared some scrambled egg into my mouth. I cast a furtive glance around the flowery parlour. People were definitely talking about me, and they wanted me to know they were talking about me. Otherwise, they could have just talked about me without looking. It's not like I would have heard – Ariana Grande was playing too loudly.

'Well, do you also know what you're gonna do for the NYU programme project? Any ideas? Thought anymore about the Malakai thing?'

I took a sip of my sour Prosecco. 'I have, actually. Weirdly, I think there's a chance I could get him to do it. You know that student that Dr Miller said was my competition?'

'Our nemesis, yeah—'

'You ladies need anything?' An almost hilariously deep baritone added accompaniment to Ariana's silken whistles. Aminah and I glanced up to see AJ (Aaron) by our table, broad smile in place. I ran my gaze across his copper-toned arm as he lifted it to push a stray loc behind his ear (there was a pencil tucked there that he did not need: he had a tablet). The Eye of Horus twinkled slightly with the movement.

I felt a soft kick on my shin from Aminah's tennis shoe. She raised a brow at me, her lips pulled back into a knowing smirk. She was challenging me. She wanted me to husk out 'nothing that's on the menu,' heavy with implication, like something out of a terrible romcom. She'd dared me to do it ten minutes ago. She cocked her head at me. 'I don't know. Do we, Kiki?'

I shrugged, 'Nothing, thank you,' deliberately avoiding looking at Aminah.

'You sure? No water top-ups? Yours is looking a little low—'Aminah's glass was still full, mine half empty. Depending how you looked at it.

I shook my head. 'I'm perfect, thanks.'

Aaron nodded and smiled, his eyes flicking across me. 'Yeah . . . Well. If you need anything. Let me know.'

'Will do!'

Aaron broadened his smile to include both of us, inclined his head ever so slightly and walked off to flirt with the cohort of Naija Princesses behind us.

'Are you kidding me?' Aminah hissed, as soon as he was out of earshot.

'Minah, please. He does that with everyone. It's part of his job. It's what keeps us coming back for undercooked eggs. Seriously, these are so runny. You heard me ask for well-done, right? It's more likely he fancies you, if anything.'

Aminah shook her head slowly at me. 'Why do you do this? You *know* you're fine, and yet you act like—'

Oh, for fuck's sake.' I let out a groan. 'This cannot be happening right now.'

Aminah's eyes widened. 'Um, excuse you?! You don't have to swear at me. I just think it's funny how you're confident enough to get with Zack Kingsford, but somehow—'

Her words were lost on me, the sight my eyes had snagged on in the café window advancing ever closer and closer. I sank down into my seat, grabbed a napkin to cover half my face. 'Minah, please. Look outside the window. Without looking.'

Aminah, immediately receiving the memo, slipped her oversized shades on and turned to look. Kofi and Malakai were walking directly opposite us, along Duke's Road, Whitewell's main shopping street. 'Oh. . . .' She relaxed instantly, and laughed as I ducked my head, studying the vegan breakfast options from beneath the napkin. There were a lot of avocados. I glared at a £6.50 avocado and matcha oat milkshake. That was new.

'*Oh*.' Aminah's voice had changed, still amused, but lower, more ominous.

'What? What was that last *oh?*' I hissed. Was the mere sight of the avocado and matcha oat milkshake making my stomach bubble, or was it the nervous anticipation of what my best friend was about to s—

'They're crossing the road and . . . yeah. Yup. Kofi has clocked me. They're coming over. I'm so sorry, babes.'

I threw the napkin on the table and sat up. 'I'm not ready for this. Is there time for me to go to the bathroom?'

Aminah pulled a face. 'I don't know. You'd have to walk past Shanti's table and while she isn't going to come up to you because that would look like she cares too much, if you pass by, she *will* pull you into it with her, and likely ask you why you made out with Malakai five seconds after you saw her get into it with *him*. Your call, I guess?'

I pressed two fingers against my temple and inhaled deeply. I was trapped between a rock (diamanté, encrusted on Shanti's pearly pink pinky) and a hard place (Malakai's chest). It was fine. When I really thought about it, running away from Malakai Korede wasn't an option. Yes, I was technically in the wrong for throwing a watery Coke and rum on his lap, but he was also – and this was crucial – an arrogant prick who admitted that he'd used me to prove a point. Admittedly, there is the fact that I also used *him* to prove a point, but *that* was not the point. He was aware of the point I was trying to prove. He was in on it. I hadn't played him. Also, I was—

'Kikiola Banjo. You are Brown Sugar herself. You do not run away from boys. Remember who the hell you are and boss up. Beyoncé didn't drop 'Bow Down' for this!' Aminah said, pointing a manicured finger in my direction and raising a brow. This was our boilerplate mini pep-talk when the other needed a figurative cold splash of water on the face. Aminah's deployment of it meant this was an emergency. I needed to get myself together as a matter of urgency.

'Yeah. *Yeah.* You're so right. Thank you.' I grabbed my champagne flute and poured Prosecco down my throat for fortification. After a scintilla of a moment, I reached out to Aminah just as she instinctively passed her own quarter-glass of mimosa over to me. A little more wouldn't hurt.

I downed it just as a growingly familiar scent wafted under my nose, a buttery sweetness of whatever moisturiser he used, tempered with a heavier, muskier fragrance, sexier; something that smelled like night-time drives to slow R&B through the city. I hated how it curled into the base of my stomach, reminded me of how his lips felt against mine. I hated how I recognised it. My body was truly unruly.

Aminah tilted her head up at them. 'Hey boys. You thirsty for mimosas or what?'

'Actually, yeah, but we better not,' I heard Kofi say as I concentrated on a fleck of black pepper on my last bit of egg. 'We're going to Prince's Park. Basketball.'

I looked up then, but miscalculated, my gaze landing on Malakai, not Kofi. And he was looking directly at me. The slip gave me the freedom to clock he was wearing loose black shorts that hung to his knee, a white tee, upon which a thin gold chain lay and a grey zip-hoodie. He looked good. Of course he looked good, and why *wouldn't* he play basketball, a certified Hot Guy sport? Predictable. Couldn't he have played golf or something?

Malakai didn't look mad or unmad. Just vaguely amused, the corner of his mouth pulled up. I didn't know if this made me mad or unmad. It would seem that we were going to pretend that everything was normal. Cool. I could do that. In fact, I welcomed that, especially knowing how many eyes were on us right then. I turned my attention to Kofi.

'Why are you coming all the way to town for basketball? We have a court at uni.'

Malakai laughed, and it forced me to look at him again. 'Last time we tried that, we drew too much attention. Beckies and Billies slowing down to stare as they walked past. It was as if they'd never seen Black people playing sport in real life.' He shuddered. 'You ever heard the word "nigger" from a look? One of them actually

121

came up to me on my way out and asked if I got in because of a sports scholarship—'

A disgusted snort jumped out of me and Malakai's eyes leapt to mine in surprise. I cleared my throat. 'That's fucked up. What did you say?'

Malakai's face was straight. 'I was scouted by scientologist missionaries while living in my small village in the nation of Africa. They knew of my prowess when I saved their camp from a lion with my bare hands. I have big dreams. I am so blessed to be the first one in my family to not herd warthogs.'

My smile slipped out. Traitor.

Malakai regarded me a fraction longer than was necessary as Kofi responded, causing both our gazes to jump apart from each other. 'Yeah, it was real zoo vibes. Made me feel like we were playing for massa.'

Aminah's eye narrowed in glittering ire. 'They're lucky I wasn't there. The cussing I would cuss would make their bodies and souls shrivel up on the spot. All that would be left is a pile of Barbour gilets on the floor.'

Kofi grinned. 'I love it when you go off.'

Aminah caught herself and rolled her eyes. 'Whatever. Look, Keeks and I are going food shopping right now and we were going to cut through the park to get to the market. We can walk along with you. We were just finishing up—'

I kicked her shin under the table, but Aminah's face remained unmoved. She was looking placidly at Kofi, my discomfort obviously of no consequence to her. I knew she thought that the best way to deal with the situation was to confront it head on, but she couldn't have been more wrong. The best way to deal with it was to pretend it had never happened. The best way to deal with it was for Malakai and I to extricate ourselves from each other's orbits. My stomach tightened as Kofi's face relaxed further, his smile widening goofily at the invitation.

'Yeah? OK! I mean, yeah OK. Cool. Calm. Let's bounce, beautiful.'

Aminah shook her head, but I detected the smile she was trying to bury under the surface. 'You talk like a tween's sitcom character,' she muttered, while making eye contact with a waiter for the bill.

Kofi laughed. 'Be my leading lady.'

Aminah rolled her eyes. 'You're a clown—'

Aminah and Kofi descended into a back-and-forth that made the awkward silence between Malakai and I louder. Eventually, Malakai looked at the table intently in careful study, stepping back a little, as if to allow him the full scope of it. I hadn't fully intended on talking to him properly yet, but somehow, I found myself asking the weirdo what he was doing.

Malakai straightened up and shrugged, swerving his gaze back on me. 'Just making sure the glasses on the table are completely empty. You know. For my safety.'

Dick.

CHAPTER 9

Prince's Park was the largest verdant space in Whitewell, slap-dab in the middle of town; so big that it also served as the divider between west Whitewell and east Whitewell. West Whitewell was where our campus was, complete with sprawling suburban-gated houses, artisanal coffee shops, cat cafés and yoga studios owned by white people with blond dreadlocks.

In west Whitewell, there were literal limits to how many Black kids they allowed in a club, although they obviously never made this explicit, having the decency to pretend that it was because they were 'overcrowded'. These clubs were full of hip-hop and white kids that rapped along to it – but when faced with too many real, breathing *Blacks* that weren't confined to a consumable form of entertainment for them, they panicked.

There needed to be just enough niggas (Kendrick said it and therefore, so could they) in the club to make them feel cool, enough dotted around, so they could feel diverse. Enough Black guys for white girls to say, 'everyone tells me I dance like a Black girl'. Enough Black girls for white guys to proclaim with jägerbomb-spiked breath that they ain't ever kissed a Black girl before, like you were the lucky one, something like *Princess & the Frog*, except the Black girl would remain the exotic curiosity and the white guy would feel transformed into something elevated, something unique, perhaps a little dangerously deviant. They needed just enough Blacks in the club to make them feel cool. Too many Blacks, however? That was going too far. Too much Black would make them feel too white.

East Whitewell – or Eastside – was where Aminah and I went to do the bulk of our grocery shopping: bell peppers, scotch bonnets, plantain, okra, rice, cheap packs of ramen to inhale during brutal all-nighters (ramen so bad that it could be used to plaster into broken ceramics. We saw it on a viral video. Somehow, this didn't stop us). Eastside is where we got our hair supplies, where Aunties, carrying swollen blue plastic bags with leaves sticking out of them, spoke loudly in Yoruba and Twi, Urdu and Gujarati. Eastside was the place where Aminah and I took turns to go to the Jamaican shop and order, faced with straight-faced 'we nuh ave dat', till Ms Hyacinth served us whatever she wanted to serve us. And Eastside was the side of the park where the basketball court was.

It was far – too far. At least a twenty-five-minute walk. It was a trek. And we had been walking down the plush park path as a foursome, Aminah and I on one side, Kofi and Malakai on the other, but at some point Aminah and Kofi had drifted ahead and together, leaving Malakai and me to hang back awkwardly behind. Technically, we could have just caught up with them, disrupted our discomfort, but that would mean severe cockblocking and apparently neither of us were that selfish. So, we'd been walking in excruciating silence for the past five minutes, the only noise being our shoes crunching on autumn leaves, kids squawking in the background and our friends' bizarre mating ritual up in front. I guessed it was up to me to make it bearable. The labour of a Black woman in this society really is unending.

I inhaled a brisk gust of fortifying air and looked up at Malakai. 'OK. Uh. I guess I should say I'm sorry for the whole drink thing. Actually, I *am* sorry. It was embarrassing. I moved mad. My bad.' I surprised myself by meaning it.

Malakai shrugged and shot me a small smile. 'Thanks. I kind of deserved it, though. I was being a dick.'

I laughed, half-surprised 'What? No.'

Malakai kicked at some leaves and rubbed the back of his neck in what was an obscenely sexy move. 'I was being shitty. I knew it. I'm sorry.' His eyes searched mine, as if he needed me to know he meant it.

I glanced away from him because their knowing focus made me uncomfortable, lasering through my skin. 'It's cool.'

Malakai cleared his throat. 'Look, uh, full disclosure? Dr Miller sent me some of your work. Your writing on pop culture and society and that essay on, like . . . what was it? The distillation of Missy Elliot's contribution to Black feminism? Where you dissected her music videos? That was mad.' His face broke into a shadow of the playful smile I'd seen the other night. 'Actually, I was kind of pissed at how good it was. Then I listened to more of Brown Sugar and that made me even more pissed.' He laughed. 'You were right. About a lot of things. And, even if I didn't agree . . . I just think you have a really interesting perspective. A cool voice.' He paused as if catching himself, cleared his throat. 'I just thought I'd tell you that. She sent it to me last weekend but she's been talking about you to me – without ever mentioning your name – since I transferred at the beginning of the year. I got kinda jealous.'

'Why, you got a crush on her?' The main function of the question was to distract myself from the fact that Malakai liking my work elicited a bloom of pleasure in me.

Malakai laughed and rubbed his chin, 'Don't you?'

'Obviously. She's fine as hell.' I made eye contact with a terrier, waddling along with its owner, 'Thank you, by the way. For saying all that. About my work, I mean.'

'Trust me, if I could have chosen to not like it, I would have.' His voice was bone dry. It struck against me, elicited a spark.

I clamped on my grin and, glancing up at him, admitted, 'I watched *Cuts*.'

Malakai's gaze snapped to me. 'Is this where you tell me all the ways you hated it as rightful punishment for my behaviour?' He was joking but he wasn't, his eyes softened with gentle wariness.

'Not gonna lie, I was kind of disappointed.' I paused long enough for the curve in Malakai's lips to collapse infinitesimally. 'Disappointed that I didn't hate it . . . It was good. Really good.

Which sucked for me, obviously, because I fully planned on going back to Dr Miller like, 'I thought you said this guy was smart?'

Malakai was staring at me, his smile sloping out wide now, rubbing the back of his neck again. He needed to stop it. Not only was it infuriatingly cute, it also drew attention to how thick, firm and muscular his arms were. Seeing them reminded me of when they were wrapped with my palms, satiny and sturdy and warm beneath them. Was I ovulating? I needed to check my period app. I blinked at him. 'What?'

'You fucking with me?'

I stared at him, trying to assess if Malakai really cared about what I, a virtual stranger who had shit-talked him on the radio, thought about him. Unless his game was so ultra-evolved that it included insecurity as a disarmament tactic in its package, his need to know seemed real.

'Malakai, if I wanted to fuck with you, I would fuck with you.'

A lady pushing a designer pushchair shot me a pointed look, like we weren't in a public place. We were still in west Whitewell after all. I rolled my eyes.

'I think you know that much about me by now. Like, it's almost causing me physical pain to say this to you.' I faked a dainty sneeze. 'Oh man. See? I think I'm allergic to being nice to you, actually.'

Malakai laughed, a surprisingly delightful, loud bark of a laugh. The air around us was cool but the force of his bellow seemed to push it up a couple degrees. 'Thank you. Seriously. *Cuts* got me into my course. I sent it with my personal statement.'

'What made you want to make it?'

'That barbershop is owned by a man I call Uncle K.'

'Ah. Super K's Kutz,' I said, recalling the name I saw emblazoned on the storefront in bold white italics against black gloss.

'Right. I kind of half-grew up there. Uncle K and my dad were old friends, from when they first arrived in England. My dad moved to Naija for work when I was seven, but before that he used to bring me along for his trims, then he took me for my first cut.' Malakai dropped a half-swaggering smile. 'Couldn't tell me shit on the playground on Monday.'

'Bet all the girls wanted to play house with you.'

'Yeah, but my true calling was football. Didn't want to be tied down.' Malakai's rogue grin grew wider at my rolled eyes. 'Anyway, when he left, my mum started taking me. When the trim was over, I never wanted to leave. I loved being there – the men were like uncles to me, cousins, big brothers. The music of it, man. The rhythm. The razors, the football, Fuji music, Motown, Highlife, the banter, the debates, even though most of the time I never knew what they were talking about. I shouldn't have known what they were talking about half the time.' Malakai lit up, the bright in his eyes so vibrant, it bounced its way over to me, grabbed the tips of my lips, made me smile.

'I used to kick off so much when it was time to go that eventually my mum started leaving me there with snacks and a juice box while she ran errands. Working there was my first job – officially at sixteen, realistically at fourteen. Sweeping, cleaning . . . running to the chicken shop with food orders. And, whatever was happening outside, or at home, that place was always safe, always

warm. And it wasn't always safe, outside. Wasn't always warm.'
I nodded and Malakai twitched a shoulder. He didn't have to say
what he wasn't saying. 'There was always love there. This like
solid form of community. Someone had a job interview? Cut on
the house. A link? Advice from the elders.'

I let a sly smile slip out. 'Oh, snap. So that's how you became
such a relationship expert? Listening to the OGs?'

Malakai rolled a low chuckle in his mouth. 'I learnt a lot from
them, generally. The film – I guess I wanted to capture the energy
I felt in that shop.'

A new side to Malakai had just been revealed to me – it was
brighter, his eyes glittering with new, fascinating refractions
when he spoke about his work, his home. I liked looking at the
dispersions of beams. I cleared my throat. 'Well. I think you
nailed it.'

His eyes shot gratitude at me. 'I appreciate that.'

The sincerity singed my guard. 'So, um, Dr Miller mentioned
a new film?'

'Oh right, yeah. Uh, this is going to sound completely nuts but
I'm actually thinking of entering a film competition, The Shades
of Motion.'

'Woah. That doesn't sound nuts. That's so cool. Isn't it one of
the biggest film festivals for new artists in London?'

'Yeah. Even being shortlisted opens up huge opportunities. *Cuts*
doesn't fulfil the requirements so I've come up with another idea.
I feel like being shortlisted would make filmmaking more than just
a hobby, you know? Make it feel legit.'

I frowned. 'Make it legit? You study it. You're good at it. I imagine you love it—'

'I love it so much, man. It's like . . . magic to me. Being able to capture life that way. Bottle it and open it up at the same time. Share it.'

A quiet fell between us. I could feel us both wondering how we got this far into earnest conversation with each other. It was too late to revert to small talk. I wasn't sure our dynamic ever really allowed for small talk, anyway. After a few moments, Malakai started to rub the back of his neck again.

'Uh, so my dad doesn't exactly know I study film. I mean my degree is technically Film and Business Studies, but still. I'm hoping that by the time he finds out what I'm really interested in I'll have something to show for it. Something tangible, you know? Just to avoid all the long talk and headache. And maybe prove something to myself too.' He shrugged. 'I mean, I probably won't even be shortlisted, and I'm definitely gonna be up against more experienced people—'

'What's your idea?'

He smiled at me, something warm that momentarily disoriented my vestibular system. I made a mental note to get iron tablets.

Malakai inhaled deeply, as if fortifying himself. 'Romance in uni. Dating in uni.'

He noted my quizzical raised brows. 'I know how it sounds. But I just feel – objectively – that romance is interesting. Especially here. It runs social interactions in Blackwell. It's part of our foundation.'

It was irritating that I couldn't argue with this. Evidently sensing this was the case, he continued. 'I feel like a lot of romance is projected or performative. Not quite a fantasy—'

'But not quite real either.'

He nodded. 'Exactly. I also think it would just be a cool way to understand women.'

I snorted. 'There it is.'

'Nah, but hear me out.' Malakai flipped so he was in front of me, half-walking backwards, his gait as smooth as ever. 'I just want to understand relationships. I'm honest, OK?' He pressed a broad hand against his chest, head ducking slightly to prove his humility.

'I don't go into them because I can't do them. But I want to understand what makes people want to enter them in the first place. What makes people realise that's what they want?' His arms were spread wide as he stated his case to me, a charismatic preacher. Had I heard his good news, that it's possible to be a player and not a dick?

'I want to understand the compulsion. And yeah, OK, if I understand gyal through it, that isn't a bad thing. Maybe I could perfect casual dating without collateral. Knowing how to attend to emotional and physical needs without—'

'Two girls fighting over you at a campus link-up?' I finished.

Malakai grinned brightly at the flat tone of my voice. He repositioned himself next to me. 'Right. Is that so bad? Figuring out how to perfect casual dating so you can approach it ethically? You know it's actually kind of a social good? The boyfriend experience

132

without the stress of actually having a boyfriend. I don't need birthday presents, I won't get jealous, but we'll have a great time together, regardless.'

'So, my gut says it's sociopathic, but your voice makes it sound reasonable, and my mind can weirdly rationalise it? Which makes me feel like that's part of the sociopathy. I think you'd be a great cult leader.'

'Mystic Malakai. That's what you called me, innit? Has a ring to it.'

'Man, you're just like . . . the worst, aren't you?'

The widening of Malakai's really fucking gorgeous smile confirmed my suspicions. There it was – the beatific smile of a cult leader. I shivered, not just due to the chilling social threat of Malakai's Fuckboi cult, but because the sun was ebbing early and the breeze was getting cooler. Stupidly, fooled by the deceptive and fleeting autumn warmth, I'd left my house without a jacket.

'So where am I supposed to come in?'

Malakai unzipped his hoodie and pulled it off, revealing smooth dark ripples of skin and sinew. He held it out to me casually. 'Your show is romance-focused—'

I shook my head at the offer of his hoodie. 'Oh no – I'm fine. Thank you. I'm not cold.'

Malakai's gaze flitted across my arms. 'Kiki, you have goosebumps. Take the hoodie. It doesn't have lurgies, I promise. If you take the hoodie, you're still allowed to think I'm a scourge to man-dating womankind.'

This brought out a short splutter of laughter. I took it from him, desperately hoping that it wouldn't compromise my feminism. 'Thank you. Won't you be cold though?'

'I don't get cold. The same way you don't sweat. Superhuman tings.'

I swished my smile in my mouth as I pulled the hoodie on, still warm from his body. It hung to my knees, his light, woodsy, vetiver and detergent scent as insulating as the inner fleece.

'My show is more than just romance. It's about . . . stopping hearts being broken unnecessarily. Preventing the mess that comes with it. Handling ourselves. Guys get away with so much and we're supposed to accept it because we're supposed to want romance, above all else, and they *know* that and take advantage of it. Monsters are bred. I'm equipping the girls with tools of protection against the Fuckboi endemic—'

'"Fuckboi endemic".' Malakai released a low whistle. 'What did you go through to become an expert in heartbreak?'

I froze. I heard his words before his tone registered; it took a second for me to realise there was no accusation. He was looking at me with soft curiosity. Nevertheless, the fact remained, it was none of his business. 'Let's just say I had an eventful time just before I started uni. It gave me a little insight.'

'And that insight caused you to call me the Wasteman of Whitewell.' His voice was dry. He was looking at me from the corner of his eye. Kofi and Aminah were far ahead of us now; we were ambling along slowly, more relaxed in our gaits, the autumn breeze blowing across our faces. I could appreciate it, now that I felt warmer.

'Tell me more about your film and what you desperately need my help with?'

Malakai inclined his head deeply in acceptance of the fact that I wasn't going to take it back and continued.

'Fine. So, I want it to be excerpts – similar to *Cuts*, but with interviews with young couples, the religious ones abstaining till marriage, the ones out in a club, the dysfunctional ones, but it needs drive. Some kind of narrative angle pinning it down. Right now, the plan is kind of like . . . a collage. Which is fun, but it's missing something. It needs context, direction, a voice. It isn't saying anything right now. And I've been listening to *Brown Sugar* and I thought, what if I cut snippets from your show? Layer it over the film so you have these two ideas of romance maybe over-lapping? We'll see where it goes. And then I thought what if you interview the couples? You have the expertise and . . . OK, now you're looking at me like I just said Taylor Swift's "Shake It Off" was better than Mariah's.' So, he had listened to my show. 'Thank God you're not holding a drink right now.'

I blinked several times, while trying to draw half-thoughts into cohesion to help me form a response. It wasn't that the idea was bad – in fact it was great, in theory – but I was just trying to wrap my mind around the fact that Malakai trusted me enough to be involved in his film. And that it would demand me actually talking to people in real life. Also, while Malakai had an undercurrent of confidence permeating everything he did, something soft flickered across his face when he spoke about his work – and, unfortunately, I found it cute.

'You can say no if you want to, obviously,' he continued, 'but you would be fully credited as a consulting producer, creative consultant – whatever. And I'd help you with what you need for your project for the NYU programme. Congrats by the way. Dr Miller told me about it and said something about us being able to help each other out and . . . You know what? Now that I am saying this out loud, I'm realising how nuts this is so I'm just going to quit while I'm ahea—'

'OK'

Malakai stopped walking. 'What?'

I shrugged. 'The concept sounds interesting. Not your Anthropological Player "understanding women" ting, because, I mean, *ew*. But the exploration of campus relationships, it's really cool. I just have two stipulations. The first is, if we win the competition—'

'Unlikely.'

'—If we win, I want forty per cent of the prize money. It's your idea but it's using my art and my really sexy voice—'

'Twenty—'

'Twenty-five.'

'Deal.' I smiled.

Malakai shook his head. 'You just played me.'

'I would have taken twenty . . . The second condition is about what I need from you for my NYU project—'

'Name it.'

Fragments of my plan began to finalise in my mind, clicking into place and turning my mental cogs. I walked ahead, then spun around to face him, beaming. 'You have to date me.'

Malakai started laughing – until he noticed the look on my face. He stopped walking, blinking at me, his smile evaporating. The notion of us being romantically involved clearly distressed him. Perfect.

'I'm sorry, *what?*'

I moved closer to him, getting increasingly giddy now that the idea was solidifying in my mind. 'Well, it will be a pretend relationship. Which, in hindsight, I should have led with, but hey, it didn't have the same bite. Stay with me,' I said as he continued to look at me as if I had spontaneously sprouted horns.

'I was playing with this idea all afternoon and it just clicked when you were talking about your film. I was thinking about everyone's reactions to that kiss on Friday. Yeah, people acted like they were shocked, but really, they were kind of turned on. Fascinated by the theatre of it. As proven by the comments on social media today.' I slid my phone out of my back pocket and took him through the same social media route Aminah had taken me on just hours earlier. Malakai stepped into me, peering down at my phone, eyes furrowed in concentration. Man, he smelled really good. I had to force myself to focus.

'See? After the initial shock, people were into it. It was entertainment for them. The display of romance was enough for them to buy into it. The drama of it. For my NYU application I need to grow my platform, build it into something bigger than it already is.'

Malakai nodded, still confused but apparently, weirdly, still with me. He looked up from my phone. Rubbed his chin. 'What are you thinking, exactly?'

I tried to subdue my excitement, but I felt it bubbling up out of me, as I slid my phone back into my pocket. 'OK, so I don't date, and you . . . well, you do. A lot. But not with the view of an actual long-term relationship, am I right?'

Malakai levelled an even gaze at me. 'Is this a trick question so you can look at me with those judgy eyes you have going on?'

'I do not have . . .' I threw up a hand. 'Judgement suspended.'

Malakai nodded cautiously. 'Fine. You're right. I enjoy the company of women, but on the mutually agreed understanding that it isn't going to be a thing—'

I kept my tone purposefully gentle. 'Huh. And how do you know for sure that it's mutually agreed upon? Like, do you sign a contract?'

Malakai chuckled. 'See, that! That right there? Judgement.'

'What! I – it was just a question!'

'You're judging. I can see it on your face.'

'What's my face doing?'

'You like . . . tilt your head to the side and then hit a man with a sugar smile. Like a knife dipped in honey.' Malakai mimicked it, batting his lashes and propping a flat hand under his chin as if cherubs came in man-size. A laugh broke out from me and I shoved him; he dramatically stumbled back half a step, rubbed the part where I touched him as if soothing a bruise.

'Fine. Sorry. Let me start again.' I cleared my throat. 'You don't do relationships! Neither do I. So, I was thinking about something I mentioned the other night—'

'Before you poured a drink on my—'

'Sure, yeah. It was about the radio show? I know I said it as a joke but Aminah was right, there's something in that. I started thinking about how interesting it would be to have a show that explores all the ups and downs and drama that happens when two people get together. Providing an insight into what guys and girls think and want. Made all the more interesting by the fact that we are two people who, historically, don't do relationships. The audience won't know it's fake and we can call it . . . something like *Gotta Hear Both Sides*. Kind of like a radio reality show. It's a format development, so will help me fulfil my requirements for the internship, boost ratings, plus, not to toot my own horn, but what better way to launder your rep than date me, the resident romantic agony sis—'

'I definitely heard a toot there.'

'It was more like a beep.'

Malakai's eyes flashed. 'You know, dating me would launder your rep too.'

'Sure. If they think I'm with you it justifies the kiss. It's great PR for both of us. The show can be a special episode we do every couple of weeks. People can write in, ask questions, we can debate and your presence will hopefully pull in the straight male demographic. Plus, Dr Miller said she wants me to step outside my comfort zone, and how better to do that than to work with someone I'm fundamentally opposed to.'

'Aw, shucks.'

I smiled and Malakai shook his head. 'Why don't you date again? It kind of doesn't make sense. You're fi—cute. You're smart and you have a reasonably tolerable personality when you're not slandering an innocent young Black man.'

I opened my mouth to reply, but there was too much and it was too dense, too heavy to haul out even if I wanted to. I pulled out the easiest response. 'I don't want to give myself to someone who doesn't know what to do with me. I . . . don't want to lose myself.'

Malakai was staring at me like he had a million more questions. The question marks were hot, piercing, and singed my skin, so I broke his gaze and looked ahead at Aminah and Kofi, hands brushing against each other tentatively, as they walked side by side, playing with the promise of what might be.

'Don't get me wrong,' I added, 'I think romance can be great in the right context, but it's so rarely the right context.'

Malakai nodded. 'I hear that.' He said it in a way that felt like he really did hear that.

We were nearing the Eastside part of the park now, my sense of smell acting like a compass – spiced scents held in the breeze, curry and patties and fried chicken.

'OK, so what's the deadline on all of this?' Malakai asked.

'How long do you think shooting the film will take?'

'About eight weeks?'

'Great. So maybe we could "break up" by the AfroWinter Ball in December? My deadline is in January, so that works well for me too.'

He narrowed his eyes thoughtfully. 'And this is what you need me to do for you to agree to work on my film? It's non-negotiable?'

'Non-negotiable,' I confirmed.

'If we do this, you know you have to socialise, right? I'm a friendly guy.'

'I noticed.'

His smile was wide. 'I'm talking parties, events . . . you have to chill with the masses in order for us to be believable. You gotta come out of your tower, Rapunzel. And not just for FreakyFridayz. You ready for that?'

Nope. 'Obviously.'

'Well then. Rapunzel, Rapunzel, let down your braids, Girl.'

I rolled my eyes.

Malakai grinned in self-satisfaction. 'Man. This is gonna be *fun*.'

CHAPTER 10

You have nine missed calls from BIG MISTAKE.

BIG MISTAKE: You moved mad on Friday. You know that? (Read)

BIG MISTAKE: Kiki, you know I got love for you still. Stop being silly. You can still be my queen. (Read)

BIG MISTAKE: You know what? Fuck you, and fuck him. You ain't that fine to be moving like this. (Read)

BIG MISTAKE: I know you miss this . . . (Click to save image)

BIG MISTAKE Has Been Blocked.

I shuddered, and immediately flipped my phone over so my screen was lying flat on the library desk, exposing my faux-marble phone-case. It was irritating that Zack was intruding upon my place of peace, Whitewell Library. It was a listed building and the oldest on the campus: ornate and Gothic, with dramatic high ceilings and looming, yawning atelier windows, which caught and refracted seraphic beams of light. It was my favourite place in Whitewell, both theatrical and practical; a place of windows and universes compacted onto pages.

Reading Zack's texts here almost felt sacrilegious. Since everything that had happened on Friday, I'd forgotten about him. He seemed so irrelevant to what had manifested from our interaction. Zack was a non-entity, a non-factor and the blurry phallic graphic he'd just sent me only compounded that.

I took a deep breath, opened my laptop and whirred it alive. I had work to do. My . . . delicate relationship with Malakai could blow my project up. We needed a concrete plan.

I picked up my phone and texted the number he'd given me on Saturday after we agreed to work together.

> **Keeks:** Hey. We need to have a meeting to figure out logistics, schedules and terms. Let me know when you're free.

There. Brief. Polite, not overly friendly, and enough full stops to make it known that I was all about the business. Just as I pressed 'send', a flyer showed up in front of my phone. I looked up to see Adwoa Baker, events coordinator for Blackwell, face grim, holding it out. I blinked at it, refocusing.

Black Lives Matter or All Lives Matter? Which is it?
A debate between Whitewell ACS and Whitewell Knights

I snatched the flyer from her. Adwoa was an ally in the Blackwell cabinet, the rest of it being made up of hand-picked members of Zack's immediate clique. Adwoa was a Politics and Journalism student who I shared an International Relations module with; she lent the cabinet some semblance of competence and was one of the few people I spoke to who wasn't Aminah. She was five foot two, with a tolerance for bullshit that matched her petite frame, sported a small bubble-gum pink 'fro and a constellation of cartilage piercings. She was also my sparring partner in seminars and was a free agent in relation to cliques.

'What the hell is this?' I hiss-whispered, as I threw the flyer, which . . . was that seriously, had an English flag juxtaposed over a Pan-African one? It was as unappealing aesthetically as it was ideologically.

'Is he serious with this? Adwoa, this isn't even a debate. Also, with the Whitewell Knights? Is he on crack?'

Adwoa pulled out a chair and sat next to me, voice low. 'I know. I *know*. And honestly? He's probably on lots of shit. I tried to stop this, but you know how it is with the rest of the cabinet. It's Zack's way or no way. Zack thinks it would be good to have an "open dialogue".'

I stared at her incredulously. 'He wants to debate Black lives with the people who had a Blackface Pimps & Hoes party two years ago? Who constantly petition to get FreakyFridayz shut down

144

because "we're not 'inclusive' enough"?' The reasons included: a) the crowd being 'aggressive and unwelcoming' and b) that it was a hotbed for drug sales. Like they didn't constantly walk around with blizzards in their pockets.

'I know, he's an idiot, but . . .' It was taking a lot of effort to balance the level of my voice with my level of anger. I shook my head and leant closer to her. 'He can't be this stupid. I mean, it looks bad and I know Zack cares about how he looks more than anything.'

Adwoa nodded in agreement. 'Yeah. It does. But between you and me, Zack is putting stipends into the cliques' pockets. The Gyaldem Council, the Vegan Cupcakes, the London Gyaldem, Naija Princesses, Bible Study Babes. The Cupcakes get to go to their little hippy festivals, the London Gyaldem throw their parties, Bible Study Babes get to take their field trips to whatever Christian singles' conference is going on in London – so they all think that Zack is doing a good job. And, outwardly, he is. The girls are happy, so they're not asking questions.'

I frowned. 'You mean questions like where the hell is he getting the money from? I know his family has bank, but I don't think his allowance is enough to support the social life of every main clique in Blackwell.'

Adwoa shrugged. 'I don't know. All I know is that he's getting away with throwing a stupid debate that discredits what Blackwell is supposed to be. I'm pissed that nobody gives a shit. I'm just the token gay they allowed in to show how "woke" they are. All they want me to do is pass out flyers on campus. These are all going in the bin, of course, but it's not going to make a difference. Not with social media.' Adwoa's voice dipped with solemnity. 'Kiki, you have one of the biggest platforms in Blackwell. You can help fight this. If you mentioned it on your show, maybe started a petition—'

I shook my head, my anger cooling to discomfort. 'Adwoa, this is bullshit. For sure. But you know Brown Sugar isn't about that. I don't do politics. There has to be another way to stop this.'

Adwoa's eyes scanned me in confusion, as if she couldn't compute what I was saying. 'Yeah. There probably is. But you're the best way, Kiki. You have the visibility. You're the only person Zack even pretends to listen to. What are you scared of?'

Lack of control. My life was clearly demarcated and I didn't need anything to make it messy. I didn't need to get into a political feud with a guy I was trying to distance myself from, and who had ammunition against me. If people knew we had hooked up it would discredit me completely, and I'd only just got a handle on the situation with Malakai. I couldn't afford exposure that would affect the show's growth.

'Look, Adwoa, if you start a petition or get someone else to, I will happily support and amplify. But Brown Sugar as a space has to remain neutral. I'm sorry.'

Adwoa rolled her tongue around her mouth and nodded slowly, sliding the flyers off the desk. 'Yeah, so am I.'

She was disappointed in me, and it stung. This was why I

worked hard to have precisely one friend. Adwoa somehow slipped through the net and now I was paying the price with this awful feeling in my stomach. 'See you in class?'

Adwoa gave me a weak smile and salute, then walked away.

Brown Sugar Show: Archives

Hi guys,

It's your girl, K, and yes, it's that time again where I break down my advice on how to manoeuvre yourselves around mandem. Now, I don't know if you lot know this, but I actually have a PhD in fuck-boiology. Yes, I, Kiki Banjo, am a doctor of this particular field of science, and I have taken it upon myself to do a quick tutorial on a phenomenon we all may be familiar with, but perhaps don't quite know the mechanics of: 'The Talk'. This is where you discuss the parameters of your relationship.

First, construction is key. The less, the better. Many people make the mistake of overloading with emojis, bulking to compensate for confidence. Trust yourself, and believe in your sauce. You don't need extra dressing. You're a snack, a whole meal and the offer of your company is a gift, a blessing.

Second. Be direct. Take control of the situation so your target has little space to manipulate it. 'You free in an hour?' is different from 'You free to talk in an hour?' The latter is powerful – you're coming from a position of strength. This is about your desire. 'You free in an

*hour?' comes from a place of need that most boys love to play with.
'You free in an hour?' could lead to a 'Maybe', which might lead to a
'What you mean maybe? You don't want to talk?' and then he says,
'About what?' A mess. We want to avoid that. Go in incisively. Don't
let these boys run you mad, my sisters.*

*Once you're talking, be clear about what you want. If that's a
relationship, be honest. If it's something else, be clear about that too.
You're not going into this for negotiation, you're going into this for
clarification. If he finds your terms unreasonable, that's absolutely fine,
it means he clearly is not the one for you.*

*Finally, sisters, go forth with the knowledge that you are the shit
and you're not about to take shit. Whether he wants a relationship with
you or not, that still stands.*

*Thank you for spending time with me this evening, it's been a
pleasure and, until next time, stay sweet.*

Yours always, K.

I pounded my fist against Aminah's door furiously. 'Aminah! Wake
up!! 999!!!'

Aminah opened her room door, bare-faced, hair wrapped in a
silk scarf and eyes wide as she wrapped her fluffy dressing gown
around herself. 'Ah ah! What happened? Did Beyoncé drop an
album?!'

'No! This is a bad 999!' I shoved my phone in Aminah's face, and her confusion melted into a slow smirk as she scanned the screen, reading the text out loud: 'You about?'

Aminah's smile widened. She leant against her door frame, took my phone and peered closer at the text, as if it could reveal more to her upon further inspection, eyes flashing wickedly. 'Malakai really sent you a 'you up?' text. Spicy!'

I'd been careful in keeping it strictly business in my first message and Malakai just jumped in with a 'You up?' text? Seemed pretty brazen to me. I couldn't understand why Aminah didn't comprehend how bizarre this situation was. She was smiling entirely too much and assiduously ignoring the fact that I was freaking out. The fact that her grin kept getting increasingly wider implied that she was *enjoying* me freaking out.

Aminah laughed as I snatched my phone back from her. 'Look, he's taking the initiative to get to know you in a regular way. Nothing wrong with that. Besides, don't you have to be comfortable with each other to pretend to be a couple for two months?'

The validity of her point was inconvenient. 'Fine, yes, sure, but this is how he wants to get to know me? You don't think this is kind of over-familiar?'

'You literally have had the boy's tongue in your mouth.'

'Notwithstanding—'

'*Notwithstanding?*'

'Why is he asking me to hang out through the construct of a booty text? At 11:30 p.m.? He couldn't ask me out for a coffee? I told you he was a Wasteman. I mean, 'You about?' Who even says that?'

Aminah bit her bottom lip in a way that looked suspiciously close to her restraining a laugh. 'Uh, someone who wants to know if you're about, innit. It's sexy.'

I grunted, rolled my eyes and walked out of the fluorescent, industrial lights of our flat hallway, pushing into her warm, lamp-lit room, ushered in with the comforting scent of coconut oil, designer fragrance and the sound of Drake murmuring from her speakers as I said. 'You're not taking this seriously.'

Aminah walked in after me and watched me sit on her plush pink bedding, hugging a fluffy fuchsia pillow to my chest. 'I think you're taking it *too* seriously.'

I shook my head. 'I can't deal with this. I have a stress headache. Also, I think I'm getting sick. I'm sweaty. My palms are sweaty. The inside of my stomach feels sweaty.'

Aminah nodded and sat next to me, pressing the back of my hand against my forehead. 'Poor baby. Did the sickness start the second he texted you?'

'What? Maybe? I don't know. I didn't look at the *time*—'

'You're nervous, Keeks.'

I lifted my head up from the pillow I had been squeezing and stared at her. 'About what?'

Aminah scooted back on her bed and folded her legs, 'About the fact that a boy you're attracted to just texted you. I know you're not used to that emotion but it's pretty normal for mortals—'

'Your logic is flawed. I was attracted to Zack and I never—'

'You were physically attracted to Zack, sure. But you and

Malakai connect. You have like a . . . *vibe*. There's a different dimension to it.'

I opened my mouth to argue, but Aminah shook her head, 'Don't bother to deny it. Don't think I wasn't watching you guys at the park being all *deep* in conversation. I swear I heard you giggle. It was like you were being pulled towards each other. Your arms kept bumping and you were wearing his hoodie—'

'I was cold. We were arranging our projects. Also, are you forgetting the fact that he admitted to using me?'

Aminah flipped a hand, shooing that little titbit away like it was an inconsequential piece of information and not potential evidence proving that the boy was a sociopath and master of deceit.

'Please, I don't care what he says. That guy likes you. I saw it in his face.'

'Maybe he's attracted to me. I have tits and I breathe. He's a twenty-year-old man. Physical attraction is separate from liking, Minah, and that's the mistake a lot of girls make.'

Aminah raised up a palm to silence me. 'He could have left you at any point to fix this mess on your own, but he didn't. Besides, you used him too. Also, I don't think Kofi would be friends with a dickhead. Kofi swears to me that Malakai's not a dickhead, and Kofi knows that if he ever lied to me, I would cut his ogede off.'

I stared at her. 'How many times have I told you that referring to a penis as a plantain is very disturbing to me. I don't like it. Plantains are sacred. Don't ruin them for me.'

Aminah smirked, and stared pointedly at my phone.

151

Aminah's erroneous thoughts aside, I figured it might as well get it out of the way. We had to meet at some point. I tapped my reply out before I could think my way out of it.

> **Keeks:** Depends what I'm meant to be 'about' for.

Aminah peered over my shoulder and grinned. 'Hey. Is that my Killa Keeks?'

I was about to toss my phone behind me, forget about it, preparing to be pissed off when he replied in an hour with something monosyllabic, when my phone chirped almost immediately.

> **Malakai:** Food.

A pause.

> **Malakai:** On me.

> **Keeks:** I prefer plates if that's OK.

> **Malakai:** Oh, you one of them boujie girls. I'll try and sort something out. No promises.

I smiled. Aminah stared at me. I rubbed my grin away and widened my eyes. 'What?' Aminah shook her head with a smirk and shrugged. 'Nothing.' My phone buzzed again.

> **Malakai:** I'll be over in 30 to pick you up.

My blood spiked. I dropped my phone on my bed like it was on fire. My palms were prickling with something hot and liquid.

'Pick you up? Shiiit dass hot,' Aminah whisper-hissed into my shoulder.

I was going to argue, but I couldn't lie, the message was charged with a confidence that sent a sharp thrill up my spine. Among other places. I ignored the spark and rolled my eyes at my best friend.

'Why are you acting like this is a real date? It's basically a field trip with a research partner who gets on my nerves.'

Aminah looked at me like she was worried I was losing my capacities. 'You didn't even respect Zack enough for him to get on your nerves.'

'Aminah, just because Malakai gets under my skin doesn't mean—'

'—that you want him *on* your skin?'

'That wasn't what I was about to say.'

Aminah frowned. 'Weird. I feel like you were.'

A reluctant grin spread on my face. 'I don't want to be your friend anymore.'

'I take that into consideration, and I henceforth reject it. So, given that you're currently in a ratty old bootleg T-shirt from Drake's 2016 tour and joggers with a toothpaste stain on, what are you going wear for your date? We have twenty-five minutes till showtime. Eight, if we take away make-up.'

CHAPTER 11

He was wearing grey sweatpants. Grey sweatpants, a grey hoodie, a white tee and that gold chain. He was leaning against a three-door, blue Toyota in the student car park, looking at his phone, the yellow streetlamps making him look like an angel decked in Nike as I approached him. I wanted to turn back immediately. My knees felt like they had been hit from behind by something blunt. I had not prepared for this. I'd washed and moisturised my face, applied barely there make-up – a slick of lip gloss, some mascara and Aminah had dabbed on my cheekbones a sample of something that promised a 'dewy Hollywood glow'. My braids were pulled into a high bun to accentuate it and I'd slipped on my standard ten-centimetre gold hoops. I looked cute, but I was not primed to *attack*. Not like him. Aminah had wanted me to wear a black, deep-cut bralet with a leather jacket alongside my ripped high-waisted mom jeans. I had refused – I wasn't about to be the love interest in a nineties'

R&B video. A nonsensical, super-cropped, magenta sweater that hovered just below my bra and showed my belly piercing had been the compromise. Now, I kind of wished I had worn the bralet. Not because I wanted to seduce him, but because he had clearly come to a sword fight with a gun. Two guns – the hoodie hugged his arms. They certainly had girth. And curves and dips to rival my own. They might have even looked better in my jeans.

I cleared my throat as I got closer to the car. Malakai lifted his head at the sound, almost looking startled to see me, his eyes skipping across my form as he straightened and slipped his phone into his pocket.

'Hi.'

I nodded 'Hey,' immediately balked at how soft and shy I sounded, so I kept my face still, slathered sarcasm into my voice to weigh it down, before continuing. 'Sorry if I'm underdressed. Prom dress was at the cleaners'.'

The smile glinted in Malakai's eyes, and I felt the potential awkwardness subside as we slipped back into what I now realised was our rhythm.

'Don't worry about it.' Malakai's gaze grazed my body again, the friction enough to make heat run from the base of my stomach to my cheeks. 'You're good. Left your corsage at home, anyway.'

I regretted wearing something that showed off my middle. What if the butterflies flew too close to the edge of my stomach, so he could see the imprints of their wings pressed up against my skin?

Malakai smiled widely and pushed himself off the car door to open it for me. He bowed with an exaggerated flourish, 'After you, princess,' the south London gait and swagger wrapping itself around his words and lodging his tongue in his cheek.

I slipped in the front seat. 'Ew. I'm not a Princess.'

'I know that. You're both Beauty and the Beast. Just wanted you to know how it feels to be given a title that don't suit you.' He shot me a tiny, sloping, dangerous smile and shut the door on my parted, wordless mouth.

Malakai manoeuvred his way around our nauseatingly picturesque university town with ease, smoothly making his way down hilly avenues lined with gold-leaf moulting trees, gently pushing the steering wheel with one hand as we drove past sprawling, gated suburban houses. The way his other hand wrapped around the gearstick brought to attention just how large it was, emphasised its sinews. I was definitely checking him out.

Malakai glanced at me quickly before bringing his gaze back to the road. 'You good?'

It was then I realised I hadn't spoken in about eight minutes. I pulled the sleeves of my sweater down to cover my hands more and folded my arms across my chest. 'Um, yeah. I'm fine. Just a little cold.'

Malakai swivelled the temperature dial towards the red arrows; an action that served as a lesson to me about lying, because my skin was actually prickling with heat.

I cleared my throat, 'So. Where we going? McDonald's?'

Malakai laughed, and his hand wrapped around the gearstick again as he deftly manoeuvred, glancing at me again before kissing his teeth gently. 'What you take me for?'

'You really want to know?'

A shadow flitted across Malakai's face. He rolled his tongue in his mouth as he pulled into a road I'd never seen before. 'OK, let's continue to withhold judgement; we're dating now, remember? That's why I chose food for our first meeting. It's universal. Best way to get to know someone is over a good meal. And I chose this time – late, with no warning – because I didn't want to give you time to overthink—'

'—how do you know I overthink?'

Another glance as we stopped at a traffic light. 'You do a lot of that on your show. And it works most of the time, but not for all things. So, I thought I'd give you a break from that. Late-night text gives you no time to think. Means you have to go with your gut. You're either in or out. And you're here. Which means you're in.'

My eyes explored the thrilling curves and angles of his profile, but I said nothing. This was alarming because I usually had something to say. It was my job to have something to say. I needed to have something to say. But he was right, there was some freedom, a rush, in deciding to dip out of campus during a weekday night. It was the same rush that came when I'd decided to kiss him.

Malakai's profile broke and shone light as he released a small half-smile. 'McDonald's? Really?'

'Everything else in this town shuts at 11 p.m. unless it's a club!'

'Maybe in the part of town you know. Also, I would never

take a girl out to McDonald's. "Big ballin', baby, when I'm courtin' you."'

I curbed the grin that immediately wanted to erupt. 'Did you just quote Jay-Z to me?! Don't do that. Also, you're not courting me.'

'"Big ballin', baby, when I'm fake-courtin' you."'

A laugh leapt out of me and I brought my sleeve-covered fingers to my mouth in an attempt to push it back in, looking out of the window at the amber and dark-green blur of trees and streetlights that enshrouded large red-brick houses with black gates – usually with two SUVs parked in the driveway.

'You're not funny.'

'Too late. I already heard you laugh.'

'It was a cough.'

'Sounded like a giggle.'

I turned to him. 'You were mistaken. I don't giggle. There was something in my throat. Do you have a lozenge in the glove box?'

'I do, but you're not getting it. I want to hear you cough again.'

'Why, sicko?'

He paused as he made a turn, 'It was a cool sound. I liked it.' His eyes were fixed straight on the road but his lips curved gently.

Heat rose to my cheeks as silence fell, but this time it was comfortable. I relaxed into it enough to notice that I had been into every song that had played in the car. New R&B mingled with old-school R&B, and as Maxwell's 'The Suite Theme' flowed into Drake's 'After Dark', I realised that I had expected that progression. I picked up Malakai's phone from where it lay in the little holder between us and tapped it alive. Sure enough, the playlist was Brown Sugar Show Presents: *Late Nights*. I usually made them after the show for my own fun, before sharing them on our social media accounts. I didn't know that anyone else actually listened to them. I made them because it was fun for me, selecting a mood and seeing where it took me. It was me at my freest, allowing myself to move according to my own rhythm, going with my instincts.

'You didn't have to play this just because you're riding with me. I know that's your thing. Studying girls to know what they're into so you can impress them with it.'

Malakai's brow quirked, as he threw me an amused look. 'Man, you are arrogant. Don't gas yourself, Banjo. It was what I was listening to before. It's a good playlist. This music is my shit. But I have to ask, did you name your show after yourself or the D'Angelo song?'

The question caught me off-guard, and I stared at him curiously for a few moments before replying. 'Uh, the D'Angelo album. My favourite D'Angelo song is 'When We Get By'. Sounds like sunshine. Sounds like how I think love feels—' I spoke before I realised what I was saying. It was the truth. But it came from a part of me that wasn't close to the surface. I regretted the exposure immediately, dreading the awkward silence that would inevitably follow. But Malakai didn't flinch.

He nodded thoughtfully instead, rubbed his chin. 'Nice choice. I have to cheat. Mine is 'Nothing Even Matters'. Can that count even though it's a duet and on Lauryn's album?'

'No, because if we were counting that, then I would choose it as my favourite, too.'

'And God forbid that we agree on something.'

I chewed my grin. 'Anyway. Why did you ask if my show was named after me? What if I was "Brown Sugar"?'

'Oh, yeah. Then I was going to say that the nickname doesn't suit you.'

I turned to him so viciously that my butt shifted in the seat. 'Excuse me?'

Malakai shrugged. 'Sorry, but, I mean, sugar is nice. It sweetens. That's cool. But you're not nice. You're more than that. You're more like . . . ata rodo.' His voice dipped into Yoruba tonality as he slid into our shared ancestral language. 'A scotch bonnet can make things less bland, adds flavour, makes stuff feel more exciting. Richer.'

I could see the glint in his eyes from where I was sat.

'—And if you're rubbed the wrong way, you can make someone's eyes water. You've gotta respect the mighty scotch bonnet. Looks inoffensive from the outside, cute, even, kind of like a berry, but it's able to bring a grown man to his knees. Should be handled with care, but it can take care of itself. '

Malakai interrupted his nonchalant tone with a little whoop. 'Hold on, this is my shit!'

He turned the volume all the way up on Anderson Paak. I could tell by the sharp pivot that Malakai hadn't thought about what he'd said. He'd just said it. Like it was true. I bit deep into his words and waited for my teeth to sink into its counterfeit charm, concocted to get something from me, but all I could taste was something rich and warm and smooth, and it spread through my chest, rushed to my face.

We pulled up in the Eastside, in front of what looked an old school diner, with The Sweetest Ting in bright-pink, shining lights.

I dipped my head in concession. 'All right. This looks cool.'

Malakai glanced at me with that wicked, smiling, sidelong look he'd perfected as he turned off the engine. 'If we're really doing this, you're gonna have to trust me, Scotch.'

The name tripped off his tongue and sank like it belonged to me, coated my muscles, made me feel relaxed. I wanted to brush it off, tell him not to call me that, but all I was able to muster was a roll of my eyes and a curl of the corner of my mouth. 'Chill out, Nay-Z.' The butterfly wings were definitely scraping the walls of my belly now and I hoped food would settle them, make them lethargic.

Malakai pulled a face. 'Oh, man. That was terrible.'

I narrowed my eyes. 'Your face is terrible.' Shit. Was I losing my touch? What was happening? Did his sweatpants neutralise me?!

Malakai nodded, 'Huh. That's funny. Because I recall you describing me as "tall and hot and dark" on your show.'

'Who said that? Not I.'

'Like coffee. "Keeps you up all night"—'

'I think I said that coffee also gives you the shits.'

'"A snack, a *beverage*"—'

'I'm not hungry anymore.'

Malakai laughed, and its force knocked out a few thousand more defences.

The restaurant was balmy and vibrant, the sweet and spiced golden-fried scent of indulgence warming our faces as we entered. It was a marriage of a nineties' Missy Elliott video and something out of *Grease*. The glossy black-tiled walls were spangled with silver specks, as if trying to approximate the starry night outside, and above us spotlights were embedded in the black ceiling (little pastiches of Malakai's eyes – I'd never seen a black so bright). Black booths of magenta pleather lined the walls, and a large flat-screen TV hung against the furthermost one, where a Donell Jones video played. It was extra in the best way, reminding me of fur coats and sunglasses in a club: superfluous, deliciously decadent, a stunt.

It was the coolest place I'd seen in my time at Whitewell, and it seemed strange that Malakai had discovered it in the two months he'd been here. People our age and maybe a little older, sat in booths, or on swivelling pink stools in front of marbleised black poseur tables, laughing, talking, bouncing their heads to the music, restrained by their own cool, or stepping up, arms up, fully dancing in their spot, freed by it. This was grounded glam, puffer jackets over body-cons, jewellery layered over joggers that were punctuated with crisp creps. It had the elegance of a queen's court.

Malakai ushered me inside, but I hung back, choosing to soak it all in, follow his lead. He walked in with a calm confidence, an urbane gait, not like he owned the place but like he belonged, comfortable in his skin. He nodded and smiled at a few people seated in the booths, spudded a few guys, threw out a few *whatsgoingonmans* and walked up to the glass counter. He leant over to clap hands with the guy behind it, an older-than-us-but-young-ish man with the sleekest shape-up I'd ever seen, an earring, and a bright-pink shirt sporting The Sweetest Ting on it.

Malakai smiled at him. 'Oga, how fa?' he said, slipping into a Lagos-boy accent that suited him. It was, frankly, obscene that his sexy came in layers that became more exposed the longer I spent with him.

The older-ish guy released a spirited grin. 'Aburo, we dey.'

His eyes drifted to where I stood and his grin melted into a warm smile. He wiped his hands on a white cloth, threw it over his shoulder and leant on the counter. 'Now, who is this queen?'

Malakai moved closer to me. 'Kiki, this is Meji – owner of this fine establishment, and my adopted big bro. Adopted big brother by force. Meji, this is my . . . friend, Kiki.'

I waved, and Meji's eyes twinkled as his smile broadened. 'A pleasure to make your acquaintance, Malakai's . . . friend. What's your full name?'

'Kikiola.'

Meji inclined his head in a bow. 'Total wealth. Complete wealth. *Pure* wealth. Sounds about right. You look like royalty. What you doing with this jester?'

My shoulder twitched up with the corners of my mouth. 'Charity. A queen isn't a queen if she doesn't give back to the needy.'

Meji released a low whistle. 'Ho ho! I like her, Malakai.'

Malakai stared down at me, his smile glinting. 'Wow. Is that what we're on tonight? OK. Cool. Good to know. Enough. Look.'

He glanced at Meji, gesturing to the black bag slung over his shoulder. 'I'm here to work. And eat. I'm making a film. Free publicity for The Sweetest Ting obviously—'

Meji grinned. 'Say less. Of course. The pictures you took for our ProntoPic page made such a difference, brother, I appreciate it.'

Malakai looked uncomfortable at the praise. 'Nah. It's nothing, man. It's the least I could do.'

Meji playfully slapped Malakai's arm before turning to me. 'A good man. He may be ugly but he has a great personality.'

Malakai laughed. 'I'm giving you two stars on Yelp.'

The man bowed, then gestured to an area in the corner of the parlour. 'Got that booth ready for you. Best one in the house. I usually reserve it for my girl and her girls, but I don't think she's coming tonight. She saw something in my ProntoPic inbox she didn't like. Someone will be with you when you're ready.'

'Needy?' Malakai's voice was low as we walked over to the booth.

I slid onto the pink pleather cushiony seat, leant my elbow on the table, rested my chin on my fist. 'We're going to eat before we get into filming, right?' I said, ignoring him. 'I'm starving. How long we got?'

Malakai shot me a tiny smile, wordlessly sliding the menu over to me. He looked at his watch. 'This place closes at 2 a.m., so a couple hours. It's almost morning, so technically it's breakfast time. Check out the plantain waffles.'

'Wait, what?' My eyed widened as I picked up the menu and scanned it. 'Plantain waffles with hibiscus syrup and chicken – an

164

option of suya or Southern fried. Akara burgers with yam fries or sweet potato fries . . . Beef suya burgers.' It was an American-Naija fusion menu. My mouth watered. There was no space for posing. My obsession was too immediate to subdue. 'This is so cool. I wonder if they make the yaji from scratch.'

I looked up to see Malakai was watching me. Heat rushed to my cheeks. I didn't need him to see me get nerdy over the composition of spice. 'Uh. My family owns a Nigerian restaurant.'

'I know. Saw it on your ProntoPic page. And yeah, Meji makes yaji from scratch. Don't let him hear you questioning that.'

I tilted my head. 'So you cyber-stalked me.'

'You didn't cyber-stalk me?'

My smile tickled the inside of my mouth, his eyes attempting to tease it out. Denial didn't seem worth it. After a silent tug of war, I cleared my throat and squinted down at the menu to disguise my defeat.

'Your niece is adorable.'

'Thanks; she is.' I heard the grin in his voice. 'My cousin's little girl . . . I liked that picture of you at the beach.'

I stared harder at the menu. I knew the photo. Barcelona. Aminahs and my first trip together. I was in an audacious blood-orange bikini that rounded and pushed my cleavage, bought with Aminah's encouragement. My arms were outstretched, and I was looking up and smiling wide. I squinted at the dessert options and released a more-prim-than-I-intended 'Thank you.'

'And I'm glad you like the menu.'

I looked up from it, to meet the arched slant of his lips. Despite it, the bright in his eyes was earnest. 'I do. How did you find this spot?'

Malakai rubbed the back of his neck and leant back in his seat. He hesitated for a moment before replying, the default lightness on his face dimming in the shadows. He cleared his throat and leaned forward again, as if gathering what he needed to tell me.

'Uh, so I'd just transferred and was wandering through this part of town looking for something that would remind me of home. It was late, around this time. Anyway, I stopped near here, taking pictures in the middle of the road . . . The chicken and doner shops look so bright in the night, like beacons. An oasis. Lighthouses. I wanted to capture that. Anyway, maybe I'm an idiot for taking pictures at night in the most policed area in Whitewell.'

Instinctual dread of what was to come cooled me as he continued, voice flat, matter-of-fact. 'They pulled up, asked me what I was doing. I said I was just taking pictures, said I went to Whitewell, said I was a film student, all of that. "Yes, sir."; "No, sir." Didn't make a difference. I wanted to spit in their faces. I kept it polite. It's funny—' the wry line his mouth pulled into compounded the fact that it was the opposite, '—it was like, the more polite I was the angrier they got. And every instinct in me wanted to fight, you know? But what good would that have done? And it's not that it hasn't happened before. Of course, it has. I'm from south. But I really thought I could have a break from that here. Anyway, they wanted to stop and search. I asked them what for and they said I was being aggressive.'

Malakai released a dark chuckle and rubbed his jaw. 'This was the first week of term and I didn't know anyone. Kofi had to go back to London for a family thing that weekend. I was alone. Like for real, alone. I don't even know how it happened, don't know it was five seconds or five minutes, but something must have happened, I must have said something – or maybe nothing was enough – but they had me pushed up against a car, hands behind my back while they searched me. Three of them. My camera drops. The camera I saved for a summer to get. Lens cracks. I feel it. Can't get to my phone to film what's going on.

'Anyway, Meji must have heard, and he comes out. Meji's kind of a big deal around here. A big brother, uncle to everyone, all the shop owners know him. Even the police know not to fuck with him. Meji went to law school in Nigeria and he's the smartest guy I know. So, Meji comes out and asks them what they're doing. They stutter. He asks them again, "What's the reasonable grounds?" And I'm shaking, man.

'I try to tell him what's going on but I can't talk. He says, "A young man taking pictures?" They stutter. He gets his phone out, starts talking about rights, how what they're doing is illegal. They let me go. The police say some shit. It's all bluster. They're scrambling. Meji ignores them, brings me back here and gives me food. He calms me down and tells me to breathe. And that's how he became my big bro. That's how I found this place.'

I sat back in my seat, the full force of what he said pushing me. My stomach was a swirl of sickness and sadness and indignation, a cocktail that caused my hand to fly over to his and squeeze, 'Malakai . . . I'm sorry. So sorry that happened to you.' But it felt weak, trite, and I felt embarrassed at how pathetic, how useless my words sounded.

Malakai's eyes dropped quickly to our hands, and he gave me a small, weakly reassuring smile, 'Thank you. It's fine though—'

I shook my head, my eyes surprising me by stinging slightly, 'No. It isn't. It's fucked.'

Malakai swallowed, and I realised his eyes were slightly glassy too. 'It's fucked. Which is why I don't get the bullshit debate the ACS is doing next month. Black Lives Matter vs All Lives Matter? Who signed off on that? Zack really is a prick, man. What does he even get out of that?'

I removed my hand from Malakai's and swallowed hard. 'I have no idea.'

A waiter came over to take our order and the ordering process gave me sufficient time to try and digest the new version of Malakai forming in my head; a version of him that roamed the roads at night trying to capture the light of a chicken shop because he found it beautiful.

'Sorry,' Malakai said, leaning forward as the waiter walked off to hand in our orders, 'I don't usually talk about institutional racism on first dates.'

I relaxed again. 'Really? Weird. I thought it was standard.' I let my eyes drift over to a booth where a boy was playfully serenading a girl along with the Pharrell and Snoop ditty playing from the speakers. She was pretending to hate it, slapping his arm just to touch him. My gaze returned to his with a twinkle. 'So, this is a first date?'

The corner of Malakai's mouth ticked slightly upwards. 'Thought this would be the perfect place for a chill preliminary meeting to get to know each other as project partners. Also, this place is a hot date spot. There are about eight couples here right now that would be perfect for the film.'

I looked around and saw that he was right. The pair I had just seen were one of many. A few were our age, some were clearly sneaking out and one was closer to Meji's age. All of them looked like they were at various stages of romance: a couple that was sitting so close to each other and looking so lustful that there was a possibility that they were violating several health codes under their table; another sharing a plate of food; one in which the woman was commanding a man to read some texts back to her, irately.

I nodded at him. 'So, you must have brought a few girls here then?'

'You're the first, actually.'

I couldn't help but cackle. 'Malakai, what do I look like? This place is sexy and opens late. We're here to be *real*, remember? Tell me the truth. You take them here, have the same routine with Meji, tell them to order the plantain waffles, drive them back to campus, fool around in your car and fire off a "Good morning, beautiful" text in the morning.'

Malakai met my gaze, eyes totally devoid of irony. 'Seriously. You are the first girl I've brought here. This is my spot. Maybe I'll come here with Kofi, but I also come here alone quite a bit. To work, to chill with Meji. Whatever. I've made friends here . . . Don't you have a spot?'

I flicked my eyes across him in quiet deliberation before leaning forward, resting my jaw on my fist. Dr Miller said I had to learn to work with others. He'd shared with me so it was only fair that I shared with him. I inhaled deeply.

'All right. It's extremely nerdy, but there's this spot in the library I like. African histories. Because no one's ever there,' I laughed. 'It's in the far corner, away from everything. I smuggle a coffee in and I just chill. Think. Sometimes there's a book involved, sometimes I'm just listening to a playlist I loaded up. It gives me . . . space.'

Malakai released a slow smile. 'Wow. That is *extremely* nerdy.'

I rolled my eyes. 'Shut up. I knew I shouldn't have told—'

'And extremely adorable.'

I shook my head and hoped it would force down the fierce flush of blood rushing to my face.

'How did it become your place?'

Growth, Kiki. You can't die from being personal. I stared at the menu once more for fortification, before looking back up at his gentle interest. 'Um . . . OK, so there was a period where my family was going through . . . a lot, and I had to take care of my little sister sometimes, pick her up from school. I knew the house would be empty when we got home and the thought of that was just . . . I couldn't deal with it, you know? She was about nine and I was about sixteen/seventeen. I'd take her to the bakery on the high street and get us two slices of Tottenham cake. I love Tottenham cake, it's still my go-to comfort treat. Anyway, I'd get us the cake and a cup of hot chocolate that we'd share and smuggle them into the local library. We'd read books next to each other, and I'd ask her questions about what she's reading, and she'd ask me questions about what I'd read, and we'd just . . . escape into these different worlds and forget for an hour, or so. I guess when I came to Whitewell, I just gravitated towards the library because it felt safe. And then I found that spot.'

I almost winced. I'd never told anyone that before and I felt acutely exposed. Why had I told him that? 'Ugh, that sounded super corny.'

Malakai shook his head. 'No, it didn't. It makes sense. When you're trying to find footing somewhere, you go to what's familiar. That's probably why I ended up on the Eastside in my first week here. Closest place to my ends.' He continued, 'Did you ever bring Zack to your spot in the library?'

Relief coursed through me as he'd tactfully avoided what I wasn't ready to show. I relaxed, furrowing incredulous brows. 'I think the library would make him combust into flames, like Trump in a church. He negates the concept of a safe space. He's a walking hazard.'

Malakai burst out laughing. 'Right. My point exactly. Your way of keeping boundaries was like . . . pre-established in the relationship. He couldn't crossover into knowing you like that because that wasn't the reason you were with him. Same way, I didn't bring girls here. As much as I may have liked them, I was trying to keep a boundary.'

'But you brought me here—'

'That's different. There are no expectations. You're not suddenly going to think that this could be something. You don't see me in that way.'

A timely reminder. I *didn't* see him in that way. And he didn't see me in that way. Not That Way + Not That Way = No Way. Still, something bothered me.

'You know what I don't get? If you like these women like you say you do, why would you put up a boundary?'

'I do like them. And I respect them. And I wanted to get to know them – have fun getting to know them. But that shouldn't have to come with some kind of unspoken agreement to commitment. I'm new here and wanted to meet people, and yes, some of those people happened to be pretty, smart women . . .'

I laughed, shaking my head, my hoops swaying with the mirth. 'Malakai, seriously, these girls aren't unhinged. They're not moving mad for no reason. They're cool and strong and maybe they didn't see your boundaries as boundaries. I totally get that sometimes people project shit onto stuff you've never said – take Zack – but I also know that you probably didn't stop them from getting the wrong idea. And that's what pisses them off, what causes confusion. They feel like they're the only ones. A bunch of women feeling like they're the only ones. That's why queens like Shanti and Chioma argue over you. And don't take it personal, but you really ain't worth it.'

Malakai sat up, eyes thoughtful. He paused to clap hands with a young-ish looking guy who stopped by our table to greet him, before turning back to me. He rubbed his chin. Again. 'I hear you.

So, when Shanti started talking about her birthday next year and things we could do together, I should have stopped that.'

'Um. Yeah. You could have tactfully guided her to the right direction. Like "It's always cool to hang out with friends on your birthday." I mean, it would suck to hear it, but it would be honest. Clear.'

'But I was trying not to be a prick. I didn't want to hurt her feelings—'

'Right, and what happened when you didn't tell her? You hurt her anyway. Look, letting people know exactly what it is in the beginning saves a lot of stress. On both sides. If anything, she'll hate you more for leading her on. Delaying it doesn't make you a good guy, Kai. And I think . . . you might be a good guy.'

The shortening of his name felt right on my tongue, like it was used to the taste, and I wanted to pull it back as it leapt out of me. It was too quick, too nimble. Malakai maintained eye contact, eyes glinting into mine with something that looked like it might have been respect. 'So, you think I'm a good guy?'

I shrugged. I hadn't realised I thought it until I said it out loud. 'I said *might*. I don't think I would be here with you if I really thought you were terrible.' I paused and let a smile lick at my voice. 'I mean you're tolerable, at least.'

He smirked. 'See, this is why "Scotch" suits you. No sugar-coating.' He hadn't noticed the 'Kai' thing. Good. Or maybe he was politely ignoring it. Also good.

'The truth will set you free,' I said easily.

'So, what was the truth between you and Zack?' He was silken with it, smooth and cool with it.

I shrugged. 'There was never any potential there. We both knew that. He only thought he wanted more of me because I didn't want him like that, and he couldn't handle it. Rejection doesn't compute if it isn't on his own terms.'

'He's a dickhead.'

As I spoke, my gaze had drifted down to the flashing flakes of faux quartz in the gleaming surface of the black table, but it snapped back up to his when I heard the frank, low brusqueness in his voice.

I traced the silvery gem imitations on the table with a sharp pumpkin coloured nail. 'And I knew that. Granted, maybe I didn't know the *extent* of his dickhead ways but . . . he couldn't hurt me. Not really. Even after the other night. I was angry, not hurt. Nothing was bruised, nothing broken. There's no way I could lose a game if I play by my rules.'

Malakai's dark eyes focused so directly into me that I felt my pulse flare.

'What made you feel like it's a game? Or is it a who?'

The waiter brought our food – piping hot and delicious smelling – and I hoped he was also going to serve us a side of distraction, but when he walked away Malakai was still looking at me, his soft gaze questioning.

I swallowed. 'A few whos. A couple whats.'

Malakai's eyes scanned me, and he obviously saw something that made him say, 'Got you – whos and whats that you don't want to talk to me about yet.'

I speared a forkful of plantain waffle and Southern-fried chicken into my mouth, partly because I was hungry and partly to delay answering him. The waffle had been drizzled with honey instead of maple syrup, the chicken infused with a perfect mix of herbs and spices, its coating crispy, the flesh succulent. It was a perfect explosion of sweet and savoury, a sublime balance of honey and spice. I wanted more as soon as it filled my belly up. It was satisfying and indulgent, enough but also greed-inducing.

Malakai smiled right up to his eyes. 'Good?'

I pressed a hand to my chest, closed my eyes and let out a little moan from the soul.

Malakai roared with laughter. 'Good, 'cause not gonna lie, I was feeling the pressure.'

I hadn't answered his question yet. I thought I'd got away with it when he started on his own food but then he paused, looked up at me, fork suspended. 'Scotch, I want you to know that we don't have to talk about anything you don't want to. I'm cool with anything you're cool with.'

I felt my bones liquify a little, easing something warm around my body. This was probably the longest personal conversation I'd had with anyone that wasn't Aminah, in my year and a half at Whitewell, and it didn't feel too long, didn't feel too personal.

'Thanks. Same. So, do you want to talk about why you transferred here? About whether it's a who or a what?'

A shadow flitted across Malakai's face, dimming his smile slightly, and he swallowed. 'It's a complicated who and what.'

'That you don't want to talk to me about yet.' My words echoed his.

Malakai's smile returned. 'Not yet. Not all of them. I can talk about a who though. She is a notable who.'

She. 'I already know she's fine.'

'She was. Is. She's also my ex. Ama.'

I perked up. This was how I would discover his Wasteman origin story, despite the fact that 'Wasteman' was no longer fitting him as well as I thought it was, splitting and slipping from the image of the new Malakai that had reconfigured in my head. It was baggy on the caricature I'd created of his player archetype, too small on the parts of him I hadn't known; like his sense of humour and the way he listened. Malakai listened with his whole face, eyes attentive and mouth patient with a penchant to curve heart-stoppingly at the right moments. He gestured at the yam chips I'd thought I'd been surreptitiously eyeing throughout our conversation. And now I discovered that he shared food. What the hell was I supposed to do about that?

I took a chip, managing to say, 'tell me everything', with it between my teeth. He grinned as I expertly tossed it into my mouth with a flip of my tongue. 'So, what happened between you and Ama?'

Malakai thought about it for a few seconds, eyes narrowed and thoughtful. 'She was kind of mean.'

I choked on a chip and had to push it down with a few frantic slurps of Coke. 'Is that it? I'm sorry, you broke up because she was mean? Have you met me? Also, I hate it when guys call girls mean.'

Malakai laughed and shook his head. 'Nah. Look, I get how it sounds. I'm not a sexist prick, I swear. Which is exactly what a sexist prick would say, I realise, but listen. You're bossy and you say shit how you see it and honestly, it's cool. I respect it. You know your mind. It's not like from a fundamentally badmind place. Ama was mean, like high-school movie cheerleader mean, you know? It was almost parody. Like, she made waiters *cry* mean. If we were at a birthday dinner and it was time to sing "Happy Birthday", she'd straight up refuse to join in. She said it was corny. You know how much effort it takes to resist singing "Happy Birthday" when you're surrounded by people singing it? Like, you really have to make a conscious decision to keep your mouth shut. She mustered that strength.'

I bit down my lip to keep from smiling. 'So why did you date her? I mean, she is who she is, so once you figure that out and you don't like it, maybe it's on you to stop hanging out with her. At some point you can't blame her anymore. It's on you.'

Malakai's lips quirked up at the corner. 'You're good.'

'So I've heard.'

He laughed. 'Uh, I guess it was familiarity. We grew up together. Our dads are friends. They work together. It was just kind of a given that we'd date and then we'd go to the same uni. She'd study law and I would study economics. We'd dated for years and she was all I knew. I thought that was what romance was. You're attracted to someone and you just power through the fact that sometimes you genuinely feel like they're a stranger to you. Like they don't really know who you are. I thought distance was normal. That's what I saw with my parents and I had no reason to think it could be any different.'

His voice had another dimension to it when he spoke about his parents, lightly detached, breezy enough to know it was concealing something heavy. I nodded.

'But you have a point.' He frowned. 'I should have ended it. I just thought that part of being a good guy was sucking it up. And we had good moments, like my parents had good moments. So, I just rolled with it, hoping that we'd just figure it out.' Something dark flitted across his eyes – it was only a split-second but it was so dark it made me miss his light. 'But . . . something happened that made me realise that life is short. Too short to be at a uni I hated, studying a course I hated, and with someone who called me childish for finally having the guts to tell her that I wanted to maybe make movies one day.'

He coughed and there was a bite to his eyes and in his voice that pinched at me. The break-up was just the surface. I decided to leave the dark alone for now.

I sat up, sighed. 'All right. You get to complain about your ex-girlfriend two more times and then I'm going to have to stop you out of feminine solidarity. OK?'

Malakai shot me a warm look of gratitude. He knew I wasn't asking what I wasn't asking. He leant forward. 'She hated *The Fresh Prince of Bel Air*. How can you actively hate *The Fresh Prince of Bel Air*?'

I laughed and felt the mood shift. 'Right. It's like not liking plantain.'

Malakai spread his arms wide in emphasis. '*Exactly*. I remember one time I showed her the most emotional episode I could find—'

'The one where his dad disappears again?'

Malakai nodded and smiled. 'Gets me every time. You know the bit where he goes—'

'"How come he don't want me, man?"' The words leapt out of us simultaneously, as if we'd rehearsed.

Malakai laughed. 'Punches me in the gut every time. She didn't even blink. Her eyes didn't even get shiny. She said it was over-acted.' He paused. 'And it's not like she was incapable of emotion because I saw her get emotional over a werewolf imprinting on a half-vampire, half-human baby in *Twilight*.'

I snorted as I helped myself to another one of his chips. 'Now I know you're chatting shit.'

Malakai's eyed widened, and his hands raised up. 'OK, so I'm not a prick for thinking that was weird. When I commented on how creepy it was, she looked at me like I was an idiot and said I was being "emotionally basic". The only person emotionally basic is Bella because who the hell would choose a vampire over a werewolf—'

'Facts. But also, my first crush was the Beast, so I'm biased.'

Malakai paused and leant back, assessing me with a comical expression on his face. As if I'd said something unhinged. 'As in The Beast from *Beauty and the Beast*?'

I shrugged. 'Yeah. He was sexy. Like, "Yo. What that snout do?" Obviously, I didn't think that then. Just now.'

Malakai seemed stunned. '*Rah.*'

I tilted my head, looking him up and down. 'Oh, what, like you're so special because your first crush wasn't a cartoon rendering of a creature that was basically an amalgamation of a wolf and a bear?'

Malakai popped three chips into his mouth. 'My first crush was on Nala, actually.'

'OK see, that's weirder than my thing.'

'How?'

'Because a lioness already exists. It's a real animal. An anthropomorphic beast doesn't exist in real life. Well, unless you count Zack. Oh shit, everything makes sense now.'

Malakai's rumble of laughter was low and rolling. I really wanted to pull my sweater off because it was warm, not just in the diner but inside my body, under my skin. My blood felt fizzy.

'I also have an excellent *Twilight* joke. Ama hated it.'

'Hit me.'

Malakai slid out of the booth, stood up in front of me and started stretching, like he was about to do a complicated gymnastics set. 'I gotta stand up to perform it.'

I snorted again. 'Oh, it's that deep?'

Malakai gave a single solemn nod, face grave. 'Yes.'

He cleared his throat as I looked at him with exaggerated attentiveness, and he bellowed, his voice deep with a Shakespearian gravitas, 'Wow, it really sucks that Bella chose the vampire over the werewolf.'

I blinked. 'What?'

Malakai's voice slid back to normal, low and gravelly, loose with a slight south London saunter. 'Nah, but do you get it? Sucks? Because of the vampire thing? They suck blood—'

'Yeah man, I get it, it's just . . . *what?* Malakai that's really, really bad.'

He rubbed his chin as he slid into my side of the booth. 'Shit, really?'

I shifted along my seat to allow him in unthinkingly, not even questioning the switch in positions. 'Dude.'

Malakai leant in closer, explaining as a professor would. 'Wait, OK then, what about: "You would have thought a vampire would have paled in comparison to a werewolf."'

The laughter had steadily built up inside me and I was doubled over, all but falling over his legs. I felt tipsy, giddy with something I wasn't entirely sure of, the butterflies now drunk on the sugar high in my belly. I clamped my hand over my mouth. 'Oh . . . my . . . gosh . . . that was . . . s-so, so bad . . . You're such a fucking dork.' My voice ended in a squeak from the strain of keeping the mirth in. I was too hysterical to be distressed by the fact that I think that what I was doing could have been categorised as 'giggling'.

Malakai was laughing too, but regarding me with some disbelief as I recovered and lifted myself up away from his legs and wiped the corners of my eyes.

'Wow. OK. This is . . . unexpected and humbling. Nah, stop laughing, it cut me deep. She said she didn't "get" it.'

I shrugged, little bursts of amusement still spilling out of me.

'I mean, I got it, Kai. It was just—' I drank some Coke to drown out the residual chuckles and shook my head, blinking at him innocently, 'You think maybe that joke is the real reason she broke up with you?'

Malakai forced his face straight. 'OK. That's enough. You know what? I take it back. You're a very mean person, Kikiola Banjo.'

An errant giggle leapt out. I feigned being emotionally choked up, flattening a hand against my chest. 'Thank you—'

'I like it on you though.'

I stirred my straw through my Coke. We were sat so close to each other in the booth that our knees bumped, reminding me of that time in FreakyFridayz before Aminah had interrupted us.

'Probably a fetish. Your ex-girlfriend was mean, but you probably just got bored of her meanness. Didn't hold the same allure. My meanness is fresh. It probably fascinates you. Maybe you like the challenge more than the person—'

'Kiki, why are you doing that?' Malakai's smile was simmering into something more serious.

I swallowed and twitched my shoulder, the air shifting to a heavier tone in the same shade. 'I'm not doing anything—'

'Yeah, yeah you are. You started talking in the abstract. Flipped the attention off you. Theorised what I said. That's what you do on your show. This isn't the show, Kiki. This is just . . . a guy and a girl hanging out. Under weird pretences, but still. We're hanging out for real. And I'm saying that I like hanging out with you.'

I held his gaze, trying to find the glint of deceit in his eyes, trying to source a clue that would lead me back to his playbook. Yet again, I came up short. I was glad I came up short. I surprised myself by wanting to come up short.

I shifted, leaning my elbow on the table and curving my palm against the side of my neck as I stared up at him. 'You don't even know me—'

'I'm getting to. I like the bit that I've got to.'

His arm was behind me, resting on the back of the booth. He was looking at me from a distinctly kissable angle. All it would take was a few inches movement from either one of us. His eyes fluttered briefly to my lips and a butterfly flipped inside. Oh no.

I sat up and changed tack.

'We should probably talk about the logistics of this. While we're here.'

Malakai looked genuinely puzzled. 'Logistics?'

'Um. Like . . . physical logistics of pretending to be part of a couple and working on your film?'

Malakai's eyes popped open as if he'd just remembered why we were here. 'Oh, right. Yeah, absolutely. Sure. I'll follow your lead. What do you think about public hand-holding?'

'Fine. Not sustained hand-holding though. Only enough for people to see, and then I'll fix my hair or something.'

'Sure. We're going to have to hang out at public events for a bit so that means FreakyFridayz, café for breakfast, maybe twice a week? House parties too. I have a few birthdays coming up and they'd be great to source interviews for the film.'

I kept my groan internal. House parties were my own form of

personal torture. 'How are you invited to so many parties? You *just* got here.'

'What can I say? I'm a delight.'

I grunted. 'Fine. Also, um, no more kisses.'

There was no getting around the fact that I was physically attracted to Malakai Korede. I was attracted to him to a degree that would have got me seriously concerned if I didn't know that we were fundamentally incompatible. While it was true the more time I spent with him, the more I discovered things I liked about him. Like how when he looked at me as I spoke it was if he was holding every word I uttered for safekeeping. But it was neither here nor there. The kissing rule was just a case of establishing professional boundaries.

'I agree.'

'Cool. Next time we meet we'll sort out our timetable. Public events, dates, *Gotta Hear Both Sides* planning, that sort of thing.'

'Hot.'

'Maybe I'll put it all in a Google calendar and share it with you for efficiency.'

His voice dropped octaves. 'Kiki, you can't talk dirty to me in a restaurant.'

'I'm sorry. I just . . . I get so carried away.'

'Clearly,' He ran his eyes across me in theatrical disgust. 'Control yourself. We have work to do.' He gestured to the camera on the table. 'You ready? . . . You get to choose who we ask first.'

I allowed my eyes to roam across the gradually thinning-out diner, stopping on the couple I saw earlier laughing just a couple of booths ahead of us. They were sat close on the same side of the booth, like us, talking in murmurs. Touching but not touching, though clearly wanting to.

I gave them a chin nod. 'Them. First date.'

'Really? Not the couple clearly doing nasty things to each under the table?'

We tilted our heads to look at the couple in question, across the aisle from us. The slow arm movements were very distressing. The girl's mouth suddenly dropped open. Mine did too, for an entirely different reason.

'*Oh.*' I broke our short, shocked silence.

Malakai cleared his throat. 'Um. I'm sorry. Is she—?'

'I think so. Good for her. Only twenty-five per cent of women are able to.'

'We should look away. If we stay looking, we're perverts.' Our eyes stayed glued to the scene.

'Um, *we're* the perverts?'

'Let's go film—'

I stared at Malakai. 'What the hell? That would actually make us perverted, Kai. That's disgust—'

'I meant let's go film the first date couple, Scotch.'

'Oh. OK. Cool. Yeah, let's do that. It's getting late.' But it didn't feel late. An hour and a half had passed and the night still felt like it was just beginning.

[Untitled_Love.Doc]
Director, producer: Malakai Korede
Consulting Producer/Interviewer: Kiki Banjo
Interviewees: Zindzi Sisulu and Xavier Barker

Kiki: You guys are adorable. You seem really, aware of each other at all times. Connected. When did you meet?

Xavier: About three or four—

Zindzi: —hours ago

Kiki: You guys met tonight?

Xavier: Yeah. And we got talking—

Zindzi: —and it's weird because the second I saw him, I knew I wanted to talk to him. And my girls were saying that I was being thirsty, that I should wait for him to come to me.

Xavier: I spotted her as soon as she came in. I told my boy that I was gonna talk to her. But, like, maybe five minutes after that, my ex walks into the party. And she's with her girls. And I was like . . . man, this shit is about to be long. I didn't want unnecessary drama. I didn't want it to seem like I was doing it on purpose—

Zindzi: I'm getting kind of irritated. Because I see him looking at me, and I'm looking at him—

Xavier: And my ex is looking at both of us—

Zindzi: And I'm like, fuck it. I'm just gonna go over there and see what's good.

Xavier: And it was good.

Zindzi: Better than I expected it to be. We just clicked. I said I was hungry, and then we came here. Which was a bold move, actually, because sometimes the vibes you have when you're around other people aren't the same when you're alone – also we literally just met—

Xavier: But the vibes were the same. Actually, maybe better – at least for me. Shit, have I just exposed myself—

Zindzi: Yep.

[Pause]

Zindzi: It was better.

Xavier: Whew. you almost killed me just then.

Kiki: What was so special about that initial conversation that made you want to see where it goes?

Xavier: It was just . . . *easy*. Just, easy.

Zindzi: That's it. There was no force to the convo – you know how sometimes at parties you force it just because you're *supposed* to flirt? And it ends up being cringe? There was none of that.

Kiki: What would you have done if you'd gone over there and it had flopped?

Zindzi: Then at least I would have known. Better to know than not, right? It's about being brave, innit. But . . . also, I don't know, I didn't think it would flop. I went there knowing – without knowing.

Xavier: Not gonna lie, I really thought she was peng. That's what first drew me to her. But maybe it was the knowing-with-out-knowing thing that made me look at her twice. Let's go with that, it sounds good.

Kiki: Where are you hoping this goes?

Zindzi: Wherever it wants to go.

Xavier: Wherever she wants it to go.

'So, it was better than McDonald's.'

We were back in the warmth of Malakai's car, but I think I would have felt warm, regardless. The cool, crisp, early-morning air hadn't shifted my body temperature – my internal central-heating dial seemed to have sprung to the highest mark, got stuck there. The first interview had gone extremely well. The couple were cute, appropriately handsy and clearly in their first flush of whatever their thing was. When we left they were making out outside, against the wall of The Sweetest Ting. The other couple had been politely asked to leave.

Malakai grinned at the road. 'Told you. Big ballin'.'

'Meji gave us our meals for free.'

'It's the sentiment.'

I smiled and shook my head. 'I had fun tonight.'

Malakai's eyes were still on the road but I somehow sensed the smile in them from my vantage point. 'I'm glad. So did I.'

'For what it's worth, I no longer think you're a Wasteman.'

I'd been preparing for some gentle gloating, for him to ask me to say it louder, but instead of the smirk I had expected to draw up on Malakai's face, he was silent for a few seconds, his face thoughtful.

'It's worth a lot.'

I tore my gaze from the road to the profile in question.

Malakai glanced at me. 'Look, I'm not saying being called out didn't suck, because it did. And I was pissed, obviously. But I think part of why I was pissed was because I was shook that you might have been right. I didn't mean to be that way, but I can see how it looked. Maybe I could've been clearer with how I approached things. Maybe . . . maybe, low-key, I knew what would happen if I was clearer.

'The girls weren't wrong to expect more. But it's like the more you invest in something the more likely it is that you're going to hurt someone. I didn't want either. I didn't want to emotionally tangle myself up with someone. I'm a mess. I didn't want to pull someone else into that. I didn't want to put myself in a situation where I could disappoint. Which I ended up doing anyway, so. I see now that that was a shitty plan.'

I frowned. 'Why do you think your default would be to disappoint?'

Malakai gave a humourless half-smile. 'Some things are in the DNA.'

Malakai was focused on the road, jaw tight, loaded, from holding on to something. I surprised myself by wanting to help him carry it. If I couldn't do that, then maybe sharing heavy of my own would keep him company with it.

'You know, the reason I took my sister to the library after school was because my dad would be at the hospital with my mum. We visited on the weekends, but she made my dad promise that he'd keep visits with us sparse. She didn't want us to see her like that. She got sick just before I started Year 12. She's OK now but back then it was bad. Really bad.'

I swallowed and looked down at the sleeves of my sweater. This was why I didn't allow myself to think about it, to talk about it, because the minute I did I was back at the kitchen table, Mum and Dad sitting my little sister and me down and telling us that it was treatable, that it was severe but that she'd fight it: we'd fight it. All we had to do was be strong. So, I was. I pressed everything down so my little sister, Kayefi, would be less scared, so my dad would have one less thing to worry about, so my mum didn't need anything else to stress over. I would be strong. I would be the strongest, if that was the only thing I could do.

I exhaled deeply. 'You know, sometimes I was so scared that I couldn't even cry. It's awful. You feel guilty for not being able to cry, but you're frozen in this . . . *fear*. You're suspended in your own sadness.'

'I know what you mean.'

I stared at him in gentle question, but Malakai shook his head. 'Go ahead.'

I cleared my throat. 'So, when I needed an escape, or when I wanted to make myself cry, I listened to music. I would listen to all this soul and R&B about heartbreak and yearning, and let it pour it out. It helped. It took me places, gave me space to look inside myself. Let me feel, when I was numb inside.'

I was speaking fast in order to avoid focusing on how much I was showing, on what I was showing, on why I was showing, when Aminah was the only person who knew this. Malakai was quiet throughout, his eyes intermittently turning to look at me, flitting between the road and my face.

'I think it's another version of "my place", music. I get lost in it, find myself in it. I think that's why I started Brown Sugar. I guess wanted to share that place.'

I caught myself. What was it about him that just tugged words out of my mouth? Something in the atmosphere between us dislodged truths from hidden places. I let out a small, nervous, possibly unhinged, laugh. '*Ugh*. Can we turn the music up? I'm sick of the sound of my voice.'

Malakai glanced at me, his strong features looking so tender in that moment that they hit me in the softest part of my heart. The junction between pleasure and pain.

'Thank you for trusting me with that.'

I hadn't realised that was what I'd done until he said it. Trust. Was that what I was doing now? Trusting people? How had he made me do that? I wanted to regret it, for that cool feeling to tell me that I'd gone too far, put myself in danger, but the warmth that was beginning to feel like default around him stayed. I liked that he didn't push, let my feelings sit, waited for me to say or not say. He had a good sense of sensing.

'I'm sorry for what your family went through. I'm really glad your mum's OK.'

'Thanks. Me too. It's weird. After it happened, it's like I forgot how to not repress stuff. I spent so long doing it, it's kind of like I can't go back. I get scared that I can't go back. I mean, it's fine for now, but I want to know that I know how to *not* repress stuff. I want that option. It freaks me out if I think about it too hard. Like, what if I never know how to do it? What if I'm permanently emotionally fucked?'

I could feel Malakai weighing my words. 'I don't think you're emotionally fucked. You're just selective with what you express. Protective. Just means that when you do choose to share stuff, it's special.'

He'd caught me with one hand, quickly, simply. My lips parted to say words that refused to leave my mouth. Malakai, as if understanding my limited capacity for this sort of talk, let the pause stay natural, continued speaking, as if he'd just made a mere observation, no judgements, no questions.

'I lied to you, by the way.'

The muscles in my stomach constricted. Malakai's gaze stayed ahead of him, and his face remained still, straight. It was ridiculous. Ridiculous that we'd known each other, what, a *week* and my body was already wrapping in on itself, guards ready to have their spikes up in self-preservation, as if it was possible for him to hurt me. He shouldn't have been able to. Weird how the tiny defiant bulb of hope made its presence known to me only when it shattered after plummeting to the bottom of me. It was fine. I barely knew him. This was professional. Friendship had seemed like a possibility and now it wasn't. It was fine. Wasteman of Whitewell. Nothing to lose.

'About what?' I kept my tone level, void of emotion.

Malakai's pause hung in the midst of Frank Ocean telling us that a tornado flew across his room. 'When I said I only hung out with you to prove a point at FreakyFridayz, I was lying. I said it because I was pissed. You said all this shit about me and I just got in my head. I thought I might as well *be* that person you thought I was. I thought I was doing something, some sort of double bluff to prove that it didn't matter what you thought of me, but I just ended up being a dickhead. And a Wasteman. I shouldn't have said that. Me lying was because, for some reason, I do care what you think of me, on some level.' He rubbed the back of his neck but kept his eyes trained on the road. 'I hung out with you that night because I wanted to hang out with you. That's it. That's the truth. There was no hidden agenda.'

He was still looking straight ahead at the road, and Malakai was usually so forthright in looking at me – even if only with tiny, discreet glances – that I knew it could only be down to nerves. The guards stood down and a surprising, overwhelming rush of ease and affection ran through me.

'Um, so do people call you Kai? Is that a thing?'

I saw Malakai relax against his seat in relief that I wasn't going to make him go further. He said what he said. I heard what he said. What more was there to be said?

Malakai shook his head. 'Nah. Not really. You're the only one who's ever called me that, actually.'

My cheeks flared. I was glad the last meal I had was perfect because I was about to shed my fucking mortal coil. 'Shit. Well, that's embarrassing. I'll stop.'

Malakai eyes stayed focused on the road. 'Why?' He twitched his shoulder. 'Don't.'

My smile had had enough of being trapped and spilled out, wide and brazen and messy, dripping everywhere. It soaked through my clothes and into my skin.

CHAPTER 12

The Blackwell Beat *with LaLa Jacobs*

What's good my fellow Blackwellians! Welcome to The Blackwell Beat, where we give you the tea, Black, no sugar. Blackwell's resident R&B relationship advisor, Kiki Banjo was seen getting frisky at FreakyFridayz when she locked lips with the newest player in town, double-chocolate fudge mocha Malakai Korede, just a few days after warning girls off him. Now obviously this smelled a little bit suspect, looked like she wanted to save dessert for herself. Had some of us rattled – we've been listening to her advice for a year, and if we can't trust her with that then what else was she lying about? Is she really about it? Well, fear not people because I've done my digging and word on the tweet is that it was just super-unfortunate timing. Apparently, Malakai and Kiki squared up to each other shortly after her show aired, him calling her out and her refusing to back down. Sparks flew

195

and enemies became baes. Cute! And I know some of us will be salty about it, but it wasn't planned and I think we all know Kiki always keeps the girls in mind. I, for one, stan the newest couple in town. I also got some intel from Kiki's camp that a new series will launch on Brown Sugar, inspired by the new romance. Gotta Hear Both Sides, will be *four episodes where the campus cuties will give us a 'he said, she said' on dating. I personally look forward to following their updates on social media, and I'm sure I won't be the only one preeing.*

This was The Blackwell Beat *with Lala Jacobs — until next time, folks.*

I pulled my earphones out of my ears as Lala signed off. So, it was official. It was a few days after the Sweetest Ting Non-Date and I'd been at the campus coffee shop, Beanz, waiting for my order, when I got a notification for a new upload of The Blackwell Beat, the quick turnover 'news channel' for all 'melanated members of the student body', which operated in front of a green screen in Communications and Politics student Lala Jacobs' room. Although she had to play an objective role for her show, she always had our back and always shouted out FreakyFridayz and Brown Sugar, being Aminah's classmate and one of the few people she actually liked. It wasn't surprising to me that Aminah had got a press release sorted and managed to give the inside scoop to The TeaHouse's rival. Aminah was good at what she did. It was a slick move that got the word out and exacted revenge on Simi for trying to mess with us. My phone pinged.

MINAH MONEY: So what you think?

KEEKS: The baddest in the game.

MINAH MONEY: Nobody in my lane 🚀 ☺ ☺ Our followers have tripled! This week's show is going to be huge! I heard Simi-the-Snake is seething at the fact that her attempt to drag has backfired. Do u like my alliteration?

KEEKS: Come thru Naija Angelou.

MINAH MONEY: Thank you. Thank you. *bows* U at ur afternoon coffee date? Ur very first one as a couple. Hot. What u wearing?? So pissed I had to leave for class before I saw.

KEEKS: It's not a date! We're not a couple! Stop it!

MINAH MONEY: Yeah, yeah, I know, but I saw that pic that someone took of you guys at dinner the other night and sent to *The TeaHouse* . . . you guys looked cozy. You were laughing lots. Also, you got like three #couplegoals in the comment section. I bet Simi was pissed, but there were four other pics of u guys online so she had to post, otherwise she'd look badmind. You guys are convincing.

KEEKS: We get along fine. I was probably laughing at him anyway. He makes a lot of really bad jokes. To answer your question, I'm wearing a mock-turtle neck black bodysuit, my tan corduroy button-down mini and calf-length boots. It's not a date.

MINAH MONEY: Sexy. That top really accentuate your tits too 😁

KEEKS: MIMI! It does, doesn't it?

I smiled at my phone just as a notification slid down from the top of my screen.

> **RIANNE TUCKER** (*GoodGirllRiRi*) has followed you on ProntoPic.

My smile swiftly froze and fell, the sight of the name ricocheting through my chest, hurling me to a place I'd thought I'd buried. My throat tightened as I stared at the tiny, circular avatar of the pretty girl with a glossy pout.

'Kiki?'

Malakai's voice almost made my phone slip from my fingers. I jumped, and turned around to see him looking down at me quizzically, and my stomach flipped at the sight of him. It was probably the distress of the moment prior clashing with surprise. Nothing to do with how good he looked in a black T-shirt and black windbreaker, those perfect-fitting jeans and his black Vans. Or his signature scent, clean and woodsy and crisp, mingling with the steamy roasted scent of coffee beans and pastry. Despite this, his presence was a welcome distraction; the frostiness the notification had brought ebbing, the dark feeling pushed back temporarily.

'Kai! Hi!'

Whose voice was that? Since when did my voice get so chirpy? It wasn't even chirpy after I'd had my morning coffee and now suddenly my voice sounded like I was a Disney princess?

If he noticed, he didn't let on, and his 'Mornin', Scotch' fell out as easy as his grin. My stomach somersaulted again. I needed something buttery inside me immediately.

'So,' I murmured as we inched forward in the queue. 'Did you watch The Blackwell Beat this morning?'

Malakai nodded and smiled, 'Yeah. She called me a double-chocolate-fudge-mocha. You know, I'm really feeling being considered a hot beverage. I'm thinking of changing my ProntoPic handle to MochaMalakai.'

I rolled my eyes. 'You're a fool.'

'Funny way of saying genius. I just want to make the most of my new social capital. My followers doubled since last week. So has the number of DM slides.'

'Yeah, so have mine.' It was fascinating, as if my new relationship status made me more accessible than I was in my perpetual singledom. My inbox was brimmed full of 'Yo, Kiki, what you sayin?' comments on IG selfies asserting that I was 'looking nice, still', with multiple fire emojis. It was as if attraction to me was validated by another man's attraction to me. That was going in the show.

Me + Newest Spice On Campus = Doubled Social Currency And Increased Perception Of Availability.

The queue crawled forward; it was peak time, purposely chosen so we had maximum eyes on us. The more exposure the better and in Blackwell, Coffee Shop Official was itself a relationship status. 'So, did you reply to any?'

Malakai raised a brow. 'DMs? Course not. I have a girlfriend who I'm dedicated to. Yoruba boys don't cheat.'

I levelled a flat stare at him. He laughed, and shook his head. 'Kiki, I didn't respond to any of them. I wouldn't jeopardise what we're doing. We're in a relationship. I'm going to be how I would be in a relationship.' His eyes breezily took me in. 'I like your turtleneck by the way. Very Nia Long in *Love Jones*. I have a mad crush on Nia Long in *Love Jones*. Actually, I have a mad crush on Nia Long generally. Anyway, I like your turtleneck.'

My entire body flushed.

He stood closer to me, bent low, lips inches away from my ear and whispered, 'How am I doing? That's what boyfriends do right? Compliment? And there are like ten other people from Blackwell right now, so we have witnesses.'

I nodded briskly. 'Yeah. Yup. Well done.'

He leant a little further back from me to assess me, before apparently quickly coming to a judgement of my emotional state and placing two large, warm hands on my shoulders. 'Don't stress.' His thumbs were resting lightly on my clavicles.

'I'm not stressed.'

I was stressed. Stressed about a deeply unwelcome blast from the past that came in the form of a ProntoPic notification; stressed that when Malakai complimented me I liked it – even though I should have known he was acting – and stressed about how convincing we would be as a couple. Faking it sounded doable in theory, but now I realised how much *performance* it would require.

Our initial kiss wasn't an act, it was very much real, too real, so real that if it crossed my mind, I had to cross my legs, but now everything I did had to be considered, calculated. Now, I was also stressed that Malakai knew when I was stressed. And stressed that his thumbs on my clavicles were conjuring feelings that were far too erotic for 10.30 a.m.

He inclined his head, levelled his gaze, squinted. 'Yes, you are. That brain of yours is whirring, I can see it on your face. You're doing your overthinking thing.'

'I'm not!'

Malakai straightened up and let out a knowing, lopsided smile. 'Relax, Scotch. I know this is our first proper time in public, but we're the only ones who know what we know. We got this.'

The 'we' whizzed around in my brain like a breeze picking up speed while on Speed when a 'next,' beckoned us forward to the till: it was our turn. I gathered myself and smiled at the barista. 'Could I have a skinny latte with one dash of vanilla, one dash of caramel syrup and, like, a *splash* of hazelnut please?' I turned to look up at Malakai, who was already looking at me, the corner of his mouth flicked up. 'What you want?'

'Do they have Mocha Malakai on the menu?'

'You're so annoying—'

'Kai Tea Latte?'

I snorted.

'OK, good. See, now you're relaxed.'

I shook my head. 'So, you want tap water or . . . ?'

'An Americano, please.'

'Oh. You're one of those.'

'What does that even mean?'

'Pretentious.'

'How is having regular coffee pretentious? I'm drinking it how it's supposed to be drunk. Why ruin it? No frills no fuss. It is what it is.'

'We get it. You're a deep filmmaker who doesn't want to tamper with the purity of coffee by actually enjoying it.'

'Oh, because I don't have dessert for breakfast? Vanilla and caramel? Really? You want a cone with that? That's not a coffee that's—'

I nodded and turned to the barista, 'Hey, Tomi, do you have anything hard enough to knock someone out with? Like a fruit scone or something?'

Tomi – one of the London Gyaldem – smiled knowingly. 'You know what? Scones crumble. An apple might work though?'

'Perfect. I'll take . . . an almond croissant and an apple. Knocking someone out will make a girl hungry.'

Malakai laughed. 'Cute.'

'I *am*, aren't I?'

Malakai rolled his smile in his mouth, his eyes dancing, 'Let me get this.'

I pushed his hand away, as I tapped mine on the card reader. 'You're getting my waffles next time we go eat.'

Tomi released a little squeal. 'You guys are adorable, man. I can't lie. I thought you were moving a bit mad, Kiki. I mean, no one ever sees you with anyone and all of a sudden you're with this one? But I can see why this happened. Shanti's just gonna have take this L.'

It was at that moment that I remembered Tomi was a sweet

girl who also just happened to be one of the biggest gossips on campus, a fact that earned her the nickname of Tell-all Tomi. And though Malakai and I had been being normal, 'normal' could be interpreted in any way once people thought you were a couple.

I let out a breezy smile. 'There ain't an L for Shanti to take. Malakai and I just . . . happened. It isn't a competition. And he *definitely* isn't a prize—'

'Hello? I'm right here—' Malakai interjected, and I shrugged.

I took my plate with the croissant and picked an apple from the basket by the till.

'You should be flattered. It means I want you because I want you. Not because I think other people want you.' I tossed Malakai the apple and he caught it in one hand, bit into it, eyes glinting into mine.

Tomi breathed a 'hot' and I turned to her with a mock shudder. 'Do me a favour, and don't tell anyone I said that please.'

Tomi laughed. 'Who am I gonna tell?'

Right.

Apparently, my girl just preed Mocha and Brown Sugar bein
    all couple goalz in Beanz. They're official, guys. It's legit.
    I think I stan, you know. #SugarMocha

I read the tweet out loud to Malakai with satisfaction– it was posted approximately eight minutes after Malakai and I had left the queue.

While on my phone, I hastily swept the notification from Rianne Tucker away. Out of sight, out of mind.

Malakai put his coffee down and choked out a laugh. 'Shit, already?'

I shrugged, and put my phone down on the faux-marble table. 'The Blackwell Gossip Industrial complex moves fast, and romance is entertainment. I guess it's anthropologically exciting that me, a weirdo who doesn't date, and you a guy who does date – a lot – are now locked into a relationship. It's almost like it propels us into celebrity status. People forget about the individuals involved and look at the projection of romance instead. Hence the couple name for us.' I paused, 'Wow, that was good. Lemme write that down.' I got my notebook from my satchel and scrawled my observations for my application essay until I began to feel the – now customary – weight of Malakai's eyes on me. I looked up.

'What?'

Malakai shrugged. 'Nothing. You're just . . . a brainiac. Which I knew before, but it's cool seeing it up close.' He absent-mindedly slid the small canister of sugar sachets on the table, and the morning light gleamed off the silver.

We were sat in the corner, by the wide window walls, giving us a view of students rushing to and ambling around on the green space in the leaf-strewn quad. It also meant that I noted the various Blackwellian members slowing down to look at us curiously as they walked past.

'All right, so,' I brought out my rose-gold-covered tablet from my bag, 'I've drawn up a schedule. Let me know if you have any questions.'

Malakai brought his bitter bean juice down from his lips. 'Oh. You were serious about the schedule thing.'

I raised a brow. 'Why would I be joking, Kai? We're doing this for a purpose. We have to be precise. We don't have a lot of time. Eight weeks to really juice this relationship thing for the show, make people believe in us and get enough material for your film. Plus, we have our first episode this Thursday.'

Malakai reclined his chair and ran a hand across his face. 'You're really taking the fun out of this, Scotch.'

'Well, this isn't supposed to be fun. It's work. My NYU place depends on it.'

'Brown Sugar is work, right?'

'Yeah. Kind of. I guess so.'

'Does it feel like work?'

'No.'

Malakai leant forward, loosely lacing his fingers together on the table. 'Right. Because you like what you're doing.'

I narrowed my eyes as I calculated the Malakai-Mathematics in my mind. 'So, you're saying that this can be fun because I like you? Because if you're saying that, I'm gonna have to call you an arrogant arsehole before telling you to go fuck yourself.'

Malakai smiled, and relaxed against his chair. 'Because we like each *other*. Platonically. We're becoming friends.'

I pulled a face. 'Don't be disgusting.'

The twinkle in his eye stuck its tongue out at me. 'I'm sorry, to break it to you Scotch. We're buddies.'

'Don't say that word around me ever again.'

'Pals.'

'I will pour my coffee all over your crotch.'

'Hmm. Interesting.' Malakai reached over to pick up my note-book and pen, and posed with them as if taking notes. 'You do the drink-pouring thing a lot. Is it a fetish?'

I kept my face straight. 'Don't kink-shame me.'

'Sorry. Also, that is not coffee it's a sundae.'

I flipped my middle finger up and Malakai clutched his hands to his chest as if he was overwhelmed with the tenderness of emotion shown towards him.

He grinned at me and passed back my notebook and pen. 'Lean into it. Let's discuss this schedule, friend.'

I sat up, and pulled up my calendar, back in the zone. 'So uh, we have to figure out milestones and situations we have to experience as a couple for it to be legit. Social events, dates—'

'Well, we've already had our first date.'

'Right, and that already got me more followers which hope-fully will translate to more listeners. We're setting the foundation. Maybe the first show will be us . . . talking about how the first date establishes the terms of engagement. Or should, anyway. How it helps to undo pre-judgements.'

Malakai leant back in his chair. 'And I learned the importance of transparency. From jump.' Which was funny because whenever he looked at me, I felt like I was being seen.

I looked back at my tablet and scrolled through my calendar. 'I'm going to share this with you so we'll sync. We'll have little things. The *Black Panther* screening is in two weeks, which will be cute. We'll go to every FreakyFridayz together, sporadic lunches and coffees—'

'We got Ty Baptiste's birthday party too, which will be a good place to cement our status and interview people.'

Ty Baptiste was ostensibly a member of Malakai's new crew and was one of the most popular guys on campus on the non-dickhead side of the social spectrum. He was like Zack's benevolent tether. His dad was an ex-footballer, but he used his wealth to spread enjoyment, like sneak-paying for group dinners and using his family country house to throw a party for about twenty-five select Blackwell members on his birthday weekend. Aminah was invited last year but skipped when I declined to go as her plus one, ignoring my protestations that she still go when she insisted she'd rather do facemasks and binge *Real Housewives* with me, anyway. I wished I could have gone for her, but the idea of it made my palms prickle like they were doing now. Going would entrench me into a social faction and I had no intention of being part of any. When you were part of something like that, the intimacy could easily sour into something that could eat you alive. There was safety on the outside. And now, I had to be inside for this whole thing to work. Ty Baptiste's party was the most inside you could get.

'He invited me to stay in one of the rooms,' Malakai said casually, as he sipped his coffee. While plenty people booked Travelodges nearby, or crashed on any flat surface or sofa, only

Ty's inner circle were allowed to stay in any of the extra rooms in the six-bed farmhouse. Malakai was inner-circle, which meant, as his 'girl', I was too. And I had to make this thing believable for the show, and the show had to be listened to for my internship. So, I had to go.

Malakai must have noted the stress on my face because he leant forward, urging me to meet his gaze. 'Hey. I'll obviously sleep on the floor or something.'

I swallowed. 'It's not that. I'm just um . . .' I inhaled deeply. It was easier if he knew. 'I just get a little nervous with intense, close social situations. I haven't had the best experience in the past.'

Malakai's brows gently furrowed. 'But FreakyFridayz . . .'

'Is open, public, and I can melt into the background. This is me being part of a group. It's different.'

Confusion still softened his face, but he nodded. 'It could be intense. We can figure out another event to—'

'No. I'll gear myself up. It's important that we're a credible couple and being at a weekend away together at one of your boys' birthdays helps that.'

'You sure? I'm cool with what you're cool with.'

I inhaled deeply and shot him a valiantly breezy smile. 'I'm sure.'

He threw me a small, lethal slant of his lips before looking down at the calendar on his phone. 'Hold up. What's this?' His brow was raised, as he read out, 'RomCon . . . The Reign of Ifekonia?'

I groaned inwardly. I'd forgot to delete it from my calendar, and now Malakai was privy to my nerdiest pursuit. I shrugged, schooled myself into nonchalance. 'Uh, that's in there by accident. It's nothing—'

Malakai's amusement glinted. 'This ain't nothing, Scotch. You've got bare emojis surrounding it. Whatever it is, it's a big deal.'

This time, I groaned outwardly. 'If I tell you, you have to promise not to laugh. For your sake. If you laugh, I will kill you.'

Malakai solemnly crossed his heart.

I sighed. 'So, "RomCon" stands for Romance Convention. It's in London. And one of my favourite book series is a romance fantasy called *The Reign of Ifekonia*. It's by this amazing Nigerian author called Idan Fadaka. I used to read it in school with my best . . . I used to read it in school. It's like this Afrofuturistic dystopian saga loosely based on a subverted Yoruba folklore. *Game of Thrones*-type shit. Except better. It has warrior kings bowing down to warrior Orisha queens during battle, uses mystical politics to explain what's happening in our daily reality.' I leaned forward, 'For instance, in the last book, *The Reign of Ifekonia: Search for the Sun*, these translucent-skinned aliens invaded the land and acted like they were sent as guardians from the Great Queen Oludumara in the land of light, when actually they came from the land of night and from the Dark Lord Eshuko and it's supposed to represent colonialism and . . .' The words got stuck in my throat, my skin warming. Malakai was watching me intently. 'I'm stopping now.'

Malakai shook his head, smiling. 'Don't. I like seeing what you look like when you're into something. Your eyes light up.'

I took a large gulp of my sweet, warm swill, as if it would push back the blood that swooped to my cheeks. 'It's weird you should say that because my favourite character is Shangaya. She's one of the main characters. She's this regular girl who works at her dad Ogunyo's metal shop, making weapons, fixing transporter vehicles. She discovers she has the power to conjure thunder and fire when she's eighteen. Her eyes become fireballs when she's angry, twilight stars when she's happy. She becomes this vigilante warrior queen. She rides a sabre-toothed panther called Tutu, because riding her calms her down when she's worked up—'

'I get it. Itutu. Coolness. Cold.'

I titled my head. 'Exactly.' I cleared my throat. 'She has a love affair with this light-guardian; a true light-guardian sent from Oludumara called Niyo. They're not supposed to mix. They're from two different classes and he's from a sect that fell to the earth ten-thousand moons ago. Anyway, I love the stories, and the author, Idan Fadaka is coming to RomCon in London for a signing. I was meant to go with Aminah. She's so cute. She's not into this kind of stuff but she was willing to dress up as Yoa, Shangaya's enemy-turned-best-friend, who has mastery over water and winds. *But*, her dad's coming to town that weekend so she can't come anymore.'

Malakai sat further up, 'First of all, that sounds really, really fucking cool, second of all . . . so?'

I chewed on a torn piece of croissant. 'So, what?'

'So, why can't you go?'

I stared at him. 'Malakai. Going to a romance convention is corny enough without going alone. Look, can we just drop it?

It doesn't matter. I returned the tickets, and it's probably sold out now.' I tinkered on my tablet. 'See? Gone from the calendar. Moving on! We break up shortly after the AfroWinter Ball in late November, and then we're done. What do you think?'

Malakai nodded in agreement. 'The ball's a great place to get material for my film too.'

'Great!' I snapped the cover of my tablet shut, slipped it into my bag, happy to be moving on from the fact that I enjoyed cosplay and romantic fantasy novels. I couldn't believe I'd left that in there.

Malakai lifted his fist over the table. His gaze jumped from my eyes to my hand pointedly. I raised my own fist so it grazed his knuckles in a kiss; a formal establishment of our treaty, our diplomatic framework confirmed. We were officially a team, for better for worse, with mutual goals at stake. Sealed with a spud.

'Shall I walk you to class, Bae?' Malakai's grin was an oblique tease.

I mock-shuddered as we got up from the table. 'No pet names.'

Malakai threw a look at me from the corner of his eye. 'So, no more Scotch?'

I slowed down as I hitched the strap of my bag onto my shoulder. I shrugged, and schooled my voice to be casual. 'Scotch is different. It's fine.' I cleared my throat. 'I like Scotch.'

Malakai tucked in a smile and crooked his arm to allow mine to link through as we walked out of the coffee shop.

'Me, too.'

CHAPTER 13

Lysha's mouth was moving. I was pretty sure it was moving. OK, yeah, it was moving, but instead of her sharp-tongued quick-paced east-London patois I heard The Internet Syd's smooth, satin voice pouring out, out of sync with the movements of Lysha's lips. Then Lysha's mouth stopped moving abruptly – Syd kept crooning, crystalline. Lysha's eyes narrowed in focus on me and before I had time to react to what I knew was coming, my girl had leant forward to abruptly pull Syd's voice from my ears and me out of my silken cocoon and into the cacophonic din of the sixth form common room. I rolled my eyes, and Lysha clapped in front of my ears.

'Yo, Kiki, you listening to me? What you wearing on Saturday? Jason's eighteenth?'

I blinked. My knees were curled up on the seat beneath me – my usual meditative position. I was zoned out before our last period of the day and we were tucked in our corner of the common room, closest to the double-glass fire-escape doors that led out to the field. We had chosen it because it gave us an excellent view of the boys playing football at lunch, without us needing to go outside, a great matinee show from a royal box seat. The Usual Suspects were in their usual positions. Lysha sat on the sofa opposite me flanked by Yinda, who periodically blew pink gummy bubbles that matched the lacquer she was coating her nails with. Her bio textbook was balanced on her knees, doubling as a mat to catch any drips and spills.

To my right, my best friend Rianne Tucker sat on Nile's lap. Wood Grove High School's power couple, our king and queen, a decree made by the two tenets of High School Aristocracy: they were both the most good-looking people in our school, and both happened to be fair. In those days, that space, the two were inter-changeable, synonymous. Coronation by way of caramel skin. They attained the tricky balance of enough detentions to make them edgy without getting excluded. They did all right in school. They weren't delinquents, but were in trouble enough to give them an air of fearless cool. That's really harder to do than it would seem, in a school with mostly white teachers.

At one point – maybe Year 11 or 12 – Nile had made moves towards me, (comments on my Facebook pictures, a few 'You look nice today you know, Keeks'); it was around the same time that boys were starting to get intrigued by my smart tongue, curious as to whether they could be the ones to soften it, if they could make it malleable enough to curve around theirs. But before I could test the curiosity, pick it up, look it over and think *maybe*, my mum got sick. I started to turn inwards. I skipped out of parties that I used to be the beating heart of (for a while my nickname was Koffee, due to the amount of living room coffee tables that were transformed into podiums when my song came on) and Ri didn't hesitate to take up the mantle. Rianne was my right hand, my ride or die, my partner in crime, and I was grateful to her and grateful for her taking up space for the both of us. There was less pressure on me to return to the person I was before – which worked out great because I had no idea who that person even was anymore. When my mum got ill, I forgot what the point of it all was, and it all seemed so flavourless, so stupid. Rebellion lost its allure, because what was I even rebelling against? It sped up the epiphany that most people have when they're in their first year of uni – when you're away from home and you're no longer living against parents you feel you need to resist in order to find yourself. I had a new respect for my ma, quick-witted, raucous laugh, could haggle light from a star, the seventeen-year-old who came from Nigeria on her own and cleaned toilets to put herself through a polytechnic and then university, before becoming a social worker and constructing a life from dust, work, faith and hope, and who fell in love with a fellow newly come Nigerian boy who really liked to cook and dreamed of opening a Nigerian restaurant, but who drove taxis because nobody would give him a job. Met at a wedding, introduced by friends. I wanted to be like the woman who put her dust, work, faith and hope with his and built some kind of life. I wanted to be just like her. And now I was facing losing her.

214

What was I rebelling against? Adolescent risk wasn't tasty when my whole life felt like it was tipping on the edge.

Which was why I said to Lysha, 'I'm not wearing anything to the party on Saturday.'

Nile laughed, 'So you're going naked?'

Rianne squared her elbow in his gut and I rolled my eyes. Since he started dating Rianne, our relationship had mutated into a weird, tentative frenemyship. I thought he wasn't good enough for my girl and he thought I was stush. He insisted that my mum being sick had nothing to do with my stushness, that I was like that before (although this hadn't previously stopped him from trying it on with me) and therefore this absolved him of being an insensitive prick who called a girl dealing with a sick parent stush.

I levelled a cool gaze at him. 'Yeah, Nile. I'm going naked. Idiot.'

Rianne threw Nile a stern look before turning back to me. 'Kiki, you haven't gone to one party this term, which I get, but it isn't healthy, man. You need to let loose. Lose control for one night. I can't go because I'm at a family wedding. Go on my behalf. Please. You even said your mum doesn't want you seeing her this weekend, after last time.'

Last time involved Kayefi bursting into hysterical sobs at the sight of our increasingly frail mother, and me having a panic attack the following Monday on the bus to school.

'I have to look after Kayefi—'

Lysha shrugged. 'Look, my little sister is having a sleepover with her mates this weekend for her birthday. I know they go to different schools but your sister gets on with mine. Our parents have met, you used to sleep at mine all the time. I'm sure it'll be cool. You can get ready with me. You can wear nipple tassels if you really do wanna go naked. Your body, your choice.'

Rianne grinned. 'See! Problem solved with Lysha's hoe couture suggestion.'

I laughed, and shook my head. 'I don't know, you guys. I feel guilty. My dad's going back and forth from the restaurant and hospital and—'

Yinda blew on her baby pink nails. 'You've been doing that too, Sis. Working at the restaurant, going to the hospital *and* looking after your sister. You going to feel guilty for being young? Listen, you been kind of a drag lately, and I get why, but sometimes it's really like we're chilling with a ghost or something. It's creepy—'

Lysha turned to Yinda sharply. 'Are u dumb Yinda?'

Yinda's wide eyes widened further 'Sorry man, you know what I mean though, innit.'

Rianne rolled her eyes. 'What Yinda is trying to say is that we miss you, we miss having a good time with you and it ain't been the same without you. Right, Nile?' Rianne's glossy lips stretched in encouragement at her boyfriend, nodding so her contraband silver hoops jangled.

Nile nodded, and gently nudged me with his elbow, 'Yeah. We all do. Who's gonna make fun of how I dress? I'll look after you. Don't worry.'

I shrugged. 'I'll think about it.'

CHAPTER 14

Whitewell College Radio, 9.30–11.00 p.m. slot, Wednesday, Brown Sugar Show – Episode 2: *Gotta Hear Both Sides*

'Look, I'm just saying that life would just be easier for everyone if people just said what they meant, that's all! Why would a girl say she's fine if she's not fine? And why am I to blame when I take her word for it? How does that make me the villain? Like, the other day we're in class—'

I rolled my eyes and said dryly into the mic, 'He's been itching to get this story off his chest. Here we go.'

Malakai had switched to my seminar this week due to a medical check-up appointment clash, which actually turned out to be perfect because it further cemented the idea of our inseparability as a couple. *So* cute, that Malakai switched to my class this one time because we'd missed a weekly lunch date and he missed me. Or so the rumour mill churned out, according to Tyla Williams, who I'd bumped into in the library as I was returning some books. Tyla Williams had never spoken to me before. Tyla Williams, who I saw had once called me a stush bitch who 'thinks she's too nice' on a leaked screenshot, eight months ago. But when we met in the library, Tyla commented, 'Michael would never do that for me, man. Once I texted him to keep me company while I took my braids out and he said, "What for? I ain't need to see how the sausage is made." What does that even mean?'

We ended up going for a coffee. She was nice. Turned out we were both going to Lagos that Christmas. We made plans to link up.

Malakai continued, comfortable in front of the desk, elbow resting against it as he leant closer to the mic. He had taken easily to his new position as temp co-host. He was charming, funny, easy – essentially, himself. Our first show had been an introduction, had been surprisingly fun, and now, in our second, we had found ourselves in a groove.

'So, listen, Kiki puts her hand up to answer a question, and she gets it *slightly* wrong. The tutor asks her to assess her answer, and she pauses. Hesitates. The lecturer doesn't wait for her to figure it out. She does that sometimes to keep us on our toes. Anyway, said lecturer poses the question to the class. Some dude answers, real condescending with it, you know the kind of shit designed to make Kiki feel like she doesn't know what she's doing. The gag is, he actually gets what Kiki got right, wrong. Kiki puts her hand up to answer, and I turn to her like, I got this, boo, because I know the answer. So, I put my hand up, as you do.'

I rolled my eyes again. He really was a dramatic storyteller.

Malakai shrugged at the mic. 'I say I *agree* with her point but she got it slightly wrong on these issues – I break them down. Now, bear in mind that I'm sitting right next to her. Mate, the second the words leave my mouth I feel the temperature drop. I'm telling you, that lecture hall was *Antarctic*a. I shivered. Man's teeth started chattering.'

I heard Aminah snort from where she was sat on the sofa and I scoffed, 'All right. You know what? The Academy Award for Doing the Most goes to—'

'You, Kiki. Because the way you looked at me – I felt shook to my soul. If I now die of hypothermia, what will you say at my funeral?' His voice had taken on an avuncular Nigerian jaunt to accentuate his theatrics.

I smirked. 'You had a good run. God bless your soul. Thank you for leaving me your grey hoodie.'

'Wow. You see? Ice queen.'

'Your hoodie will warm me up.'

'OK. Great. So, after lectures we're having lunch and I ask her if she's pissed off at me. My girl says no, she's fine, she's cool, asks me to pass the salt. As if she needed any, when she was clearly salty enough.'

I held on to my headphones and cackled. 'Wow—'

'Then I say, "Look, have I done anything wrong?" Then what do you say, Kiki?'

He passed me the small bottle of Hennessey and I took a swig, and replied, through a laugh, '"Do *you* think you've done anything wrong?"'

Malakai let out a long, exaggerated exhale. 'I say, I don't know, Scotch. That's why I'm asking you. Then she goes, "Well, if you don't think you've done anything wrong then you haven't done anything wrong, innit."'

'My voice isn't that high – why are you making me sound like road Minnie Mouse?'

'Stay with me now,' he directed his audience, ignoring me. 'Two days after this happens, we're studying together and I'm stuck on a question for a tutorial. The question is under her specialist subject. I ask her for help, and you know what she says? You know what my darling girlfriend says to me? She says,' he paused for effect, cleared his throat, '"Nah, you don't need my help. You got this. Like you had it the other day."'

Aminah cackled. I heard her say, 'My girl!' She had brought some popcorn, and was watching the show with delight. She was crunching very loudly.

Malakai shook his head at me, slow and heavy. 'Brutal. Tell me where in that story am I the bad guy? Please. My question is, why couldn't you have told me you were pissed at me and why you were pissed at me? The drama was unnecessary. I'm baffed.'

I leant into the mic and arched a brow at him. 'You done, babes?'

Malakai released a tiny smile. 'No. You also look really sexy when you're angry and that kind of made it more confusing.'

I knew it was for the show – it had to be for the show – but that didn't stop my belly from turning upside down.

'Ladies,' I said, pointedly ignoring the way he was grinning at me, goading me. I flipped him the finger and he released a soft chuckle. 'You see how they try to distract you? Stay woke. Don't let them catch you slipping. Let me break down why almost everything that Malakai said was – Minah Money, am I allowed to say it? . . . What was that? . . . Great.

'OK, so what Malakai just said was bullshit. Really ripe bullshit, from a specific kind of bull: real obstinate, meat too tough. This kind of bullshit is used for the manure that fertilises the farm used to grow male delusion. Makes it grow big and strong. I read that in *NatGeo*. True story. Mandem, listen to me. Women don't want to have to tell you how you fucked up. They want to give you time to figure out how you fucked up. Or admit that you fucked up – sorry Minah, *messed* up – because most times, let's be honest, deep down, you know.

'We're gracious angels, benevolent queens. If you just acknowledged the harm done by yourselves, it would piss us off less. So, we lead you to it, help you out without telling you – because it's not like we *like* being angry – yet still, you miss road. Wilfully. Like, you'd rather believe we're acting crazy than entertain the idea that maybe you acted up. I mean, you heard that story from Malakai's own mouth. I let him tell it to you, without interrupting—'

'—I'm sorry what? That was you not interrupting? You were like Kanye on a live broadcast—'

'—even though it is my show, and I would have every right to, I let you hear it from the horse's mouth so there would be no doubt. He *knew* the second that he had undermined me in front of the entire class that I was pissed. I knew the answer in that lecture. I was going to get to it eventually. I wanted a chance to defend myself. Even if I didn't, what I didn't need was for my boyfriend,' it tasted heavy on my tongue, not bad, but it made its presence felt, 'to basically announce to the whole class that he thought he was more capable than me. I didn't need him to swoop in like that. It was embarrassing. He wanted to look like a big man—'

'No, I didn't.' Malakai shook his head emphatically. Like the audience could see.

I cackled again. 'Are you kidding? Yes, you did, Kai. You loved it. You loved knowing something that I didn't. I saw it on your face! You were smug.'

Malakai scratched the back of his head, then nodded sheepishly. 'All right, fine. I'll allow it. Maybe I did want to look like a big man. But it wasn't to embarrass you.'

I reclined in my seat like a glam crime boss. 'Then I'm fascinated to know why.'

'I wanted to impress you.'

I sat up, forgetting we were on air, my elevated radio voice sinking back into my regular voice, becoming one. 'What?'

Malakai looked slightly uncomfortable and released a small

222

groan. 'I can't believe I'm about to say this on radio. Kiki, everyone knows you're smart. I wanted to look smart in front of you. I knew you'd have that loser by the ropes if you got the chance, but I wanted you to see that I could take him too.'

'Oh.' I sat back in my chair.

I heard a pointed cough behind from Aminah, reminding me with a jolt that I was still on air and was therefore prohibited from melting into a puddle of Henny and Fenty.

'*Oh*. Well, uh. I guess I could have been clearer. With communicating my feelings, I mean. Maybe I could have told you what bothered me earlier, and then I would have known that. Not made assumptions—'

'True, but after that whole thing in the seminar I wanted to believe things were cool, even when I knew things weren't cool. I knew you were upset with me, but I guess it was easier for me to believe you were being—'

'A cold witch.'

Malakai laughed, 'Easier for me to believe you were being unreasonable than actually face up to the—' he gestured between us messily, 'emotional shit.'

'Well, I think it was easier for me to be angry than to admit that my feelings were hurt. So, I guess we're both bad at the emotional shit.'

We exchanged a soft truce with smiles, 'Actually, emotional shit nicely brings me to another thing I wanted to say – if you don't mind.'

I shook my head, curious, not just as to what he was going to say, but about this new, fresh flavour of Kai I was being treated to — sweeter, deeper. 'Go ahead.'

Malakai sat up, his expression melting into something more sober. 'Uh, so . . . it's no secret that I'm known around campus for . . . dating a lot. And while there's nothing inherently wrong with that, it's been brought to my attention,' he avoided my gobsmacked gawp, 'that I haven't been completely genuine while doing it. I mean, I thought I was . . . I wanted to believe I was. I didn't want to deep the fact that maybe I wasn't being clear, that I was being a dick.

'Look.' He leant into the mic. 'All the girls I've spent time with are amazing and I didn't treat their attention properly. I didn't treat them like I should have done. I should have made it clear that I wasn't ready for anything serious, but I didn't because . . . it sounds shit, man, but I think I liked the attention. And I thought I was being decent for not being explicit, you know? So . . . yeah, I'm sorry. Really sorry for taking you guys for granted. You don't have to accept it, but it's important for me to say it.' He darted an unarmed look back at me, 'OK. So that's me. Sorry. Just wanted to get that off my chest.'

My breath slowly eked out of me. 'Uh. Um, OK. Woah. I did not expect that.'

Judging by the wild, wide-eyed look on Malakai's face, neither did he.

I leant back to the mic, words eventually making their way to my mouth. 'Uh, well, I guess to cap off this momentous occasion we'll play one of the greatest R&B ballads ever created. About a, um, complicated man who made mistakes he simply wants to make right. It's about pleading to the woman in your life for forgiveness, for grace. Hold tight for "Confessions" by Usher.'

Malakai snorted and shook his head, immediately looking more relaxed, his eyes softer. I laughed into the mic. 'Enjoy friends, and thank you for spending time with us this evening. This was *Gotta Hear Both Sides* for Brown Sugar, and I hope everyone got something out of this. I definitely did. I'm K—'

'And I'm Kai—'

'—And until next time lovers, stay sweet.'

CHAPTER 15

My phone was ringing. That was weird. I didn't even know my phone *could* ring. I mean, I figured that was part of its functionality in general, and I knew that it rang on Sunday afternoons which was when my parents liked to check in – after church, before lunch – but outside of those times? Eerie. My little sister preferred texting memes as her primary form of communication.

I was in my room typing up notes at my desk, dim light on, listening to music. It was Thursday, and the corner of my computer screen flashed 10.30 p.m. at me. Definitely not my parents. My dad worked late at the restaurant and my mum went to sleep at 10 p.m. sharp, rockstar that she was. I stuck my hand under my open U.S. Foreign Policy textbook and pulled the phone out from under the avalanche of notes, to see Kai's name and picture flashing at me. Something warm and effervescent rose up in my chest.

It was the day after our second show together. It had been a hit.

Aminah was over the moon. Overnight our followers had tripled, and so had our number of listeners. People stopped Malakai and I when we were out on campus, telling us how much they loved it. Even before the show, people were on our social media pages with love-eyes emojis under every silly faced selfie we posted, apparently enamoured by the dumb candid videos Malakai filmed and uploaded of me. (Me ordering coffee and him roasting me; us together at The Sweetest Ting having a rap debate – according to Meji, The Sweetest Ting had also seen a considerable boost in customers since we started tagging our location in our pictures.) Sometimes Malakai filmed our casual conversations or us hanging out on his actual camera, as a 'just in case' roll for the film.

Malakai and I had seen each other almost every day in the three weeks since we started the project. We sat together in class, got breakfast almost every morning, and texted throughout our days, but this was the first time Malakai had actually called. I turned the R&B down, slid my thumb across the screen and put him on speaker phone.

'Kai.'

His voice shot out breathless, something wild. 'All right, who the hell is this Sanasi wave-shifter guy? Is he a darkness agent in disguise? He's too handsome; I don't trust him. I mean Niyo is handsome too. "Skin like the sun was born at the depth of the ocean, dark and bright and fathomless." Jeez. Sanasi's eyes are described like ice daggers and that can't mean anything good. Why is he trying to seduce Shangaya while my man Niyo is out risking his life and salvation in a cursed galactic forest, searching for a key so they can live their love in peace? Why is Shangaya flirting back with Sanasi and letting him into the Red Earth courtyard? Sanasi is clearly a Wasteman.'

I blinked as his words configured themselves in my mind. They made sense to me on their own, but they didn't make sense coming out of his mouth. Was he really quoting a line from my favourite book back to me?

I scratched my forehead and without thinking, explained, 'Shangaya thinks Niyo abandoned her for the glory of joining the Winged Forces and she is feeling heartbroken, and when she's heartbroken she uses anger and vengeance to help heal herself. And I can't say anything else otherwise I'm gonna spoil – Wait, what is happening?! All this stuff occurs in the second book. How are you on the second book of The Reign of Ifekonia?! When did you even start reading the first book of The Reign of Ifekonia?!'

'I'm hooked, Scotch. This shit is amazing. Why don't more people know about this?'

'Afrofuturistic fantasy novels? I'm thinking just your run-of-the-mill institutional racism in the publishing industry. But . . . you're *reading* it, Malakai?'

'I know. I was shocked that I'm literate too. Yeah, started reading the books so I could see why you liked them so much. I get it now.'

I gripped the phone tighter, my breath hitching in my throat. 'What?' My skin was prickling. I folded myself up on my computer chair, tucking my knees up beneath me.

Malakai continued breezily, casually, 'They're great. Ten out of ten. They slap. The love story between Shangaya and Niyo . . .

It's weird, I'm invested. Like proper invested. Also, now I get that playlist you made called Shaniyo.'

I'd forgotten that a week before, Malakai had followed me on the streaming platform where I made silly playlists called things like 'Beats To Beat Your Face To' (Malakai had sent me a video of himself listening to it with a wave brush poised in front of his cheek like he was using it as blusher, cheeks sucked in, durag placed on his head like a wig), and 'Hip-Hop To Pop Your Ass To' (he sent me a screenshot of a Google search: How to twerk). I really didn't think he would stumble across my fantasy novel soundtrack though.

I groaned. 'Cringe.'

'Are you kidding me, Scotch? It's so good. Listening to it, it's like you're right there. You are so fucking talented.'

His voice was full of energy, and it poured over me and relaxed every muscle in me that I hadn't known was tense. I hadn't fully realised the potency of his voice until it was isolated from his body, and it was scary that whatever irresistible energy Malakai generated was so powerful that it didn't need his impressive face for it to transfer to me.

Malakai continued, voice buoyant, 'Nah, Scotch I don't think you get it. I mean, obviously you do, but this is sick. That bit at their secret commitment ceremony? Jeez! Where Niyo gives her a thousand jars of honey and a thousand jars of spice as dowry. Uses his fallen wings to carry them and lay them at her feet, saying that he lost his ability to give her moons, but even if he could, what was a moon in comparison to the light of their love? This was all he could give her, the purest things on earth, most overlooked but with the most value . . . Nah, it was nuts. My head was spinning. Bars, man. If I had Niyo's game . . . Wait. Let me even look it up—'

I heard some page flicking in the background, which bought me time as I tried to process what was happening, if this was really happening – and then his voice returned. '"Moon spice representing their ferocious passion, a terracotta hue bright enough to favour his love's eyes. Honey for their friendship, the sweetness of two spirits twined, the comfort of their knowledge of each other, happiness. The two balanced each other. Shangaya wept for Niyo's broken wing, at what he'd sacrificed for her, and he said, 'You are my flight. I can see my whole universe in your eyes.'"' Malakai skipped forward: 'Then the ceremony . . . "Shangaya dipped her finger in a jar of honey, and then a jar of spice, and gently smeared it on Niyo's lips. 'Hold them both on your tongue, my sweet Starbird, and kiss me so I can taste how my forever tastes.'"'

Malakai let out a low, heavy whistle. 'Shit. It even got me, and I'm not usually into this stuff.'

All I could manage was breathing.

'Scotch? You there?'

I cleared my throat. 'Yeah, I just . . . I'm glad you like the books.'

'They're dope. Thanks for introducing me to them. Anyway, I'm going to leave you to get back to your work.'

'How do you know I'm working?'

'You're a nerd. Also, you didn't go to the library this afternoon

230

because we went to go get lunch and you have that tutorial tomorrow.'

'Are you a stalker?'

'You do know I am basically obliged to spend time with you, right? I mean, I probably would want to spend time with you even if I didn't have to . . . to study why someone of high intellect would choose such a nasty beverage to drink in the morning.'

I grinned. 'Oh, so you *are* obsessed with me.' I leant back in my chair. 'How embarrassing for you—'

'I'm sorry, who asked who to kiss them?'

'Well, if you're a stalker, which you obviously are—'

'So, we're just gonna ignore that fact? Calm. Cool. OK.'

'Just know that last Summer, Aminah and I took two MMA classes that incorporated Beyoncé dance moves into the actions.'

Malakai released an incredulous laugh. 'What was it called?'

'Get 'Em Bodied. The tag line was "Slay While Slaying", although there was a disclaimer about how they didn't actually advocate for homicide.'

Malakai chuckled harder. 'Oh, my days. That's the sickest thing I've ever heard. Why did you stop after two classes?'

'It was technically illegal, so it got shut down. It was in a warehouse in Peckham. Anyway, my point is, I could incapacitate you via an elbow to the neck with a move from the "Déjà Vu" video. I'll have you on your knees with a move from *Power*.'

Malakai's laughter crackled in my ear like a new fire. 'If I said that I find that hot would I be breaking the rules?'

The air in my throat curved in on itself. 'Not sure we covered non-public compliments, but I think it's allowed.'

'I don't think you'd need to work that hard to get me on my knees though. Realistically.'

The casual way he said it bucked against the dive of his timbre. The impact made my pulse reverberate. In the quiet, I moved to lie flat on my bed. 'You really trying to do your sweetboy ting on me? Boy, move.'

He chuckled. 'Nah, but for real, Scotch. The more I get to know you the more I realise how much of you there is. I wanna know it all.'

I was quiet for a little while before flipping on to my front. I stared at the picture saved by his name, one I took of him as he took a picture of a basketball game in Eastside. His eyes narrowed in concentration, but expression soft, open. He didn't know I'd taken it.

'You know more than a lot of people.' That soft listening space that he always left when we spoke, like no word he said would work the way it's supposed to without my response. I swallowed. 'Or maybe it's just that I've had to let you know more, for this whole thing to work.'

'I know enough about you to know that you don't do what you don't want to do.'

My breath inched through my throat. 'True.'

Malakai's voice burred low. 'So . . . that would mean that you want to let me in?'

A path of lava pulsed through me. 'Also true.'

The pause from Malakai was oblique, precarious. When he spoke, his voice was grainy with the texture of an emotion I couldn't make out. 'Thank you for having me.' It was unexpected, and I was grateful for my prone position because my joints suddenly felt gelatinous. And then the memory of our first kiss came to me unbidden, his hands on my waist, his breath against my neck. How easy it'd felt.

The quiet stretched taut between us, and though I couldn't see him, I imagined him as still as I was, wary of movement, unsure of where to go – perhaps unsure of where we even were.

'You in bed?' I asked, finally.

Surprise jounced through Malakai's voice, 'Yeah. You?'

'Am now.'

'Why you wanna know, Scotch?'

I put him on speaker and propped my elbow on my pillow to angle my head on my palm, causing my playful, shy smile to tilt. 'Oh, I just thought that I should probably do due diligence by learning what my man wears to bed. You know, in case it comes up in conversation with any girls.'

Malakai released a low, delightful rumble. 'Kikiola Banjo. I'm scandalised. You're kinda filthy ain't you? I like it . . . You could always make something up.'

'And get it wrong? You, my friend, were kind of a slag. Imagine my shame if I say you wear boxer briefs and I get corrected by one of your ex-tings who says, "Actually, Malakai Korede sleeps in a onesie"?'

'And in this fantasy, I would change into the onesie after sex?'

'You like to be comfy.'

'Compelling argument.' A pause. 'Shirtless. Boxers.'

I imagined the taut muscle of his chest, the smooth, mois-turised skin, a sweet plane for my tongue to glide on. My core constricted. I calmly noted that I had a raging thirst-on for Malakai Korede.

'Good to know. Thank you. Good night.'

'Wait, what? Nah, nah, nah. No fair. This is a *partnership* remember?'

I grinned. 'I'm a warm sleeper, so . . .' I let my voice dip, 'I keep it light.'

'Oh. OK. I see you want me to lose my mind tonight. How light?'

The delectable frustration in his voice wound me tighter, and I was just about to answer when he made an irritated grunt and swore under his breath, cutting the tension and sending me into cold freefall. 'Shit. I gotta go, Scotch. My dad is calling me and it's better to pick up than get the stress of missing it later.'

'Hey, it's OK. Speak to you tomorrow?'

Malakai exhaled deeply. 'Yes. Put the books away soon. Watch Netflix. Night, Scotch.'

'Night, Kai.'

I hung up, vibrating, unsure of what had passed between us, but sure that I liked it. I wanted to curl in on myself as if to trap the clement heat in, but I also wanted to stretch, as if I'd just taken a deep, satisfying nap, let the energy from the good resting spread me straight, pull me taller. I was smiling. My phone buzzed – a notification pushed away at the rosy warmth that filled me, dropping down from my screen almost gleefully.

RIANNE TUCKER has tagged you in a photo.

My heart moved to my mouth as I clicked, breath hitched. #ThrowbackThursday. A picture of both of us in Year 10, hair slicked back into side-buns, held by silver-toned-snap barrettes that were there to control what Eco Styler couldn't, 99p hair-shop lip gloss slathered on as we pouted into the camera, arms slung around ourselves, holding each other tight.

Bedazzled on the throwback photo, pink and glitzy, were the words: *BFFs 4 Lyfe*.

CHAPTER 16

The Usual Suspects had been successful in their campaign to get me out. Or at least, they'd felt successful in their campaign to get me out. The truth was I'd been all or nothing, and when I decided I wasn't nothing I was determined to be all; wearing a push-up bra under my strappy top, whining on Lysha and Yinda, and then becoming the protein in a whine sandwich while Mavado told us that we were so special, so special so special, so special. And I *felt* special, braids swinging, vodka pouring. Koffee was back, on the tables, the heartbeat of the party racing to forget – doing the most to forget – the fragility of everything, especially the person who usually wore the gold star pendant around my neck.

Clear, hair-shop lip gloss had been slicked on, a touch of mascara and my mum's too-light-for-me powder pressed haphazardly on my face. I'd gone into my parents' room to retrieve it. Her vanity was a little dusty. I ran my fingers across her perfumes, her creams. I sniffed them, remembering the time her neck didn't smell like clinical sterility, of sweat and hot tears that fell from my eyes on to the hollows of her collarbone. Her neck had always been elegant, her body soft and curvy, but there had always been a stately dip in the connect between her throat and chest, queenly, an elegant deck for a gold star pendant. Now, it was emaciated with tubes coming out of it. I tried to move as much as I could, as if every hip swish and waist twist was a prayer of vitality, as if the more alive I forced myself to be, the more alive she would be. I found that alcohol lubricated my body and made this easier, made the hard edges in my mind soft, the bristles buck.

While I was stood breathless against a wall, taking a break, dizzy head spinning delightfully, Nile came over and took my hand. 'Come on. I promised I'd look after you.'

I smiled woozily and followed him to the kitchen where he refilled my cup. I leant back against a counter as people squeezed past, to and from the fridge.

'Yeah? Looking after me means giving me more drink?'

Nile shrugged as he passed me the cup. 'It's good to see you have fun, K. Relaxed, like this. Felt like I lost you for a while.'

I held still, the cup hovering by mouth. An alcoholic heat rush and hormonal heat rush combined to make me feel like I was aflame. I swayed and held tighter on to the counter. The room was pleasantly soupy.

'Bro. Bruh. Did you ever even have me to lose me?'

Nile let out a slow, sexy smile. 'I nearly did. Year 11. You were crushing on me like brazy.'

237

I rolled my eyes. '*Brazy?* Why do you talk like that? Such a beg. You're corny! And it's exactly for that reason that it was the other way round.'

'Just admit that you wanted me.'

'You wish.'

Nile's smile faded slightly, eyes giving off a metal-edged-glint as he gazed lazily at me. There were a few other people in the kitchen, but they were busy, not paying attention, music too loud to focus. Nile glanced around quickly, then stepped closer to me, whispered in my ear.

'Yeah? What if I do?'

I opened and shut my mouth, my heart pounding against my chest, his heavy, masculine heat and Christmas-present-first-grown-cologne new to me, this whole thing new to me. My mum getting sick had suspended milestones for me and, as mouthy as I was, my mouth was yet to make contact with a boy's. This was wrong, I knew it. He was Rianne's man, but everything, everything in my body wanted to be against his body, in pursuit of forgetting, in losing myself in the heat.

'Don't say that Nile. You shouldn't be saying that.' I pushed him off slightly.

Nile stepped back but his eyes remained fastened to me. 'Let's talk. Somewhere private.'

'Nile—'

'Just talk. Come on, K. We used to talk.'

So, with Nile propping up my stumbles, I swayed to an upstairs bedroom that smelled foreign, something I would later recognise as boy. We were sat on the bed and Nile seemed unable to tell me how much he missed me without rubbing the small of my back and it felt good, so good, and it was like he couldn't tell me how sorry he was for what I was going through without pushing my braids behind my neck and whispering it against my throat, and it felt delicious, so delicious. Lips moving until they were so close to my skin that he was enunciating against it. He told me through low growls how much I deserved to feel good for once, because I'd been going through it, and when he said it, it felt like the truth, it felt right, even though something felt wrong.

He said he was sorry Rianne had been distant with me lately and he attempted to make up for the distance by proxy with his hand slipping ever so slightly up my top to rub against my waist, slowly and then quickly. He said, between too-hot neck kisses, as he began to push me down on the bed, body on mine, that she was jealous, because she knew he'd liked me first and she couldn't handle it.

At the mention of Rianne's name, I'd frozen; it pulled me back to dispassionate reality, yanked me out of the fantasy of forgetting.

'No. Nah, nah, Nile.'

I pushed him off. My hand was waving sloppily, reflexes weakened by cheap vodka, 'We need to stop. We aren't doing this. I'm not doing this. She's my mate. That's my girl.'

Nile's molten eyes hardened to a blade, his smile stiffening, mask slipping. 'But is she yours? You should hear the shit she says about you. Like how she thinks it's mad that someone as blick as you could ever think you had a chance with me.'

My vision was blurry and I couldn't tell if it was the alcohol or the tears, or if maybe at this point my tears were pure ethanol, stinging their way out of my clumsily lined eyes.

'Shut up. You're lying . . . Stop chatting shit.'

'I'm the only one not lying to you, Babe. You think Lysha and Yinda ain't in on it? They talk behind your back, K. I'm the only one that's real with you.'

I was at the edge of the bed panting, everything I had tried to forget rushing to the fore, my mum being sick now mingling with being called 'blick', like being dark-skinned was as pathological as what was happening to my mum's cells, but even worse, a scourge, somehow, a sin. A sickness and a sin.

Nile posed himself as cure and absolution. He was kissing my neck again, and I turned my face so he could kiss the feeling out of me because I was feeling too much, and it didn't feel like a first kiss, no fireworks, not a candle lit, rather it was like a tourniquet around a wound to staunch the flow of blood.

It wasn't enough. Even as his hands slipped up my bra and squeezed and I let him, hoping he would squeeze all the feeling out, it wasn't enough. It was wrong, so wrong. This experience wasn't mine. It was his. He wasn't mine, he was Rianne's. None of what was happening belonged to me. I wasn't in control. I pushed him off, for good this time, sloppily but stronger now, because even though his tongue hadn't lapped up feeling, it had soaked up some of the alcohol and sobered me.

He was saying something about me not telling anyone, but I barely heard him and ran out of the room, out of the house, past Lysha and Yinda, all the way back to my home.

I'd texted Rianne the next day something to the effect of, 'I'm sorry, so sorry. Something happened. I don't know how to say this. Can I see you? I was drunk and confused. He said things. I shouldn't have done it. He said you said . . . no excuse, but did you say? Did you say that?'

It was too late. News travels fast when everyone in your community is in possession of a small rectangular computer that fits in your back pocket. Nile got ahead of the narrative quickly. I got upset about my mum so he took me upstairs to get away from it all, he said. Brother-type, no motives. I was drunk, sloppy, messy. I'd tried it on with him. I'd got upset when he rejected me – like, come on, did I expect that he'd be into me when he had Rianne. 'LOL'.

Nile had got to Rianne before I did, that night apparently. He knew I would tell her. Rianne called me words I'd only just got the confidence to think, via text. I felt like I deserved them. Red hot rage in text bubbles and then an immediate wall of ice – I'd been blocked.

The school had given me a home-schooling option for that half of the term because of my mum. I'd never taken them up on it before because I felt like I needed the normality of school. Laughable. I stopped going to school. My grades were good enough, and we were at the stage of the term where everything was essentially exam prep. Aside from exams, I didn't have to see anyone. Allegiances had been quickly drawn: Yinda defaulted to Rianne, understandably. Lysha too, on the surface, but she texted me a couple of times after a few weeks of radio silence.

LYSHA: Gotta be honest, K, this is dark shit. I know you're going through some shit but this is dark shit. I'm talking iron-tablet, dark shit bruv. But it don't sound like you. I'm worried. I shouldn't do this but you know I'm here. Yeah? I know you're not OK. Also, Nile is a prick. I don't trust a word he says. Call me.

I never called her. What was the point? People believed what they wanted to believe. I was going to leave soon, leave school behind, my mess behind. I could start somewhere else all over again and situate myself outside, never get entangled. I could keep people safe from my chaos and keep myself safe from chaos. You couldn't be caught out if you kept yourself out.

CHAPTER 17

'Screw her. What the hell does she want?'

'I don't know,' I panted.

'Why would she show up in your life after all this time?'

'I don't know.'

Aminah and I were doing our 7 p.m. Sweat Out – powerwalking around the quad – a habit we'd started since we realised we were too lazy for the gym and we hated running. We looked like two Aunties trying to snap back after a divorce, but it was effective, plus we got to wear cute workout leggings and crop tops. We did it three times a week and since we were often busy during the day, this was our time to debrief and catch up. It was pleasant, with the air newly turning crisp, and for some reason we found the deepening dusk therapeutic for our talks. I'd hoped that sweating would somehow help me release some of the tight stress that had been bound up in my chest ever since Rianne sent that friend request.

The tagging only exacerbated it. I really *didn't* know what she wanted, but the one thing I knew was that it wasn't because she was ready to forgive me, which was why I found her contact so disturbing. It was like she was trying to taunt me. It got under my skin, made me itch at a place I couldn't get at.

Aminah was shaking her head, furious, 'From what you've told me, that girl is bad vibes, Kiki.'

I swallowed. I'd scrolled through her ProntoPic profile, and her limited pictures were undergrad standard; bright and blurry club photos with her friends, some selfies – she was still so pretty – birthday dedication posts. No pictures of boyfriends though. There was a picture with Yinda and Lysha, however, captioned 'Day Ones'. My chest had pinched at it. Not necessarily because I missed them, but because I'd missed the chance to miss them.

'I don't know.'

Aminah stopped powerwalking and yanked me back, gripping my arm. 'I *do* know, Kiki. And whatever fucked-up mind game she's trying to play will not work. You made the right decision in ignoring the request. Don't mind her. You have other, more important things going on in your life, like the fact that you're going to New York next year. Which you deserve because you missed out on that internship year before uni.'

I shook my head and started walking again, soothed a little by Aminah's pep-talk, but not completely. The fact that Aminah knew everything about me was helpful, but it also meant that she could bring up things I'd rather not bring up, such as the year before we met. 'First of all, we don't know if I will for sure. Second of all, me not doing that internship was on me.'

Aminah eyed me carefully before changing the subject. 'Fine. You know what we haven't discussed? How Malakai confessed to being a dick on campus-wide radio. That's a wild move to make if he's going to return to the singles market after your experiment.'

'What do you mean 'if'? He is. Also, it could easily just be a tactic to endear the women of Blackwell to him.'

The words were uneasy in my mouth; didn't fit right on the Malakai I was getting to know. He was genuine.

I shrugged. 'Either way, vulnerability is sexy. Plenty of women are still going to be attracted to him.'

Aminah rolled her eyes (lined, because she'd said just because we're working out doesn't mean we should look like it), 'Girl, do you really think he was thinking about *that*? He sounded like he wanted the ground to swallow him up when he was confessing. You got a Yoruba man from south London to swallow his pride. Do you know what a feat that is? That was real.'

I tucked my smile back in and tried to suppress the warmth that washed over me. Aminah's eyes immediately widened in scandalised delight. 'Your face – what is that? I have never seen that before in my life. You're coy. Are you coy?' She lifted her arms with triumph into the sky, 'Ki-coy Banjo, wow, I love it—'

I looked around at the sparse courtyard and pulled her arms down, 'Could you chill a little please? Malakai and I have found a good rhythm now. I was sceptical but we're actually friends.' I thought back to our last phone-call . . . flirtatious friends, maybe, but still friends. 'That's it.'

Aminah made a choke of amused disbelief as she hitched her thighs up higher on her march, 'Oh, OK. Sure. That's what it—' Her phone chirruped, saving me from what I knew would be an inaccurate speech about how I was in denial. She sighed and zipped her grey hoodie down, pulling out her phone from her purple crop top. Her brows shot up as she read the message. 'Kofi's texting me about what colour I'm wearing to the AfroWinter Ball.'

I grinned as I hiked up my arms and legs. 'Oh, he wants to match. That's adorable.'

The Blackwell Society had a booking for the ballroom at the fanciest hotel just outside town, known for teacher's conferences, team-building seminars and Blackwell's answer to the Met Gala.

Aminah rolled her eyes, but she failed to hide her delighted grin. 'Whatever. He still hasn't formally asked, so I hope he doesn't think this counts. Apparently, because Malakai's agreed to film some of the night and Kofi's DJ-ing, they get rooms as part of their payment and Kofi wants to give us one. They said we can drive up together. What do you say?'

I shrugged, avoiding the fact that Malakai and I would be staying overnight in the same building for a second time. 'Sounds good.'

Aminah stuck her phone back into her crop top, zipped up her hoodie. 'Wow. Never thought I'd see the day where you actually attend social events with me. I mean, first, I'm gonna get to go to Ty Baptiste's party and now the AfroWinter Ball with my bestie?

If I knew all it took was you being in a fake relationship . . . ' Her smile was stiffening.

I tilted my head. 'Hey . . . Minah, I never told you to miss Ty's party, and you know this is just for the sh—'

'Show. Yeah, I know.' Her smile brightened, shining over any tiny pinpricks of unease. 'Look, either way I'm glad you're letting yourself have fun with a boy. And I don't think Zack counts. I feel like Zack was just kind of, like, a sentient dildo. A barely sentient dildo. That you didn't even bang. So maybe a barely sentient titty-squeezer. Dry-hump utility equipment—'

'All right, well, I ain't going be having that kind of fun with Kai, so—'

'Yeah, I was going to ask about that actually . . . "*Kai*"?'

I took a deep whiff of the cool damp of the air, and let the breeze hit my exposed skin. Power walking really took it out of me, it seemed, so my hoodie was tied around my waist. 'Don't you feel invigorated by the smell of the outdoors?'

Aminah narrowed her eyes at me as we made the turning that marked out our third way around the leafy courtyard. 'First of all, that's weed, sweetie. Secondly, don't change the subject. You've nicknamed each other?'

I looked across the shadows of the courtyard and squinted in the dark amber dim upon seeing two familiar figures. 'Is that Shanti and Chioma coming from the library? Are they friends now?'

'Kikiola Banjo—'

I sighed. She had full-named me, which meant there was no way she was going to get drawn away from this subject. 'It's not really a nickname, per se. It's more like an in-joke? I don't know, he said that I'm less brown sugar and more of a scotch bonnet, so I guess he just started calling me Scotch and it just stuck—'

Aminah stopped dead and I stumbled as I ground to a halt and turned around. 'Um. I'm sorry. You mean to tell me that Malakai called you *spicy*?'

I took a minute to catch my breath and undid my braids from their bun, put my hairband in my mouth and flipped my head over to tie them again in the hopes that the time it took would lead Aminah to forget about anything that was mentioned. It wasn't even loose, but I needed a distraction. Unfortunately, by the time I had retied it Aminah was still smiling at me, smugly.

'I want a boy to call me a seasoning. Do you think I can get Kofi to start calling me "Maggi Cube"?'

I started stretching. 'OK, you know what? I'm not talking about this anymore.'

'Maybe "Bay Leaf"? No, "*Bae Leaf*". Ha ha. Wow, "Scotch and Bae Leaf". Sounds like a badass modern Blaxploitation detective show.'

'So, what's happening between you and Kofi?'

Aminah's smiled slyly. 'I'm gonna ignore you ignoring me because I love you. Nothing. Still making him work. I mean I'm kind of chill about it because I already know he's going to be my husband.'

I stopped stretching my quads and straightened up. 'Pardon?'

Aminah shrugged, and raised an arm above her head to stretch it. 'I just know it. I can't explain it. I'm not even in love with him yet, but I feel like I'm going to be and it will be deep. He is sweet and kind and treats me like a princess and loves God. You know how fucking spiritual I am. So spiritual I am bi-religio—'

'Not a thing.'

'— and you like him, and you don't like anyone. I like him. We'll probably fight over what jollof rice we'll serve at the wedding because I don't know if I'm ready to have Ghanaian jollof at my reception, but maybe we'll be able to reach a compromise. When I look at him, I feel safe.' She smiled and switched arms. 'The point is, he has me. But I don't want him to ever take that for granted, so I gotta create the *illusion* of pursuit. Know what I mean?'

I bent to stretch my other leg. 'Not really, but I trust that *you* know what you mean. Wow, Minah, I knew you liked him but I didn't know you liked him this much—'

Aminah shrugged and grinned. 'Yeah, me neither. But the other day we were studying together and he casually brings out plantain chips – Dad's brand, of course – and my favourite strawberry juice drink from his rucksack. You have to go to Eastside to get that drink. They don't sell it around here. It's imported from like, Kenya. He didn't even look at me while he was doing it, he just tossed it my way and then started talking to me about the newest track he was producing and I don't know,' she exhaled deeply and spread her arms out, shaking her head, her eyes and smile bright, 'I just wanted to jump his bones right there in the study room and snuggle him. It was like, woah . . . this boy thinks about me even when he's not thinking. And I feel so relaxed around him. Like more *me*. Like I'm the greatest me. I only ever feel like that around you. And no offence, but I don't want to snog your face off.'

'That's a lie.'

Aminah inclined her head gravely. 'You're right. Come here, sexy.'

I laughed and threw my arms around her neck, kissing her cheek. 'I'm really happy for you,' I said as she playfully pushed me off. 'Kai should actually interview you guys for his film.' I paused as I noticed two figures moving closer towards us across the courtyard, just behind her head. 'Wait, that really *is* Shanti and Chioma.'

There had long been civility between the femme factions in Blackwell and Malakai Korede's presence had disrupted that. I had now situated myself firmly in the midst of that disruption, after purporting to help combat it. Chioma and Shanti weren't friends; they were from two separate cliques, and the only reason I could see for these two queens to unite was war. Shit—

'Shit!' Aminah turned around just as they reached us and immediately backed up next to me, fortifying us for attack, leaning her arm on my shoulder as if we really were the Blaxploitation detective duo "Scotch and Bae Leaf". She nodded at them. 'Chioma, Shanti. What's up?'

Shanti nodded back, her large gold earrings jangling with the movement as she wrapped her fur gilet tighter around her body. 'Kiki, Aminah, hi. We're actually on our way to dinner.'

'Hi.' I raised a brow and straightened, and Aminah's shock slid her arm off my shoulder. 'You guys are hanging out?'

Chioma laughed, her silver septum ring enhancing her already pretty smile, 'We bonded over thinking that you were a duplicitous bitch.'

I felt Aminah stiffen next to me and I surreptitiously reached out to hold her wrist to calm her down. I nodded. 'Ah. OK. I mean, that's fair. I can see how it looks.'

Shanti rolled her tongue in her mouth. 'It looked like you were being a snake. It looked like you wanted to isolate Malakai for yourself after acting like you were some kind of guru for the gyaldem.' Chioma quickly interjected, just as I felt Aminah's tongue being unsheathed and mine begin to feel heavy.

'What Shanti means, is that sometimes on the show you come across like you're not really one of us. I mean, the femme community of Blackwell *us*. Know what I mean? It's like you're this weird floater who judges us from the outside. And we didn't do that to you, by the way. We constantly invite you to shit – all the girls do – and you turn us down. Even Aminah shows up to stuff sometimes. And don't get me wrong, your advice was great but sometimes it could seem a little—'

'Like you think you're better than us,' Shanti finished for her.

An unpleasant coolness settled in my stomach. I thought my reason for reclusion was self-protection, not superiority, but despite myself I could see how warped it would look from their vantage point. Chioma nudged Shanti and Aminah straightened and took a step forward.

'OK, what's going on here? Is this an ambush?! Because I can fight and still look fine. My setting spray was expensive—'

251

Shanti shrugged. 'Well, so was mine. La Mystique; got it from Sephora when I was in Amsterdam.'

Aminah paused and stood back. 'I use La Mystique too, got it from Paris.'

Shanti's eyes glimmered beneath her lush lash extensions with something that looked like respect. 'Look, this isn't an ambush. We just came over to say that we rate the show you're doing with Malakai. You guys sound legit,' she ran her eyes across me. 'And honestly? I kinda rate you now, Kiki. Not just your advice, but, like, *you*. You sound more relaxed, like you're not judging but you're living this shit with us. Experiencing it with us. Not this self-appointed head bitch in charge who knows it all. I mean, at the last FreakyFridayz you were dancing with girls that weren't Aminah and even talking to people as well.'

Chioma nodded in agreement. 'I mean, personally, I've always known that you've had a good aura, but it has always been shrouded by something, you know.' Her voice sounded like wind chimes, a melodic scent of sweet, musky essential oils wafting from her. 'It's like you're open now. Also, you put Malakai through his paces. He's a good guy, deep down – all of us know that – but he is *tangled*. Doesn't want what he thinks he wants. Or wants what he thinks he doesn't want.'

Shanti smiled wryly at that. 'Either way, he was getting us mixed up in his mix-up. Glad he apologised though. How did you get him to do that?'

I allowed myself to relax a little with the turn of conversation and released a tentative laugh. 'Uh, that was all him. He's figuring some things out, I think.'

Chioma waved a hand. 'Please. No way he would have got there without you. Gotta say though, I was surprised by the text he sent afterwards.'

Aminah and I exchanged a glance. 'Uh,' I attempted the appearance of nonchalance, 'he texted you?'

Shanti's immaculate arches shot up. 'Oh, wow. You didn't know. He texted both of us. All of us.' At the look on my face, she smiled. 'They were apologies, Kiki. Chill.'

I'd failed at the appearance of nonchalance. I cleared my throat. 'I'm chill. I wasn't—'

Shanti smirked at my denial and Chioma spoke over it, 'Bad communication. Misrepresenting his intentions. Said we deserved better—'

'Strong agree.' Shanti's interjection was peppered with a sharp smile. 'We compared notes. All the apologies were specific to our situations. It was . . . satisfying to receive. I mean, I didn't respond, obviously, but it was satisfying.'

The new information coursed through me and counteracted the snippy evening breeze. If the apology was a performance, he would have told me about it. He wanted to do it. Defences I didn't even know I had up lowered, and I levelled a gaze at both Shanti and Chioma.

'Well you both deserved those apologies. And, I, uh, appreciate you telling me you like the show. I'm also really sorry if it ever seemed like I was judging you. I wasn't. Or at least, I didn't mean

253

to. I just . . .' I shrugged, feeling freer than I had in a while. 'I don't know, man, you're all so cool and I just wanted to keep you guys from pricks because I . . . I have been there. And I've seen how it can mess things up. But I wanted to do that without exposing myself which, yes, makes me a hypocrite. I was just intimidated, I guess?'

Shanti looked incredulous. 'Intimidated? Kiki, you're like, the most listened-to voice on campus. Brown Sugar is the only platform all the cliques are united over. You're respected here. Even if you weren't, you never gave us a chance.'

It suddenly felt harder to remember why I worked hard to not integrate fully, to remain on the watchtower on the outskirts, guarding the girls, but also guarding myself. Seeing everything but feeling nothing.

I swallowed. 'You're right. There's some, uh, friendship trauma there. I think I was worried that you guys wouldn't like me if I was *all* of me you know? Like I would let you down or something.' I inhaled deeply, and felt my tongue coiling up, ready to leap forth and ignore rationality. 'I think that's why I was afraid to admit that I was seeing a guy on campus . . .'

Both Shanti and Chioma's faces slackened, eyes widening in a way that almost made me laugh.

Shanti uttered a 'Shut. The. Fuck. Up.'

Chioma shook her head and grinned, knowingly. 'I knew it. I knew it! I knew you had a secret wild vibe about you!'

The only person who didn't seem amused by my impromptu confession was Aminah. My best friend glared at me. 'What are you doing?' She whipped back to a puzzled-looking Chioma and Shanti, 'No, she didn't. She's chatting shit.' She lowered her voice and muttered in my ear, 'Don't let this *Cheetah Girls* moment get to you.'

In the past three weeks I'd felt myself getting looser, more unleashed, trusting myself to trust and for some reason I looked at Chioma and Shanti and felt I could trust them. If they were apparently able to venture into friendship after both dating Malakai, if they could say what they thought of me to my face without any real animosity (I kind of liked Shanti's bite) then I presumed there was something in both of them that I could trust. I was good with the risk.

I squeezed Aminah's arm. 'It's fine, MiMi. It's really not that deep.' I ignored her incredulous look and turned back to Chioma and Shanti. 'So that first kiss between Malakai and me? It was just a ploy. The guy I was seeing was bothering me that night and I couldn't get him to leave me alone. Malakai noticed and I noticed Malakai noticing, and we kissed to get him off my back. It just happened. Things just kind of went from there. Turned out we actually got on, and one thing led to another.' Technically, none of this was a lie.

Shanti frowned, puzzle pieces visibly falling into formation in her mind's eye. 'Hold up. The only other guy you were seen with that night was—'

Chioma gasped, her bejewelled hand flying to her mouth, causing her multiple bangles to jangle, 'ZACK KINGSFORD?'

Aminah hissed out an angry, 'Shhh' and glared at me. 'You see now? Are you happy? This girl speaks in R&B interlude whispers and all of a sudden she is hollering that goat's name in the quad!' She put a single lilac painted finger to her temple and starred rubbing in tiny circles. 'Chioma, will you *please* keep your voice down, abeg!'

Chioma, still, evidently flustered managed to nod. 'Right, my bad.' She gestured at a nearby bench and we all congregated on it, legs squished together. Aminah reluctantly followed suit, rolling her eyes and muttering something about how this was disrupting our workout routine as she squeezed in between me and the bench armrest.

Shanti sat forward, placed two hands together in prayer and pointed them at me. 'Aite. OK. Break it down for us.'

My skin began to prickle as I told them about our nine-month fling and what had happened that night. It was clarifying into something that made my stomach queasy.

Chioma shook her head, eyes widened in defiance. 'Ew. His energy is *dark*.'

Shanti nodded grimly. 'Babe, that sounds so shit.'

I swallowed as truth and realisation began to unpick the discomfort I'd compressed. 'It was kind of fucked.'

Shanti's eyes were soft now. 'It *was* fucked. Not your fault for not seeing it. It's so easy with him. One second, you're flirting and the next it's something else you're not sure of.'

Chioma rubbed my arm. 'Right. He's a dick. I mean, even without the whole debate thing he's doing with the Whitewell Knights.' Her normally sweet, placid face grew hard. 'I wanna

256

figure out a hex for him. How does he even get away with this?'

'He's rich, light-skinned and looks like a Calvin Klein model,' Shanti said, procuring a handful of lollies from her pocket and sticking one into her mouth, before offering them to the rest of us.

Aminah nodded as she tugged the wrapper off a strawberry sphere. 'Says "diverse people" instead of "Black people". He never spoke to any of the Black boys in school. They made an effort to, as well. Did a Mandem 101 course the summer before uni with a couple of cousins and decided to do a rebrand that suited him.'

I smiled as I popped one of Shanti's lollies in my mouth. 'Did you know he once referred to himself as "perfectly blended"?'

The girls snorted. Shanti screeched, 'Like a fucking *smoothie?*'

Aminah grinned. 'Kind of perfect since his brain has no solidity.'

As the girls took turns in delightfully roasting Zack, my phone buzzed and I slipped it out the zipper of my gym leggings.

> **KAI:** Aite. A couple things.

> **KAI:** I tried to make jollof rice for dinner, but I burnt it. I think the missing ingredient was a special breed of Scotch bonnet only found in the suburbs of east London. May make your eyes water but the payoff is worth it. Will you come over tomorrow and watch me make it? I feel like your judgemental gaze will force me to be better (as well as you literally being a chef's daughter).

> **KAI:** In case this wasn't clear this is a formal invitation for you to have dinner with me tomorrow.

KAI: I just remembered you're working out with Aminah right now. Tell her hi from me and to accept my ProntoPic request. She's hurting my feelings. It's been like a week and a half since I sent it, man. Last week I literally saw her scroll past my request in front of me when we went to the movies with her and Kofi.

I made a sound that was too close to a giggle for comfort.

Shanti's brow popped up. 'That was Malakai wasn't it—'

I cleared my throat awkwardly. 'Yeah, sorry—'

Chioma's smile was dry. 'Why you apologising? You know what the worst thing about Malakai Korede is? You can't hate him. Believe me, I tried. I wanted to hate him so bad. I just never had an issue with who he *is*. I like his aura. Lots of light green in it. He's sweet, it's just that he always had a guard up.'

Shanti affirmed that with a rueful nod. 'Super thoughtful and attentive, but as soon as you ask something personal his shoulders would get all high and he'd get shifty and itchy and change the subject. I never knew what he was thinking. Every day it was like tryna do some kind of romance sudoku. A peng puzzle. Who has the time? OK, well, I did, I guess.'

It had been three or so weeks and I'd never once really felt like I had to work to know what was going on in Malakai's mind; but I still felt a form of the block the girls spoke about, the way he veered away if I asked questions about before he got here, about *why* he was here.

Shanti nodded at Aminah and me as she rubbed the arms of her black bodysuit. Fur gilets looked sexy, but weren't exactly practical when you were straddling the cusp of autumn and winter in an English town. 'Look, what you girls doing now? Chi-Chi and I were going to this new dim sum place in town – obviously, they have a vegan option – and they're doing a student discount tonight. Wanna come? Split a cab?'

To my surprise, Aminah jumped in immediately: 'Why not? This workout has tired me out and I actually want to hear more about your make-up routine because your beat is immaculate.' She flicked her eyes across Shanti's face, an everyday look that somehow shimmered, a pretty face that was shaped and pressed in a way that somehow unlocked even more beauty. 'Also, I want to know if Chioma can really work out a way to hex Zack.'

I quirked a brow at Aminah and in response she twitched a shoulder and winked. Despite her earlier prickliness, I knew the girls had won her over by their dragging of Zack and their lack of judgement towards my hooking up with him.

I smiled as we got up and headed towards the campus gates. 'I'm down too. But could we please keep the origin of mine and Malakai's kiss to ourselves? And the whole Zack thing—'

Shanti wrapped her gilet around her and looked me in the eye. 'Say less, sis. Secret's safe with us. Besides, what matters is that what you guys have is real.'

I coughed and made a general sound of assent. My conception of 'real' was growing more confused by the day. I didn't know what 'real' was anymore.

CHAPTER 18

The six-pack cardboard crate of Supermalt jangled slightly against two six-quid bottles of Pinot as I rushed through the heavy glass doors into Malakai's building. It provided percussion to the faded jumble of music flowing from open windows into the residential quad. A hall resident had gone in before me, allowing me to slip in without buzzing up. Malakai had technically invited me over to dinner, which meant it was custom for me to bring something. That's what adults did on Netflix shows about married people with dark secrets. I wasn't sure what wine would pair with jollof rice and chicken, and the attendant at Tesco Metro wasn't really that much help. So, alongside the dry white, I went for something foolproof, a staple of Naija hall parties, bought from a shop in Eastside. Personally, I didn't have a taste for it. It felt more like a medicinal meal supplement than a beverage to be enjoyed, but Malakai loved it, frequently ordering the Supermalt Float at The

Sweetest Ting, with the quip 'It's the one thing I know you won't want' – although he never stopped me from picking at his plate.

This wasn't the first time I'd been in his flat or in his room; we'd had study sessions multiple times over the past few weeks where we went over each other's projects. These sessions led to us eating pizza, watching *Twilight* and going through Will Smith's oeuvre. I'd take videos of Malakai acting out his favourite scenes (Edward first smelling Bella) and we'd take selfies that Malakai would caption with, 'study sesh with my favourite subject' to the reception of dozens of delighted heart-eye emojis and proclamations that we were #goalz.

This, however, was the first time we'd be hanging out in his room for the purpose of just chilling. This felt different. This *was* different. There was no set agenda of work, or at least no pretence of an agenda, because being real, we barely got any work done together. Either way, as I punched the upwards arrow by the lift, I began to recognise what Aminah had previously diagnosed as 'nerves'; my belly-borne butterflies flapping chaotically, palms prickling.

Was this a real *chill* date? I had no idea what 'real' meant in our context, but I knew that the pounding in my ears felt pretty fucking real.

Was it too late to cancel? I was genuinely hungry though, and Malakai had promised me that at the very least his chicken would bang.

I steadied myself as the lift doors opened. This wasn't a big deal. It was *Malakai*, for goodness' sake.

It was *Malakai*, so I was guaranteed a fun, easy time,

It was *Malakai*, so there was nothing to be nervous about.

It was *Malakai* and this was strictly platonic because he did *not* like me like that.

The door to his flat was left ajar, propped open with a shoebox. Kofi lived in the flat opposite, and Malakai often left it open so he could come through with ease, borrow some milk, some Maggi cubes. I manoeuvred myself through the door, still balancing the crate, when I heard muffled voices coming from Malakai's room. At first, I thought that he was with Kofi and was about to push his bedroom door open when I clarified that these voices sounded *angry*. The one that wasn't Malakai's was lower, gruffer and had a Nigerian lilt to its bass that made the anger thunderous.

'Malakai, you study *film?* And you didn't tell me? I have to find out from your mother that you dropped out of your Economics course at one of the top universities in the country, *months* after the fact—'

'Dad. This is also a top university. Or does it not count because it's not the same university your friends' children go to? It's the top for what I want to do. Which yes, is film.' Malakai's voice was now almost jaunty in its affability, but it was askew, a distorted funfair ditty in a horror movie.

'Olalekan, I am in Nigeria building for this family, building for my legacy, being a man for this family! You, too, should learn to be a man. Life isn't easy. You think it was easy for me after my father died and I—'

I heard Malakai chuckle humourlessly, 'Here we go.'

'Yes, *here we go*. I had to step up and hustle to help my mother provide for my siblings. At seventeen. You make sacrifices in order to be responsible. I like cameras too. Do you think I wouldn't rather have been gallivanting with my friends, taking pictures, having fun? This is a hobby. You can do a proper, solid degree, while doing that on the side. Pictures don't pay bills. Making films will not pay bills.'

'It could for me. I'm good. I work hard. Isn't that enough?' Malakai's voice was low. It sounded younger and there was a vulnerability under the frustration, the hurt in trying to prove he wasn't in pain. It sliced through me. I should have left. I'd gone past 'accidentally stumbling in on his argument' to eavesdropping a few minutes back, but I found myself frozen to the spot, holding the bag of drinks tight to my chest as if Malakai would feel the comfort via transubstantiation.

'And you could work just as hard in economics. I tried to understand when you took time off when . . . what happened, happened.'

'When what happened, *happened*?' Is that how we're describing it now? Dad, just say it. When you—'

'Malakai, I am still your father. I admit, I have made mistakes. And yes, you went through . . . something. But we all go through things. When your grandfather, Olalekan Korede, the person you were named after, the hardest-working man I knew, when he died, I found working more useful than sitting around getting depressed. You didn't even lose someone! Nevertheless, I tried to understand.

'Abi, your generation is different? So, I let you take those few months off for whatever was going on in your head. The plan was that you would make up what you missed in the summer. But you were taking your father for a fool, abi? Olalekan, this is nonsense. Your mother said you needed time "to heal". What kind of healing? Healing, kini? What happened was between me and your mother. Is it the healing that made you go mad? Because this is a mad decision, I am telling you now, son. You are being irresponsible. What kind of example are you setting for your brother?'

'What kind of example have *you* been setting? You come in here, talking about *mistakes* like you're not this destructive hurricane.' Now the pain had risen to the surface, mingled with the anger, it broke through into Kai's voice, through the air.

'Watch your tongue, boy.'

'This is the first time you're seeing me in four months. Four *months*, Dad. It only took you so long to find out what I was doing because you barely remembered you have a family here. You remembered that you were supposed to be play-acting apologetic. Even before I only ever saw you when I went to Lagos and you were barely home.'

His father cleared his throat. 'Rubbish. I introduced you to my friends.'

'You're introducing who you want me to be to them. You used to say, "This is my son Malakai studying Economics at Norchester. Did you know Norchester is one of the top universities for Economics? Only reason he didn't choose LSE is because of his girlfriend, Ama. Beautiful girl, daughter of Ekenna – my business partner. Yes, yes we are building a legacy o!" You would invite me to dinner, but then it would end up being a dinner between myself and six of your friends, and you ignore me until you tell me I need to make an effort in Lagos. That it's my home, and so, at the weekend, I go off on my own exploring with some creatives I've connected with, and when I'm back you yell at me, because "that is not what you should be doing, son! What will my friends think if they find out my son is gallivanting like an area boy?"' Malakai released a brisk, hollow chuckle. 'Dad, what were you doing gallivanting like an area boy?'

'OLALEKAN!' I felt the glass bottles in my grip tremble a little at the thunder in his voice.

'Ah. Ẹ ma binu sir,' Malakai's apology was a jaunty taunt. 'Sir, who are you building for? Ehn? Daddy, tani? Who? Is it Muyiwa who barely knows you? Or Mum? The woman who I heard cry herself to sleep over you? It definitely ain't me. Sending money is not enough, Dad. I am grateful; I am, and I am blessed, I know, and you work hard, I know, but it is not enough. Before I came to uni, I was Muyiwa's dad. I was teaching him all the things you should have taught us.' Malakai's voice was hoarse and I heard a loud thump as if he was slapping his chest. '*Me*! And I don't even know if I'm doing it right. How am I supposed to know if I'm doing it right?' Malakai's voice cracked and it reverberated through my chest. I realised my eyes were watering.

'You say I don't understand what it's like to lose a father. It doesn't feel that way.'

I should have walked away. I couldn't. It wasn't a case of being nosy – this was none of my business, I knew that – but for some reason Malakai felt like he was my business, and even though he didn't know I was there for him, I wanted to be.

When his father's voice spoke, it was quiet and crackling, the menacing spark of fire in a sleeping house. A flicker with the potential to raze to the ground, to destroy.

'I will pretend you didn't say that. For your sake.'

Malakai's laugh was dark and hollow, painful to hear, a cruel pastiche of his usual bellow that was dense with light. 'You know what's mad? I chose a business studies combination because after everything, *everything*, some small part of me thought that might make you happy. Ain't that wild?'

His father cleared his throat into pungent quiet. 'Malakai. I have paid for my errors—'

'How?'

'By allowing you to speak to me like I am your mate. But it is my job to make sure that you become a man.'

'I'm involved in a decision for my life for once. Ain't that manly?'

'Being a man is about making stable decisions. This is reckless, frivolous and indulgent. I'm worried you weren't in your right mind when you made this decision.'

His father's voice had barely risen a decibel, and yet it rung loud and clear, the words leaving his mouth like a salvo.

There was a silence that could slice through sinews.

'Yeah, you're right, Dad. I guess the months I couldn't get out of bed weren't very manly.'

'Malakai, that's not what I—'

'This decision helped make my mind right.' Malakai's voice was quiet and ferocious, but still, I heard the break in it.

I didn't need to see Malakai to see him. I should go. He didn't need me. I knocked.

When Malakai opened his door, his eyes were glistening. I could see the effort he put into pulling the fragments of his face into something resembling casualness, amiability. I wanted to tell him that he didn't have to do that.

'Kiki, hey—'

Malakai's father stood behind him, slightly shorter, in a smart, slate-grey wool coat over a white shirt and navy chinos, a business-casual demi-god. It was as if he were controlling the air in the room, his familiar, handsome face imperious. He pushed his hand into a pocket as he regarded me with gentle curiosity behind expensive frames. I saw the tension in his gaze morph into a calculated affability.

I forced my voice to sound bright, 'Good evening, sir.'

He nodded at me, the gesture almost imperceptible. 'Good evening.' He turned to Malakai, voice placid, 'Ṣé iṣẹ ẹ rẽ? Ṣe nítorí ẹni tí o ṣe fẹ́ sọ ayé ẹ nù ré? Má d'àbí èmi,' slipping into Yoruba to inquire, 'Is that your work? Is this why you're throwing your life away? Don't be like me.'

Malakai straightened, posture somehow both softened by the presence of his father, but also frigid, defensive. 'You don't have to worry about that. And you don't get to talk about people I care about like they're not in the room. This is Kikiola.'

'Orẹ ni wa, sir,' I said to Malakai's father. 'We're friends,' I repeated, as if to emphasise the point, as if to draw the battle lines, to make it clear that I was present as emotional back-up here, if need be.

Malakai's father studied me carefully before I saw the tiny movement of his mouth that could have been a smile, if you squinted with hope.

I moved further into the room, kept my voice jovial. 'We almost weren't friends though; he was competing with me for the top spot in class, which was irritating. Then I saw his short film and decided he was worthy competition, which was even more irritating as I really don't like conceding brilliance to men.' My smile was wide, bright, and the shadows in Malakai's father's eyes receded slightly, his expression sitting somewhere between bemusement and amusement.

Malakai's expression was inscrutable when I turned to him. 'I can go.'

He shook his head. 'No. No, my dad was just leaving. He has a flight to catch early tomorrow, back to Nigeria. This was a quick visit.'

Malakai's father rubbed his jaw in a gesture reminiscent of his son. 'We're not finished here.' He hesitated, and for the first time I saw a hint of uncertainty in his gaze. His eyes darted between Malakai and me. Malakai just stared at the wall behind his father's head, jaw taut, fists balled.

His father nodded deeply, more to himself than anyone else. 'Take care, son. Lovely to meet you, Kikiola. Help me keep this one out of trouble.'

'I'll do my best. But no promises.'

He smiled at me, and he looked so much like Malakai in that moment, I almost gasped. It wasn't a big smile, but it was present, enough to let me know that when it stretched it could hold the same shine as his son's. 'Your Yoruba is good, by the way.'

It was somewhere between an apology and an acknowledgement of something that had nothing to do with my skills in my ancestral tongue. 'Ẹ ṣé, sir. Ìrìn àjò áá dára.'

He patted the left side of his chest in gracious acceptance of my wishes for his safe journey, and walked out of the room, leaving a hefty, wealthy, oud scented breeze behind. It wasn't till we heard the kick of the shoebox and the slamming of the front door that either of us moved.

The smile Malakai gave me as he took the bag of drinks grate-fully, was sweet in its effort. The attempt squeezed at my chest. He put the bag on his dresser, then immediately sat on the bed, bending over, his face buried in his hands. I moved next to him, silently sitting down on his plain navy Ikea sheets. He was still, and so I thought the best thing to do was also be still. I stared straight ahead at his *If Beale St Could Talk* poster.

Eventually he spoke, his voice muffled by his hands. 'How much did you hear?'

'Enough.' I swallowed. 'You pissed?'

'Not at you.'

Malakai straightened, his hands dropping to his thighs. He inhaled deeply, then exhaled with a puff of his cheeks. His eyes were red. Malakai pursed his lips and nodded quickly, as if he was hoping the action would make the emotion ebb. He released a humourless choke of a laugh.

'This isn't how I imagined my girlfriend's introduction to my dad to be.'

I knew he meant 'girlfriend' in the false sense, in our sense, in the nonsense sense. I nudged his shoulder with mine. 'Yeah? How did you expect for me to meet him? Over four courses at our engagement dinner at Nobu?'

'Never.'

Malakai's voice was hard as he evaded my gaze, his eyes trained on the poster ahead of him. Regular Malakai would have gone along with the bit: 'Nah, on the private jet to the private island we booked for our wedding week.'

I got it. He didn't need me to make him feel better. He knew his dad, and he needed to feel what he had to feel. I barely registered reaching for Malakai's hand. It happened as I exhaled. I brought it to my lap, clasping it tight. Malakai squeezed my hand back immediately. We sat in solemn silence for a few moments, but then my insensitive stomach released a loud, obnoxious, petulant growl. *No.* I held still, hoping Malakai hadn't noticed. He didn't move either. Ignoring it seemed to work. We were quiet for a few more moments before Malakai's shoulders started jutting, slowly and then quickly and his breath leapt out in sharp bursts. I bit my lip, but it just made my snort come out nasal. Then, we spontaneously combusted. Pressurised laughter tumbled over from us, as we tumbled over each other.

'I,' *(rapid inhale and exhale)*, 'am,' *(a wheeze, some hyperventilation)*, 'so, sorry.'

Malakai got up from the bed and reached out a hand to me, his eyes brighter now, lighter now. 'All right, Nala. Let's get you some food.'

I placed my hand in his and allowed him to haul me up towards the door. He didn't let go till we reached the kitchen.

'All right. Well done. This banged.' I pushed the last forkful of moist, stewy, peppery rice into my mouth.

Malakai smiled as he rose from the dining table with both of our plates, 'We did good. And yes, I recognise it was a team effort. Don't know how I could have done it without you drinking wine and shouting commands at me.'

I inclined my head in a regal bow. 'You're welcome. I think my morale-boosting is really what gave it a moreish kick.'

'I think it was the bay leaves.'

'Who reminded you to put the bay leaves in?'

Malakai laughed and sat back down at the table, taking a swig of his Supermalt. We hadn't mentioned what I'd walked in on. Malakai deliberately left no space for it.

We'd bantered as he crushed the Maggi cubes, blended the peppers, tomatoes, onions. He'd already marinated the wings overnight in a special concoction that involved honey and assorted spices, and the aroma filled the kitchen, spicing up our laughter as the dish baked in the oven. The chicken was good, falling off the bone, the seasoning sinking through the flesh, through marrow, saturated with flavour. I was impressed. And satisfied. So satisfied I could feel myself getting sleepy. I pushed my chair back, yawning.

'Sorry.'

Malakai smiled at me. 'You want dessert? I can offer you store-brand ice cream sprinkled with Frosties while we watch an Eddie Murphy movie of your choice. Didn't you say he was your first human crush?'

I patted my stomach and stretched. 'As delicious as that sounds, I think I need to bounce. I've got some reports to fill out for the project.'

Malakai's smile dimmed, 'Yeah. Of course.'

He turned to the sink and started washing up. I watched him for a while quietly before joining him, grabbing a dish cloth and drying the plates in the rack.

'We do have one more bottle of wine. Let's start with *Boomerang*.' I released a low whistle, as I carefully dried a fork. 'Eddie was peak peng in that.'

Malakai splashed me with suds.

We weren't five minutes into the film, when Malakai brought it up. We were sat side by side, on his bed, cracking jokes, drinking mugs of wine (he, naturally, didn't have wine glasses) when he fell silent, as if trying to configure his words.

'I should explain that Nollywood drama. That's part of the deal. Communication?'

'Only if you want to. We're only playing boyfriend and girl-friend—'

'But we're not playing at being friends.'

272

The question was folded delicately into the statement. I picked up the remote and paused the TV, turning to him fully, swivelling myself on folded legs so I was opposite him.

'No.'

Malakai's mouth ticked up with a relief that made my belly flip. 'Good. That could have been real embarrassing. Because the other day I realised, that aside from Kofi, you're probably the closest person to me at Whitewell.'

My heart felt like it'd been pumped with helium, gassed, airy, overblown, too big for my body, too full.

'Yeah. You're the same to me,' I managed casually. 'Aside from Aminah. That's tragic. Should we join a book club or something?'

Malakai grinned something sweet, before he rubbed the back of his neck. 'I want to tell you. But it isn't easy for me to talk about.'

'That's OK.'

The quiet that fell between us was comfortable, a continuation of conversation. I let it lie for a few moments before I ventured into it.

'How about we sit here and watch the movie, and whenever, if ever, you feel like it, you can talk to me?'

The grateful look Malakai threw me made my chest ache. 'That sounds good.'

I unpaused the TV, reduced the volume and turned to look at Eddie Murphy's charming, bright, wide smile, as he flirted with a flawlessly coiffed babe.

'My dad actually always reminded me of Eddie Murphy.'

I turned to look at Malakai, but his eyes were still on the screen so I followed suit. 'Yeah?'

'I think that's why I loved his movies so much. Charismatic, handsome – and I know he didn't seem like it just now, but he can be really funny when he wants to be. When I was younger, I loved when people said we looked alike, loved when my mum said I reminded her of him. I liked having *something* of him. He dropped out of school to provide for his family, prided himself on being a "self-made businessman". An entrepreneur. Providing was his idea of affection.

'More than once I overheard my mum calling him in Lagos on my or my brother's birthday to remind him to call us. Then he'd visit for a week and buy us a bike that he wouldn't teach us to ride because he didn't have the time, but everything was cool. He'd kiss my mum on the cheek and dance with her in the living room to Earth, Wind & Fire and say, "My dear, everything I do is for us, I'm building for our kingdom", like everything was fucking cool.' Malakai's voice was brittle. I linked my arm through his, squeezed it against my body.

He cleared his throat. 'I started dating Ama because he encouraged it. I chose to study Economics because that's what he wanted me to study. To learn business, so I could work with him one day. I just thought it was a case of *doing* things you know? Like, I could earn him giving a shit.' Malakai's voice was muted of emotion, calculatedly casual.

'I found out my dad cheated on my mum just as I started First Year. It involved a woman messaging me on Facebook, of all fucking things. Almost the worst part of it – she sent pictures of herself in the house in Lagos. Pictures of her with my dad. I guess my dad got bored of her and she wanted revenge. It was kind of genius, actually. Because then I was in the really fun position of telling my dad that I had seen a woman draped all over him on the sofa my mum had picked out and if he didn't tell her, I would.'

His eyes were assiduously trained down, jaw tight, tense with the memory of the emotional burden of carrying information that would rupture your family and also having your hero lose his status in a matter of seconds. My whole body felt for him. I wanted to hold him.

'Shit, man.' He pressed the balls of his palms to his eyes. 'Sorry, I don't know why . . .'

I clambered up so I was sat in front of him, nestled between his legs, back to his chest. He instantly relaxed against me as I took his hands in mine and brought them together around my waist.

'You're good, Kai.'

Malakai leant his forehead against the back of my head. 'It's mad how shocked you can be by something that you were always prepped to find out. Mad how much it can still really fucking hurt. How angry you can still be. And it wasn't until then that I realised how much I was holding on to this idea of my dad. I could excuse shit because I genuinely thought he cared. I bought into the whole "building a kingdom" thing, like some cult follower. It was like I'd been brainwashed.'

'Kai, you can't blame yourself for looking up to your dad—'

'It's just, I wanted to be him so bad. Despite everything. Always cool, always collected, nothing could faze him. Life of any party. Capable. And he turned out to be a selfish mess. Cowardly. This giant became so . . . tiny. He always said he couldn't come to England because of his schedule at work, but he managed to get a flight to Heathrow two days after our call.'

'He told your mum?'

'He tried to send us out the house, but I dropped my brother at a mate's and snuck back. I wanted to be there for my mum. Neither of them heard me come in. She was screaming at him. From her gut. This mad sound. And I heard her say, "I could handle you doing it to me. I accepted it. I said, he does his job, he takes care of me. But our children? Malakai had to find out that you're a whore from one of your toys? You can't even be neat about it? My heart was not enough, you had to break our sons' too?" And it went real quiet because I guess that was when my dad realised that my mum had known the whole time.

'She goes, "Oh, you think I'm a fool like you? That's the problem. You've always thought of me as that young girl that you could easily impress. I can bring up your children but not be part of your world." You know, the worst part is that even now they're still kind of together? Nothing has changed. He's still in Nigeria, still treats us like extracurricular. I just don't know what they've worked out. All I know is that I felt like the ground shifted beneath me. I just shut down.'

The gust of breath Malakai released warmed my neck, and his arms tightened about me. It was a few moments before he spoke again.

'I clocked that so much of what I based my life on was bullshit. My relationship with Ama, my degree. All of it was to impress a man who was a liar. And I just . . . became really fucking sad. I couldn't tell what was up or down anymore. Ama was sympathetic at first . . . actually closer to pitying. But it got frustrating for her, which I get. I mean, now I realise I was having a breakdown. I wasn't going to class, didn't want to go out. I wasn't myself.

'When I told her that I was having doubts about my degree, she said I was dramatic, irresponsible, that she'd tried to be cool but this was the last straw. It wasn't even really a break-up, it was like . . . two people, finally being set free from something they didn't know they were trapped in. After we split, I couldn't figure out why I even wanted to stay at that uni. I spoke to Kofi and it looked like he was having the time of his life here. Plus, Whitewell had the perfect course for me.'

'And then, you decided to come scatter tings.'

Malakai laughed, the sound rumbling through my body. 'When I got here, I wanted to start over. I wanted to move somewhere with no expectations of me. When people have expectations, you can disappoint them. I also . . . man, I don't know how *like* my dad I really am. I have his smile, I have his eyes, who the fuck knows if I have his predisposition to being a cheating arsehole? Like maybe if I was in a relationship long enough, I'd turn out like him? I thought it was better to avoid them all together. I've seen how destructive it can be when you fuck up.

'Thinking about it, that's probably part of what the film's about. I mean, don't get me wrong, I thought it was about understanding

women, but . . . I think maybe I'm trying to figure out what relationships are? How they can work and if I'm cut out for a real one.
Trying to build a playbook to avoid failure. Just in case.'

'Kai . . . you're not a cheater and you can't inherit a cheating
gene. I just think you have to trust yourself to be who you are.
And I think who you are is good.'

Malakai's arms were still anchoring me to him, and they squeezed
in response to my words. His voice was slightly more gruff when
he spoke again. 'I haven't really talked about any of this stuff like
this before. Thanks, Scotch. For—'

'What are fake girlfriends who are also real friends for?'

There was a snug, sweet beat before his voice gently inquired,
'How can you be so sure I'm not a cheater?'

I shrugged. 'You don't hide who you are, you're open with it. I
mean, yeah, you could have been clearer on some things . . . and
you're careful about how much of yourself you show sometimes,
but who you *are* was never in question.'

Malakai was quiet for a while. 'Were you cheated on?' he asked
finally.

I found that once my truth tasted freedom it was harder to hold
captive, particularly around Malakai. 'Not exactly. I was the cheater.'

Shit. *Shit.* I wasn't meant to say that. How did he do that?
Mellow me enough for calcified secrets to soften and slip? Malakai
said nothing, but his arms didn't move from around my waist. My
heart started pounding triple time against my chest, and my hands,
holding on to Malakai's arms, prickled. I let go of them, but he
still didn't let go of me.

'Talk to me, Scotch.'

After a few moments, my stiffened back relaxed into his chest. I let everything pour out.

I looked down at my thumbnails as they smoothed over the peachy, smooth paint of the other.

'Scotch.'

I shook my head, and swiped at my streaming eyes with rough irritation. 'No. No, don't try to make me feel better, Kai. I don't need you to do that. I hooked up with my best friend's boyfriend – what kind of person does that? And then I ran away and hid. You were right when you called me a hypocrite. I think that's why it stung so much. Like, who am I to give advice when I'm capable of that?'

'Kiki—'

I stayed still, my frantic words sapping all my kinetic energy, falling out of my mouth, 'I should have known better. I'm full of shit, Kai—'

'Kiki, I want to look at you when I say this . . . Will you look at me?'

I sighed, then hoisted myself around so I faced him, legs folded over his thighs. I was expecting to see something like judgement trying hard not to be judgement, but he was looking at me with a sugar-gilded determination, soft focus. He swiped a thumb across my cheek, before running his knuckles down the side of my face, bending his head slightly, ensuring my gaze was locked into his.

'You're not full of shit, Scotch. You were going through something and you're human. It wasn't a hook-up. That prick knew you were vulnerable, and he took advantage of you.'

'I know, but I shouldn't have—'

While Malakai's eyes shone steel, it was mellowed by concern-creased brows. He reached to clasp my wrists, his grasp firm, but tender.

'Don't do that, Scotch. No buts. Would you say that if someone had written to your show? Would you have told them that they should have known better? No. You would call Nile a manipulative predator.' Malakai paused, and his eyes glinted with anger and sweetness, sugared quartz. 'And you would be right . . . I'm really sorry that happened to you. You didn't deserve that. No one deserves that. You see that, right?'

I swallowed, his words helping to clear a mental fog that obscured the truth. 'Yeah. Yeah, I do, thanks Kai, I just . . . it was confusing. That whole situation made me feel so out of control. And I spent that summer afterwards, trying to get it back. I'd actually got into an internship that summer. It was pretty prestigious and competitive and once you were in, you were in. You could go back there for grad opportunities. It started in July and the plan was to work at my dad's restaurant up until then. He was still at the hospital with my mum a lot and he was stressed. My little sister was staying with my aunt and our cousins for the summer, so this was a way I could help. But when the time came, I just couldn't go.

After everything that happened and losing like . . . *all* my friends, I just wasn't in the right headspace. The internship felt foreign, I guess. Scary, suddenly. I felt safe working at the restaurant. I kind of just wanted to hide.'

I took a fortifying breath. Malakai's thumb swirled on my wrist lightly in a tactile cypher that my pulse translated as: 'I'm here'.

'Anyway, while I was working shifts, these really cool Lagos babes would come in every Sunday. They were a group of friends spending summer in London. They used to talk loudly about their dating life. Give each other advice, that sort of thing. They tipped well. Once, they caught me listening. Or more like, once they saw me roll my eyes at something a wasteman did to one of them. They asked me my opinion on the situation and I gave it.

'Apparently my advice worked and they liked it, because they started bringing me in every week on their dating lives. It was like having friends again. It inspired me to create Brown Sugar. I couldn't make things right with Rianne, so the least I could do was stop guys doing what Nile did to the both of us – pulling friends apart. I wanted Brown Sugar to be a place where girls could feel powerful. And the music is the ultimate company. Songs about love and lust and loss. It speaks. It connects. I wanted to connect. Make people feel less alone.'

Malakai's gaze was so full warmth made my skin prickle and push out a coy, 'Corny, I know—'

He shook his head. 'No, Scotch.' He looked like he wanted to say more but he left me space to speak. I held it close to me. It gave me courage to continue.

'Um, I still didn't trust myself to be *involved,* to make friends. Aminah and I became friends by accident within the first week of uni and I'm so glad, otherwise I would have had no one. I was so scared I'd mess up . . . but I think I've over-corrected and numbed myself to the point where I've turned myself into some kind of heartless, weird, judgemental robotic *freak.*' I thought about what Shanti and Chioma had said earlier, that they'd thought I was judging them, that I thought was better than them.

Malakai tugged at a twist that straggled from the high bun tangled on the top of my head. 'Kiki, the first time I spoke to you, outside them lifts, I felt like I'd been electrocuted.'

'Hmm—'

'Not in a robotic, freak way.' Malakai grinned. 'Your energy grabbed me by the throat. You're electric. Like lightning. Bright with it. Bold with it.'

His eyes caressed my face like the flutter of a butterfly wing. 'You care so much. You feel so much. So, if you're a robot, you're one of them robots that everyone is scared will overthrow humans one day because they're so emotionally sophisticated. If you're a robot you're a really sexy, despotic one.'

I laughed, and the action further loosened the already slackened tension in my chest. Frightening, how he knew how to do that. When to do that. Merciful, how he knew how to do that, when to do that.

I smiled up at him. 'Thank you for thinking that I'm a hot, megalomaniac android. And thanks for like, um, being you enough to make this feel as easy as it does.' For being a soft landing.

'Hey.' He lifted up my hand and gently chucked my chin with our entwined hands, his gaze finding a new latch in mine to click into. 'Scotch . . . I got you.'

I smiled shyly, straightened, then exhaled deeply through the bloom of heat that rushed through me, my voice intentionally light as I said, 'Netflix and trauma. So, how does the wet mascara look around my eyes?'

'Peng. Shall we take a picture for the socials? Let the people know about the sexy night the Campus It Couple is having—'

'Yeah, which filter erases the look of emotional evisceration?'

'Alcohol. There's that bottle left.'

'Let's do it . . . Oh, by the way, since we're doing confessions, did I tell you that I think I'm friends with Shanti and Chioma now?' I reached for his television remote to unpause Eddie Murphy.

Malakai spluttered on his room-temperature mug-wine. '*What? You couldn't lead with that?*'

'Well, I'd just witnessed a very intense father–son confrontation.'

'What you just told me is *way* more stressful . . .'

And so it went, flowing back and forth together with satiny ease until he walked me home. We held hands the whole tipsy way through the forested path to my halls, the delicate moonlight and brazen campus lights finding love and making a home on Malakai's silk-over-marble face. I wasn't sure who picked up whose hand; all I knew was that we were holding each other's for no reason.

At the door to my halls, Malakai still didn't let go. We talked like we did, laughed like we did and he didn't let go. When an errant yawn from me alerted us to the fact that it was 3 a.m., he laughed and murmured, 'Sweet dreams, Scotch.'

It was a self-fulfilling prophecy, because that night I would close my eyes and think about how he'd said that before he squeezed my hand and I pulled him into a hug and his arms pinned me so close I could feel his heart racing through his sweatshirt. His face fit into the crook of my neck like it belonged, his nose brushing up against the skin between my collarbone and throat, eliciting a spark in my heart and between my legs. He released me so slowly, like he was giving something up by doing so. His hand dragged currents across mine as he surrendered it, palm to fingers to tips, before lifting my hand so his lips could graze my knuckles like a feather on fire before finally letting it go, because, no kissing, I'd said no kissing. I couldn't remember why anymore.

CHAPTER 19

The Saturday morning of the following week, I was awoken by an aggressive buzzing sound. I hauled myself up on the bed and picked up my phone to be informed of two things:

1.   It was 9 a.m.; far too early for any normal human being to be calling on a Saturday morning.
2.   Malakai was not a normal human being. Deep down, I might have known that already.

We were both at FreakyFridayz the night before, and we'd only got in five hours ago. He should have been as tired as I was. I rubbed my eyes and blinked at the caller ID for a few moments to establish that I was indeed seeing what I thought I was, before picking up.

I groaned. 'Why?'

Malakai ignored my warm greeting. 'Aroa, Shangaya.'

I frowned into the morning sunlight streaming into my room. 'What? Are you still drunk? Why are you saying good morning to me in Fekonian? Are you that much of a Reigns geek now that you're speaking the language? Ugh, I've created a monster—'

'Come to your window.'

'Mate, if this is a Rapunzel situation, my braids are tied up with a headscarf. The lifts in this building work fine,' but I was already scrambling up off my bed, walking to my third-storey window by my desk, squinting against the autumn light, curiosity and excitement propelling me.

'Can you just – I'm tryna do a ting. Can you let me do the ting?'

I laughed. 'OK, I get that being my fake boyfriend means you gotta try to be romantic, but I think Romeo and Juliet roleplay is a bit much. Particularly as they were both just basically horny idiots who—'

I stopped as I spotted Malakai in the courtyard between the student hall buildings. He was Niyo. Well, he was dressed as Niyo. He must have hit up the seamstress Aunties in Eastside because somehow he'd got the deep scarlet material needed for the cloak that Niyo wore in the book. Niyo's cloak had ancient celestial characters written on them – Malakai had re-created it through cutting out and sticking some black material to the cloth, following the patterns in the book. It wasn't perfect, but it was an impressive attempt; particularly for someone who, I'm pretty sure, had never watched *Project Runway* before.

He was wearing crisp white trousers from what looked like

one-half of a traditional Yoruba outfit, ṣokoto, the precise kind
that Niyo was described as wearing. He also happened to be topless. This made sense for Niyo who existed in a tropical fictional
ethereal universe, but not for Malakai who was in a southern
town in England. It was about twelve degrees. It must have been
uncomfortable for him, but I was grateful for the choice. It allowed
me to see, with clarity, his gold chain glinting on the deep brown
of his chest, mimicking the protective amulet his character wore,
but more importantly, gave me a full view of his lightly-defined
six-pack, which, though not specially acquired for the occasion,
I appreciated anyway. His skin was deep and smooth and glinted
in the morning light, a sight for sleep-addled eyes, and just like
that, I was alert, energetic like I'd had ten hours of sleep. He had
sprayed his hair gold, in homage to the fact that in the story, Niyo's
curls had been fashioned from sunbeams. All of this combined to
somehow amp up his already unbearable levels of sexy.

I bit my lip. 'Malakai . . . ' my voice was a whisper. 'What are
you doing?'

I saw him shrug. 'We're going to RomCon. I found tickets on
the black market. Kidding. I took the wedding photos for this guy
who works in the marketing department of a ticket company, and
he said I could shout him for tickets whenever. Turns out they're
doing the tickets for this event. Our train leaves in an hour and a
half by the way. I got you slices of Tottenham cake for the journey.'

I couldn't breathe. 'Kai, are you serious?'

'I mean, I didn't bake them. I definitely got them from the
bakery last night, so they might be a little stale.'

'Not the cake. I mean, yes, the cake, but also the trip . . . Kai, it's too much!'

His voice was easy, jovial. 'Oh. You think this is for you? I have a bunch of books that need signing.'

I snorted and my eyes misted. Something in my chest swelled. I felt like I was being lifted by the sheer force of the butterfly wings batting within me. 'I can see your nipples from here. Could take an eye out.'

'Yeah, it's cold as fuck. They can double as weapons since I didn't have time to make his lightning staff. I'm gonna wear a T-shirt on the way there, but I just needed you to get the full effect. I also got a nose ring.'

I pressed my forehead against the window and Malakai tilted his head, angling it in a dramatic pose and, sure enough, I saw the tiny glimmering sliver of Niyo's characteristic thin silver piercing. 'Incredible.'

'It's definitely going to turn my nostril green. Worth it, though. I look sexy. Tupac is in Cuba, shaking. Be honest, does the gold hair make me look like Sisqó?'

'I don't know. Do the "Thong Song" for me right quick?'

When Malakai did, immediately bursting into the chorus, clutching his fist, I snorted. 'Yes. It's cute, though.'

Malakai's grin competed with the autumn sun, and instantly I was overwhelmed with an unidentifiable force that was strong enough to cause me to hang up, grab my key and rush out of my flat braless, in my crop top, jersey booty shorts and slippers, outside into the crisp November air and jump on to a surprised Malakai who apparently had been trying to call me back. I threw my arms around his neck, buried my face into it.

Malakai was only momentarily surprised; his arms instantly circled my body, pulling me to him, almost lifting me up, my T-shirt hitching a little, so my skin was against his skin. It was cold, but at this contact heat seared through me, making my pulse whirr. As we pulled slightly away, our rapid exhalations misted up and mingled in the tiny space between us; our arms stayed around each other.

'Kai, I don't know what to say. This is one of the sweetest things anyone has ever done for me. I can't believe you're standing in front of me in cosplay right now.'

Malakai's dark eyes shone and he was doing a shitty job at hiding the bashful grin spreading across his face. 'I'm kinda into it, you know. I think I pull this 'fit off.'

It was true. It was kind of scary, actually. He looked exactly how I imagined Niyo to look; Regally handsome. Kind.

'But,' he continued, 'as you know, Niyo is nothing without Shangaya. According to my calculations, you have forty minutes to get dressed. I already know you have your outfit. You ready, my Fireflower?'

I did already have my outfit. His use of Niyo's pet name for Shangaya made me smile. 'I don't think I'm ever going to get used to you going full nerd on me. But,' I released him, and started backing my way towards my halls, 'that ain't the question. The question is, are *you* ready for me as Shangaya?'

Malakai raised an eyebrow as he followed me into my building, shooting me a slanted smirk as he murmured, 'Oh. Rah. You think you got it like that, Scotch?'

'Nah,' I said, adopting Malakai's own swagger and mimicking his self-assured tone of the night we kissed, 'I know.'

'Are you sure you got that on camera?' I stared at the message on the page of my copy of *The Reign of Ifekonia: Search For The Sun*, eyes blurred and wide.

Malakai grinned at me from across the café table and nodded, 'Yes, Scotch, for the one-hundredth time, I have the film of Idan Fadaka signing your copy.'

'And the bit where she froze when I said my name and said it sounded familiar? When she said she remembers me from a panel she was on last year, because my question was so – what were the words she used?'

Malakai's smile widened. 'Incisive and thoughtful.'

'Incisive and thoughtful. And then what happened? Just to verify—'

'She said you made a beautiful Shangaya.'

'Oh my God, Kai. I know I'm being annoying, but I can't believe today happened!'

Malalakai shook his head, the movement somehow making the twinkle in his eyes glint sharper.

'Not annoying. I love seeing you like this.'

'Nerdy?'

'Yes.'

I threw a sugar sachet at him and he caught it with a hand, laughed. 'And happy.'

We'd been at the convention for half a day and it had been packed with panels and talks that Malakai was surprisingly engaged in, following me to every discussion that caught my interest, excitement and giddiness bouncing me all over the place. Malakai, it turned out, was the belle of the ball, his sharp beauty and height coupling well with his costume and character. He drew flirtatious stares and requests for photos, and Malakai, ever the ethereal prince, was always pleasantly game, smiling brightly for each snap, accepting each compliment with grace and enthusiastically talking about his character. When I went to meet him in the convention centre corridor after visiting the ladies, another Shangaya was talking to him, braided wig flipping over her shoulder as he handed her back her phone. My stomach swung low at the sight, breath moving stilted through my throat, irritated that I felt this way. I defaulted to the sacred chants I'd been using to pull myself together recently:

Malakai and I are friends.

This is a project.

Malakai does not like me in that way.

Malakai and I flirt because flirting is part of our friendship DNA.

Yes, we had that . . . moment the other night, but it probably just happened because we were both feeling vulnerable.

I decided to evolve the lengthy, clumsy, unpoetic chants for the occasion.

And, he isn't even here in the capacity of my fake boyfriend; he's here in the capacity of Friend. We are outside of the jurisdiction of the project, and he is free to do whatever he wants.

Just because he is dressed as my literary crush and therefore the literal embodiment of many an erotic fantasy, doesn't mean I can project.

Fuck, why is he so cute?

Malakai caught my eye, smiled and the chants became undone, because sure, we weren't together but did he really have to be so bold about flirting with someone in my presence? I felt like it lacked some couth, it wasn't cute and actually, fine, yes, I was jealous. Maybe it was because of the roles we were playing today, but how would he have liked it if I was all over another Niyo in front of his face?

My steps stuttered like my pulse did, and I slowed as it sped up. I waited until she left before forcing out a breezy smile. It didn't feel breezy upon release, however, it felt like a fucking gale force, a prelude to a storm.

'So, was that another Shangaya trying to taste your forever?'

Shit. I immediately wanted to pluck the words from the air and stuff them back into my mouth. My cheeks burned. I had been quoting the book, but I belatedly realised how wrong it sounded and unfortunately that wrongness mitigated my already question-able breeziness. I had all the easy breeziness of a hurricane.

Malakai shot me a slightly bemused look. 'I don't know about that, but she did ask me for my ProntoPic handle.'

I nodded and smiled wider, like the chill, carefree, unbothered girl I was, clamping my jaws down to contain the clump of aorta that had made its way to my mouth. The rest of my heart sank down to the pit of my stomach, squashing all the butterflies.

'Uh huh. That's, you know . . . ' I laughed, putting my hand on my hip to further denote casualness. When I realised it probably made me look like a stern Auntie, I dropped it. 'What's cool about this kind of place and what I personally love for you and for everyone else, including myself —' Why couldn't I talk like a regular human being? What was wrong with me? Oh God, was I having a stroke? A jealousy-induced stroke? '—is that you get to meet so many interesting new people.'

Malakai shrugged. 'Yeah. I guess. But, when I told her I had a girl she didn't want my handle anymore, so—'

I blinked. 'You told her you had a girl? Why?'

Malakai looked bemused. 'I told you I'd act as if we're in a real relationship and that's what I'm going to do. Do you want churros? I saw a pop-up churro stand somewhere.'

I added more chants.

Malakai's just method. He's focusing on the role of Boyfriend for our mutual academic success.

Ignore the butterflies. They're dumb and brainless and metaphorical.

It's probably a gastrointestinal issue.

I consume a lot of sugar and dairy.

Crushing on Malakai would be as fruitful as crushing on Niyo.

As we sat down and gorged on hot churros, I felt like I was floating, like I'd acquired the powers of the character I was dressed up as. My costume was much more subdued than Malakai's – he'd chosen the most extreme version of his character to embody. Mine was a slick, patent-pleather coat that fell so it hemmed the heel of my combat boots, high-waisted leather leggings and a black crop top. My eyebrows were more arched, deep black, framed with amber-like, stick-on gems, my lips painted wine, eyeshadow earth reds and sunsets. The costume had a placebo effect on me, making me feel all-powerful, all-capable and completely satisfied. Malakai's eyes brushed mine in a slight sweep.

'You really do make a beautiful Shangaya.'

I swallowed my smile. 'Thanks, mate.'

Maybe if I verbally reminded myself that we were just friends, it would be easier to kill my crush. I cleared my throat. 'When do our interviewees arrive?'

I'd got the idea to film at the convention – even though we were technically out of the physical remit for the film, I thought we could find a couple our age to interview, add a new dimension to the documentary. Malakai was immediately into it and picked out a couple while queuing for our churros. He'd got chatting to a guy who'd been brought to RomCon by his girlfriend, and who, apparently, had been instructed to order the exact same coffee specification as me, for her.

'Any second now. I think this one will be good; it's a dope idea to interview here, Scotch. It's so weird that his girlfriend likes the exact same kind of coffee-scented syrup like you, though—'

'First of all, shade noted and ignored. Second of all, I know, right? I wonder what else we'll have in common. Do you think she's also in a relationship to boost campus radio show ratings?' I muttered playfully.

'Chances are high. That's a pretty common relationship model. We ain't that special,' Malakai's gaze shifted; he nodded at something just beyond my head, grinning. 'And here they are now—'

'See! He's dressed up! Why couldn't you dress up?' the girlfriend's voice was teasing as she approached.

'Didn't want to steal your shine, baby.' Her boyfriend's retort was shot out smoothly before he theatrically, comedically, lowered his voice – presumably in the direction of Malakai, 'I thought I told you to change before we got here? Man's showing me up.'

Malakai laughed. 'Sorry Bro, but I'm feeling it.'

Malakai had got up, his default, easy manner radiating off him as he welcomed them. I, however, found myself glued to my seat, the multiple layers of leather sitting with a new weight on my skin, my mouth dry, chest twisted tight. The girlfriend's voice had an unmistakable familiarity, one that tugged and unravelled compacted memories, pulled at an unholy mix of sadness and inexplicable joy, an old, sophomoric, naive joy, the one that came with memories of learning a dance from a Beyoncé video on YouTube, secretly getting our belly buttons pierced together and perfecting our coffee orders together through trial and error before sipping them through straws as we strolled through our local mall on Saturdays. I had trained myself to feel nothing and now I found myself frozen by the avalanche of emotions that I'd forced away.

'Scotch,' Malakai was saying, gesturing to me. 'This is Amari and . . .' He faltered as he saw the expression on my face.

I wrenched myself up, turning to face our interviewees, and confirmed what I already knew.

'Rianne.'

The girl's wry smile dissolved instantly. 'Kiki?'

Malakai's eyes popped open as he looked back and forth between us. 'Oh. Oh, fuck.' The boyfriend just looked confused.

Rianne hadn't changed that much. She had the same beauty. Her nose was pierced now, like mine was, and her loose curls were left natural, buoyant around her face. Her dress was deep-blue and skimmed her curves to the floor. She was dressed as Yoa, subduer of the waters, Shangaya's mortal enemy-turned-ally-turned-friend. I felt like I was going to faint.

She turned to the boys, who were stood still, unsure what to do as they looked on, trying to figure out if they were in the midst of war. All I knew was that I had an instant stress stomachache. I was going to pass out.

'Hey . . . can we have a few minutes, please? If you don't mind,' she directed the last part at me.

Malakai turned to me, eyes horrified; he pulled me aside, lowering his voice, 'Kiki, I had no idea, I swear. I am *so* sorry. We can just drop this . . . Are you OK?'

I shook my head slowly, feeling stunned. 'Of course, you had no idea. I glanced at Rianne, who was watching us. 'I think I have to talk to her. I'll be fine.'

296

Malakai reached out to gently squeeze my elbow before nodding at Amari and finding a table nearby.

'It's good to see you, Kiki. Here, of all places,' Rianne's smile was so forced it was perplexing. 'I mean, I guess it makes sense if you think about it. We were obsessed with those books at school. Do you remember when we used to spend ages on those fanfic sites? God, how did we manage to pretend we were cool?'

I exhaled deeply and rubbed the bridge of my nose. Then it was as if I erupted. 'Rianne, what do you want? Like, what was the friend request about? Why are you tagging me in old pictures? Why are you acting like we're just two old friends catching up right now? Is this some kind of weird extended revenge plan, because I am sorry, I said it then and I'm saying it now. I just—' I was speaking faster now, trying to get words to outrun the tears I felt burgeoning, stinging my eyes, 'I'm sorry, I was drunk and then he was giving me more alcohol and then before I knew it, I—'

It took me a while to realise that Rianne was shaking her head frantically, her own eyes glistening. She reached out and grabbed my wrist. 'K, K . . . Fuck. I'm so sorry.' Wait, what? 'That's why I sent the friend request, that's why I tagged you in that picture. I just didn't know how to reach out to you. I've been so ashamed. I acted really, really badly—'

'Rianne, I get it—'

'No. No. I was wrong. I should have heard you out. But, Nile had this hold on me, you know? He told me that you'd been after him for a while, and I was an idiot not to have seen it. He was a manipulative prick, Kiki. He's the one that told me to block you

297

and, I don't know, he just had this way of making me feel like I was an idiot. We went out for maybe two, three months after that, and I really lost myself. And, at first, yeah, I was so, so pissed at you. But inside it never made sense to me. You wouldn't do that.'

'Ri . . . I was really drunk, and he was saying all this stuff and before I knew it, we were kissing, or he was kissing me, and then I pushed him off but he kept – I *swear* I pushed him off.'

Rianne's hold on my wrist tightened; her eyes were shiny. 'Stop. I know. I know. You don't have to rehash this for me, I promise. His version didn't make sense. I kept asking him what exactly had happened and he would get so mad, so I'd drop it. One time, we were having some argument about a cheating rumour – that turned out to be true, by the way – and he goes, "Fuck, why was I even loyal to you when Kiki tried it with me? I should have let her keep going. She was better with her tongue than you, anyway." Then, it was like something clicked. Like I'd been under some fucking spell and it had broken.

'I thought about the way he acted with me and put two and two together. And I *knew*. Fuck, Kiki, I have been feeling so sick about how I treated you. And you were going through so much and I was so selfish. I let him get between us . . . I'm sorry.' Her voice broke.

I flipped her hand so it was in mine. The relief I felt at her words, her understanding was soured by the nausea that rose at the thought of what she must have experienced with him – the anger at what he'd taken from us. Taking a deep breath, I squeezed her hand. 'Ri, it's OK. He messed with both of us. I'm just glad that you got away from him.'

Rianne's eyes filled further. 'There were so many times I wanted to call you. I wrote so many messages that I ended up deleting before I sent them. Our break-up really sucked for me, K.'

I swallowed, but still the words barely made it out of my throat, 'Yeah. It really fucking hurt for me too. Nile said . . . that you called me things. Really shitty things behind my back.'

'He was lying. Kiki, I swear. I never spoke badly about you to him, ever. He would say anything to gain power. The most fucked up shit.'

Her eyes were naked, earnest, desperate and once again I was hit with how thoroughly evil Nile had been. Her voice hovered above a broken whisper. 'What did he say I said?'

I swallowed and shook my head, knowing she would feel worse with this revelation.

'It doesn't matter anymore. Man. I think I lost my mind for a bit after the whole thing.'

'Same. I totally understand if you hate me.'

The nausea receded. 'What? Ri, whatever happens you're always going to mean a lot to me. I love you. I didn't stop.'

The tears spilled over from Rianne's eyes and she squeezed my hand back. 'I love you too, K. Can we like . . . start over, maybe?'

'I'd really like that.'

Rianne and I had grown and all the places we used to fit into one another had been filled or had evolved, the gaps sealed. We might not ever be best friends again, but there was potential there.

Hope. And now that we'd cleared away the debris of the past, we had access to the memories we'd created together and we could build something new on that foundation.

'I can't believe we're dressed as Shangaya and Yoa, sobbing at a convention centre coffee shop,' I muttered, as I drew a paper napkin from the silver dispenser on the table and dabbed the edges of my eyes with it.

Rianne snorted as she swiped beneath her eyes with her thumbs. 'Yeah, I know, man. Although when you think about it, it's pretty poetic. Also, speaking of coffee, I should have known it was you when I met a guy whose girlfriend had the same order as me. Does your man take the piss out of it too?'

'Yeah. A serious lack of taste.'

'Except when it comes to us.'

I snorted. 'Obviously.'

[Untitled_Love.Doc]
Director, producer: Malakai Korede
Consulting Producer/Interviewer: Kiki Banjo
Interviewees: Rianne Tucker, Amari Kamau

Kiki: What drew you to your partner?

Rianne: So, I was about a year out of what I now realise was a pretty emotionally abusive relationship. I lost . . . important things to me. Including myself. I made bad decisions. I was pretty fucked up from it, not gonna lie. I had trust issues, intimacy issues – all of it. I didn't date for my entire first year of uni. Like, at all. Anyway, I went away to work at this summer school in Kenya. When I got there, all the Aunties kept on saying that I needed to meet the other British uni student working there, that we'd get along so well. He was on a short break in Tanzania. The kids kept on saying that I was their second favourite teacher after Mr Kamau. That really pissed me off – I mean, me, second best? I hate competition!

Kiki: I know the feeling. Especially with a man. Gross.

Rianne: Right? *And* I gave them lollipops!

Amari: That's bribery, Babe. So as soon as I return, everyone's telling me that I need to meet Rianne. The kids are telling me she looks like a princess, the Aunties have already started buying their wedding hats – it's a lot of pressure, but then I meet her and bruv, I'm done for. Gone. Obviously, she's gorgeous, but she was also great with the kids, just so kind and patient.

Rianne: Amari came and I'm like OK, fine, fuck, he's a bit of me. You know my type, K – don't he look like my type? That other prick wasn't my type, but Amari?

Kiki: Yeah, it's like you built him. You always said your type was rap with a dash of R&B and a sprinkle of soul.

Rianne: Exactly. He's like the embodiment of that. Sweet, sexy, kind. Everyone was happy around him. He brought joy to any room. It's just that I wasn't in the right mindset. I went there to work. At first, I barely spoke to him—

Amari: Well, there was that time you said 'excuse me' on your way to the bathroom at a bar during a staff social. I remember that because the guys asked me if I needed a glass of water.

Rianne: This is the thing, I knew that if I talked to you, I wouldn't want to stop. I was scared of that. One day I caught him filling up the cookie jar in the staffroom with my favourite kind. I always wondered why we never ran out of them, and then I realised.

Kiki: Why didn't you initiate conversation, Amari?

Amari: So, I'm usually a confident guy. I never struggled with babes before . . .

Rianne: Chill.

Amari: But with this situation I just sensed . . . that I should wait. Wait till it felt like she wanted me to speak. But even without speaking, we connected. We made fun of the same things. I know because we would clock things at the same time and immediately find each other's eyes. You know that feeling? At first, I thought they were trying to hook us up because we're the only two Brits, right? But it was more than that. Well, we were the only Black Brits. There were a couple white English people, but the Kenyans weren't huge fans. Can I say that on

here? They were just doing way too much – you know, one of
them was wearing an Africa pendant.

Rianne: That's actually how we got together. We were just sitting with each other in the staffroom while I was scrolling my
phone, in silence, when the guy with the Africa pendant came
in. It was the first time we'd seen it. He was real posh, on a
"gap yah", talking about how he couldn't wait to tell his friends
back in the UK that he'd found a new spiritual home, and that
didn't we feel so connected to nature out here, like in a real,
base, *animalistic* sense. And the entire time, he kept touching
that fucking pendant. It was so bait that he wanted us to say
something. To compliment him. Anyway, as soon as he left, we
bust out laughing. Like howled. Then, Amari goes—

Amari: 'If I steal it for you, would you get a beer with me?'

Rianne: And I go, 'He probably sleeps with it on.' Amari says that
that just makes things more interesting.

[*Rianne grins and plucks a gold necklace out from beneath her neckline*]

Amari [*grinning back*]: Reparations.

Rianne: But honestly, even without him stealing from a man who
used to speak in some beg 'African accent' that sounded like a
hate crime—

Amari: I think it was a hate crime.

Rianne: I would have gone on a date with him. What I liked about him is that he didn't force anything. He gave us the space to happen.

Amari: But it was mostly the jewellery, right?

Rianne: What can I say? I'm a gold-digger.

The next morning, I was woken up early by a stream of dawn flowing into a room that was not mine but felt as safe as my space. I found myself warm, secured against a chest that was rising and falling softly against my back, Malakai's sweet tiger-cub snores were the only sound in the room.

After we got back from the convention and changed, Malakai ordered The Sweetest Ting to his place, where we indulged while watching old R&B videos, discussing the logistical issues of pleading for a woman on a street in the rain. It got late and our words slowed. I was already curled into his bed and Malakai offered to sleep on the floor, but I told him not to be silly, that it wasn't necessary, I trusted him. Then he'd offered to put a pillow between us and I'd said that it was cool, that it wasn't necessary, I trusted him. Why did I trust myself?

Half-asleep, I'd moved back, body curved in a tentative question mark. He didn't wake up, but he did respond, shifting closer to me, his breath tickling the nape of my neck. It felt too natural, too easy, too comfortable. The reasons around the comfort felt like they would be hot to touch, that they could burn, so I left it alone, but the comfort itself warmed me so I let myself settle in it.

I was lying there in joggers and not much else. During the night I had removed my cropped sweater to reveal my bright pink bralet. Malakai was shirtless but had kept his own joggers on too. I could feel his heart ticking away against my shoulder blade. When I reached over to pull his arm around my waist, he immediately fastened on to me, shifting his other arm behind his pillow, pulling me in closer, his lips just below my lobe.

'Scotch.' His voice was drowsy, delectable hot honey rumbling through my ear and directly to my core.

I swallowed, suddenly uncertain. 'Should I go?'

'Do you want to?'

'No.'

'Then I don't want you to.'

Then his lips were nipping at my ear, sending a shiver through the delightful loophole of our 'no kissing' rule. I was moving back against him and I could feel the depression and extension of his bare chest against my back, agitating my heart rate further, a throb that dropped below my waist as it rotated in a rhythm that he immediately, excruciatingly, matched. His hardness speaking directly to my softness and turning me molten in the places where it mattered. Malakai's teeth scraped the soft of my lobe, tugging it with a tender surety.

I felt myself becoming feral.

I swivelled under his arm to face him and, fuck, dawn suited him, landed sweet on him, and the narrow column of new sun made the blaze in his focus more intense. My stomach flipped, my pulse skipped, my breath tripped. His too-respectful hand remained on the incline of my waist, his thumb searing circles into my skin. I was just about to ask what is this, what is happening, what have we started? – when I saw a glimmer of something cross his face, a flash of something, something like – apprehension? It sent a nervous knot into my stomach despite the tie between us winding tauter and tighter by the second.

Malakai held my gaze, in a space I couldn't figure out the dimensions of, face inscrutable. His thumb stopped its hypnotic circuit on my hip. Then he removed his hand from my waist, dragged his knuckles down the side of my face, and said, 'Uh – actually . . .'

Heat fled my body. 'Oh.'

He swallowed. 'Maybe this isn't a good idea, what with your project and the film and us working together. It might confuse things—'

'Of course. Totally. You're right.'

I swiftly got up, grabbing for a sweatshirt that wasn't where I thought it was. Was it possible to die of embarrassment? I was sure it was happening. I was about to die in a fucking hot pink bralet. At least it made my tits look great. Not great enough for Malakai to want to kiss on them though. Would he speak at my funeral? '*Sweet girl,*' he would say with a tasteful glimmer in his eye. '*But I just wasn't into her like that.*'

Malakai sat up, and the soft, apologetic crease between his eyes felt like hands tightening around my throat. He ran a hand across his head. 'I'm sorry, I didn't mean to . . .' He trailed off, as if lost for words.

Didn't mean to *what?* Have me feeling like I would go insane if I didn't have his mouth on me? I almost laughed. Instead, I fished my sweatshirt from under the covers. 'Oh my gosh, please don't worry. *I'm* sorry.' I pulled it over my head and got up. 'I shouldn't even have . . . it's cool. And you're right. It would have been a bad idea. A terrible idea.'

'Kiki.'

I shoved my feet into my shoes and grabbed my phone and key card, still searching inside for my dignity, feeling around for the shape of it. I grasped at something with its semblance, crossing the room where I turned to face him, my hand curved around the cool of the metal door handle. Malakai's hand flew to the back of his head; he looked like he felt bad, like he felt sorry, and I hated it. I wished his rejection was more brittle; it would have been easier for me to cut it cleanly from me. But this, whatever this irritatingly soft thing was, was clinging on to me, tacking on to my fingers as I attempted to peel it off. It was more brutal.

'Erm . . . we're still on for this weekend at Ty's, right?'

In my mortified haze, I said something like, 'Yeah! Sure!' – too light, and garishly bright, like cheap jewellery. I know I blurted out something about an early seminar we both knew I didn't have before running back to my halls, as fast as my Ugg knockoffs would carry me.

CHAPTER 20

'What's up with her today? She didn't stay up long enough to give us a breakdown of all the Missy Elliot productions between 1995 and 2005.' Shanti's wry husk flowed through my sleep-addled brain from up front in the driver's seat of Mimi the Mini Cooper (christened after Mariah, Shanti informed us).

'Oh, she and Newbie had a fight or something. They'll figure it out. I mean it's not like he did cosplay for bants. He's *into* my sis,' Aminah's voice piped up from beside me. My mind was still too muddled to refute this. I hadn't told Aminah the details but she was Aminah enough to detect that something was off and not to push it until I was ready.

I slowly blinked my eyes open behind the oversized sunglasses I'd slipped on to keep the sharp winter sun from them. And to hide my puffy, sleep-deprived eyes.

Shanti shrugged, as she smoothly switched lanes on the

motorway so we were in the right lane to turn off towards Ty's country house, 'He better not fuck this up with her. Somehow, I know it was his fault.'

Chioma turned and reached back for the box of doughnuts situated between Aminah and I. 'Which one is vegan? The Pistachio White Chocolate? Cool.' She picked one up, 'Yeah, probably. Man, boys are idiots.'

Aminah hummed, 'Tell me about it. Yesterday Kofi was moaning about the fact that I called him bro in front of his boys at FreakyFridayz. He was all, "Minah, I ain't tryna be your bro. Why you tryna play me like that?" Play you like what? Bro is a neutral term of endearment.'

Shanti snorted. 'Yeah, not gonna lie, I'm with Kof on this one. "Bro" is the kiss of death.'

Chi cackled. 'Do you hate his guts, Aminah? There are kinder ways to let him down.'

'Meenz,' I said, fully awake now. 'I can't lie, that's pretty savage.' I stretched and pushed my sunglasses up to look at her. 'But then you're probably freaked out a little by how much you like him so called him "Bro" to distance yourself from your own feelings.'

Aminah raised a brow. 'Oh. She's alive? Where were you at FreakyFridayz, hmm? Maybe if you were there you could have an opinion.'

I dipped into what was left of the box of doughnuts. 'I was tired.'

Aminah didn't waste a second. 'You were hiding.'

Aminah and Chioma stared at me. Shanti also pointedly glanced

309

at me in the rearview mirror. I ignored them, and the truth, chewing slowly on my pistachio iced pastry.

Malakai and I had met at every FreakyFridayz by default for the past few weeks: it occurred seamlessly, and whoever arrived first got the drinks and waited in our booth in the Cuffing Corner for the other to join. We would then people-watch, sip, talk, tease, or play our new favourite game – Which Celebrity Could You Feasibly Seduce? – where we answered the titular question before breaking down how exactly it would occur. Our last round involved me and Trevante Rhodes at a house party (he would overhear me thoughtfully critiquing his last film and be intrigued) and in an impressive display of self-belief, Malakai's fantasy saw him seducing Doja Cat, while he filmed her tour documentary.

I'd skipped yesterday's FreakyFridayz though to recalibrate and to begin the work of convincing myself that what happened with Kai wasn't a big deal. Not only was the rejection still too raw, but I was pretty certain Aminah would curse out Malakai's entire lineage. Despite my humiliation, I didn't think it was entirely fair that his great-grandchild be doomed to hideousness and a lack of rhythm just because he didn't want to make out with me.

I exhaled and shifted uncomfortably in my seat. 'I . . . we need space' – which was the truth. Aminah pressed her glossy lips together, arching her brows so high they met the rims of the Dior sunglasses perched on her head, but she said nothing.

I had no idea what I was supposed to do. Sustained space from Malakai was unfeasible at this time. Brown Sugar's listeners were up by forty per cent, and we were now the third most-listened-to show on campus. A few more weeks and it stood a chance at being Number One, which would make my place on the programme a shoo-in. There was also the guilty fact that Shanti and Chioma didn't know the technicalities of Malakai and my relationship yet, something that had proved increasingly difficult the closer I got to them.

I swallowed. 'I just want to get through this weekend, man. Link-ups like these aren't my thing and now Malakai and I are weird and—'

Shanti made a loud retching noise and glared at me through the rearview mirror. 'No moaning in Mariah, unless it's from me hooking up with a spice! Not only do you have *us* this weekend, you also have a footballer's mansion with a hot tub.'

Aminah nodded. 'Dassrite. We got tequila, you look cute and Ty said in the group chat that we're gonna do nineties–noughties karaoke, the era you're the most annoying about—'

'And,' Chioma's voice fizzed, 'I made vegan brownies last night. They're in the boot.'

Chioma sighed into the silence she was met with. '*Weed* brownies, guys—'

A whoop, a holler and a 'why didn't you say so?' whipped the air in Mimi into a joyful frenzy that jolted through me and slid over the unease I felt about Malakai. I was going to a social event with a group of girls for the first time in a long time, and in the place of the stomach-tightening trepidation I expected, came a thrum of warm comfort. I didn't want to climb out of my skin or burrow myself further into it, I felt safe within it, with these three girls.

I laughed. 'You're right. My bad. Sorry for being a downer. Killa Keeks officially activated for the weekend.'

'There she is!' Aminah grinned.

The girls' trills escalated as I connected my phone to the Bluetooth and selected a Destiny's Child classic. 'And she is feeling,' the beginning disparate twangs of the songs filled the car, before we simultaneously shout–screamed, '*So good!*' A song title: a proclamation. We dove into the lyrics, punctuated by giddy giggles, hair flicks and a lot of pointing as we informed an invisible nemesis that we were doing mighty fine.

'Lads, the *QUEENS* have arrived! Make yourself decent!' Ty's muted voice leaked through the wide doors of the stone farmhouse, a surprisingly elegant, nouveau-riche architectural concoction of both glass and stone, as they fell open and revealed his broad grin and handsome face. He was in his usual weather-ignorant attire of shorts and a T-shirt, apron that read *'Mr. Good-Lookin' Is Cookin'* teetering across his broad torso.

While his father was a football star, Ty was an English-lit studying, towering, bulked-out-gentle Adonis, who preferred chilling with his Blackwell crew to the chaotic raucousness of his rugby team, who were known to make 'jokes' about the reason for his strength on the field (he was Black! That was the joke.). His golden face glowed as he beckoned us into the warm amber crush of the house, scented with the expensive candles his mother owned, the

312

faint aroma of BBQ, and a cocktail of colognes — within which Malakai's rose to meet me, clean, inviting and excruciating. My skin pricked.

'You're the first squad to arrive.'

Squad. I was in a squad now. I waited for the anxiousness to find me. It didn't. I smiled at Ty as he took off his backwards-placed cap and bowed deeply before us.

'So glad The Blackwell Baddies are here to save me from these barbarians.'

I quirked a brow. 'The Blackwell Baddies? Is that what we're called now?'

'Well, that's what Shanti referred to you guys as when I asked what time you'd all be getting here.'

Ty was generous with his smile, but he gave more of it to Shanti as he took in her cute, curve-hugging, pink athleisure co-ord. It was clear he wasn't as concerned about our group's arrival as he was about hers. She smirked and smoothed a hand over her sleek ponytail, 'Our presence is a present—'

'Kiss your ass?' He paraphrased the end of the bar with a twinkle all of us caught.

Shanti's response was an expertly cool gaze. She passed Ty her overnight bag. 'Where does your dad keep his scotch? Don't cheap out on me, Baptiste.'

She swayed past him, and Ty followed her through into his own house, entranced.

Aminah, Chi and I were exchanging smirks when Kofi appeared with a tray of libation. 'Welcome to The Chateau, ladies.' He nodded at Aminah as she took a tiny glass of clear liquid. 'You all right, mate?'

Aminah almost choked on her shot, eyes wide at Kofi's impressive pettiness but he'd already turned to me. 'Keeks, Malakai's been in a mood since we got here. Whatever is going on with you two, fix it. You don't want to lose me in the custody battle.'

'Nothing is going . . . '

Malakai emerged from the wide hallway, and my words stumbled and fell down my throat at the sight of him in his basketball shorts and hoodie, the scruff on his jaw. His casual fineness was quite inconducive to my plan of extricating myself from my feelings. I hadn't seen or spoken to him in a few days, and the shape of him instantly fell into a space I hadn't known was there. I felt the inexplicable need to climb on him. His hand flew to the back of his head, his eyes soft, hesitant. I downed my shot, hoping it would push my heart back to its proper position.

Kofi gave me an unnecessarily pointed look before ushering everyone to the living room. When Malakai reached to take my overnight bag, our fingers brushed; a streak of heat shot through me. Unhelpfully, it seemed the other night had only made me more physically sensitive to him, a drop of water driving a parched desert wanderer rabid.

'Hi.' Probably detecting that I was a horny monster, he stood back, for his safety.

I swallowed. 'Yo.' *Yo?*

'You didn't show up at FreakyFridayz last night.'

I shook my head. 'I got caught up with work. My bad.'

314

He held my gaze and I held my breath, the quiet sitting awkwardly between us. Thankfully, somewhere in the house, the group started to play a game.

I raised a brow and forced myself to speak. 'Did I just hear the words "tequila pong"? It's 12 p.m.'

Malakai released a quarter-smile. 'You know how bars are open at 6 a.m. at the airport? That's what this place is like. Time doesn't exist. Anything goes. Ty's already insisted on a barbeque, doesn't give a fuck that it's ten degrees. He's calling this party the "Blackwell Bacchanal". After I googled "bacchanal" I got kinda shook.'

The straightness of his face bypassed the tension and tickled a sexy snort out of me. His eyes sparked in surprise at my pig-in-heat giggle and his smile widened a little before he paused and took a half-step closer to me. 'Listen, I know this weekend might be a lot for you and it isn't your thing, so if you ever wanna bow out or take a break, just shout me. I'll make an excuse and we can go somewhere.'

The newly re-erected protective bars around my heart bucked and bent. He'd disarmed me so swiftly; I never saw it coming. I needed to see it coming.

'Thanks, but I'm good. I got my girls. Besides, this is a relationship, cementing outing. We have to be here together, because which self-respecting Blackwell woman leaves her man alone at a Ty Baptiste party? Especially if that man is Malakai Korede?' Something in Malakai's eyes flickered and I cleared my throat. 'I gotta play it smart.' I took my bag from his grip and stretched a smile on my face. 'Go join them, I'll drop this in the room.'

I tapped his arm in what I hoped was a casual and friendly manner and moved towards the stairs.

'Kiki.'

I didn't turn around, focusing instead on the incredibly expensive-looking chandelier above me, my words rushing out, stumbling over themselves, clumsily stretching out tangled conclusions. 'Malakai, it's calm. No stress. You didn't want to kiss me. And even if . . . a part of you wanted to kiss me, you changed your mind. You're entitled to do that . . . physically wanting to kiss someone and mentally wanting to are two different things, and I respect that. And I get it, because let's face it, the reality of it . . . of *me* is messy.' I took a deep breath. 'My ego is bruised, but that's all it is. It was for the best, anyway. You don't have to explain yourself.'

I didn't think it was a terrible speech, considering. The main points were conveyed. I was above the drama and I was evolved enough to accept rejection. I would have got an easy pass if this was a seminar presentation.

Malakai cleared his throat. 'I was gonna say that our room is the second on the right.'

I closed my eyes and willed the chandelier to fall on me. When it refused my command, I nodded in grim acceptance. 'Noted. Thank you.'

I walked primly up the broad, spiralling staircase with the firm knowledge that I needed to get thoroughly drunk tonight.

'Keep still,' I wound my arms around Malakai's neck and hitched my legs tighter around his waist. His grunt reverberated through his chest to mine and his hands slipped under my legs for a firmer grip, but he continued hopping from one foot to the other. Our faces were inches apart, so close that our hot tequila tainted breaths were mingling.

'The hell are you doing?'

'Warming up.' He decided to dip and stretch a leg with me still clamped on to his chest like a marmoset on a branch.

'It's a race to the end of the room where I have to direct a blind-folded you to a table that holds a shot of tequila that you have to pick up with your teeth and pour into my mouth without spilling it. You don't need to warm up for that. Light work.'

Malakai smiled and, despite the silk scarf I had used to tie around his eyes, I could see the spark in them.

'I'm an athlete, Kiki. Let me do my ting.'

I rolled my eyes.

'You just rolled your eyes, innit.'

'How do you know?'

'I don't need to see you to see you.'

My belly twisted. *Fucker*. Bold of him to say those words while we were in a position where it would only take a slight consensual shifting for there to be a real risk of pregnancy.

While it was true that I had entertained, tiny, vignette fantasies of climbing on Malakai like I was a squirrel scurrying up an oak tree, this wasn't quite how I envisioned doing it. Malakai was a finalist in the Lit-Lympics, a competitive event founded by

Ty Baptiste, in which participants had to partake in a series of athletic challenges that ended with one or more shots of alcohol. The prize was the main bedroom with the en-suite hot tub with a consenting partner of one's choosing. The notion of group games usually made my blood turn icy, but due to the high stakes of this particular one (the hot tub) and the fact that Malakai's participation necessitated my involvement, here I was. As the second of Ty's three dress codes had been 'beach chic' (he had turned the heating up in the house to create a tropical Sussex microclimate), I was wearing a neon-yellow-sleeveless crop top and stone washed booty shorts, while Malakai had unbuttoned a red, blue-and-yellow geometrically patterned shirt which was paired with board shorts. His bare skin bumped against my chest as he warmed up.

'You're just flexing for your mates.'

Ty was currently doing squats with Shanti fastened to him, keeping count. Kofi had made up with Aminah after she gave him a shoulder massage to prep him for the previous event. Right now he was doing some kind of intricate warm-up dance footwork while Aminah smoothed down her hair. Neither of them had their blindfolds on yet. I'd made Malakai put his on early as a safeguarding precaution for myself. Eye contact was still too dangerous.

Ty's family conservatory was large, running almost the entire length of the house, and all pool tables and exercise bikes had been cleared for this last event. More people had since arrived for the party and so each side of the floor-to-ceiling glass room was lined with Blackwellians with red cups in hands, buzzed by the notion that Ty might actually be beaten by a newcomer.

Both Malakai and I had had more than a couple of drinks by now, muddling through interviews that got easier as the alcohol released dormant flirtatious energy that ran hot over the awkwardness. I knew I was supposed to be uncomfortable, knew that I was meant to be mad at him for playing with me like this, but I allowed myself the indulgence of feeling the sweetness of the lie before I repressed the instinctive quickening of my pulse. This was a performance and Malakai was nothing if not a showman – the playful hollers and whistles couched us so warmly it made me feel cold. All Malakai was doing right now was running drills to flex and train flirtatious muscles. He was trying to avoid Fuckboi atrophy. This was purely medical. I was a physiotherapist.

I grabbed his chin and a hold of myself. 'Focus. I need you to get into beast mode. Our main competition is Ty. He has Shanti, and he's gonna wanna show out for her. He has something to prove. Kofi will be too flustered by Aminah's proximity to focus.

'We have to win this. We're gonna have them eating dirt. Well, this house is super-clean so, like, licking the marble.' I paused. 'We're gonna have them getting mild poisoning from the disinfectant, just a couple of trips to the bathroom, nothing major.'

There were a couple of silent beats until Malakai breathed out. 'You're kind of a competitive sociopath, aren't you Banjo?'

'Shut up.'

'I like it.'

'Anyway, I'm gonna hoist my butt slightly up to alleviate the pressure on your—'

'Kiki, chill. I got you.' He gripped tighter onto my thighs.

'You better have. I'm at a really juicy part in the latest Ifekonia book, Shangaya and Niyo are in a mountain cave. They just had a heated argument and they're definitely about to have angry sex. The hot tub would be a perfect place to get into it.'

'I'mma get you that horny reading hot-tub time, Scotch.'

It was the first time he'd called me Scotch since the other night. It sank into me, sat warm under my skin, made my heart buoyant enough to jump to my mouth and push out a smile that I didn't tuck in fast enough. I was grateful he was blindfolded. The potency of whatever permeated the air between us seared through my confusion over the other night.

'All right sistren, brethren, them-thren.' Chi, our self-proclaimed gamesmaster, gathered our attention. She was perched on top of Ty's dad's home bar in the corner of the room, a bottle of tequila in one hand and a karaoke mic in the other.

'On your marks!'

I had a last-minute anxiety spike, imagining being dropped on my ass in front of the Blackwell elite and having it immortalised in gif form on Simi's blog.

'You better not let me go, Kai.'

'Get set!'

Malakai bent his knees slightly, his hold on my thighs firm.

'Already made that mistake the other night.'

What?

'Go!'

320

After our triumph was declared I untied my scarf from his eyes and they were ready for me, waiting for me, searing through my flimsy resolve to not let him in again, because who was I kidding, he was already here. My chest had grown a hook for him to hang his smile on whenever he came around. He reduced all half-reconstructed walls around me to magma. I was in trouble, had been in trouble since I first set eyes on the kid.

The party around us began to roar back into action, as Ty clapped his back in good sportsmanship, as the tunes picked up pace and volume under Kofi's resumed authority, and as my whirling literary analysis of Malakai's words gathered speed. *Already made that mistake the other night.* I hopped down from him, but his hands stayed on my waist and my arms stayed around his neck. He opened his mouth to speak, but then Chi was pulling my arm up from Malakai's neck, looping hers through mine and dragging me away. Shanti promised that they would return me in one piece while pushing a cup of something syrupy and potent into my hand. Aminah loudly commanded Kofi to play our newest favourite song.

Then we were dancing, and the lights dimmed and my thoughts became looser, and though it became harder to grip on to what Malakai had said, the taste of it stuck to the roof of my mouth, and I realised that there was something sweet there, something intoxicating there, stronger than what was in my cup. As I rolled my tongue around its possibility, I got more excited. But then there was the burn. The thrill quickly got chased with fear. He could have just been playing, saying things just to say things. I looked across the room and he was with his boys by the drinks;

he caught my eye and stole a heartbeat. There was too much to lose here – my head, my heart.

I was getting waved right then and my girls were waved, and it rolled under us and merged with the rhythm to pull us into the middle of the room. We went with it, hand in hand in hand, weaving through a crowd that had somehow doubled in size within the last hour. I lost sight of Malakai but found myself in a cluster with the girls where we fell into moves that called and responded to each other, that were in conversation, hips calling each other's to come join, and I found myself laughing. I was here, with my girls, and our hair was swishing, and our booties were teasing gravity and we were whining on each other and delighting in each other. I was in this. I wasn't on the outside anymore. Our laughter was a featuring artist on every banger and it made it better. We rapped, we sang, we rolled and we dipped as our bones became tender with the heat of the beat. The chandeliers in the garden house shimmied in appreciation.

Ty bellowed, 'The Blackwell Baddies in-fucking-DEED', gassing us, knowing we didn't need gassing, gassing us knowing it was surplus because our energy was self-generated. Phones whipped out to film the movie we were all in and Kofi chose a song just for us, the rhythm bowing for us. Then, a hand on my waist. I turned around and Malakai addressed a question to the group while barely looking away from my face.

'Sorry to interrupt ladies.' He smoothly avoided someone kicking him on the makeshift dancefloor while gbese-ing to Burna Boy. 'You think I can have her back now?'

Aminah rolled her eyes. 'Temporarily.'

Malakai bowed. 'Many thanks.'

Chi smacked my ass and Shanti stuck her tongue out as Malakai took my hand and drew me to the corner of the room, and I floated through, high and happy, panting, feeling pretty.

He ran his eyes across me, his smile faint. 'This looks good on you, Scotch.'

I leant against the wall. 'What does?'

'Everything.'

He took a moment.

'I owe you an explanation.'

The tempo had switched through the speakers, and a grown and sexy Afrobeat song flowed through, playful, soulful, sensual, created for slow misbehaviour. I wanted this moment to stay still for a while – there was no denying what was between us right here and now and nothing he said would have changed that.

'Yes, you do. Dance with me first.'

Malakai blinked and then smiled something hot and narcotic and sweet. He took my hand and pulled me forward, his hands moving to my waist, as I slowly rotated it. His gaze followed the motion, transfixed, my hips his North star, and I turned around and pressed my back against his chest. The beat acted like a catalyst to whatever chemical reaction was occurring, had been occurring, would be occurring within us, causing our bodies to answer the questions our mouths were too nervous to ask.

My back arched gently and Malakai's hands curved across my hips, pulled me slightly closer to him.

'I'm sorry Scotch.' Malakai's breath was hypnotically warm against my ear, his grip still tight on me – the song had changed but the tempo remained the same, giving us an excuse to stay like this.

I swallowed. 'What for?'

'Making you feel like I don't want you.' He stopped moving, spinning me around so I was facing him, his hands still resting on my hips.

'Kiki, I want you. Been wanting you. And I wanted you so bad the other night. The reality of you isn't messy, it's . . . man, it's perfect. I'm the mess. That's why I got freaked out. I mess things up, Scotch. If I fuck this up, I will never forgive myself. This isn't a casual thing to me. You're not just a link to me. You're *it* to me.'

His sentences were fired in searing, sharp bullets as if he didn't speak them quickly they would melt in his mouth. Malakai was looking at me, eyes bright and wild, yet stricken, apparently waiting for me to weigh up the truth of what he just said or figuring out if it was light enough to haul it back to him without me noticing. Too late. It was out there, too heavy to throw banter over, too impactful for us to revert back to how we were before.

Words were not at my disposal at that moment, and the only thing remotely resembling solid thought in my mind was the internal siren instructing me to kiss him. As I curved my hand around his neck and his face inched closer to mine, a bellow shattered the delicate spell above the room.

'Hear ye, hear ye, the KING has arrived. Yo, Ty, did my invite get lost in the post or something?'

Who else would pronounce their own entrance? Who else

would command people to bow in their presence? Who else could make the butterflies in my belly, flutter down and curve their wings around each other in protection? And who else would roll through with Simi in front of him, the harbinger of chaos, wearing a glossy, demure smile on her face and a floor-length, red body-con with a thigh-high slit?

Zack Kingsford walked into the room, a bottle of Cîroc in his hand, smile wide, eyes scanning the party until they found mine. He winked.

CHAPTER 21

'Never have I ever hooked up with more than one person in this room.' I stiffened and Malakai muttered, 'You have to be fucking kidding me.'

The party had migrated to the Baptistes' Moroccan-style family room and while it was nice being curled up against Malakai at the foot of a sofa, we also had the misfortune of being sat opposite Zack.

Simi was shaking her head at him. 'You're really so fucking crass, Zack.'

'And yet,' I said, angling a sharp look at her, 'you brought him here.'

Simi shrugged. 'Whatever happened to community spirit?'

Aminah's eyes narrowed and Shanti rolled hers from the sofa they were sat on, bracketed by Kofi and Ty. Chi cleared her throat diplomatically.

'We're not playing 'Never Have I Ever', Zack. We're playing the numbers drinking game,' Chioma said with a tight smile from her position cross-legged on a cushion.

Since his unceremonious entrance, Zack had succeeded in making everyone feel slightly uncomfortable. He rolled through the party with his crew and without shame, feeling like a jurisdiction unto himself, knowing that Ty was too peaceable to say shit. Ty didn't like trouble, and so, though his smile dimmed a little, he welcomed Zack in, let him divert the party to another gear. Ty figured we would get the drinking games Zack suggested out of the way before continuing the party, just to shut him up. This was, of course, under the misguided notion that Zack wasn't obsessed with the sound of his own voice.

Zack hadn't said a word to me since he'd arrived, but he was always near, always talking around me, beside me. Malakai had taken my hand, squeezed it, looked me in the eye and said, 'You sure you're OK, Scotch? We can go.' And I'd replied, nah, that there was no way I would leave anywhere because of Zack. Now I slightly regretted that decision as Zack repeated his question and necked his drink, looking straight at me.

'Come on,' he grinned. 'Can't only be me who's shared the love.'

He wasn't expecting an answer; he just wanted my attention. He also wanted to remind Malakai that he'd accessed me first.

Zack directed his gaze at Malakai. 'Ayy, that's right. Who was it again? Chioma, Shanti and some others, you been about, innit?'

He was trying to rile Malakai. I felt him tense, but his voice remained level as he looked at Zack. 'Is there a point to this?'

Zack laughed. 'No vex. Look, man, I'm just trying to get to know you. There must be something special about you to make you the first guy on campus that Kiki claims.' Zack had strangely mutated the way he spoke when talking to Malakai, slackened his tongue to mimic Kai's Naija-flavored south London accent. It made me feel queasy.

His eyes roamed over to me. 'Because you're picky, innit? Any man that's had a chance to be with you is blessed.'

I held his gaze. 'Anyone want a snack? Crisp bowl is empty . . . I'll be right back.'

Aminah shifted to follow me but I shook my head. Malakai's brows furrowed gently.

I forced a smile out, murmuring, 'I'm good. He's gonna wait a minute and then follow me out. Let him. I need to deal with this by myself.' Malakai didn't look convinced, but he released a tensed jaw nod.

I'd just emptied a bag of Chilli Heatwave Doritos into a large far-too-fancy crystal bowl in the sprawling farmhouse kitchen when I felt his presence behind me.

'You're a prick, Zack.'

I put the bowl down and turned around, leaning against the counter to look up at his infuriatingly easy grin. He bent forward to grab a crisp and pop into his mouth. 'Don't play like it's not what you like about me.'

'I promise, I like nothing about you. Why are you here?'

He shrugged a shoulder. He was, of course, wearing a muscle T-shirt. He technically looked good because he always technically

328

looked good. Everything was measured to the sum of Handsome but all I felt for him at this moment was revulsion. His pretty made my teeth ache, his cologne was suffocating and his eyes had a sickly shine to them. Was it possible for a vagina to invert?

He stepped closer to me. 'Ain't it obvious? Kiki, I'm here for you. I'm not an idiot. You kissed him to make me jealous and it worked. Not talking to you is killing me.'

It was a premise hinged on the baffling delusion that we ever talked in the first place. I smiled sweetly, 'Then die.'

As usual, my words didn't land. He was living in his own American teen soap opera. This was a pivotal moment in Kingsford Valley. He squinted, reaching out to caress my face. I shifted and his hand dropped.

'I fucking hate seeing you with him. You can drop the act—'

'Zack, I'm with Malakai because I want to be with him.' The lie didn't taste like one.

'Babe.'

'I'm very close to a bread knife, right now. It's serrated.'

'We can do this for real, this time. I see you, going to parties, *out there*, now. Imagine us doing that together? Ruling this place? Every king needs a queen.'

I snorted. 'You're a democratically elected leader, but since elections are coming up, maybe not for that long. There are a few more people contesting this year, innit? I saw on the blogs. People aren't happy with your policy of being useless. Speaking of, what the hell are you up to with the Whitewell Knights? How long do you think you can play both sides for?'

Something in his gaze shifted, but he carried on smiling at me. 'I'm trying to strengthen our foothold in Whitewell. Form an understanding. Blackwell just needs to see the vision. You can help with that. Together we're a dream team. You endorse me on your show, maybe I can have you on my platform as VP. I mean you have amazing ideas, and—' He stopped as the cackle burst forth from me.

Why did I ever think Zack wasn't funny? Zack was fucking hilarious. He didn't even have what it took to be less transparent, he didn't have enough personality to couch his shallowness in. Before, he wanted me because I'd rejected him – it was purely about possession and pride – but now it was because I was a tool for him. My feelings were just a tedious obstacle to manoeuvre around till he reached his goal.

I stepped closer to him and started speaking extremely slowly. 'Zack, let me make this as clear as possible for you. I don't want you. I won't ever want you. You are not going to use me to win this election just because I have a few hundred more followers on ProntoPic and Brown Sugar's numbers are going up. And, you need to back the fuck up right now, before I grab the kitchen knife behind me and make this party a murder mystery.'

Zack moved back, but only slightly. 'You're crazy.'

'I am.'

'It's sexy.'

'Get away from me—'

'Kiki.' He reached out to grab my arm just like he'd done at FreakyFridayz, but his hand dropped away at the sound of the firm male voice behind him.

330

'You didn't hear what she just said?'

Despite knowing I could handle Zack, my heart flipped at the sight of Malakai. It wasn't that I thought Zack could hurt me, but it was his imposition on my space, the fact that he saw rejection as a game he could win. Confusingly, Simi followed him in, for no other purpose, it seemed, than to bear witness to drama.

Now, Zack stepped away, back straightened, chin angled up. 'Chill, man. We were just catching up. Reminiscing, right?'

The anger roiled in my blood. 'You're fucking sick.'

Malakai had walked further into the room, standing next to me and opposite Zack. His voice was calm and low but there was fire trapped in its cool, an inferno trapped in steel. 'Yeah, I think you're done here.'

Something ugly flickered in Zack's eye, a glimpse of what was beneath his pretty. His smile was a snarl. 'You know, it's mad you and I aren't boys. We have a lot in common. We're handsome, have the same taste in women.'

Malakai stilled. 'Walk away, man—'

Zack picked up the beer he had placed on the counter and shrugged. 'Relax. I'm going. But come to me for advice whenever you wanna know how to make Kiki feel good.'

'Zack, what the *fuck* is wrong with you?' He was so predictable in the worst ways but Malakai had pushed himself forward from the counter, angling himself so he was in front of me. His jaw clenched as if he was trying to contain something. 'Talk about Kiki one more time.' Voice placid, a cobra quiet in its coil.

Zack laughed.

The fact that four of us were missing from the main party must have rung alarm bells because, in that moment, Aminah, Shanti, Chioma, Ty and Kofi entered the kitchen. I was holding on to Malakai's wrist, and felt his pulse quicken; the air in the room soured and thickened.

'Kai, he isn't worth the energy.'

Kofi had moved in closer, eyes narrowed, and the girls tried and failed to pull me from Malakai's side. I'd noticed that Simi had picked up her phone. Did she really hate me enough to live tweet my drama?

'Zack, go home.' Ty's usually affable demeanour had shifted, as he levelled a glare at Zack that made it clear why his opponents were terrified of him on the field, the full bulk of him seeming magnified. Malakai's fists were balled tight. It was as if his whole body was vibrating in restraint.

Zack smiled menacingly, and gestured to the room. 'Shit man, everyone's so tense. Chill. I'm just being friendly to the new kid. I'm just saying I can be like . . . ' his smile widened, 'your tour guide or study buddy for Kiki. I can give you tips. I know all the right spots to make her—'

It happened in a blink. Malakai leapt towards Zack, making him drop his beer, grabbing him by the shirt and shoving him against the kitchen island. Though Zack attempted to fight back, Malakai had him pinned. The boys moved to break up the fight just as the girls successfully disrupted my attempt to reach Malakai, pulling me away. Two of Zack's boys belatedly entered the kitchen, too drunk to make out what was happening, but somehow figuring out that it might be too late to save their man after seeing Ty's involvement. They made noises that approximated macho aggression and pretended to try and get involved just in case anyone clocked their cowardice.

Malakai breathed hard, his fist hovering as Ty and Kofi held him back. He eventually dropped it with reluctance but maintained his grip on Zack's shirt. He lowered his voice. 'Let me not catch you fucking breathing in her direction again.'

Kofi released Malakai, his eyes on Zack. 'We won't hold him back next time.'

Ty stood between Malakai and Zack, ensuring he was towering down over him. 'We'll help.'

Zack made a strangled sneer of paltry hypermasculine bluster as he pulled himself up and readjusted his shirt. 'Whatever man. Pussies. Party's dead, anyway,' before summoning his boys to leave. He nodded at me, 'You know where to find me.'

I released a false, wide grin and chirped, 'Rot in hell.'

Simi, clearly bored by the absence of a true fight, had already made her way out. The boys made sure Zack and his minions were moving along while the girls assisted with a chorus of cusses: Shanti shouting, 'Shoo, motherfucker,' as Aminah released a string of Yoruba curses and Chi made sounds that might have been a summoning of malevolent ancestors. A strange lump formed in my throat as I watched them, and I felt my eyes start to fill.

'You OK?'

I turned to Malakai to see the wild fury in his eyes had now mutated to soft concern. I exhaled heavily. 'Yeah, I just . . . I haven't really had a group of people . . . friends, stand up for me before. It means a lot. And I hate that I brought all this drama here.'

Malakai's brows creased, as he reached for my shoulders, holding them with gentle hands. 'Scotch, we care about you. A lot . . . And you didn't bring the drama. Zack did. I'm sorry I didn't listen to you about not following you, I really did try and wait it out, but I couldn't sit there knowing you were alone with that fucking creep. Are you sure you're OK?'

'I am. Thank you. I just . . . I don't feel like going back to the party.'

Malakai nodded slowly. His unaddressed confession was now radiating heat. 'Yeah. Me neither.' He drew his eyes across my face and all our unsaids swirled about and made it stickier, harder to breathe. Questions hung in the air, dripped onto our tongues, made us thirsty. 'I have a lot of footage from tonight, and we got enough interviews. Would it be super-unsocial if we—'

'I think we should claim our prize. Ty said the main bedroom has an eighty-eight-inch TV. Has all the streaming apps. The bed is Alaskan king-sized.' I gestured at the huge kitchen with the equivalent of a Tesco Metro stocked on every counter. 'And I think we're good for snacks and drinks.'

Malakai released a small, sweet smile that trilled a charge through my veins.

'All right then. Afterparty. Just us.'

CHAPTER 22

I flopped down next to where Malakai was reclining on the giant bed, leaning up on his elbow. The bounce of the mattress jostled me, so my bare thigh grazed his leg and my arm pressed against his. Everything stilled.

He turned to me and smiled, the amber light from the bedside lamp warming his face further as the movie we'd put on – *Brown Sugar*, as a half-joke – burred low on the colossal flatscreen. His eyes sent a thrill through me as they skipped across my form. 'You should keep that shirt.'

I'd forgotten to pack my pyjamas in my confused state, so Malakai had loaned me a T-shirt while he had changed into his sweats. His shirt skimmed me in a way that somehow made me hungrier for him. A sudden urgency wrapped an idea around my tongue. 'Let me do you.'

Malakai froze. 'What?'

'Let me *interview* you.'

I slipped off the bed and padded over to the grand mahogany desk at the corner of the Baptistes' main bedroom, picked up Malakai's camera and flicked it on. I beckoned Malakai over, and he sat on the chair in front of me. I perched on the broad desk and lifted a leg so my foot rested beside him on the chair. His gaze jumped to my thigh – inches from his face – then back to my eyes.

'Malakai Korede.'

'Oh, we're really doing this?'

I smiled as I tilted the camera towards him. 'It's your turn.'

'That angle is really bad—'

'It's arty.'

'It's wonky. Also, the lighting.'

I switched on the reading lamp on the desk. 'There. See?'

Malakai laughed. I cleared my throat theatrically, then said in a crisp, journalistic tone, 'Malakai Korede, I have a few questions to ask you. The first being . . .' I let my eyes wander from the lens to his face, '. . . you sure you like me?'

The sudden blaze in Malakai's eyes answered me before he said, 'Yes.'

Still, I needed to make sure this new ground was sturdy before I stepped onto it. I swallowed, forced myself not to whisper. 'No, I mean . . . are you *sure* sure? On a scale of one to ten, where would you rank your certainty?'

Malakai got up from the chair, standing between my legs. 'Eleven.'

I leant back on the desk, lifting my other leg so it was on

the stool, effectively bracing Malakai between my thighs. 'That's impossible.'

'You're impossible, so it's possible.'

Malakai's eyes flashed into mine. He took the camera from me, switched it off, carefully placed it on the desk. He stepped into me, our chests now bumping, our faces so close together I could swear I was getting tipsier by the champagne on his breath. It tasted potent. His eyes scanned my face, his hand lifting to it, cupping my cheek.

'You are everything, Scotch. I like your mind. I like seeing it work up close. I like your eyes, especially when you're rolling them at me. Yeah. Just like that. I like how you see things. Adds colour to how I see things. I like that when you're listening to a song you love, you close your eyes and let it take you places. I wanna go wherever you go to.

'I like your mouth.' His eyes dropped to it and I felt my lips tingle. 'Not gonna lie, I'm kind of obsessed with your mouth. How something so spicy can be so sweet. I like it when I make your mouth laugh.' My lips curved in response.

'I like your skin.' He picked up my hand and swiped his thumb across my wrist. 'I like feeling your pulse race beneath it. I like the person beneath it.'

I discovered the words 'knees going weak' was not a silly, sentimental little saying, but a literal phenomenon. My joy was barging against my gates of caution, demanding freedom.

'My pulse?' I said, my tone light. 'You being a vampire would be really inconvenient right now.'

Malakai smiled. I needed to joke to find my footing in this new place we were in. Vulnerability made me nervous. He knew. He gave me the space. 'That's why I said all the anti-vampire stuff before. Needed to throw you off the scent.'

He swept his thumb across my cheek. 'How you feeling?'

'I feel like . . . ' I paused. The truth felt steady in my mouth. 'You're the only guy that's ever held my hand without the intention of getting something from me. You just hold my hand to hold it. To hold me. Like you like doing it or something. And it scares the shit out of me, every time, because I like you doing it. Because I don't want you to let go. It feels good and safe and right . . . you feel right to me.'

My voice faltered, buckling under the weight of my words, worried that it was more than he wanted from me, that I had shown too much. My eyes flicked downwards, but Malakai tilted my chin up, looking at me in a way that sent shockwaves through my body. His hand slipped around to my back and pulled me closer to him.

'I'm not playing with this, Scotch. This ain't a game to me.'

I swallowed. 'Me neither.'

My hand glided up the ridges and dips underneath the thin cotton of his shirt. Despite the tension on his face, a flash of mischief skittered through it, making him look impossibly sexier, as he inched closer to me, lids heavy.

Malakai's propped his hand around my neck as his mouth brushed against my neck, my jaw and my ear, staggering my breath, making the air buckle and spasm in my throat. Then, his lips landed on my cheek. He knew precisely what he was doing.

I laughed. 'Oh, come *on*. Give me more than that, Kai—'

I felt his lips curve against my skin. 'OK.'

Then we were kissing each other like we were oxygen, consuming each other, growing stronger. Malakai tasted like all the things I liked: cognac and chocolate, honey and spice. Sweet, sharp, smooth, soothing, stimulating. Familiar and thrilling.

This was different from our first kiss. That was introductory Chemistry 101. Our tongues lapped and laved and our teeth bit and grazed, kissing with messy grace and hunger, and my thighs wrapped firmer around his waist, responding to his firmness against me and driving us both crazy with pressurised swirls that he matched, falling easily into my rhythm, harmonising with my pace.

I'd never wanted anyone so bad. My hands travelled up and down his chest, enjoying the heat of his skin against my fingertips, enjoying how I could feel his groans reverberating through them, how I could taste his groan in my mouth. I smiled into his groan reveling in the taste of how I made him feel. I needed to feel more of him. I broke away from him for a second and watched him watch me as I slowly pulled off the top I was wearing and tossed it to the floor.

Malakai's breathing got heavier and so did his eyes, their weight causing them to drop from mine and move across my body like he had uncovered a treasure thought lost. Slowly, across my breasts, my stomach, my hips, his eyes left searing trails where they travelled. I imagined them as glowing lines, criss-crossing on my skin, amber against brown, like he was drawing constellations on me, or drawing constellations from me. Stargazing, gazestarry. My stomach flipped and dipped. The pulse between my legs became more incessant at the feel of him getting firmer.

I smiled against his lips. 'I can put the shirt back on if you're uncomfortable.'

Malakai's eyes slowly rose to mine and smiled indulgently, wickedly, making the fire in me roar. He curved his hand around the back of my neck. Our breaths married, his lips moved against mine. 'Kiki Banjo, you are a problem.'

He tried to slip his tongue inside my mouth but I gently pulled away, lifting the edge of his shirt, slowly peeling it upwards, revealing the smooth, rigid, creamy deep of his skin.

'Come solve me then, innit.'

Malakai's smile slanted and he pulled away so he could yank the shirt over his head and throw it to the side like it was something fetid and unholy. He was back with me in a second, hands spreading around the breadth of my thighs and lifting me up, drawing me close to him like I was something sacred. My arms twined around his neck, the feel of his skin against mine, his heat taking me up to a higher level of thirst and I kissed him wanting to sate it.

He walked me over to the bed, kissing me back all the way, matching my appetite. He sat down on the edge of the bed and dipped his head so his mouth was on my neck and then my collar bone, and then lower to the soft, cushiony curves of my chest, and I was delighted to note that his lips really were all that they had seemed on my mouth, full and accommodating and bossy, commanding my body to yield to their softness. My body did as it was told.

My hands wandered over the smooth muscular terrain of his back as I kissed up his shoulder, up the slopes of his deltoids till I reached his neck, sucking and nipping like a starved, wild thing until Malakai let out a low growl, wrapped his hands around my waist and switched us around, so I was on my back. We moved further up the mattress and he laid on his side, hovering above me, breathless.

'Shit, Scotch,' Malakai's voice was low as he leaned his forehead on mine. His smile grazed my lips. 'You're mad sexy. You know that?'

My laughter came out in tiny, bubbly and breathless spurts. 'I had a hunch.' I slung an arm around his neck, whispering against his plush lips, 'You're OK too.'

Malakai chuckled, and I loved the sensation of it reverberating through me. He arched a brow. 'I'm OK?'

I shrugged, purposefully pulling a casually unfussed face. 'Yeah. I mean you *aite*. Cute.'

Malakai levelled an incredulous look at me. 'Cute. You're really calling me *cute* right now?' He glanced down at the very, *very* sizeable protrusion in his sweatpants. 'Right fucking now?'

'Aw. You are so adorable when you're being all hyper-masculine *shit*—'

I bit my lip as Malakai skipped his hand down my stomach slowly and began to knead through my knickers. Just as I opened my mouth and released a breathy sound, Malakai ate that moan, catching my lips, kissing me deeply, indulgently, like I was something to be savoured – like he could slow time itself down with every languid flick of his tongue, every rogue suck of my lip, as he continued to massage my now-considerably soaked panties. I writhed against him and dug my fingers into his hair. Malakai pulled away, eyes heavy-lidded, but questioning, lips bumping against mine as his fingers moved in swirls against me. 'Tell me.'

'Kai.' His name was a moan. I could see the effect on him, in the flash of his eyes, and I could feel it pressed into my thigh, so pleasingly. Every vaguely sexual experience I had before this was lust-by-numbers, erotic-by-rote.

'Kiki, I need you to tell me if you want me to feel on you.'

I could tell Malakai was enjoying torturing me like this because of the slight curl of his mouth. I nipped his lip in vengeance, and his smile just became wickeder. 'Feel in you. Because that's what I want to do. I wanna feel how *cute* you think I am.'

I ground desperately against him, biting my lip, his words almost working as much magic as his hand was. My arms wound around his neck so I could drag him over me, his leg nestled between mine. I kissed and sucked at his neck, my hands slowly massaging his chest, sweeping my fingers across his rock-hard nipples. Malakai released a low snarl and pulled back. 'Nice try. Witch. Almost had me. You're good. But that's not an answer.'

Expecting me to speak when he was doing what he was doing to me might have been the only truly mean thing Malakai had ever done. I was just heart and nerve endings set alight. I felt exposed. Vocalising the exact thing I needed him to do to me made me shy. Yet it was exciting, my need rubbing shoulders with my coyness, the tension challenging me to step up.

I slipped my arm from around his body so I could slowly spread and smooth my hand down my stomach. Malakai pulled back slightly and watched my hand's journey, transfixed. It stopped when it reached the tropical junction between my legs, joining Malakai's. His eyes jumped up to mine, blazing bright. Our gazes were still fixed on each other when my hand moved over his, taking it to slip it under the waistband of my panties, pressing his palm hard against me. Our breathing instantly became even more erratic, Malakai's eyes a hypnotic black hole that held all my deepest, most desperate desires. His touch made a home in me.

Malakai's voice was gravelly with tension, 'Showing me works too.'

I released a gust of a giggle. 'Do you think you can take over from here?'

'I got you.' Malakai's smile was roguish delight and he kissed me hungrily as he gently pushed a finger inside me. I immediately gasped and bucked, the delicious sensation ricocheting throughout my body, tip to toe. He was agonisingly slow with it, making me coil up with exquisite tension. He was doing it on purpose, I knew, because he drew back, eyes glinting mischievously.

I managed to choke out a strained, 'Dick. *Petty.*'

Malakai's smile broadened and he eagerly slid two more fingers in, varying the pace, pressure and depth, making my hands fly to his back, sink my nails in, making his name in my throat a mew of anguished bliss. '*Kai—*'

When he spoke, his voice was husky with frustration. 'Do you know what you do to me when you say my name like that, Scotch?' Which, of course, made me grind up against his hand more. If it was anything like the way I felt when he called me 'Scotch' then I was basically deific.

I arched my back and bent my arm to unclasp my bra so his hand could do what it was doing with no restrictions. His free hand travelled and explored the newly exposed territories, caressing, tweaking, acute and thorough in the pleasure. It was glorious torment. I slung a leg across his waist and writhed against him. His smile melted into something more tense, focused, arousing. Aroused.

I was moving chaotically against him as his fingers increased in pace, conjured tides, stretched me delightfully. He looked so good and so sweet in the dim lamp lighting, the muted gold marrying into his dark skin that I kissed him harder, even more messily, wanting to taste as much as I could. Malakai pulled away only so he could cover a nipple with his mouth, lapping me up, hungry, grazing with his teeth.

'You. Taste. So. Good.' Each word was punctuated with a punishingly pleasurable hard suck.

'More.'

A menacing grin against my skin. 'More who?'

'*Kai.*'

His mouth did the same on the other breast, continuing his

heavenly censure, while his hand took over the other one, making sure there was no neglect, conscientious in his caressing. I was losing my mind. There was no time, no space to be embarrassed. I just wanted to feel, let my feelings be noisy. I'd spent so long hushing, ignoring them. His lips moved to sear the skin between my breasts, then my stomach, soft, sweet, scorching, embossing his lips across me, down, down, down, till he stopped – his eyes flew to mine in question.

'Keep going.'

He gently nudged my thighs further apart with his face and kissed the soft flesh on my right and left. He was deliberate with it, left enough space between kisses for me to start to get indignant, impatient, before he was back on me again. He pressed his lips against me through the thin material of my lacy briefs, the heat of his mouth making me buck, before he looped his fingers through my waistband. I arched, helped him move my panties down my thighs. Then, finally, *finally*, all my nerve endings standing up in applause, his mouth replaced his fingers, the transition smooth, his tongue swirling and thrusting expertly and angrily inside me, until my hand was spread across his head, moving frenetically against him. Malakai was a lion's snarl of delight, his mouth pushing warm winds that forced my teeth to sink into my bottom lip. He was starvation coming home to a banquet.

The words that flew out of my mouth were illicit, raspy sounds that only seemed to galvanise him, a circuit of pleasure. I felt like I could taste light if I wanted to, hear yellow, see the future. Then a sensation like no other, a pleasure and heat I'd never felt before, bloomed and rippled across my entire body and I came undone, clamped up, squeezed at my chest, moved raggedly against him, against the bed sheets. I flopped down limp, sweating, spasming, panting, in a state of disbelief. How did that even happen?

Malakai shifted up, and moved so his chest was covering mine, the weight of his body feeling like the ultimate comfort blanket. He stared down at me, eyes dark and coruscating, the corner of his lips kicked up as he scanned my face, his breathing as jagged and irregular as mine. His thumb scooped a rivulet of sweat from my forehead and he casually examined the droplet.

I frowned. 'What are you——?' I stopped, fascinated. He rubbed his thumb, my perspiration, his meticulous work, on my bottom lip and sucked it into his mouth in a slow, exquisite kiss that made my core tighten again. It was depraved, it was divine.

He brought his forehead to mine. 'Thought you didn't sweat?'

I laughed and pushed his face away from mine. 'You're,' *pant*, 'the,' *pant*, 'worst . . .' I was amazed I could even talk: I'd just orgasmed with a guy for the first time. Ever.

And there was the fact that no one had ever looked at my body like Malakai looked at my body. Because Malakai didn't just look at my body, he looked at *me*. And he heard me. He listened with his hands and his eyes.

I swept my thumb across his jaw and tugged at the waistband of his sweatpants. He'd given me something. Maybe I should give him something back. Just as I began to slip my hand down his waistband, his hand flew to my wrist, held on to it.

'What's wrong? Don't you want to——'

'Do you want to?'

I hesitated. I wanted to in the abstract. I *knew* I wanted to. I wasn't sure if I was ready to right *then*, but—

Malakai gently moved my hand away and planted a kiss on my collarbone. 'We have time, Scotch.'

I sat up and watched him quizzically for a moment, then retrieved and slid into my panties, grabbed my bra, refastened it. Was I being rejected? *Again?!* I moved a little further from him on the bed.

'Um, you sure? Because I feel like I got the most out of . . . that. I'd get it if you felt like maybe I didn't reciprocate enough?' Oh my gosh. I was bad at this. I was *so* bad at this. Malakai made me feel powerful but also sensitive. Like my heart was comprised of a billion tinier hearts. Why was I acting like such a dork? I cleared my throat.

Malakai's brows furrowed. He was looking at me like I was nuts but also like he wanted to hold me. He was looking at me like I was a meowing puppy. 'What? OK. No. Stop. Can you get over here? You are way too far away from me right now.'

I closed the space between us, climbed on him and sat across his legs, thighs bracing his. 'Hey.'

Malakai's eyes were angel down. 'Hi. Look, Scotch, I need you to know that I got a *lot* out of that. You were amazing. And it feels good to make you feel good. I like making you feel good.' His gaze harboured a faint, diluted version of the same blessed wickedness they had when his fingers were inside me, conjuring electrical storms within me. I got an instant sharp trill between my legs. Realising how much I liked Malakai made me realise how much I wasn't quite ready. It was a big deal. It would be a big deal with him. I just got a hold of what this thing was between us. I needed to secure myself more before we increased the weight of it. I didn't want to lose balance.

'So, just know that. Whatever you decide you want to do, make sure it's totally on you. Not about me.'

I cleared my throat. 'Yeah, I know. And I think I was just caught up just then. I, actually . . . I don't think I'm quite there yet. I mean, I'm on my way but—'

'You don't have to explain, Scotch,' he brushed braids from my face, 'We can go as slow as you want. I'm ready when you're ready. I'm gonna be here,' he smiled, 'Trust.'

I swallowed and stared at him. Hot stinging tears sprung to my eyes. My chest felt full and lighter at the same time. This was mortifying. I was crying like some kind of virgin nerd. I mean technically, yes, I was a virgin, and OK, yes, I was kind of into fantasy cosplay, but I wasn't a 'virgin nerd'. I was a virgin bad bitch. Also, I could drive. I was no Cher Horowitz. Plus, I wasn't crying *because* I was a virgin bad bitch. I was never ashamed of that. There was no shame in that. Sexuality doesn't define either way. I knew that. I was crying because – why the hell was I crying?!

Malakai drew his head back from me, eyes widening with panic. 'Oh man . . . Kiki? You OK? It's not that I don't want to, I promise – shit, am I making sense?'

He was adorable. This made me want to cry more. He looked so sweet and so stressed. I kissed the corner of his mouth. And then his jaw. Then his ear.

'I know you hate being called cute but you're really fucking cute.' I smiled at Malakai's mock frown, which made him impossibly cuter, and whispered against his lips, 'And sexy. Not every guy can be both. I happen to like it. A lot.'

'Yeah?' He murmured his smile into my mouth. His delight tasted like mine. 'Well, I like you a lot, Kikiola Banjo.'

It felt as good as all my best feelings melded into one: iced lemonade on a hot day, the first time I listened to the album *Lemonade*, hot Lagos rain on my skin while riding a bike around my grandad's compound when I was twelve, finding a £5 note in the pocket of a jacket, sun between my shoulder blades, a bookmarked pair of shoes on sale, someone cancelling plans I was dreading, the taste of ripe plantain fried golden, the way Frank Ocean repeats 'pleasure' on 'Pink Matter' but somehow more. Somehow wider, somehow deeper. Something that was part of me now, fusing into my skin and into my soul. It made me feel like I was floating, flying and falling at the same time. Like I was ascending while rooted safely. Before I got the chance to analyse it further, Malakai was kissing me again, and I was kissing him back.

CHAPTER 23

'You look . . . chirpy.' Dr Miller's red lips curved wryly as I placed a coffee cup on her desk. Her room smelled of the bergamot- and tea-tree oil-scented steam emanating from the diffuser she had in the corner of her chicly decorated office, all Swedish ergonomics, wooden imitation-Bantu sculptures and succulents.

'Oh, you must be mistaken, Dr M. This is my usual look of urbane insouciance. You know what it must be?' I plopped myself down in the seat in front of her. 'I switched up my nude lip gloss.'

Her lips twitched as she raised the cup to me in thanks and surreptitiously pushed a brown paper bag of mini-flapjacks towards me.

I grinned and popped one into my mouth as she said, 'Well, the new lip gloss suits you. I like it.' She clicked on her laptop key so it whirred into life and brought up the documents she needed for our catch-up.

'How are you finding your partnership with young Mr Korede?'

I tried to eat my smile but I felt it spilling out of me, just like the warmth emanating from my chest, almost keeping me as snug as Malakai's hoodie, which I was currently wearing over tights, and which I'd taken from his room, where I'd spent the night tangled up with him in his bed.

It'd been a fortnight since Ty's country house and I'd been walking around like I'd swallowed a star; fiery, celestial, delightfully volatile and beaming everywhere. It felt like we were supposed to be this way, like our connection had been prepped for this progression. Spending our days together held new pleasure, liberated to do all the things we had to do to keep up the pretence without the souring tinge of pretence – and with the addition of other things that weren't allowed under the stipulated rules – like his hand squeezing my knee during lectures, like kissing in the quad, like him calling me 'baby', like me liking it. We were also, to our mutual delight, discovering the *many* creative ways we could enjoy each other before I was ready for sex.

I couldn't articulate this to Dr Miller for obvious reasons, so I cleared my throat and hoped to push back the heat in my face. 'The partnership is going well, I think.'

Dr Miller nodded briskly. I thought I caught a glint in her eye though it might have been wintery sunlight beaming through her office blinds.

'Good. I believe your partner thinks so too – his film is coming along very nicely. You two work well together. I can see that your voice adds something special to his film and I'm pleased by the progress you're making with your application project. The audio reality show was a novel conceit. It's warm, it's engaging and your listeners have more than doubled.'

The clip of Malakai and Zack's scuffle had been almost definitely recorded and leaked by Simi, with evident glee in seeing me in the midst of the mess. Mercifully, it had backfired, with the hashtag #MMAMalakai spinning around campus alongside gifs of Zack stumbling comically, slow and impotent. Our subscribers had gone up. As I allowed the warmth of the praise to sink in, a sound coming from the window threatened to distract me completely. If I listened closely, I could detect the words 'Whitewell Knights.'

I blocked the noise out and focused on Dr Miller's inscrutable expression.

'This is all perfect for your application.' Dr Miller paused and I heard the loudly silent *but*. 'Kiki, what would the internship mean to you?'

I opened and shut my mouth. It was supposed to be an easy question, but it rolled heavier in my mind than anticipated. 'Freedom? It's hard to explain, but I had the opportunity to do something like this before and I missed out on it because I was a – a smaller version of myself. Now, I feel more confident. Ready. I feel more *me*. Like I'm hiding less.'

Dr Miller sipped her coffee and nodded, with a glimmer of a smile. 'People connect to authenticity. Make sure, whatever you do you centre what feels right to you. That's where integrity in media comes in. It's not always pretty, but that's what connection is about.' The sound coming from the window got louder. 'The truth.'

'We Don't Debate with Hate! We Don't Debate with Hate! Goodnight, Whitewell Knights!'

There was a chain in front of the student union building where the studio was. Or rather, a human blockade, holding up placards, headed by Adwoa and some renegades from Blackwell. I spotted Chioma and Shanti. Other students slowed down to take pictures, videos, join in the chant or taunt. A group of white boys, in pastel oxford shirts and sweaters with little riding horses embroidered on the top right corner, crowded around. The Whitewell Knights. They looked stressed, cheeks red, periodically running their fingers through their hair, standing with their hands on their hips and occasionally saying things like, 'this is just savage', 'ridiculous', 'preposterous', 'this is why we need the debate'. Campus security were encircling the premises menacingly, but technically they couldn't do anything. Protest was our right.

Malakai, Aminah and I slowed down as we approached the building, working our way through the crowd – it was show day, we were on in an hour and had planning to do. Aminah swore under her breath as she shoved a James or a Spencer out of the way.

'I get why we need to do this, but we have a show. How long are they gonna be here for?'

Malakai had been holding my hand. He aimed a hard warning look at a Francis who tried to get in my way. The Francis slinked off. Malakai shrugged. 'As long as they need to, probably. I dunno, I think this is really cool. They're not listening, so we make them listen. We gotta disrupt them.'

I moved so I was slightly ahead of them. 'Let me get at Adwoa, see what's up.'

Adwoa caught my eye, and dropped her protest arm, face softening from the grim determination it had previously been positioned in. She passed her megaphone to someone and took us both from the furore, pulling me round the side of the building.

'Adwoa, what is happening?'

She was panting, wild-eyed. 'Kiki. I quit the cabinet. Today. You wouldn't believe the shit that went down since we last spoke. I went snooping. Found that Zack is getting sent money to hold this debate. None of which, of course, will go back to Blackwell.'

My breath hitched. 'Wait, what?'

'Zack's been having meetings with the Whitewell Knights. Remember last year, when we booked the main hall for Reni-Eddo Lodge and when she came to speak, it weirdly, coincidentally, turned out that there was an administrative fuck-up and the Whitewell Knights had booked it for that pseudo-intellectual nationalist guy? Zack got paid off to cancel it.'

'Hold up.' I blinked, trying to process this. 'Zack has been sabotaging us the whole time?'

Adwoa grabbed my arm. 'Kiki, he has been going to the meetings. I've been working on this for months. I have a mole. Zack is such an idiot. They're good to him, so he thinks of course, they can't be racist. But it's great PR for them. They've been using him this whole time. Did you know that Zack's dad was a Whitewell Knight too? They always find one so they can keep up the pretence that they ain't a fucking klan. He's a legacy.

'Zack was somehow smart enough to find a way to be in power and also take money. He has president of a society on his CV and he also gets to pocket money and connections from helping out the Whitewell Knights. He's going to get his pick of fellowships, internships, graduate jobs – whatever he wants.'

I stumbled back. It was clear now that Zack's brand of dark was layered, any depth he had directed to being the world's biggest prick.

'Shit, Adwoa. I mean, well done, but *shit*. You found this out all by yourself?'

Adwoa shrugged. 'Nah. My girlfriend's a professional sleuth. She has a blog. She helped dig. Did some undercover work with him. He had extra money to buy her stuff, and he couldn't help but brag.' She rolled her eyes as the noise of the protest escalated. 'I know we have to do something and out him to everyone, but she can't expose him because her platform isn't far-reaching enough and the institution won't take it seriously as it's a gossip site. If we swing at him, we can't afford to miss. Look, Kiki, I have to go. I'm sorry this is getting in the way of the show but—'

I shook my head. 'It's fine. Actually, I think I have an idea. Let me help.'

The idea solidified as the words left my mouth. After his antics at

Ty's house, it was clear that Zack, in general, was an infection who needed to be neutralised for the good of Blackwell. If he behaved like that towards me, what were his actions like towards the First Years who flocked around him, mainly for social currency? He was addicted to power and ownership, and it made him a perpetually unsatisfied monster. It would be messy and I'd have to run it past Aminah as it would put Brown Sugar's recent success at risk – getting involved in politics was almost a sure-fire way to plummet listenership – but I had to do it.

'Yeah?' Adwoa didn't bother to hide her surprise. It was understandable considering my track record.

I looked back at the burgeoning crowd. Malakai had found a placard and Aminah was looking at her watch, rolling her eyes.

I nodded. 'Tag me in.'

Whitewell College Radio, 9.30–11 p.m. slot, Thursday, Brown Sugar Show

'What's up, sweet things? It's your girl K, and we're gonna be doing something a little different today. As you may have noticed, the musical theme of this episode has been a little militant – rap in war mode – because I'm tryna get us ready for something.

'I want to talk about the Wasteman of Whitewell. You see friends, what I got wrong before is *who* this Wasteman is. This ain't no Bogeyman shit, this is real. He is in our midst. See, his

Wastemanosity goes far beyond the scope of being a dick to the gyaldem – and make no mistake people, that is *still* included. That alone would be enough. But not for him. This man is greedy with his fuckery, and yeah, I said fuckery because this is a *fuckery*. Fresh out the factory. This guy is sophisticated in that respect – maybe only in that respect, yes offence, yes disrespect – his badmind reaching to affect us as a community. I'm talking about none other than our dear Commander-in-Chief, Zack Kingsford.

'Some of you are already unhappy with him, I know that. I hear that. You were outside protesting, and now you're outside blasting this show on the speaker. You're exercising your right to be heard. It's our right *not* to have our rights be the subject of debate, pro-testing against the sanctioning of hate. The fact that Zack allowed this to happen is a disgrace, but what's even more disgraceful is the fact that he's been taking money from the Whitewell Knights to sabotage his own community.

'Events cancelled and moved, and the things that *do* happen aren't sorted by him. Black careers day? Adwoa organised. Fashion show? Shanti Jackson. Open mics? Chioma Kene. And remember the hurdles those women overcame? How Adwoa struggled for a permit to get the Black careers fair until she started saying words like "discrimination" to fight for the cause? How Shanti could only get permission for her Afrocouture Fashion Show if she agreed that she'd also have white models for "diversity"?

'And, I'm sure we all know that FreakyFridayz would not have happened if I hadn't broached the idea in public. Zack didn't leave it to me because he was generous, he left it to me because he thought it was gonna flop. None of these endeavours have flopped. AfroWinter Ball didn't flop because Simi Coker, baddest on campus, has chaired it for two years running.

'So that leads us to question: what exactly is *Zack* running? Because it ain't Blackwell. Adwoa just quit so what do we have left in the cabinet? A corrupt president and his bum-licking cronies. The real Wastemen of Whitewell.'

I could hear the cheering outside the building, my voice reverberating across the quad. I leant into the mic, emboldened. 'Fear not fam, because I think I have a solution. A new cabinet. A Blackwell run by the people who actually run tings. We've looked into the society laws and if you all call for a new order on the student portal now live on our website, we can hold a by-election. How you feel about that?'

I looked back at Aminah, who was assiduously monitoring the comments on the Brown Sugar page on her tablet, eyes focused behind her designer glasses. She had been sceptical of the idea at first because of the anticipated drop in listenership, but now she smirked and whispered: 'They feel very good about that.'

The faint uproar from outside the building confirmed it. We grinned at each other.

'Well, all right then. Anyone can run, of course, but right now I have some people who would like to put their cases forward. And in the coming weeks anybody who would like to put their name forward for cabinet positions can come state their cases, right here, on the show, if you all agree to an election. But for now, I would like to introduce: the Presidential candidate, Adwoa Baker; Events

Secretary Candidate, Shanti Jackson; Student Liaison Officer candidate, Chioma Kene and Press Officer candidate, Aminah Bakare. We're not gonna let the Wastemen win.'

I sat back, spun my chair around as Adwoa – who had been sitting next to me the entire time – started her manifesto with a rousing bellow of 'What's *good*, Blackwell?'

On the sofa, Shanti, Chioma and Aminah all grinned widely, thumbs up, hands put together in reverence, in celebration of a new era. I looked up at the camera Malakai was pointing my way with a grin. He'd wanted to film it just for my records: 'to remind yourself how sick you are, in case you ever forget'.

'Oh my gosh, Kai.' I was beside myself with glee as I let myself into Malakai's room, slipping my sneakers off, 'On the way here I saw the Whitewell Wailers doing a melodic, a capella rendition of "Niggas in Paris" on the quad, but instead of "niggas" they said "*suckas*", as if that would make it any less of a hate crime. Anyway, instead of saying "married Kate and Ashley", the lead nerd goes, "married *Kiki* and Ashley". And winks at me. I know you're sad you missed it, which is why I recorded it for you. Man, you are so lucky to have me in your life.'

Malakai scooped me up at the door and kissed me hello, and despite its default knee-weakening properties, I tasted something amiss in the kiss. He released me and gave me a smile that tried in earnest to reach his eyes before he sat on the bed, pulled me on to his sweat pant-covered lap. 'I really am. And I'm not surprised that you have Glee Club nerds serenading you in the middle of campus. Show me the video.'

I pulled back a little. We had an ongoing competition about who would catch the most egregious showcase from a Whitewell performing arts club in the wild. Last week he'd seen an operatic version of Beyoncé's 'Brown Skin Girl' performed as a show of 'intersectional-feminist-solidarity' by a bottle-tanned girl called Imogen, and was moved to hysterical tears. This reaction was underwhelming to say the least.

I frowned and held his chin. 'What's wrong?'

Kai dropped his eyes to my lips in an act that was more avoidance than lust. 'Nothing, I'm just pissed you beat me—'

'*Kai.*'

'Seriously Scotch, I'm good.'

I swallowed, stoically accepting one of my worst fears realised. 'OK, Malakai if you're suddenly not into this you have to say. This is your out – you don't have to spare my feelings.'

Malakai's eyes snapped sharply to mine, brows creased with incredulity. 'Woah. What? Scotch, nothing like that.' He kissed my shoulder. '*Never* like that. How could you think—'

'I don't know what to think because you're not talking to me. I know something is up,' I said, even as the surge of hot relief washed over me, detangling the pre-emptive knot in my belly. I released the breath I hadn't even known I'd been holding, but I still sensed something askew.

Malakai cleared his throat, reluctantly bringing his eyes to mine.

The glint of vulnerability in them pierced my chest. 'It's really not that deep. I just, I uh, told my dad that I got that summer job as a runner at the production house. And he said he couldn't believe I was passing up working at his office in Lagos to be a glorified "houseboy".'

Malakai released a hollow, gruff laugh as I rubbed his back, my heart cracking a little just as I knew his own had. 'And I don't even really know why I told him. Why what he thinks still matters to me. Why I think that if I win the Shades of Motion competition, or at least get shortlisted, then maybe he will begin to take this shit seriously. Me, seriously.' He shook his head, rubbing a hand across his face. 'It's pathetic, really. Can we just forget ab—'

'I got you something last week. When you told me you got the job. It arrived this morning.'

I shifted off his lap and reached for the gift bag tucked into the tote I'd dropped on his bedroom floor. Malakai's brows furrowed in mild curiosity as I passed the gift to him. I beckoned him to open it with a gentle jut of my chin. 'Spoiler alert. It's a framed picture of me.'

Malakai grinned as he opened the bag, the smile falling away as soon as he saw what was in it. He lifted the gift from the bag, stared at it, eyes flitting from shock to wonder to gratitude, eyes getting increasingly shinier. My heart grew ten more sizes at his expression.

'*Scotch.*' His voice was a rough choke.

It was a filmmaking clapperboard. In white marker, I'd written,

'Untitled', next to the name of production, and 'Malakai Korede', beside 'Director'. The date was his birthday.

I curved my hand around the back of his neck and let my thumb sweep across the sweet valley of his cheekbone. 'Here's the thing, Kai. You don't need your dad's co-sign to live the life you want to live. You don't need anyone's co-sign. You do what feels right to you. You're a filmmaker, OK? And for what it's worth, I'm proud of you. It's not easy to step outside a path laid out for you. It's pretty brave, actually. You're figuring out your freedom and it's inspiring. And one day that's gonna be a real production clapperboard with your name on it.'

Malakai still hadn't said anything, his gaze a hypnotic twilight.

'Obviously, if you'd prefer a framed picture of me that could be arrang—'

Malakai shut me up, kissing me with a ferocious sweetness that rendered me hot molasses. The kiss was so excruciatingly, exquisitely soft, so full with delicate, but robust feeling, it made me want to cry.

I felt myself recline, the full force of that feeling pushing me back, my arms wrapping around his neck and pulling him down so his delectably warm weight pinned me to his bed and I felt his heartbeat sear through his T-shirt. I sucked his bottom lip, and that seemed to set something divinely feral loose within him. His tongue licked with passionate and precise persistence in my mouth, like enough wasn't enough, and I got wetter, got wilder, while the lovely, *lovely* thick length of his hardness pressed against me. It sent me savage as I wrapped my legs around him and ground my hips.

He tasted so dizzyingly good, so intoxicating, it felt like my consumption should be regulated. Just before the last remnants of our minds were lost, Malakai pulled back slightly to lean his forehead against mine, breath ragged. He pecked my lips sweetly, like he couldn't help it.

'So, you liked it?'

'Scotch, thank you. It's the second-best gift I've ever got.'

'Second? You shitting me? What's the first?'

Malakai bumped his nose so tenderly with mine that my breath stopped to bow in my throat in reverence.

'You.'

CHAPTER 24

'I've never seen this place so rammed.'

The Sweetest Ting was teeming – Meji was so happy to host us he'd turned a blind eye to the liquor being poured into Sprites. Ty, Shanti, Chi were up by the front, dictating their song suggestions, while Kofi curated a video playlist for the several-inch flat-screen on the wall. Malakai was busy talking to some Third-Year film students about *Cuts*, the direction of his next film, lenses and frames and other things that made his eyes light up even more than their natural brilliance. I had thrown a little campaign social to generate heat before the upcoming election and the event had blown up into a party before my eyes.

Aminah sipped on her Coke. 'Omo, you're popular now. Get with the programme. Hot girl on campus. Belle of Blackwell. People want to be wherever you're at. After I posted the ProntoPic story of us here, my inbox was blowing up. They're especially

364

interested in you after you put Zack on blast the other day, and yes, while I was sceptical about you making Brown Sugar political, and, yes, we are yet to see how it will affect our audience numbers in the longrun, it's for the greater good. You're helping them stick it to the Wasteman.

'And it's bringing people together because *look* at this place. You ever seen this many different social groups come together and mingle ever? You got a Bible Study Babe flirting with a reformed roadman doing Sports Science, and I don't think she's trying to convert him—'

'Unless, speaking in tongues suddenly means something different.' I hitched a brow as said couple brought their lips together in the crook of the corner most booth.

Aminah was right, factions had folded together, and it was so seamless, I'd barely noticed it, cliques separated and mixing. Blackwell seemed more fun this way, more alive, less confined. I had put my internship in slight jeopardy but somehow I didn't feel an inclination to spiral; something was shifting in real life. It didn't matter how big our audience was, but who they were. People who cared.

Aminah handed me a jerk chicken pop and held hers up so we could smash them in a toast. 'You did this with Brown Sugar. By announcing a new committee with all the girls, you were signalling something new, validating something new.'

I shrugged. 'Maybe, but Brown Sugar would be nothing without you, and the marketing and the managing.'

Aminah waved a hand of dismissal while nodding at the same

time, her long lashes accentuating the twinkle in her eye. 'We're a power couple, babes. Let's just say that,' she nudged me, 'even when you're reconciling with old frenemies.'

'Wait. You were feeling a way about that?'

I'd told Aminah that Rianne and I had been texting since we'd met at RomCon and she'd been nothing but cautiously supportive, while still harbouring a slight protective grudge, while encouraging of my peace. Like a mother whose child had taken up a hazardous sport.

Aminah shrugged. 'No, because it would be insane of me to wonder if your best friend from childhood, with great bone structure, with whom you have nerdy pursuits in common is going to replace me.'

I grinned. 'Yes. It would be. I'm glad I made up with Rianne, but you're my life partner and your roasting of my nerdy pursuits keeps me balanced.'

Aminah pinched my arm. 'I bully you because I care. And I need you in my life to take me to quaint bistros like this to keep me grounded and cool.'

'It's a diner.'

Aminah nodded without an iota of recognition. 'Don't know what that is, but this is cute. I like the vibe.' She flicked her gaze above my head and her eyes flashed teasingly. 'Ho ho, *man*, he just can't stay away from you can he? If this is what he's like before you guys have smashed—'

'*Aminah.*'

She wriggled her brows and somehow managed to elegantly

climb over me and out of the booth just as Malakai reached us. 'Newbie,' she greeted Malakai stoically.

He bowed his head. 'Lady Aminah. You gonna accept my ProntoPic invitation now?'

Aminah shrugged. 'I feel like there should be some boundaries between the spouse and the sidepiece but sha, make it past the three-month mark and I'll consider it.' She strutted away towards where Kofi stood, eyes eager.

Malakai grinned as I scooted over for him. As he sat, he passed me my requested illicitly mixed rum and Coke and slung an arm around my neck. 'I think she basically just said I'm like a brother to her.'

I laughed. 'I heard it.'

Malakai cast an eye across The Sweetest Ting, a broad smile lighting up his face. It lit me up too. 'I always feel so at home here. With you. Ama would have never liked a spot like this—'

I bristled. 'So? Why are you even thinking about her right now?"

Malakai's eyes jumped, alert. 'I'm not. I'm just saying I'm glad I can be me around you. I couldn't do that with her.'

I'd piled my twists on top of my head and he gently tugged at a straggling twist from my Ankara headwrap. I stayed silent as I tried to work out the arithmetic of what he'd just said. The slight tension was displaced by an overwhelming scent of peony and mild disdain.

Simi stood by the booth. She tapped an elegant, milky clawed finger on Malakai's shoulder, chiming, 'Girl chat! I am sure you don't mind.'

Terrifying. I would have wondered why Simi was really here, but both reason and rhyme were beneath her, buckling under her powers of chaos. Malakai hesitated, his eyes flitting between Simi and me, before I hitched a shoulder. I once saw in a wildlife documentary that the best thing to do when facing off a wild lion was to stand your ground. Stay calm. Do not bend.

Malakai whispered in my ear, 'Safe word is "Malakai, you sexy beast."'

He scooted out of the booth. 'That's a sentence – and you're the worst.'

Malakai grinned as he backed away. 'I know.'

My smile remained on my face till I turned. Simi was now sat opposite to me, and her signature mild disdain had manifested into a smirk and a slight cock of her head. 'You and Malakai are kinda cute.' She sipped her drink. 'Especially considering you first kissed him to make Zack mad.'

Not quite true but still I froze, the blood rushing from my cheeks. 'Wh–what are you talking about?'

Simi's smirk widened as she brought out a rose-gold flask and poured whatever was inside it into her Coke. She took a sip of it and released a sigh of contentment that only worked to pull out goosebumps on my skin.

'*Better*. But now,' Simi continued, paying no heed to my question, 'it's clear that there is something real between you guys. I didn't know what the end game was for both of you. I thought maybe you wanted a fast-track to popularity, and Malakai saw you as a ticket to cementing himself in Blackwell society.' She ran her eyes across me. 'But you don't need that. I mean, you're not on the same level as me, obviously, but people rate you for some reason. It's the reason people turned up here the night Zack is throwing a party in a pathetic attempt to regain public favour since you announced his contest on your show. Brava by the way.' She brought her hands together in two staccato slaps. 'Nice work.'

My brain was too slow to catch up with all that had happened with Simi and all I managed to muster in response was, 'I didn't know he was throwing a party tonight.'

Simi flashed a sharp smile. 'Irrelevant. You're siphoning his power away, and that, sweets, is a good thing. My point is, it doesn't matter why you and Malakai got into this thing. It's real now.'

I stared at Simi, stunned into mortified silence, and she laughed. It wasn't unkind, and it was the first time I had my defences low enough to actually hear it properly. It was rich, husky, perhaps . . . warm? Was it ever really unkind or had I just presumed it sounded unkind?

'Kiki, I am a gossip blogger, a journalism student, and I'm gonna be an MA student next year. I'm the best in my year. I saw you and Zack that FreakyFridayz and I knew you had been hooking up. I was gonna step in, but I saw that you had it handled. Then you and Malakai had it handled.' Her smirk widened. '*Really* handled.'

I blinked, trying to digest all the new unexpected pieces of information, chewing slowly, trying to extract sense from them. 'Wait, so why did you drag me the next day? And bring him to Ty's? And leak that video to make me look bad?'

Simi's was unruffled, an easy smile on her glossy lips as she reclined and sipped the mystery cocktail she'd just concocted. 'I needed you away from Zack so I could do my job properly. And I figured he wouldn't mess with someone who'd publicly embarrassed him. He's vain. I came with him to Ty's because I overheard him saying he was going to crash and I thought if it was with me, I could at least help to control the damage. I filmed and leaked the video to make *him* look bad. Which he did.' She sighed, apparently finished, the need to explain herself to me a tedious inconvenience. 'Look Kiki, I knew you'd be able to handle some infamy as collateral.'

I nodded slowly as embarrassment cleared the way for elucidation. My eyes widened, suddenly finding their way to Adwoa as she chatted to Chi in another booth. She'd said her girlfriend was a blogger.

'Were you investigating him?'

Simi saw where my eyes had drifted: she gave a slight nod, 'Right. By "dating" him. Well, by flirting with him enough to make him think we could date. I mean, we never did anything, but for guys like Zack the promise is enough. I'm Simi Coker. I have currency. That turned Zack on. I needed to get close to him to get the tea. I couldn't continue to watch him fuck up my legacy. I worked hard when I was in office, and I watched him undo everything I worked for.' She leant closer, eyes, diamond and flint.

'He severed all the connections we built, all the events we did with ACSs across the region. He wanted us isolated so he could do what he wanted to do, which was to have it all completely under his

370

control with racist Whitewell's institutional backing. He's corrupt as fuck. Which is why I never really understood why you were hooking up with him.'

I shook my head, trying to process the fact that Simi had partly orchestrated a systematic takedown of the most powerful boy on campus, that she was possibly – possibly – one of the coolest girls I knew. 'If you knew I was hooking up with Zack this whole time, why didn't you blow my cover?'

Simi looked me up and down like she was seriously considering the question. She found her answer and punctuated it with an elegant twitch of her shoulder. 'I don't really know. I think you remind me a lot of myself when I was younger.'

It didn't seem like an opportune time to point out to Simi that I was only about fifteen months younger than her, so I decided to focus on the other truly shocking element of the statement, which was that Simi looked at me and saw similarities. All this time, I thought when she looked at me, she felt a visceral sort of, if not loathing then at least scorn: an Auntie who has spotted your bra strap slipping at church.

Simi's darkly lined eyes were looking at me analytically, like some kind of queen of ancient, deciding which village girl should be her handmaiden. 'I knew you weren't hanging out with Zack for popularity because you did your best to hide it. I just could never figure out why. I guess that's why I took it out on you sometimes. You're smart. I hated seeing you waste your time on him. At one point I wondered if you were in on it with him, but it didn't make sense. It didn't match who I know you to be.'

I tilted my head. ' . . . and who do you know me to be?'

Simi took a bite of a yam chip from the sharing platter in front of me. Another surprise, as I'd never seen her eat carbs. I'd assumed she subsisted on the blood of First Years.

'A leader.'

I stared at her, trying to detect a hint of mockery but found nothing. Simi was a lot of things, and while she did sensationalise the truth sometimes on her blog, she wasn't a liar. She went on facts. She didn't give compliments.

After a few moments, I asked, 'You fucking with me?'

Simi rolled her eyes. 'Look, I may not have always liked you, but I've always rated you.'

'That why you called me Poetic Injustice?'

Simi chuckled at her genius. 'OK, that was funny.'

Unfortunately, it was, but I couldn't let her know that. I schooled my face to remain mock-straight.

Simi cackled harder, but in an attempt at peacemaking she shoved her drink towards me. I didn't need it, but out of diplomacy, I took a sip. I immediately choked. 'Did you put vodka *and* rum in this?'

She shrugged. 'It needed a kick. Anyway, come on, Kiki. A little bit of rivalry is fun. I was toughening you up for your future. When I leave undergrad, I'll need you to take over as Boss Bitch of Blackwell.'

'*Boss Bitch*? That's not a political post.'

Simi was irritated by my slowness. 'Yes, it is. It's just unofficial. But aside from that Adwoa and I have been talking.' I liked that she felt comfortable enough to drop Adwoa's name with intimacy, like she'd always said her name to me.

'And what Blackwell needs is a strong presence to keep everyone accountable. Adwoa's a great organiser, but she doesn't want to be president. Ask her. She's only doing it because you flat-out refused when she asked you, and we don't have better options. But I think you should do it. I'm going to warn you, *Brown Sugar*'s listenership might take a dive when you go all campaign-y, but I will help you boost it. My touch is magic.

'Kiki, I have watched for two years as Zack has run my kingdom to the ground. But he's been stressed the fuck out since the announcement. He's scared of you. That's why he threw a desperate party tonight. *You* have a community mandate and, more importantly, you care. You had the balls to call for a snap election. You're a powerful girl and that's the only kind I fuck with.'

In a weird turn of events, it turned out I might like Simi. I felt warmed, although, that might have been the lethal tincture she had mixed. She stared at me oddly, frowning. 'Ew. Please don't cry. It's embarrassing, and I will have to rescind my co-sign. Will you run?'

I weighed the notion in my mind and the horror I'd expected to detect wasn't there. It intrigued me, sank into my thoughts better than anticipated. 'I'll think about it.'

A genuine smile glimmered on her lips, just as her phone vibrated. 'Good, because—' the smile faded as she squinted at her phone and scrolled. She looked up at me, stricken, before her eyes darted up and around the room. I followed and saw that everyone else's attention was drawn to the white glare of their screens, their faces morphing from blurry, casual joy to intrigue to discomfort, to looking at me with scandalised curiosity or, worse, like I was an imposter in their midst. The restaurant was hushed now, harsh-edged whispers were taking the place of the loud squawks and bubbles of enjoyment. My blood pounded hot warning into my ear, I felt like I could chew it.

Steel slid over Simi's face – not unsympathetic, but briskly business. 'Kiki. Listen to me. Your moves now are important. Don't bend. Don't cave. Remember, Zack is petty and small. He's retaliating like this because he's losing.'

Something was definitely wrong. The music playing from the speakers seemed to have warbled, distorted, slowed. People were either looking at me or pretending not to.

Aminah had showed up from nowhere and was grabbing my hand and pulling me out of booth, saying something like, 'Let's go now Babe, everything is OK'– which let me know that things were very much not OK. Chioma was grabbing my jacket and Shanti got my bag, and then I saw Malakai in the corner of the room, his eyes ripping away from his phone and immediately rushing towards me, assuring the girls that he would take over, that he would take me home.

Outside The Sweetest Ting, the cold slapping up against my skin so hard it felt like a relief from the anticipatory heat in my body, I told everyone to please, *please* let me look at my phone, that I needed to face the source. Aminah tried to swipe my phone from me, and Malakai tried to convince me that it was best that I waited till we got back home.

'Give me your keys, Kai.'

Helpless against my glare, Malakai did as told and I immediately got into his car parked up outside The Sweetest Ting, locking the doors as Aminah tried to get in. Something told me I had to be alone for this. I looked at my phone.

PRONTOPICLIVE

@COGNACDADDY

Wassup guys [gentle, self-aware friendly chuckle and wave], it's Zack Kingsford here, your President, and I like to think brother of Blackwell. It's been a while since I've done a broadcast. I've been quiet. Been reflecting. There's been a lot of drama lately. A lot of accusations being thrown about. A lot of misconceptions. I've sat back and watched them because lions don't concern themselves with the affairs of mice. Nelson Mandela said that. He was also a great leader. But I just feel like enough is enough, and I feel like I owe you all the truth. We're a family.

The first truth is that the debate with Whitewell Knights is truly just a way to open up dialogue and to really make our presence known within campus. How can we progress if we don't unite? As you know, I myself am of mixed-race heritage being both Black and white, and I consider myself a real emblem of what can happen when we put our differences aside. The protests against the debate are further proving stereotypes. That we would rather struggle than seek peace. That struggle has become our identity. Let's step away from that. Like my hero Nelson Mandela did, I am trying to bridge gaps.

The second part I want to address really is . . . awkward for me. [Another chuckle, that quickly dissipates. Soft, vulnerable eyes appear.] I really don't like to make the personal political but it seems that I have no choice. Kiki Banjo's platform Brown Sugar has been used to disseminate false information and to instigate a coup. I haven't been worried because I know I deserve to be where I am. However, it is important to know that her platform isn't neutral. Kiki Banjo has her own personal vendetta against me.

Kiki and I were embroiled in a relationship for a while. Entangled, if you will. I ended it, and unfortunately Kiki has taken some time to adjust. It saddens me because I really did respect her, but it seems she is seeking vengeance by slandering my name and getting the members of her coven to do the same. It has become a witch-hunt. They want to lynch me. We saw an example of this, with her encouraging the thug, Malakai Korede to attack me last weekend. It's a shame because I was truly trying to forge peace. Can we trust someone so manipulative? Blackwell fam, please don't pay the lies any attention. Do the right thing, vote for Zack King . . . sford. One love. Oh, and evidence of our relationship will be posted on my ProntoPic stories, to prove my integrity.

I hadn't sent any pictures of myself to Zack, but apparently, he had taken one of me, in my bra and panties, as I was pulling a dress on one time. You could barely make out my face, but, if you wanted to see me, you could. I wasn't crying. I couldn't. My muscles had stiffened, the air in my lungs, dense.

Malakai was knocking on the window saying, 'Scotch, come on.'

I unlocked the car. Aminah rushed into the back, squeezed my shoulder. I don't remember much, but Aminah's sweet assurances that she was already working on the picture being taken down, as if that was a remedy against screenshots and shares. Malakai was saying that he would kill Zack, but also, confusingly, that none of this mattered, which made me so angry, because if none of this mattered then why would he want to kill Zack? The irritation at the lie was something grounded that I could hold on to, so I held on to it, because the idea, the fact, that *this* was happening to me again, that somebody had wielded me against me in some kind of ego trip to fix their reputation, was too much for my mind to process, it would have plunged me in way too deep. I had to stay afloat. So I clung on to my anger at Malakai's well-meaning attempt at consolation, till it cloyed in my mind. My mouth was salty. When he said, cautiously, gently into the silence, 'Kiki, please say something,' I replied, 'Don't do anything to Zack that could get you suspended. Promise me.'

Malakai's jaw tensed but he nodded. 'OK.'

Then I asked him to pull over so I could throw up.

CHAPTER 25

I threw my phone on the industrial carpet of the library, forcing myself to not tap the replay button again. I hitched my knees up and leant back against the shelves, my head resting on some books about Bantu civilisation. Speaking of Southern Africa, Nelson Mandela's estate should sue Zack for his audacity. It's one thing to smear my name, but conflating Nelson Mandela's legacy with your fuckery while you're doing it? Unforgivable.

The video had already hit over one thousand views and I was pretty sure a good number of them were mine. It was masochistic, I know, but somehow, fully analysing and processing the attack was the only thing that could give me anything close to relief. This was a calculated, vicious, aggressive ambush. Zack had known he was going to do this, known that the longer he held back, rock in a slingshot, the harder the knock, the further the reach, the deeper the wound. If my integrity was up for question, then so was the re-election, and so was everyone who had anything to do with me – anyone who had come on the show as part of their campaign tour. I'd potentially messed things up for the whole of Blackwell. Simi's suggestion that I run was now quite poetically comical. Brown Sugar's subscribers were in a precarious flux since Zack's broadcast, and way lower than I would need to get into the NYU programme. I was fucked.

It had been two days since it happened and the library was the only place I'd left my room for. I missed lectures and seminars and screened dozens of calls and messages from Chioma and Shanti. Aminah was all but holding vigil by my door. Malakai had come by, but I told him I needed space. He left and couldn't have been out of the building before he sent the message:

KAI: I got you, Scotch. Know that. X

Nothing would make me feel better. Nothing that anyone could say could make me feel less stupid for letting the same thing happen to me twice. The one thing I swore to myself I would never allow to happen. The minute I let my guard down, let myself get involved in Blackwell society, I was paying for it, and everyone else would pay for it too. Life was far easier when I didn't talk to anyone but Aminah – unless it was unseen and through a mic and about what it means when a guy doesn't like your pictures. I couldn't believe that somehow, a guy had managed to weaponise his attraction to me against me again, like some kind of poisoned kiss that would always lead to my social demise.

My eyes were stinging again, filling again. I had been sat in my secret spot in the library for at least two hours. Thankfully, there were plenty of things to keep me occupied. I was equipped with books about colonialism, Yoruba masks, the matriarchy in ancient African cultures, and half a granola bar. I'd already eaten today so if I saved the granola bar until tomorrow then maybe I could hide out here for like two days. Nobody would ever find me.

I reached behind me and pulled a book out at random. *Heaven on Earth: Divine Power in Ancient Yorubaland*. Maybe I could tap into my inner celestial being and transcend this situation totally, and rewind time so I was curled up in bed with Malakai, because I missed him, I just didn't know what to do with us anymore, us felt trapped underneath the emotional debris of Zack's chaos.

'Kiki—'

My latent powers must have been super potent because I hadn't even turned the first page and they'd already been activated. I'd willed myself to hear Malakai's voice. With a little bit of training, I could really run the world. I turned the book around. Was it some kind of grimoire?

'Scotch.' The voice was louder, and I looked up to see Malakai stood in between the two bookshelves. My heart leant into its compulsion to leap at the sight of him, whatever the circumstance. Malakai sat next to me on the floor. The moment his arm curved around me, I turned to him, curling my legs over his, as he leant his chin on my head, my body furling into the comfort of his energy. I inhaled deeply, taking in his scent, letting it soothe.

'Look Kiki, I know you said this was your safe space but the

380

girls were getting worried. I was getting worried. I thought I'd try. Do you want me to go?'

'No.' I sniffed and untangled myself from him, crossing my legs and swivelling so I was facing him. 'Kai, I don't know what to do. It wasn't like all of it was a lie. But if I admit that some of it is true then people are gonna think that all of it is true and then there's that fucking *picture*—'

Malakai picked up my hand and let his thumb rest on my wrist. My pulse rose up to kiss it. His eyes went steely, and I could tell he was containing himself for my sake. They dropped to focus on his thumb rubbing circles on my skin, as if in meditation, to calm himself down.

'Kiki . . . the only reason I haven't fucked Zack up is because I promised you I wouldn't.'

I shook my head, 'I don't need any more drama and I don't want you to get in shit.'

Malakai nodded and looked up. 'Fine. But, Kiki, the picture was immediately reported and his account has been suspended. Aminah was on it immediately. And I'm not gonna tell you what to do because I can't do that. But what I do know is that you have the strongest voice I know and I think you should use it.'

The little energy I had left was used to laugh. I felt drained. 'Who's going to believe me? And now Brown Sugar and my summer programme is in jeopardy because who the hell is going to listen to me giving advice with my fake boyfriend, when I've just been exposed as the biggest hypocrite on campus? I need a sustained high level of listeners and – what?'

'Fake boyfriend?' Malakai's thumb had stopped its circuit on my wrist.

I blinked and rubbed my forehead. 'You know what I mean—'

'Nah, I don't really, Scotch.' He shifted back. 'This thing between us ain't bigger than the show?'

I froze. 'Are you serious right now? The only reason we decided to do this was for the show and your film. Obviously, now it's different, but—'

'Is it? What is this to you? Because not gonna lie, it kind of feels like this thing between us only exists to you in relation to Brown Sugar.'

I almost recoiled, tilted my head to the side. 'I'm sorry. Are you asking me what we are right now? Right fucking *now*, Malakai?'

It was belated, slow in boiling, but I realised that I was angry. Raging, in fact. The hurt had subsided and now I was pissed at Nile, at Zack and, apparently, at Malakai for treating my attention as some kind of leverage.

Malakai's eyes flashed with something that looked a little like hurt. 'Kiki, I'm just saying . . . it lowkey feels like you've had one foot out of this thing since we started. Like you've been waiting for a reason for it not to work. Why did you ask me if I was going to end this the other day? Did you want me to?'

I swallowed, something ugly forming inside me. I could feel it, stinging and agitating its way into becoming. It was the same way a boil formed to fight an infection, gathering every toxin together to expel it. In this case the infection was how much I liked Malakai Korede. So much that even now, I just wanted to call the fight off, put my face in his neck and be held by his warmth. But I needed to protect myself. Malakai probably thought that what he felt for me was real – the same way Nile wanted me during the moment, the same way Zack had chased me – but it would melt away soon, be proven a fallacy and a fantasy and I'd be punished for letting my guard down. I couldn't let that happen again.

'I don't know. Maybe. Malakai. We're attracted to each other. We hooked up. And maybe you want that to mean something more than it does – maybe that's why you compared me to Ama.'

Malakai ran a hand over his face and stood up, 'You have to be fucking kidding me. I knew you were pissed at that.'

I stood up too, and realised I really was pissed at that. It reminded me of Nile's desire for me being contingent on the fact that I wasn't Rianne.

'Do you like me because I'm not her?'

Malakai's shoulders dropped and his eyes softened. 'You can't think that's true, Scotch.'

I hitched a casual shoulder. 'I don't know what's true. Like, do you want to be in a relationship so bad to prove that you can actually be in one? Is it even about me?'

Why was I saying this? Why was I doing this?

The words stung on their way out of my mouth, overflowing like something rotten. When they hit the air, they sounded fascinatingly cold.

Shock and hurt coalesced grotesquely on Malakai's face. It almost knocked me off-balance, almost made me want to eat my words immediately, force them down, but I didn't. I let them sit, rancid in the air between us.

His gaze bolted into mine, eyes raw, glacial, slicing right through me. 'Don't act like I made this thing between us up. Don't fucking do that.'

I forced my voice to come out strong, but I heard the crack of my heart threaded through it. 'Kai, I don't think we're ready for whatever we think this is.'

Malakai stared at me like I'd lost my mind. Maybe I had. 'Why do you sound so reasonable right now? Like what you're saying isn't nuts—'

'Like . . . when you're emotionally freaked out your initial response is to shut me out. You wanted to enter the film contest to prove something to your dad . . . what if I'm just an extension of that? I'm not your therapy, Malakai.'

He held still and ran his eyes across my face. Then he rolled his tongue in his mouth, and across his lips, as if to rid himself of words he might regret, maybe to wipe away any residual feelings or maybe to clear his palette for the truth of what I said. My eyes were filling up and my stomach was turning, but I forced myself to continue pushing stinging words out.

'The film is mostly done, and—'

'Yeah,' His eyes dropped to my chin, his hands had slipped into his pockets. 'Let's just call it.'

I could feel the atmosphere between us tilt. I knew I asked for this – the fact that I didn't want this meant that I needed this – but this didn't stop me feeling like I was sliding downwards with

384

nothing to grip on to. I had said words I did feel and didn't feel and let them tangle up together. The emotional cacophony was making me nauseous. But I knew however I felt then would be better than how I would feel if I let myself enter us fully, and for him to later turn from me, rip it from under me, make me feel like an idiot for even believing in us. I wasn't ready to risk it. I was right not to risk it. Because he obviously agreed with me.

He was nodding, barely looking at me. 'We just met two months ago. And we got lost in the game we were playing.' His voice was cold, mechanical, precise. 'And maybe I did want to prove to myself that I'm different to my dad by being with you. And maybe this . . . thing was something you used to make yourself feel better about what happened to you in school.'

I almost smiled through the sharp pain lacerating me. Finally. The dagger, the one I'd imagined being suspended in the air, waiting for Malakai to pick up and twist in me. It was a relief that he'd picked it up. The sentence hung in the air and Malakai's eyes mellowed with regret immediately, shiny. His anger crumpled. He ran his hand across the back of his head.

'Shit. Scotch, I'm sorry. I didn't mean—'

'You did. And don't call me Scotch.'

The air between us stilled and cooled. Malakai levelled me with a sharp gaze that made my heart whir and then stop. He hit me with an empty half-smile that hooked into and pierced my chest.

Then he laughed humourlessly, a frigid chuckle that turned my bones brittle. He rubbed his chin, looked at the floor.

'OK. This is . . . I'm going to walk away now.' He started to back away, and regret flooded in, so quick and heavy I almost staggered with it.

'Malakai, wait—'

Malakai shook his head. 'Nah, you're right. We got caught up. I got caught up. That's on me. I am not . . . I'm not made for this. Not right for this. It's cool, Kiki.'

His voice was so forcibly light I had to blink a couple times to readjust myself to the darkness that I realised had fallen around us. He was looking at me without looking at me, somehow seeing past me while staring into my eyes, and it hit me square in the gut, causing a seismic shift in my heart, crushing the butterflies that had taken up residence in there since I bumped into him outside the lifts two months ago. I wanted to grab his face and tell him that I was chatting shit, that there was no game, just us, but instead I watched him turn around and walk away. When his footsteps grew faint, I realised that I was out of breath, and that I was panting, and then I was sobbing.

CHAPTER 26

'Is she even in there?' Chi's voice flowed under my bedroom door, through the scent of burning incense and wispy R&B.

'I assure you,' I heard Aminah say, 'she's in there. I can hear Jhené Aiko playing faintly, and the tape I put on the door to let me know when she's left the room is unbroken.'

'What's that smell?' I could hear the wrinkle in Shanti's button nose.

'Incense,' Chi said immediately. 'Sandalwood and frankincense. So at least I know she read my message about the best thing to burn when you want to cleanse negative energy.' She knocked. 'Babe! I brought crystals too! Amethyst!'

'Please, abeg,' Aminah was saying, her voice snapping into a brisk upper-class Lagosian lilt 'none of that juju shit.' She thumped on the door with what sounded like a closed fist. 'Kikiola, if you don't open this door right NOW, I will call your mother. I have had enough. Do you want me to stress Auntie out by informing her that her eldest child is having a meltdown?'

Low, but effective.

I flipped my covers, stared at my ceiling, and allowed the tears that had been filling my eyes to blur a little, before I blinked them away, slumped out of bed and shuffled towards the door. When I clicked it open, Aminah was standing in her house athleisure with a hand on her hip and a wrap tied around her hair that contributed to the vague feeling that she was about to beat my ass. She was flanked by Chioma and Shanti, who were armed with wine glasses, a bottle of rosé, and a tub of ice cream.

'Cute pyjamas.' Aminah ran her eyes across my tartan shorts and slouchy grey sweater. 'Have you changed out of them in the past three days?'

'I love you guys, but please I . . .'

I pinched the skin at the bridge of my nose and attempted to close my door. Aminah stuck her pink fluffy socked foot in the door frame. 'Absolutely not. This, my dear, is an intervention.'

I opened my mouth to say I didn't need one, but all that escaped was a sharp sob.

Aminah's face immediately slackened, 'Oh baby.'

And that was all it took for me to burst out crying and collapse into her.

It had been nine days since Zack's broadcast and a week since what I now recognised was my break-up with Malakai, and I was forced to admit that my method of trying to pre-emptively avoid hurt by cutting ties with him had possibly been short-sighted. It had caused acute physical chest pain and every time I thought of him, I had a sweet, sharp soreness, like I was comprised entirely of a tangle of ulnar nerves.

I missed him so much my stomach twisted with it, the grip made tighter by what we said to each other, precise shots fashioned from intimate knowledge, constructed to maim and fashioned from our own pain. It replayed in my mind like a horror movie, and familiarity didn't lessen the sting. Not only had I potentially lost my show, my admission to the NYU programme, and the respect of Blackwell, but I had also lost one of my best friends again, and this best friend happened to be a very good kisser. I missed the fact that I felt like I had my own personal sun when he looked at me.

'I said some really horrible stuff to him guys,' I said as I sipped at my £6 rosé, cross-legged on my bed. Aminah was cuddled up with me, Shanti was sat by my desk and Chioma was busy, strategically positioning crystals around the room. 'Really, really mean—'

'OK and he said shit to you too. You were mad at each other. So what? You'll figure it out,' Shanti muttered as she scrutinised the contents of my make-up bag.

'Doubtful.'

I wanted to apologise, but every time I tried to type it out, his words of dismissal weighed on my fingers. '*We just met two months ago*' pressed on my thumb till it backspaced the whole message. We got lost in the game; it was an idiotic fantasy. That was all. I was still angry too. That he saw the relationship instead of me, that I was a tool to rectify daddy issues. It was for the best. I shook my head as if to rid myself of the now-familiar pinpricks of hurt and loss.

'Anyway, it's not just the Malakai thing. It's the elections. I've messed it up for everyone contesting against Zack. Everyone who I stood with is sullied by association. And I really want to apologise to you guys for being an emo bitch this week. I was embarrassed. By everything. Embarrassed by Zack, embarrassed by how sad I feel about Malakai, embarrassed that I've messed things up for Blackwell.'

Aminah released me and sat up. 'First, I don't mind you being an emo bitch if you let me into your room. Second, there is nothing to be embarrassed by. Zack is a prick who shall be dealt with – and you and Malakai have broken each other's hearts.'

I couldn't help but laugh bitterly into my wine glass. 'Malakai's heart is not broken. I granted him his freedom. I'm sure he's grateful he dodged a bullet.'

Aminah waved a hand in the air and kissed her teeth. 'Please. Kofi told me that Malakai's been a moody prick since you last spoke and refuses to talk about what went down. He just keeps saying, "It is what it is", which, like . . . what does that even mean? Because what is *it*?'

I digested this alongside a spoonful of cookie-dough ice cream. It paired oddly well with the wine. I would need some Pepto-Bismol later. Aminah was biased. Malakai being in a bad mood could easily have stemmed from a dent in pride. I refused to entertain the sadistic glimmer of hope that he was as cut up about us being over as I was.

'And as far as Blackwell goes,' Chioma sat and stretched herself along the foot of my bed, 'You didn't mess anything up. Everyone thinks what Zit did is dark.'

My mouth curled genuinely for the first time in a while. 'Zit?'

Shanti nodded, 'If you checked the group chat you would know that that's our new name for him. And exactly. People mass-reported his account and Aminah's pretty much scoured the Blackwell socials to check that nobody's sharing the image. She's convinced everybody that it would bring shame to them and their families to keep hold of it.'

Aminah put the bottle of rosé between her legs and twisted it open to pour herself a glass. 'Shame is a powerful tool. Anyway, people are just confused because you disappeared. It just doesn't seem like you.'

Chioma shrugged, 'Maybe she just needed to align herself.'

Aminah snorted, 'If aligning herself was only running out the room to get pizza from the door.'

Something was bothering Aminah, I could tell, her chuckle was soft and sad, but before I could press, Shanti, interjected with a point of the tube of eyeliner that she'd procured. It was then I realised that she was examining every piece of make-up I owned before tossing those she deemed unacceptable into my wastebin.

'There are some dickheads, but I think mostly people just wanna know what's going on. We'll all be pissed if Zit's fuckery actually does manage to affect the election and permanently fuck with Brown Sugar ratings, but I don't think it will. Before this, our campaign was going great, and the other candidates are really putting the work in with their social media campaigns, which is good for us because it means legitimate competition and enthusiasm for things to change. Also, I feel like the whole Blackwell set-up had shifted. Like, you get to uni and you just gravitate to the people who are most like you on paper, right? But I'm more than just bundles and perfect brows.'

I laughed, 'Your brows really are perfect though.'

'Thanks babes, I'll do a tutorial just for you.' Shanti took a sip of her wine as I tried to figure out the exact ratio of insult to kindness. I figured it was exactly equal. Equal meanness and kindness tipped friendship into sisterhood.

'But seriously,' Shanti continued. 'You enter into these groups and they become cemented and you feel like you can't leave them, and then you're hanging out with people who you don't even really like.'

Chioma shrugged, 'Honestly, I really don't vibe with a lot of the vegan girls; one time I switched to regular deodorant because the natural shit made me smell like . . . well, shit, and they acted like I was single-handedly murdering the planet. Also, they're not that fun. I realised that I have a lot more fun hanging with you lot. I love you guys.'

I smiled. 'I love you too,' my smile faded and I exchanged a loaded look to Aminah that she instantly translated. She gravely nodded her agreement. 'Which is why I have to tell you guys something.'

Shanti quirked a brow and Chioma froze. I inhaled deeply, and proceeded to tell them the real origins of Malakai and I. When I was finally done, Shanti and Chioma stared at me in blank confusion while Aminah sipped her wine in a rare moment of silence.

'Um. Did you guys hear me?'

'We heard you,' Shanti said, with the eerie grin.

Chioma shrugged. 'Yeah Babe. You and Malakai were in a fake relationship to help you boost ratings for Brown Sugar to help your summer programme application in exchange for you collaborating with him on his film—'

'But then you were actually in a ting,' Shanti finished with a glint in her eye.

'Uh, right. And I didn't mean to lie to you guys, and I didn't expect to become such good friends with you and—'

'Lied to *us*?' Shanti smirked wider. I repressed a shiver. 'Oh honey. Thank God you're pretty!' She shot a look at Aminah. 'Does she genuinely think she was in a fake relationship this entire time?'

Aminah released a confusing cackle. 'Babe, I know. It's mad.'

Chioma snorted and her hand flew to her mouth, her clinking bracelets and bangles adding percussion to Summer Walker's crooning.

My brows furrowed. There was a joke being told that I wasn't in on. 'Know what?'

Aminah continued as if I hadn't spoken, and waved a manicured hand in the air, 'She'll come to it eventually.'

I blinked. 'OK, I have no idea what you guys are talking about but I'm *trying* to apologise.'

Shanti swatched lipstick at the back of her hand. 'Babygirl, it's fine. Thanks for telling us. I get why you didn't though.'

Chioma smiled. 'Right. You didn't know we'd become gang. We know you, Sis. It wasn't like, malicious.'

Shanti shrugged as she tossed a nail polish bottle. My relief at their grace was strong enough to refrain from pointing out that I loved that colour. 'We still love you, or whatever.'

My heart filled with warmth, the comfort of being seen and known displacing anxiety. 'You guys are pretty fucking amazing.'

Shanti shot me a flat look. 'No shit. Also, the plan was kind of genius. And it technically worked.'

Aminah nodded. 'Yeah, before . . . everything . . . we were up by sixty per cent.' She patted her own shoulder elegantly in congratulations.

'Plus,' Shanti continued, 'You fucked Zack *up*. Thinking about it, Zit wouldn't have done all this if he wasn't intimidated by you. He's literally printed out his face on flyers with a caption that says *You know what to do*. Dude is terrified!'

Chioma nodded gravely. '*Shook*. Your power is potent, Queen.'

I felt myself returning to myself a little, the brightness of my friends forcing some perspective, easing the clouds. The self-pity was receding to reveal a gleaming fury that was primarily for Zack and his audacity.

Aminah scrutinised my face. 'OK. I see some colour coming back to you,' she paused, 'Metaphorically. Good. Because AfroWinter Ball is next Saturday and I'm going to need you to be ready for it. Kofi is still giving us his hotel room so . . . '

The mention of the ball gave me a genuine, hearty laugh that I was grateful for. 'Oh. I'm not going to that.'

Aminah's brow arched. 'Are you joking?'

I smiled and my chin jutted out incredulously. 'Are *you* joking? Going to the ball was something I was doing because I was with Malakai and it was part of the whole deal. Going to it now would just be humiliating.'

Aminah flipped both her palms up. 'You're unbelievable.'

'Um,' Chioma's voice was quiet and tentative. 'What's going on?'

Shanti gently reached over for the ice cream tub I was holding, grabbed a spoon and returned to her chair. 'I think they're having a domestic?'

I shuffled a little further from Aminah to assess her. 'Meenz, what's wrong, because I feel like you have something to get off your chest.'

Aminah sat very still and then started blinking rapidly at me in a very alarming manner, as if she was malfunctioning. Then she raised a hand and through her long extended lashes she pincered me with eyes hard with love. 'Kiki, this is not OK. First, you shut me out for a week and now this? Why is Malakai the only reason you want to socialise? Was I not enough? You didn't come to the AfroWinter Ball last year, and even though I went with some girls from my course it was shit without you! It's a pattern! You bail on the most fun stuff in uni because you get shook! And I get it, but it's time you let it go, OK? I am tired! Ó ti su mi. Sis, I am not going to let you miss out on this. Fuck, I am not gonna let myself miss out on a good time with my best friend. Which, by the way, I have. So many times for you.'

I blinked, stunned, her words sitting cool within me, sending up spindles of shame. 'What? I never asked you not to go to events.'

Aminah rolled her eyes. 'No, you never did. Of course, you never did, you would never do that, but you think it's fun for me going out without my main? Most of these bitches are dull as hell.'

Her eyes drifted to Chioma and Shanti and she flashed them a quick, dazzling smile and rose a pacifying hand. 'Not you guys, obviously. Other bitches.'

Shanti was texting with one hand and had a spoon in the other. She didn't look up from her screen. 'If I thought you were talking about me, this spoon would be shoved down your throat, my darling.'

Chioma flicked her wrist in a rolling motion. 'This dialogue is healthy. Continue.'

'I love how much you've grown, Keeks.' Aminah's voice was gentler now, 'And I love that everyone gets to see the Kiki I adore. Your real nature has shone through; you bring people together. Look at Brown Sugar, FreakyFridayz! The elections that are happening! Blackwell is so much closer because of that. So, be part of what you bring together. Stop fighting it.'

I nodded, feeling my nerves soften, my edges curve, my breathing slow. She was right. I could do this. I was also being selfish – it was just cowardice. I wasn't someone who hid anymore.

I poked her shoulder. 'Hi. Have I ever told you that you're the love of my life?'

Aminah beamed and wiggled on the bed before pulling me into

a tight hug. 'Yes, but it's good to hear it again. Sorry I had to go savage on you.'

I laughed. 'Please. I needed it.'

'All right.' Aminah sat up, tone brisk. 'Lovefest done. Now that I feel like you're getting back to normal, I'm gonna need Killa Keeks to awaken.' She clicked her fingers in my face before picking up my phone from the bed and unlocking it with the passcode I didn't know she knew.

I squinted and hissed like she was dropping lime juice on a wound. 'No. Please, I'm not ready.'

Paying no heed to my resistance as I sat back on the bed, Aminah shoved the Brown Sugar inbox in my face. This seemed particularly cruel. I wondered if her showing me hate messages was like that training montage in *Creed II* where Rocky made Adonis punch the air over an open flame? Was she trying to toughen me up for the fight of my life? I blinked at the screen, ready to shove it away, when I saw the first message:

Solidarity Queen! Don't know what happened with you and Zack but we miss Brown Sugar.

I took the phone from her and scrolled. There were more messages like this — sandwiched, of course, between the expected misogynistic comments, but still, there were far fewer of those than I'd anticipated. And then something else that made my breath hitch and my hair stand on end. Messages from girls who had also dealt with Zack, who said that he also took pictures without their consent, that he lorded it over them, taunted them with the pictures if they broke things off with him or challenged him.

My palms were sweaty and I snapped up to shoot an inquiring look at Aminah. She nodded grimly.

All the remaining desolation drained from my body and was replaced with an all-consuming compulsion to kill, and if not kill, then to maim. My jaw clamped together. It was one thing to do it to me, but the fact that he'd been getting away with doing it to other girls . . . that he would likely go on to do it to other girls. The sadness that had stiffened my bones fled, the rage made me feel supple, fluid, and I felt myself melting into someone I recognised more. I'd allowed too many men to drive me to contort myself into a diminished version of who I was and could be. He had attempted to make so many women feel so small, so he could feel big, and it was going to be my pleasure to ensure we trampled him underfoot.

Aminah gasped and clapped her hands together. 'Oh, it's happening.'

Shanti smiled, something conspirational and curious. 'What's that look on her face?'

Chioma nodded sagely. 'I think she's summoning energy from the crystals.'

Aminah shook her head, 'Nope. That's Killa Keeks coming back with peppeh. What's stage one?'

The plan was configuring in my mind, becoming solidified as something I needed to do rather than something I could do. It was sealed with fury and conviction. There was no choice in this.

'I need to meet with Simi.'

Aminah raised the back of her hand to my forehead. 'It's gonna take a while for her to fully recover, poor thing. Take your time Babe. You're delirious.'

CHAPTER 27

From: S.Miller@WCU.ac.uk
Subject: A Notice

Ms Banjo,

I have heard about a recent ruckus on campus and I know you have exempted yourself from class for the last two seminars. I want to send you a pertinent reminder: You are an intelligent, powerful young woman, and any situation that makes you feel diminished is deceptive. Your power is in your truth. Stand in yours. Be loud in yours. The numbers for your show have dropped, but I am proud of what you have done with your voice regardless. I am also proud of your contribution to Mr Korede's film. I have seen the rough cut. It is beautiful. You make a wonderful team.

I hope to see you next week in class.

Warmly,

Dr M

I was going to vomit. I'd been fine on the drive down with the girls – more than fine – all of us singing loudly, badly, to my playlist. It was fun, possibly one of the most fun times I'd had in uni, and for forty minutes I'd forgotten about things like heartbreak and social pariahdom. But it was clear to me now that those feelings were just hibernating till we pulled up to the car park of The Pemberton, where I was faced with Blackwellians stepping out of cars, dripping with sauce, posing for the cameras and poised for drama. My plan had kept me steady until this moment, balancing me out when I considered that showing up to the biggest social event on the Blackwell calendar might be too exposing and undoing for me. I told myself that there was too much at stake for me not to do it, and yet here I was, nauseous, palms and pits prickling, frozen by the car as the girls buckled shoes and did last minute spritzes of setting spray and perfume. I was receding into myself again.

I wasn't ready. I wasn't ready to see Malakai. He was hired to film, so I knew he would be here logically, but emotionally I couldn't comprehend the idea of seeing him. I'd missed him so bad that every time I saw something that reminded me of him I felt an alarming twinge in my chest. Turned out everything reminded me of him.

After a few moments, when the girls had finished preening, Aminah noticed me leaning against the car. 'You OK, Keeks?'

'Mhmm, sure. I just . . . ' I fanned myself even though it was around 13 degrees, 'I need a moment.'

Aminah stepped closer to me, regal in her strapless purple pencil-legged Ankara jumpsuit paired with black, barely-there, heels and a compact, deep, violet gele that decorated her head. She'd gone over to a salon on Eastside to get it tied. She hooked a finger beneath my chin. 'I know being here is overwhelming . . . and honestly, for all the shit I gave you . . . it really is tough being here with everything going on. But your plan is so great and I am proud of you and I love you and you look too fucking good to waste this outfit. Blackwell is not ready.'

I'd foregone a coat for the sake of the look, not wanting to sully my yellow Ankara two-piece outfit – covered in majestic blue and red birds of paradise taking flight – with something as tedious as pneumonia prevention. The sweetheart neckline crop top hugged and pushed what needed to be pushed, and my high-waisted skirt cinched and accentuated the curve of my hips. I couldn't wear a *coat* over this, it would be an insult to my ancestors.

I smiled. 'They're not.'

'Have you guys finished making out?' Shanti was raising an impatient brow at us as she locked Mariah's doors. She was in a blush-pink structured iro-and-buba style fit, wide sleeves with geometrical shapes cut out at the hem, the softly glittery blush wrap-skirt cinching her waist, gele decorating her head like a crown, Chioma was wearing an elegant jewel-green chiffon Nigerian bubu, cascading to the ground, wide and ethereal, giving her wings.

Chioma waved us over as Shanti said, 'Considering I took the time to get each of us special phone ring lights for tonight, you guys are being very disrespectful wasting precious selfie time.'

402

Chioma smiled and inhaled deeply as she gazed at the three of us. 'I have a good feeling about tonight, girls. Good vibes, good energy. Sweetness and sisterhood in the air. Can you smell that?'

Aminah took a whiff, her expertly highlighted nose tilted up to the early moon. 'I can smell weed and . . . suya? Simi may be many things, but she snapped with the catering.'

Chioma winced 'As long as the veggie option isn't carrot sticks and hummus again.'

Shanti playfully rolled her eyes, artistically shadowed to mimic a summer sunset, 'Maybe you should grow up and eat meat. You've had worse things in your mouth.'

Chioma gasped, and I cackled and linked my arm through hers, 'Speaking of. Who do you have your eye on tonight?'

Shanti nudged Chioma in placation. 'How about AJ? He's coming tonight, saw it on his ProntoPic story. Doesn't he play djembes in some postgrad Afro-fusion band? Sexy as fuck. Thick muscles. Thighs that could crush a coconut. Pounding those drums with finesse. Imagine how he'd pound your—'

I squealed, 'Ashanti?'

Shanti cackled, 'Whatever. He's premium red meat though,' she shot a teasing look at Chioma, 'Not suitable for veggies.'

Chioma shrugged. 'Maybe I'll make an allowance for tonight. Gotta get my protein in somehow.'

Aminah, Shanti and I gasped in glee before we all collapsed into filthy squawks, heels clicking a happy, haphazard percussion as we made our way to the hotel.

CHAPTER 28

'm still not sure about Simi's involvement. How do we know we can trust her for sure?' Aminah's voice was angled with dry scepticism as I situated myself behind the DJ deck on the stage where Kofi had configured a complicated technical set-up for live broadcast, and ignored the curious looks being thrown my way.

'Look, the pop-up Brown Sugar episode was my idea. Besides, she wouldn't let me take up any extra attention at AfroWinter Ball, *her* event, if she didn't think it was necessary. You know she hates sharing the spotlight. She believes in this. And she's been really cool these past few weeks.'

Simi had been checking in once a day to ensure I wasn't bottling it, and to also remind me that she doesn't back losers, and her reputation was at stake too. So, she was supportive like a vaguely emotionally distant aristocratic parent of a perpetually disappointing child. She'd sent out a memo to the Blackwell populace as soon as I'd told her what I wanted to do.

THE TEAHOUSE

Wassup Blackwellians, it's your girl Simi, and looks like Kiki Banjo is coming out of hiding to give us some sugar for the tea we've all been dying for, with a special Brown Sugar episode at the AfroWinter Ball! Get your tickets now! Proceeds as always will go to the Sickle Cell Foundation. Looks like it'll be a night of glamour, drama and mess, and I for one cannot wait. See you there!

Simi might as well have called it 'Kiki Banjo Tells All'. She insisted she needed to make it sound salacious to draw people's attention, and perhaps she was right. The room was packed, and as I gazed across the room from the stage, I felt a little woozy from all the looks being thrown up at me in anticipation. It was strange looking down at them, shiny and colourful and beaming. I felt separate, and it didn't feel right. I didn't understand how I ever felt right before, pre-emptively cutting myself off from connection, choosing to feel nothing to avoid feeling hurt.

Aminah twitched her shoulder and sipped on a Lagos Island Iced Tea (same as a Long Island Iced Tea but generously free-poured), while passing me a Dakar Daiquiri.

'Fine, I trust her if you trust her. Plus,' her eyes drifted across the room, 'I have to admit the girl knows how to throw an event.'

Draped upon tables were mock prints of traditional patterns

from different Black nations, each one named after a capital city; Chi and Shanti were sat at ours, Addis Ababa, with Ty and AJ hanging on to their every word as Kofi vacillated smoothly from Amapiano to Afrobeats. It was an Afrotopia, Nkrumah's dream, compacted into a mid-sized event hall often used for corporate seminars.

It was while eyeing the room that I noticed a ripple in the atmosphere of the hall. I craned my neck to see who had entered to cause the shift, the thickening crowd turning towards the entrance. Simi stepped in, resplendent and refined in a strapless pink Ankara ballgown that puffed out at the waist, glitter eyes, looking like both the competition and the prize, and on her arm was Adwoa in a black tux with kente trimmings. Dapper, head half-shaven, crisp, with intricate cornrows criss-crossed on the other side of her head, cumulating into a ponytail of plaits.

I grinned, as Aminah gasped. 'What?' She turned to me, eyes wide and incredulous. 'You knew and didn't tell me?'

I shrugged. 'I didn't *know* know. Besides, I didn't think it was for me to tell.'

Aminah leant against the table and rapped elegant fingers beneath her chin as she squinted at the couple in fascination and awe. 'This is such an iconic relationship reveal. Dramatic, glamorous. No questions need to be asked because this is the full statement. PR genius. I think I like her so much more now.'

Simi kissed Adwoa on the cheek before immediately snapping into organiser mode and making a beeline for the stage. The crowd parted for her, her power and ironic imperviousness to gossip searing through it, her sharp eyes terse and deeply painted lips pulled into a brusque line. She hitched the skirt of her dress up as she floated up the stairs and towards the table I was sat at.

She flicked a vaguely approving look at my outfit, before nodding briskly, 'OK, so you know the schedule? Dancing, chilling, and then you're on for half an hour while dinner is being served, just before the AfroWinter Ball royalty announcements. I have all the technical stuff set up. Are you set? Because I really can't deal with you bothering me with questions throughout this thing.'

Aminah took a sip of her drink and muttered, 'I've changed my mind about the last part.'

Simi ran her eyes across Aminah, 'By the way, I don't want any extra drama tonight aside from the one that I have agreed to, so if you're going to fight with your little DJ about how he's flirting with Zuri Isak right now, please wait till after the party, because music is kind of necessary to this whole thing.'

Aminah's face fell and we turned to look at the DJ booth to see that indeed, Zuri Isak in a dress fashioned from kanga that boasted a deep plunge and a fitted silhouette was tilting her head and pointing to Kofi's deck in a way girls did when they were asking questions about things they didn't give a shit about to cajole a man's attention. Zuri slipped in front of Kofi and he leant over to her to show her the various buttons and knobs, then, in a devilishly artful move, she turned around so their lips were precariously close to each other, and giggled. If I wasn't loyally horrified, I would have been incredibly impressed by the smoothness of her technique. Aminah and I gasped simultaneously.

My mouth dropped open. 'What the fuck?'

Aminah's voice was level and dark. 'Is he serious?'

Simi sighed as if this was all slightly plebian theatrics. 'All right, well. I'm going to go and make sure everything is going OK at the voting station. I've made precautions to ensure that Zack hasn't got to the counters and promised them access to his table at FreakyFridayz, but best to keep across it. I'll see you later.'

She hesitated before putting a light hand on my shoulder and squeezing, then swiftly and elegantly sashayed away.

Aminah scratched the side of her nose and smiled widely, nodding rapidly, terrifying with faux nonchalance. 'This is why he's a DJ, innit.'

I chilled. Earnest use of British *slang?* She was beside herself.

She pulled up a chair and sat beside me. 'Of course he's good at spinning when all he does is spin lies and deceit.' I refrained from saying that DJs didn't actually spin records anymore.

'Why wouldn't man wanna be a music producer,' Aminah said, 'when all he knows is to push people's buttons?'

Aminah was jabbing the air with sharp acrylics, eyes narrowed, making her lashes look like fanned daggers as she stared in the direction of Kofi. Indeed, when I turned to pree what she was looking at so I could tell her that it surely wasn't as bad as it seemed, I was faced with Kofi's arm around Zuri as she held a headphone pad to her ear. Kofi's gaze flicked towards Aminah's almost imperceptibly, before turning back to Zuri.

I bit my lip. I didn't think I'd ever seen Kofi give attention to a girl that wasn't Aminah. 'Huh. OK. Yes. He's trying to make you jealous. Which is a really dick move that doesn't sound like Kofi. Did something happen between you guys?'

Aminah's mask of fury shook a little, and I caught a glimpse of something softer. She took a hold of it, fixed it properly on her face and frowned. 'Why does something have to have happened? Why can't you just accept that he's being a prick for no reason?! Stop trying to rationalise this Kiki, this isn't one of your Brown Sugar dilemmas. Is it because you made up with Rianne that you're feeling all kumbaya?'

I looked at my best friend and saw the hurt that she didn't want me to see. I leant in closer to her and held her hand. 'Do you want it fixed?'

'No. I hate him.' But her eyes were glistening, anger weakening.

I nodded, hearing her loud and clear. 'OK. Then we'll fix it. Walk me through it.'

Aminah sighed, 'All right. So, um, we were talking by the bar when Osi came up to—'

'Osi, First-Year Osi?!'

Osi Ummoh was the last guy that had got Aminah stressed – a Theatre Studies student, as tall as he was vacuous, actor by study and actor by personality, presenting himself as the perfect boy-friend to Aminah and three other girls on campus simultaneously. He didn't cheat but he was close enough to it to drive Aminah to distraction till the trance broke.

'Yes Keeks, that Osi. So, we were right next to him, and I had planned on ignoring him, but then he was all "Hey, Disney, looking good," and you know Disney was his nickname for me, right? Because he said I reminded him of a Disney princess. Anyway, I rolled my eyes, yes, but I smiled a little you know? Because Osi is still fine as hell. Then he was like, "I miss you. It would be good to catch up these days," and I was like "What we gonna talk about? How you fucked up a good thing?" and Osi was like "Maybe". And then he smiled and walked away. That was it! That is all that happened. And then suddenly Kofi starts acting all weird, just moving mad awkward, and says, "What was that?" And I said, "What was what?" – and he goes, "Aminah, are you serious right now?" And then it's time for his set to start and I come here and then the next thing I know he's basically smashing Zuri Isak on top of his decks!' Aminah paused to take her breath and skip a look across me. 'OK what? What? Why are you looking at me like that?'

'Um,' I folded my hands together on the table, 'I just want to clarify that Kofi was there the entire time that this interaction occurred with Osi?'

Aminah looked less indignant. 'Uh, yeah—'

'So, I just wanna break it down. Kofi was stood there as you flirted with your ex-boyfriend? Who didn't acknowledge his existence? And you didn't bother to introduce Kofi.'

Aminah swallowed. 'When you put it that way it sounds bad but . . . we aren't even technically together.'

'Uh huh. So then why are you pissed that he's flirting with Zuri right now?'

Aminah's face fell. 'Oh shit.'

'Do you want to be with him or not?'

'Obviously!'

'Who is it obvious to?'

Aminah's lips parted to speak but nothing came out. I moved closer to her, squeezed her arm. 'MiMi, Kofi has always been straight up about his feelings for you. He probably thought you guys were getting closer to getting to be a thing and then, well, you kind of mugged him off. Tell the truth, you knew talking to Osi would make him a little jealous right?'

Aminah shrugged. 'Yeah, but that's our thing! He chases, I tease.'

'So maybe he's tired of chasing. Maybe he thinks that this is just a game to you.'

'We talk every day! I even made him a cup of tea once!'

I nodded. 'Oh yeah. That time he came round with your favourite Chinese food because you were working late on some coursework and he knew you were running on fumes.'

Aminah stared at me. 'Whose side are you even on?'

I laughed and grabbed her shoulders, shook her a little. 'Yours. Always yours. And that includes not letting you get in your own way and helping you accept that shit doesn't have to be complicated to be real. Like, you already know you want to be with him – why do you think there has to be work involved to validate it, you know?'

Aminah rubbed her temple. 'Wow, I am sobering up quickly. I'm gonna need a Timbuktu tequila shot after this. I hear you. I really do. I just feel like if there's no work involved then he won't appreciate me enough. I see how my dad takes my mum for granted sometimes. You should hear how he speaks about her. I mean, he loves her, don't get me wrong, but he's always like, "She's safe, she's reliable, I can always count on her, she keeps the home running". As if she's some kind of generator, expending energy to keep everyone else running. But what about her energy? I just feel like if Kofi has to put work in, he's more likely to, like, cherish me. I want to be cherished.'

'Meenz. Kofi is obsessed with you. And besides, you cherish yourself. I cherish you. And if it turns out that he doesn't treat you how you should be treated then you have the option to bounce him out your life. And I'll kill him.'

'Thank you.'

'But you have to at least try. You have to take the risk.'

Aminah sniffed and dabbed the corners of her eyes with the edges of her palms. Excessive alcohol made her extremely emotional. 'Shit. You really are good at this.'

I grinned. 'I know right, being in a fake relationship that turned into an ill-fated real relationship gave me true insight.'

Aminah burst out laughing, which I found a little rude since I was doing some really deep, introspective emotional reflection and unpacking. 'Um, what's funny?'

Some residual giggles were still falling out of my best friend's mouth and I waited (im)patiently for her to get them all out. I almost preferred it when she was crying. Aminah shook her head slowly. 'What's funny, Keeks, is that you're still saying *fake relationship*.'

'So?'

Aminah tilted her head to the side, 'Oh. Oh, honey. That was never, ever, a fake relationship. If that boy was ever faking how he looked at you, then Daniel Kaluuya better watch out because there's a new, fine-ass Oscar-winner in the village.'

I followed her direction to see Malakai filming people talking by the bar. He slowly moved with the camera and landed on me. He froze. Even with the distance I saw the latent heat in his gaze. He nodded infinitesimally at me in greeting, so tiny that I could have missed it, so tiny that it was heavy.

'Hi,' he mouthed.

'Hey,' I mouthed back.

I allowed myself to risk the headrush of fully taking Malakai in. He was wearing crisp, navy trousers and a kaftan, tailored to perfection, and even at my vantage point, I could see the intricate, twirling embroidery on the lapel of the high neck, see the way the material fit around his thick arm in a way that made me want to grab on to it and swing like fruit ready to drop, before I did drop into his lap where I could pull him closer and kiss him. His thin gold chain winked at me, conspiring with the gleam of his cufflinks.

All of me leapt and unfurled and unleashed, all the missing all the anger, all the hurt all the . . . that heavy, soft thing, the pink matter of the matter. Fuck. I was falling, had fallen, when had I fallen? Was it a process, or was it an instant, or did time warp and rupture around us? Because whatever we were defied physics. Which was why falling in love with him had felt like I was shooting up and above and was light and full but not weighed down. I was in love with him. I was in love with a boy that I had thoroughly fucked it with.

Someone tapped Malakai's arm, asking for a picture, and he tore his eyes away from me. I was breathing hard, my pulse pounding in my ears, feeling an odd storm of happiness at the sight of him and heartbreak at the loss of him, because somehow, I knew that our argument was both of our insecurities colliding, that the mess wasn't the sum of us, the sum of our possibility. It was part of it, and that was OK. We were beauty within the mess. I pushed him away because I was scared he would hurt me and he let me because he was scared of the same. We were too scared to talk it through, lashing out to protect ourselves and hurting ourselves in the process. What was it that he had said when he walked away from us? That he wasn't made for this? Wasn't right for this? I should have said, that we would learn how do this together. That he was so sweet and so kind with this. He's so right for me it's like he's made for me. I think I'm right for you, Kai. I think we operate at a higher frequency when we're together. Our energies fuse and we become supernovas. I think we have so much more to share and to give. I think we've barely even begun. To not give us a chance would be a shame, a waste, a tragedy.

I took a large gulp of my drink. 'Oh my God, Aminah. I think . . .'

Aminah had been watching me and she pinched my waist. 'I know.'

'What do I do?'

She scraped her chair closer to mine and leant her head on my shoulder. 'Take the risk. Be my Killa Keeks.'

414

'What's good Blackwell? Welcome to the first ever Live Brown Sugar Session, an episode made in conjunction with tonight's AfroWinter Ball – thanks again, Simi, for this opportunity.'

Simi raised a glass elegantly from her table, and looked around demurely at her constituents, accepting silent praise.

I forced smooth joviality into my voice and let the words melt over the mic as my skin prickled from the spotlight on it, the intensity of eyes on me making my nerves spark. There was a light smattering of cheers, conveying curiosity more than excitement.

I put the mic on the stand and clapped my hands together. 'So, normally, I'm reading you guys' confessions and giving you my feedback. But I think for this episode it should be the other way round. I'm sure you all watched the video that our dearly beloved petty king Zack released last week, and I'm sure you all have some questions. I thought I'd lay it all out now.' I inhaled deeply. 'Uh, first of all yes, it's true, Zack and I hooked up for a few months.'

Oh, now the crowd had found their voice?! Gasps and murmurs vibrating through the hall, people turning to each other, whispers of 'I told you so' and 'rah' rippling through the room. Zack wasn't here yet apparently every year he arrived just before the AfroWinter Ball royalty was announced. I cleared my throat.

'But uh, contrary to what he implied, I did not catch feelings. Actually, if there is one thing I have a violent allergy to, it is feelings for Zack Kingsford. Like, even saying that sentence is making the inside of my throat itchy.' I coughed a couple of times, and the crowd's laughter grew warmer. I grew bolder.

'It wasn't a relationship. It was just, well, I don't know what it was. I want to say it was fun, but honestly? When I really think about it? It really wasn't that fun.' I shrugged. 'It was a means to an end, but actually . . . well, I never achieved the end I hoped for if you know what I mean.' Guffaws now and knowing hums from the girls. 'It was an end I could have achieved by myself. With less talking.' I pulled a face and it pulled in more laughs.

'Thing is, Zack thought he could get away with his lies because he thought I would be too freaked out to tell you guys this. He banked on my silence.'

I pressed the clicker in my hand and the projector behind me flickered alive. It flashed screenshots of texts that dozens of women had sent me with their names and photos blurred. Clear as day though, was Zack's number, alongside aggressive texts in which he taunted these women, threatening to expose explicit images of

416

them. The picture that Zack had posted of me was in the middle, unblurred. There was a collective sharp inhale, some murmurs, some heckles. I almost buckled. I looked to the side of me to see Aminah making an OK sign with her fingers and gesturing to the two emergency shots of tequila she had waiting for me.

I took a deep breath, wet my lips and continued. The crowd had settled now, hooked on to my every word.

'Some of these pictures were sent, and some were taken without consent. Either way, none of these women deserved to be taunted with them or blackmailed. He is weaponising our sexuality against us. Zack Kingsford is a misogynistic pig. Silence emboldens him. He is weak and afraid of the truth. He's afraid of us. Our voice.

'And aside from this, he has his own agenda and it has nothing to do with the good of Blackwell. If he wants to cosy up with the Whitewell Knights to get fast-tracked into being a token Black mascot at a soul-sucking law firm, well, be my guest.' The audience was electrified again, thunder looping through the room. 'But what we won't allow him to do is use Blackwellians' integrity to do it. We are better than that. We deserve better than him. Whoever you vote for next week, just please bear that in mind. We deserve a leadership that cares. We aren't a mechanism to feed somebody's ego.

'We're a community, a movement and a family. Family don't sell each other out. Family are honest with each other, and when we're not, we put our hands up and come clean. So, I'm coming clean, and I really hope you guys will give me a fresh chance and Blackwell a fresh chance in the upcoming elections. Let's make the right decision for our family and rid ourselves of the real Wasteman of Whitewell. I want to thank all the amazing women who trusted me enough to help share their story. You're incredible. And I would also like to note that the screenshots have been reported to the university board by us.'

There was uproarious applause, foot stamps and, while I was tempted to be bolstered by the energy, I knew I hadn't finished. I waited till it died down to add, 'Um, also . . . I really, really appreciate you all for supporting *Gotta Hear Both Sides*, but I can't be a hypocrite anymore, so in the spirit of transparency,' I inhaled deeply and my gaze roamed the crowd to see Malakai stood at the back of the hall, looking straight at me, a hand in his pocket, face carefully inscrutable.

'Malakai and I didn't start off as a couple,' I nodded at the harsh, hushed shock that flowed through the tables, 'It's kind of a long story but . . . we pretended to be in the relationship for *Gotta Hear Both Sides*. And I thought . . . there was no risk in faking because I really didn't think Malakai and I would work.'

Malakai was now looking at his phone, eyes hard. Was he even listening? He glanced up at me for a second, expression unreadable, before he turned away and walked out the doors of the ballroom. In some kind of weird display of masculine solidarity, some other male members of Blackwell left with him. Was that Ty and Kofi? My heart cracked. I had to stay. This was bigger than us. I felt sick. Was I shaking? I heard a heckle from the crowd.

'I'm sorry, you basically lied to us? For weeks? And we're meant to be cool with this?' The sentiment caught on and the tone of the crowd was more nebulous. I curled my hand into a fist in order to retain my nerve.

I shook my head, 'No you're not meant to be cool with it. It was a shitty thing to do. I didn't respect you guys like I should have. And I think, I . . . thought everyone else was performing romance so what I was doing wasn't technically wrong. But the truth is . . . you lot are so cool and so brave for just going for it. Letting yourself *feel*. I missed out on so much for so long because I was scared of doing that.'

The tables were silent, looking at me contemplatively, trying to figure out whether they hated me or not. That was fair. Aminah attempted a slow clap that Chioma and Shanti tried to join in on from their table, but it quickly dissipated into a weak patter when they realised nobody was willing to build it to an applause.

I wet my lips. 'Uh, so, anyway . . .'

Someone put their hand up and Simi signalled for the mic to be passed. I said it was an open forum and anything went. The person was Zuri. I instantly regretted the decision.

'OK, I hear the political shit, and we care, and we agree that Zack is a Wasteman but . . . back to you and Malakai, you were faking this whole time?'

I'd committed to honesty, and there was a picture of me in my underwear on the screen behind me so I figured that there wasn't much more to expose. Malakai had left the room, but the truth was still the truth. Blackwell had told me so much about themselves. I owed them the same vulnerability.

'Well. No. We became a real couple. And . . . actually, I don't think I was faking any of it. I just didn't know that at the time. From the moment I met Malakai it's like something fundamental in me *knew*. He's thoughtful and gentle. He has a stillness that calms me. He's infuriating and he makes really corny jokes, and he makes me smile even when I don't want to. Especially when I don't want to. And I tell him he's the worst, and he is, because he's annoying, so fucking annoying, because there is no hiding when I'm around him. Completely fucks up my guards.

'He's the worst in the sense that he's the best. And I think I lashed out at him because I was scared of how much I liked him. It's kind of a mess. But I've decided that I'm good with that. Sometimes beautiful things get messy. Mess is OK. I learnt about myself. I've learnt to let myself enjoy things. I've also learnt how cool it is to like someone and be liked back.' I released a wan smile.

'I've learnt to trust that I can be liked with no agenda. Knowing that in theory is different to knowing that in practice.' I inhaled deeply and pushed out brightness onto my face, dug up from my reserves. 'So . . . are we good? Or do I need to spill *all* my tea right now?'

The audience seemed to forgive me, and more congenial murmurs filled the hall, quiet discussion loosening the tension just as Aminah rushed to the stage. She grabbed the microphone from my grip while I stared at her in confusion.

'Hi, all! It's Minah Money on the mic! Producer and PR extraordinaire. Wassup? OK, so as you know, this is a Live Brown Sugar Session with a twist. Later on, we're allowing people to send questions, put their hand up, or call in to ask for advice or request a bop. But first, we have a sponsor that would love to play a message. OK. Thanks!'

Aminah winked at me and assiduously ignored my mouthing of 'What the fuck?' She nodded at Simi who had somehow situated herself behind the tech desk without me knowing. Simi nodded professionally and the lights dimmed further as the screen behind us blinked, changing from Zack's exposure to . . . my heart flipped and my stomach dipped.

Untitled appeared in stark white letters across a black backdrop. I already knew it was a clip from Malakai's film before it started rolling. It was even more stunning than what I had seen in the edit suite. Gorgeous vignettes of tessellating-toned, brown-skinned people, kaleidoscopic sizes and shapes that formed a deep, rich, bright texture, their voices overlapping and then separating to tell their stories. Blackwell denizens at parties, in the push and pull of attraction, swelling up with it till it made their skin glow with it. In campus cafés, at the libraries, on the quad. People in the audience laughed and cooed as they recognised themselves.

And then, there was my voice, speaking on a neo-soul instrumental that Kofi composed, 'You know from the songs I've listened to . . . I feel like relationships are in the seeing. I think everyone just wants to be seen and to find someone who they enjoy seeing. Like . . . seeing them brings them joy.' And then, Malakai's camera was on me, laughing at one of our dinners at The Sweetest Ting, me sticking my tongue out at him across a lecture hall after he surreptitiously brought out his camera, me slicking lip gloss on my lips in my mirror, the reflection showing him mouthing a 'damn' that I rolled my eyes at, my smile repressed. My chest felt tight, in a good way, like my heart had expanded, filled all the way up. 'And isn't it a trip,' I said, 'when you find someone who you like seeing and who sees you?'

Now, I had taken the camera from Malakai, filmed him putting his durag on, swiped it to film him while he was watching *Boyz n the Hood*, by his hero, John Singleton, the focus on his face, his mouth shaping his favourite lines, his eyes lighting up with inspiration, the bright in the deep. I'd focused on his lips.

'It's such a miracle that people write songs about it. People pine for it. People get scared and sabotage it. People plead for it back, fists clenched, breaking it down in the middle-eight. Man, I just feel like the whole thing . . . the love thing . . . demands that you're brave. Seeing people for who they are can be scary, that's like . . . full investment. Responsibility. You have to care and be committed to the care. And you gotta care even while preparing for the fact that they're not going to fit into your idea of perfection. Is it worth the risk? I don't know. Only you can know.' A pause, and then I say while laughing, 'Shit that was deep. Now here's the "Thong Song", one of the greatest love songs of all time.'

Malakai had filmed during Brown Sugar. I'd got up and mouthed the lyrics to the 'Thong Song' with passion, eyes squeezed, fists closed, looking completely goofy and completely happy. I bit my lip and laughed. I liked seeing myself like that. I liked seeing Malakai see me like that.

Then, there was Malakai sitting in a booth at what I recognised as The Sweetest Ting. It looked like he was filming himself. He rubbed his neck and leant forward.

'So, uh, when I started making this documentary, I really thought relationships weren't for me. I almost approached it like . . . a wild-life documentary, right? I wanted to observe and understand why people would put themselves at risk of hurt like that. Why they would want to be tied to another person. Why anyone would even try. But then I met this girl.' Malakai smiled to the camera, his eyes so full of something so warm and heavy and precious, my own started to fill too. 'I met this girl with the sharpest, sweetest mouth and the biggest heart. Soft and tough and shy and bold. Beautiful man, so beautiful. And . . . she made me want it. Really want it. And I figured . . . that's why people do it right? Be vulnerable and shit. Because they want to be close to the person who makes it worth it. It's about connecting with someone who makes you want to try. And she made – makes me want to try.

'And me and this girl had an argument. It was rough. We both said really harsh things to each other, I dunno. I . . . my skin was inside out for her and that was the first time I really clocked it. I got scared and I backed her into a corner. She was going through something, and I didn't give her space to feel that. I was thinking about myself. I always say that I got her. But when she needed me . . . I didn't have her in the way I promised myself I would always have her. And I'm shook I lost her because she is the best thing. The best fucking thing.

'Anyway, I've been wracking my brain trying to figure out how to let her know how I feel, and then I remembered, in one of her shows she said, that it just has to be true to you, just has to be real. Say it in the way you know how. So this is what I know. I know how it feels when I get the perfect shot. When the light hits a certain way, and someone's expression is the perfect display of emotion. It feels like you've hit on something sacred. That's how I feel when I look at her. She's the perfect shot. And the perfect shot isn't about something being flawless, it's about the truth. She's the truth to me. Clarity. The world is *doable* when she is near me.'

Composure was threatening to leave my body. 'Kai.' My voice was a hoarse, vocal stumble. Blackwell was enraptured, camera phones up, interest piqued. I was frozen to the spot.

'I also know how my favourite movies make me feel. They pull me in and pull me out, I am totally in their world, but they also make me look in. I watch them and feel home, I watch them and feel like I can never know enough, I watch them over and over, always ready to discover the universe they create. That's how she makes me feel. There's a whole universe in her and I would be so lucky to live in it, explore it. Over and over.'

The film stopped. Aminah cleared her throat into the mic. Her eyes were glistening, and she surreptitiously pinched my waist. 'OK. Well that's it from our sponsor. Now we have our first call.'

She smiled at me and passed me the mic, as if I were capable of working right then, as if my brain was capable of coherency. She nodded at me with such command that I found myself saying, in a choked-up voice, 'Hi. Welcome to Brown Sugar Sessions. What's your song request?'

Malakai walked through the doors, phone to his ear, hand in his pocket, looking directly at me, into me, revitalising the butterflies, gaze moving like a defibrillator. The crowd turned around to see what I was looking at and immediately dissolved into low whoops and cheers, braps and bloops and gun fingers.

'So I was thinking, "When We Get By", D'Angelo. You know it right?'

I was going to faint.

'Vaguely.'

'See that song,' the voice said, 'sounds like sunshine to me. Sounds like how I think love feels.'

I shook my head and bit into my smile. 'Corny.'

'Rude.'

I snorted.

'But then I wondered – and I guess this is my query,' Malakai continued, 'if, even that song isn't enough. Maybe this demands the greatest love song of all time. And I wondered whether if I arranged for the Whitewell Wailers to perform an acapella version of the "Thong Song" for her, the girl I can't get out of my head would forgive me for being a dick.'

I laughed at the in-joke. 'Well, objectively, I think she's sorry for being a dick too. And that you're already forgiven. I think a performance from the iconic Whitewell Wailers would help, but just in case you can't secure the third-place finalists in the regionals for the National University Non-Conforming Singing Group Competition, we can just play it.'

Malakai nodded. 'Sure, sure. Except—'

My jaw dropped, as a strong, baritone hum of *bum-bum-bum-bum-bummm* immediately burred through the doors of the ballroom, quickly followed by twelve of Whitewell's second-finest choral group, walking towards the stage, dressed in white tees and black trousers and solemnly informing me, in pristine harmony, that my dress was so scandalous, that there was a look in my eye so devilish.

Malakai's smile was wide and he shrugged, eyes bright with mischief as the hall exploded into whistles and cheers and my eyes watered and I was laughing and I couldn't believe how much I loved this ridiculous man.

I turned around and Aminah was grinning wildly as she shooed me off the stage. I hopped off and was followed by trails of 'GET IT, SIS' as I twined myself through the tables to where Malakai was by the doors.

The Whitewell Wailers found an engaged and appreciative audience in Blackwell, and everyone was up on their feet, clicking in time, and it smoothed over the atmosphere, subduing all residual animus, warming the air. With everyone suitably distracted, Malakai and I were essentially alone. We both paused, the silence comfortable, hot, tingling with energy, faces firm in their self-aware coyness.

'Hey.'

Malakai brought his phone away from his ear and slipped it in his pocket, releasing a slow, delicious half-smile, and drank me in indulgently. 'Hi.'

'Thank you for the serenading.'

'They're complete divas. Wanted a rider. Hot water and lemon. Massages.'

'I blame *Pitch Perfect*. By the way, did we really both do public declarations of affection just now?'

'Embarrassing, innit. I can't believe we've become those people.'

Malakai grinned and stepped closer to me, and further into our comfort. 'Can we talk about how you buried that prick? You're incredible. I am so proud of you. You're kind of my hero, Kiki Banjo.'

I smiled because I couldn't help it, smiled because I didn't want to help it, even if I could.

'I thought you'd left.'

Malakai shook his head, 'Nah. I got a text that Zack had tried to enter the building. I had to go deal with it. Had an AirPod in and I was plugged into the live show the whole time, so I heard everything you said.'

I felt my lips part in shock. The boys leaving with Malakai suddenly made sense. I noticed slight creases in Malakai's otherwise-crisp kaftan. 'What did you do?'

Malakai shrugged, 'Stopped him from getting in, innit. I promised you that I wouldn't do anything that would get me in trouble with uni, but technically we're out of the university's jurisdiction.' His eyes glinted and my knees got weak and I made the executive decision to not ask any more questions because truth be told, I didn't give a fuck about anything but us right then. Zack could choke.

'Scotch . . . please believe that when I say "I got you", from now on, I mean it. I'm not gonna slip on that again.' His gaze blazed into me with a ferocity that branded his words as truth in my heart. I trusted him.

I nodded. 'I know.' I reached up to trace the intricate embroidery on the lapel of his kaftan, before flattening my hand against his heart. 'And I got you.'

Malakai smiled, placed his hand over mine, before picking it up and tenderly tugging me closer to him. 'You know, Meji kicked me out of The Sweetest Ting the other night because he said I was "bringing down the vibe". He said he likes me better when I'm with you. I said, Well shit, I like me better when I'm with you.'

His eyes, as ever, black diamonds, coruscated and lit me up from under my skin. His arms slid around my waist, pulled me till my body was flush against his and I melted, butter cupped in a palm, silk between his fingers. I curled my arms around his neck.

'And the other day,' Malakai spoke, blithely, 'I burned plantain for the first time in my life.'

I gasped.

Malakai nodded gravely. 'I know. It was difficult for me. But do you know why I burned it?'

'Tell me.'

I was thinking of you. I got lost in thinking about you and I forgot that I was frying plantain. That's when I realised that I must be in love with you. Like . . . insanely in love with you. No one else could distract me from plantain.'

A truth I knew viscerally, but its expression made me feel like I could pluck stars from the sky and wear them on my ears. Like my blood was a liquid giggle. His broad hands wrapped around my waist, heat and pressure agitating the butterflies into chaos. His gaze dropped on to my lips, found something there that made its journey back to my eyes more arduous, lids heavy. In the heat of us, I was sweet and golden and hot and soft like perfectly browned plantain. I was so fully me, so safe in me. I lifted my hand to his face and bumped my lips with his.

'I can't believe I'm in love with a guy who burns plantain. Worse still, the fact that my boyfriend burnt plantain hasn't made me love him less.'

Malakai's face was the first stretch of sunlight in spring. His gaze blazed and beamed like something the ancients would build temples for. He curved a hand around the back of my neck in precious possession. 'Scotch. Before I lose my mind—'

Malakai's smile spread across his face and all over me, and when he scooped me so my chest was against his, his arms holding me tight to him, everything fled from existence but us. I might have heard some whoops and hollers, but I wouldn't have been able to tell for sure. I was elsewhere. I was happy, I was here. His heat melded into my heat and created an alchemy that metamorphosed the butterflies into a bird of paradise, and I was taking flight with it. This kiss, this *this*, this us, tasted like indulgence and sustenance. Our tongues moved like we were each other's rice and wine, twirled with the ease of drunken, fed hips. In the kiss, I tasted him and I tasted me and I tasted what we were and what we could be. It tasted like honey and spice, twined.

The music faded and Simi's voice echoed across the hall, the lights dimming dramatically, and focusing on the large stage where the DJ booth was situated. 'Mandem, gyaldem, peopledem, pay attention, for the portion of the night you have all been waiting for has arrived.'

Her regal demeanour soured a little as her eyes narrowed at something at the back of the hall. 'Um . . . who is in the photobooth? Fuck's sake, what is wrong with you people? I'm all for sexual liberation but we are literally in a hotel right now. You have options. Look, who is on health and safety duty? We have to disinfect that now. Ugh. Chanel, can you sort that please? Don't do that face. Whose earrings are you borrowing tonight? Thanks, Babe. OK.'

Simi swung some hair out of her face and recomposed herself a shimmering, glossy smile painted across her face again like she'd never been interrupted. She delicately cleared her throat. 'OK. So. It is time to announce this year's AfroWinter Ball royalty. The winners get crowns specially ordered from China, a bottle of Prosecco to share and a two coffee vouchers for Beanz worth £50, and were voted by you, the polis of Blackwell, tonight. Like I said earlier as the polls opened, not only does the AfroWinter Ball royalty have to serve looks, they also have to represent who we are as a community. I hope you chose wisely. And the winners are . . .'

Simi fluttered a serene look across the hall before opening the envelope in her hand.

'Aminah Bakare and Kofi Adjei!'

'*Hello?* . . . Where are they? . . . Oh my God! Are *they* the people making out in the photobooth?'

430

When We Get By

The Blackwell Beat *with Lala Jacobs*

What's good Blackwellians, and welcome to The Blackwell Beat with Lala Jacobs.

Our sources have just informed us that Zack Kingsford, the recently disgraced former president of Blackwell, is being investigated by the university for corruption and harassment after Kiki Banjo's exposure of him at the AfroWinter Ball. Her accusations amplified the protests lobbied against him in the past month, making it impossible for them to ignore what they have been ignoring for months.

Simi Coker provided a damning dossier to the university bosses. The news has gained traction across campuses nationwide and it is possible that the university's fear of embarrassment has forced them to act. The Whitewell Knights have formally disbanded and have been condemned by the university. Zack Kingsford has been expelled from campus.

THE TEAHOUSE

Well Blackwellians looks like the presidency might just get a whole lot sweeter.

In a shocking turn of events, following the Live Brown Sugar Session (that was far, far too corny for my tastes), Blackwellians have collectively called for Kiki Banjo to put herself forward for interim president and Adwoa Baker has withdrawn herself from the race, putting herself forward for the vice-presidency instead.

If Banjo does win, I hope she and her boyfriend manage to keep their making out to themselves because frankly I'm sick of seeing that much of their tongues in communal spaces and it's unbecoming for a leader to engage in that much PDA. Seriously, it's gross. We get it. You're in love. You're not the only ones.

I am sure Adwoa Baker will make a fine vice-president if their cabinet wins. Some may say the vice-president's role is more important than the president's, a more strategic position. The team, including Aminah, Shanti and Chioma, call themselves The Dahomey Amazons, after the all-bad-bitch military regiment in the ancient kingdom. They are up against . . . an all-male party called the Kingsford Kollective (really? OK. Sure.). And the Pow Party (I am seriously so confused – is this some kind of dance competition from an early 00s' movie?!).

Best wishes to all involved.

From: L.Davis@NYU.com
Subject: Brooks Media & Arts Institute, New York University

Dear Miss Kikiola Banjo,

Congratulations! We are pleased to inform you that you have been granted an unconditional offer and full grant on our Cross-Media summer fellowship program. We look forward to seeing you in July.

Faithfully,
Loretta Davis
The Dean

ACKNOWLEDGEMENTS

In Yoruba culture, twins are called Taiwo and Kehinde. Taiwo is physically the firstborn but is thought to be the spiritual younger child who was sent out by the eldest to 'taste the world' or 'try the world' first. Kehinde, the eldest, is born second, after their spiritually younger sibling has confirmed that the world should be ventured into. In other words, after Taiwo has informed Kehinde that the world is worth living in. There is a hope embedded in this lore. The notion that despite the darkness of the world, some hope can be detected, some light, some joy, some goodness. That living in the world is worth pursuing.

Love in Colour is the Taiwo to *Honey & Spice*'s Kehinde. *Honey & Spice* is my spiritual firstborn, conceived years ago, living with me through many transitions in my life, growing and deepening as I matured. While I planned for *Honey & Spice* to be my first book, *Love in Colour* came along and altered those plans – and *believe me* it took some convincing! *Honey & Spice* was my firstborn! However, I am so glad that *Love in Colour* came first, because it encapsulated my mission statement, confirming why I do what I do, why I am who I am. It was an introduction, a taster of the many flavours of romance and love I explore and revere, and it affirmed that not only is there a space for the stories I want to tell but a community for it. When I came back to shaping and building *Honey & Spice*, I was bolstered by the many things *Love in Colour* had taught me about my craft and my subject matter, by the people who held those stories close to their hearts and breathed life into it by loving it. So, I would like to acknowledge *Love in Colour* and all that came with it for tasting the world first, and telling Honey & Spice that there was space for it, that the world was ready for it.

In all that, my faith propelled me, so I would, as always, like to thank God who is love, who is light, who gave me the compulsion and the need to create, to craft, to imagine.

My perpetual gratitude and love to Mummy and Daddy, Olukemi and Olufemi Babalola, whose unwavering love and support and belief in me has given me a confidence that has propelled me through the darkest and hardest of moments. I can do what I can do because of you. If you never doubted me, how dare I doubt myself? Thank you, Daddy, for your WhatsApp blasts of every single bit of news that has my name in it, and ensuring everyone who has met you knows that your 'dear daughter' is an author. Thank you so much for answering every random message asking for elucidation on Yoruba grammar and diacritics immediately, and with such intellectual vigor and patience! My professor! Mummy, thank you for your no nonsense tenderness, for giving me words that help to piece myself back together when I feel scattered, for reminding me who I am. Just knowing I have your blood in me, that you are part of me, makes me believe in my capabilities. My therapist! Thank you, parents, for always trying to understand even when you don't, for your eager curiosity about my world even when it seems far from your own, thank you for sharing it with me. The joy is making you proud.

Katie Packer! My dear KP. Book doula! Thank you so much for believing in this world as much as I do, for understanding this world as much as I do, for asking the questions that helped me enrich it, develop it, challenge it, so it could be the best version of the story I could produce. Thank you for settling my nerves and being so capable even when I am having a meltdown! Thanks for understanding the need for Beyoncé references, thanks for understanding when I need time, and thanks for your effervescence and love. I am also glad that we always know when we're in editor mode and diva/writer mode, so the lines don't get blurred! But I am also glad when you know that I need a friend. You have a sharp eye, and you are such a force, and I can't wait till you run tings! KP, Bad B.

Elle Keck! Thank you for being in my corner and throwing your confidence behind both *Honey & Spice* and *Love in Colour* – it truly means the world that you wanted to broaden out their community, and that you understood all the cultural references that were so precious to me and helped form the flavour of the book. I always felt like I was in safe hands. I wish you all the best, always. Julia Elliot, thank you for taking over from Elle so seamlessly, with the same passion and enthusiasm! Grateful for the immediate trust you helped foster, and I don't take it for granted.

Thank you to everyone in the Headline and William Morrow

teams for all the energy, belief and enthusiasm thrown behind the book.

Juliet Pickering, my Angel Agent! I am so grateful that I embarked on this rollercoaster with you next to me. *Honey & Spice* has been part of my dream for so long, before *Love in Colour*, and you always believed in it, always saw what it could be, even in its infancy (the blobby, distorted, embryonic stages that make me cringe upon revisiting). I can't thank you enough for taking a chance on me. Thank you for being my advocate and friend (and sometimes manager), thank you for patience (this is a running theme . . . I have a lot of meltdowns) and thank you for your counsel – and your gentle pushing. Your wisdom and generosity is something I cherish, and I am blessed to have you on my team.

Jessica Stewart, my endlessly patient TV agent – thank you for understanding how much this book means to me, and allowing me the space to work through it with no pressure – despite having other engagements! It means the world that you support me holistically, and it really helps reduce the aforementioned meltdowns.

My beautiful friends, my chosen family. I love you all. Amna Khan, for knowing my essence, and never questioning my dreams and always seeing them with 20/20 vision. From adolescence to now, you have been by my side, with spiritual understanding and a deep knowing of myself that kept me grounded. Charlet Wilson, your heart is so golden and such an inspiration, and your kindness and support is such a galvanising force – from a mug that says 'Bolu Babalola puts the lit in literature' when my first book wasn't even out, to framing a book cover for a silly little story

I wrote when we were 22. Dreaming big is easy when you have friends who see your dreams as reality. Asha Mohamed – thank you for reading the cringe stories I wrote during 'private study' in 6th form and thank you for liking them and actually wanting to read them (even if you didn't actually want to . . . thank you for lying about wanting to read them). You helped confirm that this is all I wanted to do – to write worlds people can believe in, to write worlds that make people think about the world, people, our feelings.

Daniellé Scott-Haughton! Thank you for being my big sister and my pastor – your fortification is not only sororal but spiritual, and I thank you for knowing when I need to be held, for giving me clarity when all I can see is my creative anxiety. Thank you for always being a single frantic call away (I have a lot of meltdowns, OK? I'm an artist). Candice Carty-Williams, my darling CCW. Your guidance is invaluable – thank you for knowing that sometimes all I need is a, 'I know it's hard. And guess what? You will do it because you can.' Folarin – cuz, bro, thank you again, for proof-reading 'Netflix & Chill', that short story that got shortlisted for a competition, that got me signed to my agents. Thank you for never doubting. Sase!! My wifey. Thank you for being an endless source of laughter and light since we were 7 to now. Grateful to have you by my side, and to be your sugar daddy.

Groupchat edition: a source of laughter, encouragement and reprieve. All pockets of supremely talented, wickedly funny, and ridiculously kind women (they are also hot).

PPE: I cannot say what these letters stand for, and if you ask I will say they stand for Platinum Praying Energy. One thing is for certain though: you are platinum babes.

Twisty Bobcat Pretzels: Grateful that all of you are in a different timezone to me, because it means that even my allnighters are punctuated with joy and a meme, a well needed break.

I hate it here: thank you for being a place where I can purge out all the things I hate so I can return to the world as at least an ostensibly well-functioning person.

I don't know how to name this one, because it's the brain and lightning emoji? But it explains a lot because you are both a source of light and intelligence.

My bestie-cousins! Shoutout to BIOgraphy – Ore and Ibzy for allowing me the space to be my goofiest self, for laughing with me till we're crying.

My blood sisters Bomi and Demi – thank you for your support and love and the fact that we don't need to say much to know what it is. Gang gang.

Beyoncé – obviously. An artist dedicated to her craft and meticulous with her vision – a constant inspiration.

From London to Lagos to L.A., I have been graced with family, and what a blessing it is, to not be able to fit everyone in this section. I trust you know who you are. I truly have been gifted with so much love and support in my life, and I want you to know that even if you haven't been mentioned by name, you are so valued and appreciated.

Last but not least, I would like to thank my readership and my work's community who have messaged me about my work and have helped carve a space for my voice and the stories and worlds I have dreamed of crafting and building. You breathe more life into the work than I have ever imagined. Thank you for seeing me. God bless you.

Love always,

B x

.